KAPLAN'S PLOT

ALSO BY JASON DIAMOND

The Sprawl: Reconsidering the Weird American Suburbs

Searching for John Hughes: Or Everything I Thought I Needed to Know About Life I Learned from Watching '80s Movies

KAPLAN'S PLOT

A NOVEL

JASON DIAMOND

FLATIRON
BOOKS
NEW YORK

KAPLAN'S PLOT. Copyright © 2025 by Jason Diamond. All rights reserved. Printed in the United States of America. For information, address Flatiron Books, 120 Broadway, New York, NY 10271. EU Representative: Macmillan Publishers Ireland Ltd., 1st Floor, The Liffey Trust Centre, 117–126 Sheriff Street Upper, Dublin 1, DO1 YC43.

www.flatironbooks.com

Designed by Omar Chapa

Library of Congress Cataloging-in-Publication Data

Names: Diamond, Jason, author.
Title: Kaplan's plot : a novel / Jason Diamond.
Description: First edition. | New York : Flatiron Books, 2025.
Identifiers: LCCN 2025004257 | ISBN 9781250385918 (hardcover) |
     ISBN 9781250385925 (ebook)
Subjects: LCGFT: Novels
Classification: LCC PS3604.I154 K37 2025 | DDC 813/.6—dc23/
     eng/20250410
LC record available at https://lccn.loc.gov/2025004257

Our books may be purchased in bulk for specialty retail/wholesale, literacy, corporate/premium, educational, and subscription box use. Please contact MacmillanSpecialMarkets@macmillan.com.

First Edition: 2025

10   9   8   7   6   5   4   3   2   1

To the grandfathers.
Bernard Kaplan z"l and Julius Meerbaum z"l: Thanks for showing
me the right way.
Barry Goldsher: Thanks for showing Lulu the right way.

a kind of promise my dead
will never be finished with me.

—RAVEN LEILANI

KAPLAN'S
PLOT

1

CHICAGO, 2023

According to his mother, Elijah Mendes was a born skeptic. Elijah didn't personally believe that was true, but Eve Mendes maintained that her son had come into the world filled with doubt, that she realized it the first and only time she tried to breastfeed him.

The way she recalled it, Elijah swatted away the nipple with his tiny hand, looked at his mother, stopped crying for a moment, and wrinkled his brow before refusing Eve's second attempt at feeding him. The nurses said that some babies were fussy and needed more coaxing than others, but there was something about the way Elijah looked at Eve that she couldn't get over. She believed her son had slipped past the data, doctors, and millions of years of human evolution by coming into the world questioning everything.

Eve first told Elijah that story the night of his bar mitzvah. She admitted that she wasn't exactly in the right frame of mind when she came up with the bit of infant psychology about her newborn, that she was under the influence of drugs she'd been given for the intense pain and the adrenaline that was cascading down her circulatory system like a raging river. If she could have done it all over, she probably would have waited longer and made a different decision about how to feed her son; but the look, she said, was very real.

Telling personal tales was a bit out of character for his mother, but then Eve doubled down with an unheard-of second admission: she was uncomfortable. The whole ceremony marking Elijah's journey from childhood to accountability as an adult in the eyes of the God of his forefathers felt "off," she said. Eve and her husband, Peter, weren't observant, so the bulk of Elijah's time spent in Jewish houses of worship as a boy amounted to a few visits to Temple Beth Shalom, a synagogue twenty minutes up Lake Shore Drive from the part of Chicago where he'd grown up. Once, it was for the funeral of a distant cousin on Peter's side, and then another visit for a night of "Israeli and Palestinian friendship, music, and food" his parents took him to after the 1993 Oslo Peace Accords, which offered some glimmer of hope in the region that would be violently snatched away yet again just a few years later.

Elijah's bar mitzvah was held at the Chicagoland Sephardic Center on the city's far North Side, a favor to Elijah's grandfather and Eve's father-in-law, Sonny Mendes. The boy loved his grandfather, who the doctors initially said had a few months left to live when Elijah was ten but who ended up sticking around longer. Sonny pleaded with Eve and Peter for his youngest grandson to have a bar mitzvah, saying it was his dying wish. He didn't make it to see his dream come true, but Elijah wanted to fulfill the promise. So with a few months to go until his birthday, a tutor named Udi was hired to give a crash course in Hebrew and what to do during the ceremony, the rabbi at the Center agreed to host since Sonny was one of the congregation's founders, and the date was set. Peter cried as his son stuttered through his *haftarah*; Eve was mostly confused and unmoved since her own bat mitzvah had been entirely in English. Afterward, Eve and Elijah found themselves sitting alone together at a big round table while Peter and the guests stacked burekas and heaped mounds of couscous onto their plates. That was when Eve turned to her son and explained her theory of his inborn skepticism. Maybe she brought it up to break the silence, but as a well-known lightweight, it was more likely the three glasses of wine she'd drunk. Eve told her son the story of his birth like it was the funniest tale she knew but stopped short of adding that she never understood *why* he looked at her that way, and how first impressions truly are the lasting ones. That look of wariness wasn't simply about the nipple; her son didn't trust *her*, she'd decided. And unlike the regret of choosing to bottle-feed him that she made in an opioid haze, Eve held on to the belief that her only child viewed her with doubting eyes and never got over it.

More than two decades after Elijah's bar mitzvah, as mother and son thumbed their fingers on the white cloth that topped their table at Gene & Georgetti, Eve again considered filling the time between the endive salad they ordered but barely touched and their entrees with another very big fact. Although she didn't believe in some Jacob Marley afterlife where she'd be made to wander forever with the chains of burden she had forged in life around her neck, Eve was plagued by the idea that she'd be dead in a few months and there was so much unsaid between them. Even though she'd hoped to avoid it, the prognosis that her life was coming to an end did indeed get her to start looking at things differently. It was the clarity purchased by imminent death she'd heard so much about, and it annoyed her greatly.

There was also hunger, a feeling that was brought on by the weed she had started vaping throughout the day after she'd been deemed terminal. She told Elijah how she wanted chicken Vesuvio from the venerable old steak house; he didn't think it a good idea to eat there given how her stomach still rejected half the food she ate. But she was craving the dish only people in Chicago seemed to know about and swore the stomach thing came and went.

Instead of bringing any big admissions up, Eve walked outside to take a hit from one of her vapes. Elijah had never known his mom to get obsessive over things like varietals of wine, or what continent her coffee beans came from, and she didn't have a bucket list of places she needed to see while still alive; yet she was hell-bent on knowing and trying all the different cannabis strains available at the dispensary.

While his mother refreshed her high, Elijah nervously tapped his fingers so loudly on the table that the server walked over to ask if everything was OK. He apologized; the tapping was involuntary, something he did when whatever medication he was taking too much of to keep his anxiety under control did a good enough job of helping him forget he was nervous. There was something he wanted to talk to his mother about, and nothing drove him crazier than waiting to start a conversation with her. He often psyched himself out when he had too much time to game out how a talk could go, no matter how big or small the topic, because Eve had a way of taking hold of the wheel and steering the discussion in the direction of her choosing. She'd often treat even the most mundane conversation like an interrogation, picking out specific words Elijah used or asking questions about the smallest details. Eve hated psychoanalysis, but Elijah believed Freud would have found his mother's ability to see deeper meaning or metaphors in common nouns fascinating. Even a question as simple as "How was your day" could provoke a weary look from Eve, and possibly the dreaded response of "why." It was as if he was hinting at something else when he'd ask his mother how her day went. It was like that with small talk and big conversations. If Eve accepted his reason for asking, she'd give him her answer. If she didn't feel like having a conversation, then she'd swing the wheel violently and crash the whole thing into an entirely different topic.

Things had been a little different since he'd been back in Chicago: Eve had been considerably looser and more outgoing, and that threw Elijah for a loop. She smiled at her son as she walked back inside, tucking her vape into her purse. The entrees arrived just as she sat down. Elijah caught a whiff of the white wine the chicken and potatoes had been cooked in and asked his question.

"Can we talk about your book? I told you I wanted to help you with it," Elijah said, noticing the smallest bit of softness in his own voice. The look on his mother's face before she answered told him all he needed to know.

"Why?"

"I thought you've been working on it," Elijah said.

"What brought this up?"

"What brought it up? I've been thinking about it. That's all."

"You've never cared about my poetry," Eve said.

"I don't care about *any* poetry, but I care about you." Elijah knew that he was dead in the water, but still made one last attempt to survive the ordeal. "Besides, this isn't another book of your poems—it's a memoir. I'm curious to read *your story.*"

"What do you want to know? You can ask me anything," Eve said.

Elijah didn't have an answer, but he was enticed by the option of asking his mother *anything.* That opportunity had never been offered before, and for a moment, Elijah dwelled on the possibility that maybe for once he could have a normal conversation with his mother about something . . . anything. He cycled through the mile-long litany of topics he had stored away for decades, from the truth about how his goldfish *really* died when Elijah was six to why Eve's parents had settled in a neighborhood known for its famous university, which churned out one Nobel laureate after another, even though one of the few bits of information Eve had ever shared with her son was when he was sixteen and she said her mother's education stopped as a teenager when the Nazis showed up in her home country and her father didn't have any secular schooling at all. It was her way of saying how proud she was of her son for being a good student without using those words, but when Elijah asked what she'd meant about his grandfather who'd died long before he was born, she simply told him, "Oh, you know what I mean," and that was it.

After she finally got comfortable in her seat, Eve stared at her son for a moment. Her eyes were bloodshot; he couldn't tell if she was angry about something or lost in a haze. Then something else in the restaurant caught her attention.

"Oh, that's . . . I forget his name, but he's my favorite weatherman to watch because he's wrong so much," Eve said, her mouth stuffed with bits of chicken and capers. Elijah had never seen his mother talk while chewing, and it made him feel uneasy. "It's so odd he's wrong and the other meteorologists are usually close to right. I'd imagine he has the same equipment as the guy on WGN or Channel 5. Is he just a bad weatherman?"

Along with his mother's declining table manners, Elijah was still trying to get used to a lot of things that had changed since he'd last visited his hometown, including Eve's stoned ramblings. Her weed intake started with a few puffs a day after the doctors said it would help ease some of the pain from chemo, when there was still hope that treatment could help. When she called Elijah a few months later with news of another tumor, she joked, "Soon my entire body will be sponsored by cancer," and then laughed for twenty straight seconds. Elijah felt numb; the only question he could conjure was to ask how much of the joint she'd smoked. After that, every conversation was filled with his mother's dark jokes and meandering observations that he wasn't comfortable interrupting because it felt especially rude to stop the dying from talking while they still could. But Elijah was bored as he stared at the skirt steak he didn't really want.

"Are you going out tonight? I saw they're doing a series on that director you like at Music Box," Eve said. Despite having plenty of closer options near her home, she only liked seeing films at the old theater up near Wrigley Field. Elijah used to complain about having to take a trip to the North Side when he wanted to see a movie, but realized that she was right, that seeing anything in some newer, corporate Cineplex just wasn't as good.

Elijah said he wasn't in the mood, an answer that would have sufficed when he was younger. From there, Eve's mouth would crook to the left, her eyes followed the brows on an upward trajectory, and she'd usually add a slow, disappointment-cloaked "OK," but that was always the extent of it. Eve was never one to prolong a conversation unless it was absolutely necessary, but things had changed.

"Oh, come on. It's that one director. You know who I'm talking about," Eve said. It was a familiar phrase of hers—*you know who I'm talking about*—and her son had once calculated that one out of three times he did, in fact, know who she was talking about.

Elijah played along like he always did. He started naming directors off the top of his head, each one followed by his mother saying "No." After it wasn't Altman, Soderbergh, "that guy who did *Harold and Maude*," Spike Lee, Billy Wilder, or Elaine May, Elijah tapped out and changed the topic.

"I really don't like going out here. I don't know what it is, but Chicago just feels so . . . devoid. The problem is I don't know what it's devoid of. I just try to enjoy myself here and . . ."

"How is it *devoid* of anything? It's one of the great American cities!" Eve's voice had gone up a notch or two above what Elijah was used to, especially in public.

"Sorry, Ma. I didn't realize you were cultural attaché of Chicago now. It's just that time away made me see how provincial this place is. It's an island in the middle of . . . the middle. I'm not saying the Bay Area is perfect, but at least there's more around. Chicago is a great town, don't get me wrong. I just never really fit in here. It's better to save money, anyways."

"Oh, shut up," Eve said with a stoned giggle. "You're a millionaire. You've got nothing to worry about."

"I *was* a millionaire. Past tense," Elijah said with an eye roll.

Between multiple lawsuits brought against Elijah and his former partners, and then the divorce, there was enough in his bank account to cover a year's worth of rent in a big city. He thought he'd be able to cut down on the number of hours lawyers billed him by just giving everything to his ex, but they still charged him an Ivy college tuition's worth in fees just for telling him where to sign on a bunch of contracts. He was nearly broke.

"In the Bay Area I'm barely above the poverty line," Elijah added. "Scraping by. A real blue-collar Joe."

He looked at his mother and noticed she was breathing heavily, and her face had turned a deathly green. Elijah waved the server over to pay the check, but she said that the lady had given him her credit card when Elijah was in the bathroom. Eve always did that, and it drove him nuts.

As soon as Eve's signature was scratched on the bill, Elijah threw her coat over her shoulders and they rushed out the door. He'd seen his mother turn the same shade a few nights earlier as they ate a take-out pizza, and he didn't want to experience the same result that followed, but he timed things wrong. Just as they stepped onto the pavement, Eve vomited straight at him without any warning. She apologized; he said it was no problem. They drove home with the car windows cracked, the frigid Chicago air overtaking the cranked-up heat. The traffic on the expressway was mercifully light on the way back to the house that both of them had grown up in. Eve's father bought the place before she was born; Elijah had grown to know every nook and cranny, the notes each step upstairs creaked in, and the way the wind was blowing depending on where the draft was coming from. The home was at the end of a leafy block, a stately old Victorian redbrick with columns that sat over the porch and front door; there was a conical roof in the front that always made Elijah think of an old clown's hat, and a great weeping willow in the backyard. Eve had wanted her son to start a family and take over the home the way she had, but he didn't want the house with its old pipes, wiring that needed replacing, and the funk of memories forever stuck in the walls, of Eve's parents passing, then Peter's mother and father, Eve's sister, Peter, and in an undetermined, but short time, Eve would join the list.

The problem with knowing when you're going to die, Eve reminded her son every single day after she received the terminal prognosis, was that there was so much to do. That seemed strange to Elijah, given his mother's agnostic beliefs. When Sonny passed, Eve told her son death was eternal sleep, a forever of nothing. But with her own end approaching, she'd taken to organizing everything in the home. Boxes and papers were all over the place. Elijah had a hard time navigating it all.

"I saw some video with a guy who said he got his baby's puke out of his jacket with a mix of vodka and water," he said as he rummaged through the shelves.

Eve pointed to a cabinet at the end of the kitchen island by the wall. Elijah opened it and found a dust-covered bottle of Smirnoff with a small puddle left in it. Next to the bottle was a pile of mail. Elijah grabbed the stack of envelopes on top.

"Hey, Ma, what are these? They're all from . . . the Greater

Chicagoland Hebrew Benevolent Society? And they're all addressed to 'The Mendes/Kaplan family.' You haven't gone by your maiden name since when?"

"That's where I keep mail I'll get to," Eve said.

"Yeah? When? This one is from two months ago," Elijah said as he opened one and looked over the letter. He opened another. "This is from last month, and here's one from last week."

Elijah couldn't tell if his mother was ignoring him or actually didn't hear what he'd said. He started reading the latest letter out loud.

"'Dear Mr. or Mrs. Mendes. If you could please respond to my last letter, I would greatly appreciate it. I'd call or e-mail but I don't have your contact besides this address listed in our records from the 1980s. Again, this is to discuss some of your father's things we have here at the office that I'd like to make sure you get instead of us throwing it out when we start reorganizing at the end of the month. Thank you again, Rabbi Zev Ginsburg.'"

"Like I said." Eve yawned, then got up and headed for the stairs up to her bedroom. "I'll get to it."

"Can you at least tell me what it's about?"

Elijah walked toward her and tried to put the letter in his mother's hands, but she didn't take it.

"It's some property in the family name. It's a long story. Nothing too interesting," she said without turning around.

All Elijah had ever heard about his parents owning property besides the house was when they went in with some friends on a summer cottage in Wisconsin that they visited twice and then decided lake life wasn't for them.

"We *own* the property this is addressed from? It's right by UIC. How much money is that worth? It's gotta be . . ."

"I don't know, Elijah. Can we talk tomorrow when you drive me

to my appointment? I'm exhausted," Eve said without stopping to wait
for her son to answer.

The next morning at 7:00, Elijah walked downstairs expecting to see
his mother ready and waiting for him. If she got any sleep, it was for
a few hours in the night and then he could hear her waking around
3:00 or 4:00 and pacing aimlessly. He wasn't sure what she was doing in the early hours of the morning, but he knew she usually went
downstairs between 5:00 and 5:30, then sat at the table reading for a
few hours. Eve held fast to her routines, so it surprised him when her
figure was absent from the same chair at the table she'd always sat
at for as long as he could remember. He called out to her, but got no
response. He noticed a note on the fridge held up by an "Obama '08"
magnet.

> Felt like taking public transportation to my appointment since
> the weather is decent. I'll see you later.
>
> —E.M.

The way she signed her initials so elegantly, with the little dramatic swoosh of ink shooting out from the bottom right point of the
M, was the thing that always kept Elijah from thinking too hard about
how Eve never once signed any note to him with "Love" or "Mom."
After hours spent talking about it in therapy for fifteen years, he tried
his best to stop reading into why his mother did things the way she
did. He could move on from the signature; it was the note itself that
bothered him. Classic Eve, Elijah thought. She probably didn't want
to talk about whatever that letter he'd read was about and figured
avoiding it would end the conversation. He'd seen her use that move
on his father a hundred times, and Elijah had fallen for it himself

on a few occasions, but this time she'd overlooked Elijah having no job, no life, no friends, and no plans in Chicago. He had nothing but time. The app on his phone showed an early-morning traffic mess on the Dan Ryan, thirty-two minutes to get to the destination he knew should have been an easy twenty-one. He considered avoiding the expressway, but then doubt crept into his head about whether he could still navigate through the city of his birth. He went with the first option, taking 94 North, up the city's most clogged artery toward the Traffic Circle of Doom, which had been renamed as a tribute to the first woman mayor in the city's history a few years earlier. Elijah inched a half mile over fifteen minutes toward the section where the Dan Ryan, Eisenhower, and Kennedy expressways all smashed into one another, and he couldn't help but wonder who Mayor Jane Byrne must have pissed off in life to have one of the worst parts of the city named after her.

After driving seven miles and a few extra feet over the span of forty-two minutes, the app told Elijah he'd arrived at his destination. He didn't see the address that he'd gotten off the envelope for the Greater Chicagoland Hebrew Benevolent Society on any of the buildings, and just assumed that the old neo-Byzantine building with its marble columns and the big Star of David etched into the stone above the entrance was the place he wanted.

Just as he was about to get out of his car and go inside, Elijah caught a glimpse of himself in the rearview mirror. He couldn't believe how terrible his skin had gotten in such a short amount of time. He'd forgotten how Chicago's weather stayed firmly planted in winter well into springtime. His face was ashen, lips were constantly chapped, and he swore he'd developed at least two wrinkles on his forehead. His ex had always tried to get him to use moisturizer, but there was just a part of him that couldn't take seriously all the "repair cream" and "facial fuel" she bought him.

Maybe it was another thing he should have listened to her about, he thought as he pulled the flesh around his temples back and dwelled on gravity's impact on his skin before another thought took over: what was he doing going to an old synagogue in the morning? The thought crossed his mind that it would be hilarious if he'd lived an entire life devoid of any religion, and his mom throwing up was what set Elijah on a road to living a pious life. He'd heard stories about people finding God in the oddest places, but none of them involved vomit. Outside the car it had started snowing—how quaint, he thought. He picked the wrong jacket and didn't have a hat to keep his head warm. The gentle Bay Area weather had softened him too much.

When Elijah got out and took a closer look at the place he'd assumed was the synagogue, he saw one, then another person in expensive black workout wear walk up the steps and into the building. He looked at the cool grayish-blue sign above the doors, the letters VTL spelled out on it in a white font. He figured the VTL CNTR gym sign must have blended with the gray Chicago sky and snow flurries whipping around and he'd just missed it. He walked in and was greeted by a smiling blonde in yoga pants and a hooded sweatshirt that said "Always on Grind Time." Elijah asked if there was a Jewish temple nearby; she seemed confused by the question and said she'd just moved to Chicago a few weeks earlier. One of her co-workers, a guy whose arms and shoulders looked like a mountain range when he stretched out, told Elijah to walk back outside and turn right.

"Try two doors down," the tanned and toned trainer said. "I see all those old guys with the hats and . . ." He pointed at his own neatly groomed beard. "Either they're Jewish or Amish."

As Elijah walked out, he could hear the two talking about him. The guy said something that made the girl laugh. The only word Elijah could make out in the conversation was *Jews*.

He walked in the direction he'd been given. Next to the synagogue-turned-gym sat a small, squat, one-floor building. There was a heavy chain locked on the door, and there weren't any windows save for a few pieces of thick dark glass that made it impossible for anybody outside to look in. On the ground in the doorway, the remains of words spelled out in tile in Hebrew and English were barely readable. The Hebrew was all but gone; above them, the Roman letters *S*, *C*, and *H* were chipped and worn. Elijah cleared some dead leaves and garbage with his foot to reveal an additional *V*, with a *Z* missing part of its bottom. The address on the door said 1253. He was looking for 1257. A new condo that looked like it had been designed by a five-year-old, with a top floor that jutted out like a triangle that was sitting atop a square, was 1255. The hideous new architecture that was supposed to convey *modern* was spreading like a disease all over the city just as it had in San Francisco. Elijah complained a lot about having to be back in Chicago, but he'd always loved the buildings. Even the ones that weren't grand and ornate usually had some sort of charm.

The building he was looking for, the one that housed the office for the Greater Chicagoland Hebrew Benevolent Society, was hardly charming. How a developer's wrecking ball had missed it was hard to figure out. He opened the door to the place he guessed had once been a convenience store and found a group of Hasidic men conversing with one another at a table. A few plastic bottles of seltzer, some pastries, and prayer books made up the spread. They all turned to see who had walked in and looked at the stranger with fearful eyes.

"This is private property," a fat man said. He was the only one still wearing his fedora inside. Elijah always liked their hats. "No trespassing."

Elijah asked if they could tell him where the Greater Chicagoland Hebrew Benevolent Society was.

The men all looked at one another and started talking quietly in Yiddish. The fat man with the fedora on was their designated speaker. He pointed at a door to his left. Elijah nodded, walked over to it, and pressed the doorbell button as the Hasids stared at him in silence. When it buzzed and Elijah walked into the other room, he could hear them start chatting loudly as soon as the door shut behind him. The room he walked into was basked in gray, with a single lamp providing the only electric light. There was an old woman wearing a wig that didn't quite fit her head sitting behind the desk. She was reading a book with Hebrew on the cover. Elijah walked to the desk.

"Is Rabbi Zev Ginsburg available by any . . ."

"Who are you? We don't have any appointments," the old woman snapped. Her wig shifted from right to left.

Elijah apologized. "I tried calling, but . . ."

"Are you a Mormon? Jews for Jesus? We told you not to come here anymore!"

"I'm responding to his letters to my mother."

The old woman eyeballed Elijah. Her tone didn't soften as she told him to take a seat.

"Does he want to know my name?"

She ignored him and pressed a button before going back to reading her book. Elijah walked toward the chairs. There was a fine coat of dust on one of them. He put a six-year-old copy of *Time* on the seat and was about to sit down when a stick of a man walked out from a door behind the woman's desk. His yarmulke was so big over the back of his head, it almost made him look less bald. He wore a faded black suit that desperately needed a tailor's hand. His beard was black with electric streaks of white and went down to his chest. Elijah wasn't sure if the man spoke English or not, so he waved.

"Hopefully you're from the gas company. We've called *six times*," Rabbi Ginsburg said without looking Elijah in the eyes. The way he repeated "*six . . . times*" not only verified that his English was perfect, but Elijah could detect an accent native to the region.

"My mother is Eve Mendes. You wrote to her about some things," Elijah said.

The rabbi pulled at his beard. Crumbs of food and small particles of dust floated out of it. Elijah couldn't tell if he was in his forties or seventies.

"Interesting," Rabbi Ginsburg said unenthusiastically. He was either tired, annoyed, or both, Elijah deduced. "You're Rose Kaplan's . . ."

"My grandma?"

"Your grandma? I don't know," the rabbi said. "Was she?"

"I never met her," Elijah said.

Rabbi Ginsburg thought for a second. He squinted his eyes as he tugged again at his beard. "Are you . . ."

Elijah was prepared for the question he'd been asked countless times, especially by other Jews, and said "No" before the rabbi could ask it. People had wondered if he was everything from Mexican to Algerian; some thought he was Muslim and from the Middle East, while a girl he dated in college said Elijah looked just like a picture of her great-grandfather back in Sicily. Even he always had to pause before checking off the race box on forms, often just leaving it blank and hoping nobody cared to look. "Not adopted," Elijah said. Just saying that almost always shut down the conversation, but the rabbi looked confused.

"I was going to ask if you're Mizrahi," he said.

It surprised Elijah that somebody got it right on the first try, but he understood if anybody would, a rabbi was the most likely to. He apologized, then asked to be reminded what Mizrahi meant.

"Where is your family from. If they're from Ukraine or Poland they're Ashkenazi. If they're from . . ."

"Oh yeah, right," Elijah remembered. "My mother's side was

from Eastern Europe. Half my father's family was from Egypt and Morocco; his mother's family came from Puerto Rico. She converted, though. Her ancestors had been Jewish in Spain, but they were, I forget what you call them . . ."

The rabbi rubbed his fingers down his mustache to smooth it down. "Thank your credentials," he said.

The crack cut the tension. Elijah wasn't used to talking about his cultural background much. He usually found that leaving people guessing was easiest, but when another Jew realized what he was, a pang of insecurity about being Jewish but not *Jewish* would rattle through him. The rabbi, however, seemed unfazed.

"As I understand, your grandfather bought this property long ago, and had made an agreement to let us stay here," Rabbi Ginsburg said.

A look of self-satisfaction crept across Elijah's face as the conversation turned to business. The rabbi may have been a man of God, but real estate was an unholy discussion. In his head, Elijah conjured up visions of Michael Jordan and Kobe Bryant taking over basketball games and dominating their opponents. He tried to channel that energy as he started speaking.

"From what *I* understand . . ." Elijah spoke with the sort of confidence he'd seen from billionaires talking down to millionaires. He straightened his shoulders and looked around the room. Everything was covered in dust. There were spiderwebs covering cobwebs. He could hear at least three dripping sounds from different places. "I bet the college would love to put up housing here."

There was a time in his younger, less cynical years when Elijah would have been disgusted if he heard somebody say what had come out of his mouth. But as he got older and found success he started to adhere to the belief that business was business. It was difficult to imagine just giving away a piece of property so some Hasidic men could pray, and the Greater Chicagoland Hebrew Benevolent Society could go on doing . . . whatever it was they did elsewhere. Elijah was going to ask if they were a nonprofit and what their mission was, but the rabbi had other plans.

"Follow me." Rabbi Ginsburg didn't even wait a second before turning around and walking back through the door.

Elijah brushed past the old woman, who shot him a death glance as he walked by. He went through another door that led to a dark, narrow hallway. The farther they walked down, the more it felt as if they were descending. They reached the other side and entered what looked to be a very expansive basement with a few dim light-bulbs hanging from the ceiling that lit the entire space, which was filled with boxes and cabinets. There was a framed painting of a very old rabbi on the wall but little else for decoration save for dust and rat traps all over the place. Rabbi Ginsburg searched ferociously, moving boxes that looked like they could throw anyone's back out until he gave out a loud "Ah-ha!" He motioned for Elijah to come over, then began pulling papers and folders out of the box, stacking them on top of one another until it looked like they'd topple over. He examined one of the papers and started explaining how almost a century earlier the society had been entrusted with the care of the building they were in. "The organization was founded in 1886 to help alleviate some of the burden on Jewish immigrants coming from Eastern Europe."

He handed Elijah a photograph of the structure dated 1921. Save for the brick-paved roads and streetcar tracks, it looked like not much else had changed.

"It was built as a mikveh around 1907," the rabbi said before realizing Elijah didn't realize what that was. "A ritual bath. They added a sauna a few years later, and eventually a certain element followed: criminals. Gangsters, politicians. Eventually, the neighbor-hood changed and the Jews started moving away. There's no documentation on exactly when the Schvitz closed that I could find, but it was between the expressway being built right near here in the early '60s and the 1980s."

It was obvious the civic history lesson was leading up to something. Elijah wanted to figure out a way to speed things up but felt strange hurrying a man of God.

"A few years ago, one of our younger board members with deep pockets said he wanted to renovate the place and make it a mikveh to help convince other Orthodox Jews to move nearby. We didn't hear a no from your family, so the renovations finally started last year."

Elijah asked what had happened to the synagogue, as Rabbi Ginsburg found the box he'd wanted. He pulled it down and put it on a table near them. The cloud of dust that flew out all around it looked like a soul escaping a vessel after years trapped in purgatory.

"It was a church when it was first built, then the Christians moved, and the Jews took it over. Then the Jews all moved away, and it became a church again for Spanish-speaking people in the 1970s. Numbers were so low a few years ago that the archdiocese sold it to some guy who had hoped to turn it into luxury condos. That guy went to prison on wire fraud and extortion charges when they took down that one state senator, so it sat until it was purchased for nothing, renovated, and that gym moved in."

The way the rabbi's face contorted when he said "that gym" made Elijah feel guilty that he'd recently signed up for a week's trial at the VTL CNTR near his mother's house. He could have just used his old membership at the YMCA, where he'd learned how to swim as a boy, but the last party he'd attended in San Francisco was thrown by the VTL CNTR founders when they went public, and he felt some sense of gratitude since hardly anybody invited him out after the very public downfall of the startup he'd co-founded. Nobody wanted the former *chief experience officer*—a job title he didn't even quite understand—of a failed company around, and he didn't really blame anybody for that. Successful people can't stand failure, he'd once heard; they worried the bad luck would rub off on them. For such a godless group, the technocrati of the Bay Area were superstitious, so if anybody from the world he formerly inhabited even acknowledged that he was still living, Elijah felt a deep sense of goodwill toward them.

Rabbi Ginsburg pulled some folders out of the box and laid them on the table. "I don't understand why you just couldn't go to my mother's house. It's not that far of a drive," Elijah said as the rabbi looked at some papers.

"I attempted that," he replied as he pulled out another small stack of forms. "Your mother wouldn't open the door. She yelled something about how she was still undecided about God and told me to go away."

That sounded about right, Elijah thought.

"My reason for contacting your family was because I wanted to give you these things, but I also hoped you'd see how vital this place is to the community."

"Which community is that? I just saw a couple of old men," Elijah said as he flicked a dust bunny off his arm. "I don't understand why you consider this specific place necessary. Was there some sort of miracle or something performed here?"

For the first time during their conversation, the rabbi looked at Elijah like he was an idiot.

"No, Mr. Mendes. But there was a bit of a mystery, and it involves your family. On the first day of demolition, we found a room that looked like an old office. There was a safe in there. I know a guy who can open them . . ."

Elijah couldn't help but let out a chuckle. In a city like Chicago, even a rabbi knew a guy who could crack a safe. Elijah picked a folder up and gave it a dismissive look.

"There was nothing of value in there, but I have an interest in history, so I took the folders and papers back here and looked through them. I'm still unsure what all this is and hoped maybe you or your mother might know. Or maybe that you'd want to keep this since it's part of your family history."

Rabbi Ginsburg spoke fast with an affect that was a mix of Chicagoland and the Talmudic titter-tat with which Elijah sometimes overheard impressively bearded Orthodox Jews speaking, which came from years of poring over laws set forth by scholars from centuries ago. It was the echo of a people forever debating. That was the thing Elijah felt most connected to when it came to his own Jewish heritage; he found comfort in the idea that it's all just one big, ongoing question.

Rabbi Ginsburg excused himself. He needed to get some tea. Elijah picked a sheet of paper with a lot of numbers and little one-word notes that didn't have any meaning to him out of a folder. He looked at another one; it had a date at the top: August 12, 1957. It was the draft of a letter to a local alderman looking to get extra fire hydrants added around Maxwell Street. The chicken-scratch signature at the bottom was Yitzhak Kaplan's.

Rabbi Ginsburg returned holding a chipped mug with a tea bag string hanging from the side.

"Yitzhak Kaplan was my mother's father," Elijah said. He studied the paper again. "My grandfather. These were his things?"

"Yes. But now it belongs to you," the rabbi said before taking a sip of his tea.

Elijah found himself moved but dismissed his nostalgia and steadied himself to get back to business. What were the things in front of him besides pieces of paper that may have touched the hands of a man he was related to but knew little about?

"I did a little digging into your grandfather's history," Rabbi Ginsburg said. "He was—interesting."

Elijah wanted to ask what the rabbi meant by "interesting," since he'd always been curious to know more about the man who died more than two decades before Elijah was born. He knew Yitzhak Kaplan was an immigrant, and Elijah had once heard his other grandfather talking about Eve's "criminal father." When he was a little older, Elijah asked his father what Eve's father did for a living, and Peter said, "He was a businessman," with a look on his face that even his young son could tell meant there was more to the story. The problem was, if Peter wasn't going to tell Elijah all of it, Eve certainly wouldn't fill in the missing details. So he just forgot about it and went through life accepting there was a gap in his family story that he'd likely never fill. It just felt easier to move through the world not letting the mysteries of the past hold him back.

"I appreciate this, but I still don't understand why you need *this* building. I'm sure your organization does great work, but can't you do it in another place? Up in Rogers Park there's that big Orthodox population—but here, there's just a lot of college students," Elijah said.

Rabbi Ginsburg nodded solemnly. "Last I checked, Jews go to college. Many, many great ones have, in fact. Some even teach at them, if you can believe it."

The closest to a rebuttal Elijah could get was "I mean, sure . . ." Then he stopped. The old business instinct to keep 'em talking as long as possible, to make their heads spin with facts, real or bullshit, likely wouldn't work with a rabbi.

"Before you decide, there's something else that belongs to you," Rabbi Ginsburg said as he motioned for Elijah to follow him back toward the door they'd walked in through. They went through the office, past the old lady with the wig, who didn't even look up from her book, then out another door that had been painted in a shade of gray like the concrete wall, almost like it was purposely camouflaged. It led to the back of the building. They walked through an alley, then made a turn and came upon what looked like a small yard that was covered in growth. It felt out of place in the middle of Chicago, almost like a lost land, vestiges of the prairie. There was a little path and a gate with a sign on it that read "Cemetery for the Greater Chicagoland Hebrew Benevolent Society," and remnants of a fence around the area, but most of it had collapsed or was buried underneath broken branches or debris. The rabbi turned to Elijah. There was a playful grin on his face as he asked if Elijah believed in ghosts. Elijah said he didn't, but if they did exist, he imagined they likely lived somewhere down the path in front of them.

"There hasn't been a burial here since 2012," the rabbi said. "We have a few recurring donations and we're close to getting landmark status. A friend's son is helping us with grant writing and one of our trustees is the grandfather of the new senator, but most of the people buried in the cemetery are great- or great-great-grandparents of people who moved away a long time ago."

They walked past dozens of graves, some of them broken and toppled over, a few so weathered from the decades of harsh rain and wind that you couldn't read what had been carved into them. One had graffiti on it: a spray-painted swastika that somebody had tried their best to rub out. They watched not to trip over vines or get pricked by thorns, until they came to what looked to be a mound. Anywhere else the sight of the earth curving upward might be commonplace, but in the flatlands of Chicago, it made Elijah pause. It didn't seem natural because it wasn't.

"Man-made. It lines up with the building we were in, which was built on a slant into the mound. It's a very strange construction, but it was done for a purpose," Rabbi Ginsburg explained, stopping for a second before leading Elijah to the side of the mound. He pointed to a handsome gray stone mausoleum with a Star of David at the top, and below it, etched into the rock, was "Kaplan," his mother's somewhat common maiden name.

"Jewish law states a body must be buried in the ground. When your grandfather wanted this built, they came up with a plan and bought the entire lot in front of it, put up the building, then put it in the care of our organization. It's not a traditional mausoleum where the bodies are stored inside the walls. The bodies are in the ground, not too far from where we were standing in the basement a few minutes ago."

"My grandfather *owned* this cemetery?"

"He bought it in the 1930s, a real mitzvah to keep it going through the Depression. And now you're the owner," Rabbi Ginsburg said. "A family business. You should be proud."

The rabbi walked over to the mausoleum door. He took a key from his jacket pocket, undid a heavy lock that held a thick chain in place, then opened the cast-iron door, its patina almost matching the grass of the man-made mound. It creaked open in a deathly manner that fit the setting. Elijah walked in and turned his phone's flashlight on. The mausoleum was still and cold, a tight chamber that hadn't been entered in decades, occupied only by the dead and whatever beasts managed to crawl in. Elijah tried not to think too much of it. He moved his light around but didn't see much until he aimed it at the corner toward the back. There was a small plaque. He walked toward it to get a better look. There was Hebrew he couldn't read, and then, after a second of adjustment, his eyes made out the name in English just below them.

"Who is Solomon Kaplan?" Elijah asked.

"That's the question. There's no record of a burial here. We can account for every single body interned here except the ones in this mausoleum," Rabbi Ginsburg said as he pulled out his phone and turned on the flashlight.

"You said 'ones,'" Elijah said. "As in multiple corpses are in here?"

Rabbi Ginsburg pointed his light toward the opposite corner.

"More plots. There's room for five in here. The records say that one in the corner was filled sometime in 1958, but that's all I know.

I couldn't find a record of any burial. There are no notes about a ceremony, and I even looked in the library's newspaper records; no funerals are listed that aren't accounted for with gravestones."

Suddenly Elijah felt he was being put in an uncomfortable position and began to wish he'd never opened that letter. They taught children the story of Pandora and her box early on for a reason, he thought.

"I understand my grandfather purchased this, and there is somebody in here with his last name, but I honestly have no idea who Solomon Kaplan is."

The rabbi motioned for Elijah to step back outside. He pulled out his phone and scrolled on the screen with his finger for a second. He found what he wanted and handed the phone to Elijah. It was a picture of a brass plaque on a wall. "When they were pulling out the seats of the shul to make room for the weight machines for the gym they put in, somebody saw this plaque."

Elijah read it out loud.

"'From Yitzhak Kaplan and Solomon Kaplan, in memory of their parents and sister. Moshe, Raisel, and Chava. May their memories be a blessing and may their ancestors know their names.'"

"They were brothers," Rabbi Ginsburg said. He waited a moment for a reaction.

"Oh," Elijah said. He was balancing trying to find the right words to say and how to feel. He was at a loss for both. "I . . . I wasn't aware he'd had a brother."

"Your family never talked about him?"

Elijah shrugged.

"I see," Rabbi Ginsburg said.

"It's complicated," Elijah said.

"Families often are," the rabbi said.

2

ODESA TO HAMBURG TO CHICAGO, 1909

"Don't start with your crying," Mother snapped to one of her children hidden below the floor. "Now isn't the time!"

It was the dreaded second night of attacks. The hope had been that the vodka would run out, and that the gentile neighbors would all be too tired to do any more rampaging after one evening. That was often how things worked with the flare-ups. Usually, there'd be a few broken windows, a couple of stolen cows, some small fires, fingers broken, a cracked rib or two, and some teeth knocked out. Then, the next morning, the Jews of Odesa would emerge from hiding and try to get a sense of what was to come. It was a lot of guesswork and bet hedging. Would there be another evening of violence or not? And if not, how long until the next thing—there was *always* a next thing. Then there was the decision of whether to clean up right away from the previous evening or not. If they cleaned, then the Jews ran the risk of some local who was still drunk from the night before thinking it was an opportunity to start things back up. If they didn't, then the soldiers might come around and start trouble because of the mess. Whether they cleaned or didn't, the Jews would eventually all go back to their homes, lock their doors, and wait for the sun to go down. Prayers were whispered as weapons—axes, broken chair legs, and anything else that could be used as protection—would be readied in others. More often than not, life would go back to normal. The Jews would return to being despised second-class citizens again, but that beat being punching bags or shooting targets.

Glass shattering somewhere on the eastern side of the neighborhood signaled the start of the second night of horrible festivities. It was followed by a concerto of sounds: a woman's scream, then a thunderous bang, followed by a chorus of shouts in Russian. Within thirty minutes, one home and a small shul had gone up in flames. There was calm for a few moments; the street outside was empty and silent until the sound of something being dragged across the dirt could be heard approaching. A few people looked out their windows to see if it was over, only to witness one of the locals parading the streets with a pig on a leash, yelling for the Jews to come out and kiss the swine.

"Kiss your god, you Hebrew heathens," the man shouted. His voice echoed up and down the street, signaling for the other gentiles to follow him. More than two dozen men armed with pitchforks, torches, knives, and anything else that could cause damage and death came charging after. They began smashing everything and everybody in sight.

"These asses," Mother said. "Drunken Russian apes."

Soldiers had carried out most of the attacks during the initial evening, giving the whole affair some feeling of order and official business. It was a controlled riot; the army wanted to keep the havoc to a minimum. The point was to make it look like the tsar was taking action and that the good gentiles had nothing to worry about, that it was Jews who were again causing whatever of the country's latest ills they were being—falsely—blamed for. They were the ones causing the trouble, and the instigators would be rooted out if they had to kill every single hook-nosed rat in the empire.

Thankfully, a Jewish soldier from the area had slipped a note to the rabbi a day before things started that he should get the Torah and anything else he could from the shul as far away as possible because there would be fires and the synagogues were sure to be on the list of places to burn down. The hope among the Jews was that if it was official, maybe they could bear the brunt of it, grit their teeth, then clean up and go back to living like they usually did, but they always prepared for the worst. Some of the elders could recall 1859, the year Greek sailors stormed the streets during their Easter holiday, chanting "Death to the Christ killers!" More than a few adults had been around in 1871, and every man over the age of thirteen had been put on alert countless times since Nikolashka's coronation in 1896. But after the attacks of 1905, when it took nearly two weeks to give the stacks of dead Jews proper burials, there was no telling what could happen.

To the boys under the floor, it was impossible to tell one night from the other—it all bled together. Mother made them stay underneath the house, telling them they could come out when she was certain things were safe. They lived on the dirt, sitting on an old potato sack and sleeping under a thick blanket. They'd go to the bathroom in the corner, then use a little shovel head to bury it in the earth. The only information they had was what they'd heard their father report after the first night died down: mostly clubs and bricks had been used, but no gunshots had been heard. Besides some injuries and fires, a few chickens and horses had been stolen, but no reports of deaths.

The second night was different from the start; it sounded almost right outside their home. The boys tried to listen to what was being said by Mother and a neighbor who were directly above him. Somebody had thrown dynamite, but it wasn't certain who. The older boy called out to his mother, but was told to shush.

"Unless you want your head chopped off by a Russian," she whispered in her harshest timbre. Her normal tone was one that expressed her unending annoyance with the universe and everything in it, but the one she answered her son in was the most severe voice he'd ever heard her use.

The boy, Yitzhak, didn't quite understand the concept of death and what it entailed, but he knew that he *definitely* didn't want his head separated from his torso. He knew dying meant you were gone, but his sister Chava had been gone for over a year, and she wasn't dead. Yet the idea of his body without a head made sense, so he did as he was told. He hunkered down with his younger brother, Solomon, and after a few hours of trying to decipher the noises, the smaller boy was able to fall asleep and stay that way through the steady stream of violent rumblings. Yitzhak stayed awake. His eyes remained wide open; closing them wasn't even an option. He wanted to cry, but figured that would only lead to a beheading, so he bit his lip until it bled and whimpered in silence. The sounds came and went, leaving horrible silence to fill in the gaps. At some point—Yitzhak figured it was midnight after the clanging of nearby church bells—there was a commotion nearby. He listened as his father screamed at some men outside, begging them to leave his house alone. Mother echoed her husband, adding in a few curses for good measure, threats that the men should grow onions out of their asses and maggots should hold weddings in their bowels and invite all the worms they knew. It seemed to hold the men off for a time, but then came the sound of something smashing up against the house, followed by a scuffle. Yitzhak heard Mother screaming inside the home. A man shouted something in Russian, followed by the sound of footsteps pounding across the floor, right above the part the older boy had his ear pressed up against. A man let out a sinister laugh, trailed by more of Mother's cursing; she called him a cow fucker, a devil, a piece of excrement, all in the local language and not in the Yiddish they spoke inside the home. There was some sort of commotion, and that's when Yitzhak covered his ears and barely whispered a prayer to keep him and his family safe.

The wood above his head vibrated, there was a loud bang, then more vibrations until everything stopped suddenly with what sounded like something hard with a soft inside being split. It was an ugly noise, one that probably left a mess, like the sound of a pile of gooseberries being stepped on. It was silent, then there was a collapse, and something crumpled to the floor. The boy pulled his hands away from the door. There was nothing. No movement and no sounds. The younger brother was somehow still asleep through all of it, and didn't notice the little bit of liquid falling from a crack in the floor and onto his potato-sack blanket. It was a single drop. Then another. Yitzhak counted three seconds and then watched as a small trickle started coming down without pause. He watched for a few seconds until the door above him flew open and he felt his bladder empty from fright. It was Mother. Her face had speckles of blood all over it.

"Yitzeleh," she whispered. "I need your help."

"Where is Papa?" Yitzhak asked.

"No questions. Wake Solomon. Get him up here."

He shook his little brother awake. The boy tried to cry, but his older brother slapped him.

"Mama needs us," Yitzhak said.

Solomon had kind eyes and chubby cheeks that old women loved to pinch, but the frown on his face made it look like he was having gas pains. He tried to ask a question, but Yitzhak raised his hand as if another smack was coming, then he told his brother to stop acting like a baby and get up through the hole in the floor. Solomon jumped up out of the hole, and as soon as his head popped above it, he let out a piercing shriek and got back in the hole.

"You baby," Yitzhak admonished his brother. "It's not that difficult to get up there."

Yitzhak pulled himself up and to the floor of the home, and his eyes instantly met with the gaze of a dead man. Yitzhak was about to scream, but Mother put her hand over his mouth. She looked down at her son's urine-soaked pants and rolled her eyes. There was a knife straight through the dead man's skull.

"There's no time for foolishness," Mother said in a manner even sterner than her normal tone. "Help me put him in the floor."

The dead man was scary, but Mother was terrifying, so the boys used their small frames to hold the dead man's arms as Mother pulled his legs. She was slight, but Yitzhak had watched her chop wood for fire more than a few times and witnessed her help a neighbor pull his cart out of the mud by herself. She pulled the man's body down and had her boys push him. Just before his full body was in the little room under the house where they normally kept any extra vegetables they had, where the boys had been hiding, Mother whispered to get the knife.

"You want the knife?" Yitzhak asked.

"Yes. The knife," Mother said.

"The one in his head?"

"Are you a fool? Yes. The one in his head."

"Pull it out?"

"Yitzhak, there's no time for this. That's my best knife."

"Mama, I don't think it's kosher anymore," Yitzhak said.

Mother reached up from the hole and pulled her son down by the ear and shouted, "The knife!"

Yitzhak looked at the man's head and the cleaver sticking out of his forehead right above his open eyes.

"Papa's a butcher," Yitzhak pleaded. "He can't get you another one?"

"Do you know how hard it is to find a good knife?"

The boy took a deep breath and closed his eyes. He bent over and gave a little tug.

"It isn't budging," he said.

"Pull harder!"

He pulled with all his might, and the blade finally came loose with such force that it sent Yitzhak crashing backward. His mother pulled the rest of the body down into the hole. The boys listened as there was a bit of rustling, and then their mother poked her head up. There was a noise outside; footsteps approached the front door. Mother hurried them back into the cellar.

"What? Mama—the dead man!" Yitzhak protested.

"You will be a *dead child* if you don't get down there!" she hissed.

The boys scurried down into the hole and had to sit on the dead man's corpse. As soon as Yitzhak closed the door over their head, Mother let out a shriek that came from the southernmost part of her stomach.

"It's just your father," she said. "Idiot. Frightening me like that."

The boys leaped out from beneath the floor and threw their arms around one of their father's tree-trunk legs.

He tussled their hair. "There isn't much time," he said. His eye was swollen and he had a fat lip. "The Kaufmans—all of them gone. Their entire house burned. The bastards even shot their old goat."

Mother clutched her chest and shouted, "May their memories be a blessing." Then she yelled for God to make the killers crawl on their bellies until they died, and for them to have no rest in their graves.

Papa nodded solemnly and said, "Amen."

Yitzhak knew the goat his father spoke of. He'd always hated that decrepit thing. It would always yell out a sound that sounded like the boys' father's body whenever he ate too much cholent on Shabbos. Except the animal only screamed at Yitzhak when the boy walked past it on his own. The goat hated the boy, and Yitzhak was happy the beast was dead.

"There is another casualty in this story," Papa added in a grave tone. "His wagon was stolen."

A hush fell over the entire house. Yitzhak felt vomit creeping up from the lowest depths of his stomach; he tensed his muscles to keep it down. Mother sat down in a chair, rubbed her forehead, and mumbled something that could have either been a prayer or a curse. It was often difficult to tell with her.

The wagon was the way out of Odesa. The plan had been for Kaufman's oldest boy to take his sister and mother, along with Yitzhak, Solomon, and Mother, west to a local Jewish group that had promised to give them shelter until it was safe for them all to board a ship. Yitzhak and Solomon's family already had their sister in America; Chava had gone to Chicago to live with an uncle who helped her get a job sewing buttons. The plan had been that the brothers and Mother would join her while Papa stayed behind and took care of trying to sell his butchering business. There had been so much hope and in just a few words it was all dashed away.

"There is another option," Papa added.

"Yes? Why the suspense?" Mother asked. "You want to audition for the theater—do it after we're safe!"

Papa cleared his throat, a sign Yitzhak knew meant that Mother would not like what she heard.

"Rozenbaum . . ." Father started.

"No," Mother said as she crossed her arms and shook her head defiantly.

"Would you let me finish?"

"No," Mama repeated.

"Rozenbaum . . ."

"A hoodlum!" Mama shouted.

"Rozenbaum tells me there is room on board the ship that's in the port, the one being loaded with wheat. It leaves in two hours."

Mother's eyes widened. She hit her husband on the head.

"Why did you waste all that time getting to the point? Time is of the essence!"

"Because you wouldn't shut up!"

"Let's get our things. We will leave immediately," Mother said as she grabbed the suitcase that she always had packed with a change of clothes and a few other necessities.

Papa demanded she stop, but Mother just kept packing. Papa punched the table with his big reddish fists that he used to slice into bovine flesh and muscles day after day. The boys had never seen him get mad like that.

"Can you just shush? Please," he said.

Mother threw her hands up in disgust.

"No women allowed on the ship," Papa said. "The boys can go, but we will have to find you another way to leave. Rozenbaum will be on board. He'll look after them. The Jewish Aid Association people will be waiting when they arrive and will help them book passage to America."

"I will get word to your brother and Chava," Mother added.

"Best of luck hearing from that daughter of ours. Four months and no letter," Papa replied. "We may as well sit shiva for our daughter."

Mother jumped up out of her chair and toward Father. Her open palm planted itself perfectly across his cheek. She spit three times. "You chicken's asshole," she shouted. "Don't say such a thing!"

As Papa rubbed the pain out of his face, Mother bent down and looked at her two boys and asked about their schooling.

Papa shrugged. He tried to whisper to his wife, but the boys heard him say, "Solomon is still too young and it's not as if the other one is some great scholar. He can pick back up once he's in America. There are fewer distractions there, I'm sure. It will be easier for him."

Mother nodded. She wiped away the tears from her eyes and started gathering a few things for the boys to take with them. She asked what they would eat on the journey.

"Rozenbaum assures me . . ."

"*Feh!* Rozenbaum. Once they're out to sea that thief will probably throw them to the fishes and steal their things!"

Yitzhak had heard his mother say plenty in that tone of voice. He knew whenever she said anything in that flat, resigned way he shouldn't take it to heart. Besides, he was excited about spending time with Rozenbaum. He had introduced himself to Yitzhak as "Uncle Rozy" when Yitzhak was just a boy, and although Mother swore he wasn't a family member, Yitzhak couldn't help but notice the man had a strong resemblance to his father. And unlike Mother, whenever Papa brought up Rozenbaum's name or saw him in the street, he'd smile and nod graciously. Papa had a different opinion. He often reminded his wife that Rozenbaum was not only one of his best customers, but he was one of the men who had the money to bribe local officials to stay out of Jewish affairs. How he got the money was the problem, Mother would argue. In a city of crooks and swindlers, Rozenbaum had attained a status as especially untrustworthy. Exactly what criminal activities he took part in nobody could say, but he was known for his importing business that dealt in whatever exotic goods he was able to get his hands on at any given moment. Tobacco from Turkey, olive oil from Italy, French wine. He even once gave Papa a small bottle of vodka that he claimed came from Sweden. When Papa drank it for the first time, he said it tasted like any other vodka he'd ever had, but the unmarked bottle still was brought down only for special occasions.

Yitzhak was always fascinated with Rozenbaum. He didn't dress like the other Jews; he was always in his nice suits and shirts with a perfectly white detachable collar and colorful ties. He had a thin mustache, a bowler hat on his head, and a walking stick he claimed was from a famous shop in London. They called him the Dandy of Moldavanka.

"Mama," Yitzhak whispered. "We will be OK. I will look after Solomon."

Mother smiled. She pinched Yitzhak's cheek.

"My Yitzalah. It's not your little brother I'm worried about. You're fragile as an egg yolk."

The boys weren't sure how long they'd been at sea. They lost count after three weeks. All they knew was that they didn't see Rozenbaum once the entire time they were on the ship. When they arrived in Hamburg and were waiting to get off the ship and onto the next one that would take them to America, they finally saw him from afar. He looked to be in a rush, his normally crisp and clean shirt was crumpled, unbuttoned, and untucked because his pants were in his hands. A group of men chased behind him. When they caught up to him, they beat him before tossing him into the water.

"He cheated at cards last night," Yitzhak heard somebody say as they walked the long pathway down to the dock. There had been about twenty Jews in total who all lived in cramped quarters that hadn't been designed for human habitation. It was a space where surplus wheat would normally go, but the harvest was lower than expected, so the captain made up for it by charging people to use it to get as far away from Odesa as the ship could take them. There were no beds or blankets. Yitzhak and Solomon slept huddled up with each other every night; their heads shared a sack of potatoes that grew more comfortable with each passing evening as the spuds softened from rot. When they finally made it down to the port and the other Jews were all accounted for, a woman walked toward them and spoke in a type of Yiddish that Yitzhak had to really listen to understand. It seemed the other Jews were also confused.

"She's practically speaking German," Yitzhak heard one man whisper.

The woman smiled, waited for a second, then told the Jews to follow her.

The brothers followed and made their way to the next ship. The man waiting at the foot of the bridge looked down at Yitzhak and Solomon and asked where their parents were. Yitzhak's instinct told him to say they were coming. He lied because he had to, so it wasn't a sin, he told himself.

"You two share a bed. Number Twelve," the man growled.

Yitzhak and Solomon hurried their way up the bridge and onto the ship. Somebody yelled "Jews to the left," so they marched for a few moments until they found a room with a dozen bunk beds crammed together. A one-eyed man handed the boys a thick wool blanket that smelled of smoke and had red stains on it

"Somebody was eating borscht in bed," the one-eyed man said. He flashed a weak, toothless smile.

The boys had seen borscht stains before, but they'd also seen plenty of blood on fabric, being the sons of a butcher—both knew it was the latter. Yitzhak asked the man where the bathroom was. He'd been holding it for an hour but couldn't wait any longer. The one-eyed man pointed at a bucket and said to wait until the boat was at sea to dump it overboard.

People kept to themselves on the ship out of Hamburg. The tight steerage room was dark and damp. A group of Hasids prayed in a corner;

their wives and daughters slept in one row of bunks with a makeshift curtain on each side. In the bunk next to the boys, there was a woman from Bucharest who asked the boys where their parents were. She was pretty and clean. She wore lipstick and smelled like flowers. Talking to her made Yitzhak blush and he couldn't get an answer out.

"Back home in Odesa," Solomon said.

"Odesa? You must be very tough," the lady said.

Neither of the boys knew much of anything beyond their town unless a rabbi had come from there. The only reason they knew the word *Champagne* was because it was the region of France where Rashi had come from in the eleventh century and the Baal Shem Tov was from the north somewhere a few days' journey from Odesa, but the name of the place always escaped Yitzhak. The boys had no concept of what people thought of their hometown.

"There are so many gangsters and thieves there, I've heard," the woman added.

Mother always talked about people that the boys had to steer clear of: Rozenbaum, of course, but she also said not to make eye contact with any of the men who played dice for money in the alley near his home. There was the little hut down an alleyway nearby that she said was where the anarchists did their plotting, and Mother said to never go near it. The sailors who were in town for a few days were always to be avoided, but there were also thieves who blended in effortlessly with the locals and could rob anybody of anything if they didn't pay attention. Mother told her boys the best trick was to never trust anybody, and Yitzhak took the advice to heart. Even speaking for too long with the pretty lady from Bucharest at first felt dangerous to him. Solomon, meanwhile, was an amenable child who had no problem making friends with anybody, and it drove Yitzhak crazy. He'd always admonish his brother, repeating Mother's advice that one day he'd talk to the wrong stranger and end up kidnapped and be forced to live as a slave in the catacombs that were said to exist under the city streets.

It didn't take long for Yitzhak and Solomon to learn nearly all they felt they needed to know about life on the ship. Keep to themselves, try to get to the bathing area as early as possible because it smelled awful by noon, and that the food was especially terrible. The hard black bread was served with schmaltz that had an especially sour taste and left Solomon's stomach hurting, the only vegetables available were raw onions, and the beef at dinner looked like brown string, so Yitzhak went for the other option that he assumed was a stew of some sort. It only took one mouthful to realize he was very wrong, that it was salt pork in baked beans. He'd never had *treyf* before, but he knew that the taste in his mouth wasn't kosher. The salty, sweet flavor was swine. He kept eating and said nothing. When his little brother asked for a bite, Yitzhak couldn't oblige the boy and bring him into the sinful world to which he had crossed over.

There were rules that people were supposed to follow. There was water for bathing, and water for drinking, and you never wanted to mix them up. You weren't supposed to go above deck, either. There was a sign that had been written in multiple languages and posted on the wall that read, "The people in first and second class PAID for the luxury. Do not leave the area you have been assigned to unless given permission." The rumor around the bilge was that one man, a Pole from some nameless town, had broken the rule in the early hours of the morning. He was caught trying to steal some bread and roasted meats from the empty kitchen by one of the crew members, and promptly thrown overboard.

On the second day, the people below deck were told they were allowed to go up top, but by no means allowed to journey past a white line that had been drawn in chalk across the ship that signified the little part they'd been allotted. The space could barely fit more than a dozen people, yet nearly seventy-five were crammed into it. The boys were wedged out by the adults and were about to go back to their bunk downstairs when Yitzhak's eyes widened. He grabbed his little brother by the arm, pointed, and asked if Solomon recognized the curious man with a neat little mustache that curled at the tip on each side who was about to pass by them. His small black eyes and the way he seemed to be nervously surveying everything around him reminded Yitzhak of almost all the Jewish men of Odesa, but he wore a pince-nez on his eye, a bowler hat atop his head, a gray suit jacket with a vest underneath, and a purple shirt and white tie under that. His trousers were a darker shade of gray from the jacket and with a checkered pattern. The sun reflected off his freshly shined black shoes. He looked out of place walking around steerage. Yitzhak couldn't contain his curiosity, and Mother wasn't around to tell him not to talk to somebody he didn't know. He told Solomon to ask the man why he dressed the way he did. His little brother shrugged his shoulders and obeyed Yitzhak's orders. The man scoffed at the question.

"What way should you expect me to dress?"

He spoke Yiddish, but with a flair that sounded French—or what Yitzhak believed French sounded like. Yitzhak didn't know how to answer besides "Nicely."

"Why should I not dress this way? These are my clothes. We're on a ship crossing the ocean. Would you ask the King of England or Baron Rothschild why he dressed the way he did if you saw him walking on this boat?"

"I suppose not. But you're neither one of those men," Yitzhak said.

"How would you know? Have you ever seen Baron Rothschild in person?"

"He hasn't. I know he hasn't," Solomon said. Yitzhak elbowed his brother in the ribs.

"It's just that you look like somebody I know," Yitzhak said. "Do you have a standing order for cow liver whenever it's available?"

The man's eyes lit up.

"The butcher," he said. "Astonishing. Kapovitch the Butcher is your papa. I should have guessed I'd find some landsmen on this ship. Where is your father? I'd love to say hello."

"Odesa," Solomon said. Yitzhak gave him another elbow and told him to quiet down.

"Ah. I see. Your mother?"

"Odesa," Yitzhak answered ruefully.

"Well, then." The man stuck out his hand. "Hershel Kaminsky. My friends call me Hershey and I'd rather not know what my enemies say. And you're . . . Yitz and Sol. Right? I'm great with names. I never forget them."

In Odesa, calling a man by a shortened version of his name was a sign of respect and camaraderie. It made the boys feel like grown-ups. They asked their new friend what he did for a living.

"I'm a writer. No doubt you haven't read me. I'm sure anything that could make it back to Odesa would be suppressed by the tsar and his philistine friends. Now, tell me, are you two going to be butchers like your father?"

Yitz had never thought about what he wanted to do when he was older. The choices he was presented with were either hacking meat from bones or spending his hours poring over holy books, and neither seemed appealing. But Hershey seemed proud of what he did, and Yitz heard the way the adults talked of intellectuals; the men who wrote for the newspapers were local heroes. Everybody read books, he reasoned. It was what the rabbis, the tsar, Bolsheviks, Mensheviks, anarchists, Jews, gentiles, and everybody else had in common. Being a writer sounded like a safe profession, so that's what he said he wanted to be someday.

Hershey ruffled the boy's hair. "You'd better get working on your English before you start applying for jobs. All the Yiddish newspapers in America are socialist and they pay their writers like peasants. That's why when I've made my mark in Chicago, I plan on living in New York. That's where playwrights go to find success. Chicago is a fine starting city, I'm told, but New York is where you go to get rich."

The boys looked at each other.

"Our sister is in Chicago, but we don't know where it is," Sol said. "Rozenbaum was supposed to take us there, but . . ."

"Rozenbaum! That good-for-nothing," Hershey said before spitting on the ground. "A bum."

The hatred for Rozenbaum stirred a memory of Mother in both boys. They both fought the urge to cry for a moment until Sol gave in. Seeing his little brother in tears made it easier for Yitz to suppress his own sobs.

Hershey looked at the boys. They were so innocent and lost. He, on the other hand, had strayed far from the path of righteousness—taking up with prostitutes, enjoying the occasional cigar on Shabbos, and gaining a taste for pork schnitzel—that if he were to show up back at his old yeshiva with his mustache and the smell of *treyf* delicacies secreting from his soul, they'd brand him a heathen. But Hershel Kaminsky still believed in doing good for others. Making mitzvahs was the one thing about his religion that still made sense to him. And what better way to start off on the right foot in America than a first-rate deed? And not just for anybody, but for the butcher's children! Kapovitch was a mensch. He basically saved Hershey's family after their father died. He didn't charge them for at least six months, but never treated them like beggars on whom he took pity. Whenever Hershey or his brother would go for their meat, Kapovitch would take their order, prepare it, always add some extra before nodding, chat for a moment, then send them on their way. He never asked them for payment, and when they finally could take care of their large tab, he smiled and told them not to worry, that it had been settled.

Along with the do-gooding and favor-returning, Hershey had once caught a glimpse of the Kapovitch sister in the nude when she was bathing in the canal and he'd been able to picture her bosom ever since. Surely running into the helpless boys in the middle of the ocean was facilitated by some divine force. It was a sign. Hershey was meant to help the pair of brothers. He told them that when the ship docked in New York City he'd accompany them to Chicago and help them find their sister. She'd be thrilled to see her brothers, but Hershey imagined the look on her face when she caught a glimpse of him, all grown up and worldly, and no longer the sickly yeshiva boy he'd been in Odesa.

As the ship approached America, all the people on board cheered. Some cried, a few prayed. Hershey looked nervous. Yitz heard him mumble "God laughs while men make plans" under his breath.

"Not to frighten you, but a man just told me what could happen if they suspect we aren't related," Hershey said to the boys. "The word is that children who don't show up with a parent or some older relative risk getting sent back. But don't worry."

The brothers looked at each other. They were sure they could survive the gauntlet of Ellis Island, but the Virgil who was to guide their quest didn't seem so confident. Little did any of them know that they'd be rushed through one humiliation after another and wouldn't have time to dwell on the fear of being sent back.

The man at the first desk asked Hershey several questions; the last was whether he was a socialist or an anarchist. He said no. The man smiled at the boys and asked, "Is your papa here a Bolshevik? We can't have any of that coming into our country."

The few words that the brothers understood were all ones their mother had told them to never even mutter in public; just mentioning revolutionaries like Lenin or Trotsky in public could land a Jew in Siberia, so they shook their heads no. The man waved them through to pass to the next tribunal, the one with the doctors in their white coats telling them to strip. As Yitz pulled his pants down, he caught a glimpse of a woman on the other side of the room as she accidentally walked past the curtain that separated the men and the women. Yitz saw her full naked body for a split second, enough time for his *schmeckie* to pop right up. It had happened more than a few times, but never like that, not in front of anybody. All the grown men laughed as one of the doctors pushed a cold stethoscope to the boy's chest.

"Don't worry about it. Happens all the time," the doctor whispered in English. Yitz didn't understand and thought the man was mocking him.

The final man they had to see was the one with the stamp. The boys gave him their documents and he noted in English that their names weren't on it.

"Name? Yitzhak and Solomon Kapovitch," Yitz said.

The man shook his head and mumbled to himself. He wrote something down on each of their documents, stamped them, then handed them to the boys. Hershey looked at what was written down.

"It seems that you're Yitz and Sol *Kaplan* now," he said.

They were on the train to Chicago two hours later. The ride was long, but all three slept the entire way—even Yitz. The rush from Ellis Island into Manhattan, seeing all the buildings and people moving at a speed he didn't know was possible, took what little energy he had left in his body. His first hours in America felt almost like the time he'd had a fever and sworn the entire house was spinning and the earth was shaking while his mother said blessings for the sick and dying over him.

At some point during the train ride, Yitz awoke and looked out the window. He saw only blankness but felt the speed at which America was passing him by. It was Yitz's first time on a train. He was bolting into the future faster than he could have ever imagined. It felt good, a motion that mimicked how the inside of his brain felt. Always shooting quickly forward without much cause for stopping.

When they finally made it to Chicago, Yitz and Sol thought the grand stone train station was a castle. Hershey looked at the address of where the boys' sister was staying. It was the same street his brother lived on: Maxwell. The numbers were so close to each other that he assumed it would be an easy drop-off, so the trio stepped out into the unfamiliar city with hope in their hearts. They were greeted by a cacophony of bangs and crashes, the symphony of progress; new buildings were going up in every direction and so many people rushing up and down the sidewalk that Sol asked if they'd mistakenly wandered into a parade.

They roamed for three hours trying to find their way. Hershey tried asking people for directions, but most of them kept walking; one spit in his face and said, "Go back to where you came from," and a woman with a pile of makeup on her face told him she didn't give directions, but that she could show him a good time for a price.

"Why don't you want a good time?" Yitz asked as they walked away. "What's wrong with a good time?"

"Nothing," Hershey told him. "Just no time for one."

They went in circles until Sol noticed they passed by the same old man with an eye patch selling fish heads three times and decided to take matters into his own hands. He walked up to a tall man in a brown suit.

"Mister," he said using the little English he knew. It came out as "Mistah," and when he said the name of the location, he replaced the *w* with a *v*, asking for "*Maxvell* Street."

The man bent over and looked the boy in the eye. He snickered. "You wanna go to Jewtown, kid?"

He had a wide pink nose that made him look like the hogs some of the gentiles kept in a field right next to a small shul back in Odesa. The rabbi complained to the owner after he walked into the holy hut one morning and saw one of the pigs defecating on the floor, but the gentiles just laughed at the rabbi and started slapping him in the face.

"Jewtown is that way," the pig-nosed man said. He pointed a finger at a sign. "That's where you filthy rats go."

"Jewish? Yes," Sol said with a smile on his face as he pointed in the same direction.

"Go be with the other vermin, you little snot," the man said as he turned and walked away.

Sol knew to say "Thank you" before he walked over and told Yitz and Hershey what he'd found out.

They got on one trolley, then another, then a train that went aboveground, giving Yitz, Sol, and Hershey their first real look at the sprawling city that never seemed to end, and they made it to Maxwell Street. The scene was so familiar that Yitz wondered if they'd been traveling for so long that they just ended up back in Odesa. It looked just like the Jewish market there, except surrounded by taller buildings.

"And this is much dirtier," Sol said as he pointed at a man who had just clubbed a rat the size of a cat to death and left the carcass there as he chased another one.

"What's that smell?" Yitz asked. He pinched his nostrils.

"Which one?" Hershey asked.

They soldiered through the crush of peddlers and beggars: young women buying, old men haggling, chickens letting out final squawks before having their throats slit, rats moving confidently at the feet of the humans. Yitz tried to understand what was going on around him, but there was so much to take in, and it all moved like flashes of light.

That first time walking down Maxwell Street was the greatest thrill of Yitz's young life; it was the most terrified *and* happiest he'd ever been. Nothing made sense, but it all impressed the wide-eyed immigrant boy. Sol had to pull Yitz by the arm because his older brother was so busy looking around.

"This is it," Hershey said as he pointed at a building with a sign over the front door that said "Bakery."

They walked in and asked the old man behind the counter if the boys' sister lived there.

"Chava? That idiot. She meets a man, some Bohunk. They left me a month ago—I get two days' notice. Two days I had to fill the room!"

The boys were confused. Yitz asked where the uncle she'd been staying with had gone.

"Poor Mendel. He died—may his memory be a blessing. Four months ago. Coughed himself to death," the man said. "Now, you buy something? I need to make money, you know."

Yitz and Sol hadn't eaten in almost two days. The hunger pains that shot through them made it difficult to mourn an uncle they hardly knew and not knowing where their sister was. Hershey bought three pretzels and gave each of the boys one. They walked outside and ate them while trying to make sense of everything they saw around them. Hershey took a bite, then had an idea.

"We're going to see Avi. He'll know what to do," he said.

They walked down to the address where his brother and mother lived, then solemnly up the stairs to the third floor. The boys trailed behind Hershey and noticed he was shaking. When they finally got to the door, he tried to steady himself but Yitz noticed the slight tremble in his hand. Yitz asked if he was going to knock, but Hershey looked as if he might faint. He couldn't bring himself to knock on the door, so Sol shook his head, and without saying a word, the younger brother stepped forward, balled his fist, and banged on the door until footsteps could be heard marching heavily on the other side. The locks were undone, and there stood Avi Kaminsky, tall, straight, and sturdy. His face was chiseled, his black hair was almost all perfectly parted to the right side, a dramatic line separated what was combed to the left. The shirt he wore was perfectly white and his shoes shined like polished gems. Yitz and Sol had never seen a Jew like him before. So proud. So healthy. He smiled at his brother and shook his head before embracing Hershey in a hug that looked like it could squeeze the life out of a man if he held it long enough. The two men stepped back and looked at each other for a second, then Avi noticed the two boys.

"You jerk. You didn't tell me I'm an uncle," he said.

"We're from Odesa," Sol said.

"The butcher's kids," Hershey added.

"Kapovitch? The Meat Mensch of Gospitalnaya Street? Where is he?"

Nobody said a word. Avi understood what that meant. He pulled at his suspenders.

"They can stay with us while they figure things out. Mama will love having more boys to cook for. It'll be a mitzvah." He winked at Sol and Yitz, then pinched his brother's cheek. "We'll find something for them to do."

As luck would have it, Avi had a knack for finding young boys employment. He had several who hung around hoping to make a couple of bucks doing this or that so they could help out their family, but because of the Odesa connection and his warm memories of their father, he looked after Yitz and Sol. He gave them a place to stay with Hershey and his mother, and they got to spend more time around Avi than the other boys, but the Kaplan brothers still had to work like everybody else.

It was mostly little jobs: shining shoes, mopping and cleaning the windows of the *banya*—that the men of any importance along the strip referred to as the Schvitz—where Avi had a small office he worked out of, scooping up the horse and dog shit on the sidewalk, and delivering envelopes and not asking questions. They also trailed the rag pickers who all scoured the heaps of trash for stray bits of cloth, old buttons, scraps of metal, or anything else that could be cleaned up and resold. The pickers who worked around Jewtown each had to pay a weekly fee to Avi for the pleasure of sticking their hands in piles of rotten food, broken glass, maggots, and other assorted waste in hopes of finding bits of fabric, copper, bone, or anything else that would get them a couple of cents, and it was Yitz and Sol's job to let Avi know if they were keeping anything for themselves.

Avi's crew of younger guys did the sort of work grown men couldn't be counted on to do. People called them "Avi's Boys," and they were his eyes, ears, and occasionally the ones called upon to do some of the dirty work that didn't involve heavy lifting or hard punches. Early on, it was Yitz, Jabby Wiessman, Westy Mendleson, Jakey Jake Malamud, and Avigdor Foxman, who everybody just called Foxy, because it sounded better than his real name and the shortened version was already owned by Avi.

Sol was also one of Avi's boys, but it was different with him. He longed for *something*—he wanted to be a butcher like his father and *his* father before him. Yitz would tease him about his aspirations, saying he had so much more potential beyond wrapping up cow liver and tongue for old ladies to cook on Shabbos. Even though he was the youngest, Sol was the one all the other boys feared the most because of his strength. Avi called him a little piece of granite and had him box in a few matches with boys who were a few years older than him, each bout ending in a knockout within seconds. If somebody dared start anything with him, they ran the risk of Solomon the Battering Ram running toward them, knocking them over, then pounding them until they begged for mercy. Yitz thought his little brother was going to be a prizefighter, but no—he wanted to slice brisket. Avi said he respected anybody who wanted to work, and promptly made sure that the boy was given a job three days a week training with Mendel the old blind butcher, then he'd work for Avi the other four days.

Sometimes the work was fun, like when Avi told Yitz and some of the others to get with a few of the Italian boys to stand on rooftops and throw firecrackers at supporters of the mayoral candidate Peter Wilholm, who was vehemently anti-Jewish and anti-Catholic. He'd said if he won, he'd push for a quota on immigrants who practiced anything but "good, old-fashioned Christianity," and Yitz loved watching his supporters scatter as the little explosives rained down on them from above. Then there was the time Avi had Yitz and two other boys light an entire delivery of newspapers on fire as a sign to a distributor who wasn't paying his dues. The guy caught the boys just as one of them was about to strike the match. He swung wildly, getting Yitz just across the bridge of his nose. Yitz heard a cracking and could feel the warm blood dripping down his face as he ran for his life.

"I think you've got what it takes, kid," Avi said later that night as he examined the swelling around Yitz's nose. "The good news is I don't think you'll need a doctor for that."

Yitz was so relieved that he didn't see the hand shoot toward his face until a finger was in his right nostril. Avi moved fast, realigning the bone and cartilage with a flick. It was the worst thing Yitz had ever felt, shooting from his face all the way down to his toes. He let out a loud shriek, felt himself about to cry, but looked at Avi standing in front of him. Some tears welled up and dripped down his cheeks as the adrenaline raced through Yitz's body, but he held out. Avi smiled as he swiped a match across the wall that he used to light his cigar. He took a few puffs, then pointed the burning cherry so it lined up right between Yitz's eyes. "Odesa makes tough boys," he said.

3

The soulless glass cube disguised as architecture sat in the middle of a part of the city where countless pigs and cows were sliced up into steaks and chops for over a century. It felt a million miles away from secret graves and long-lost relatives, Elijah thought as he rode the elevator to the top floor of the building.

He got to the doors and waited to be let into the Sergei Chicago Holdings office that looked out over the entire South Side. The firm was named after the founder's favorite childhood hockey player, a fact that always reminded Elijah that Raphael Razumov-Augier was a rich kid who'd taken the small fortune his father had amassed by shady means after leaving Russia in the late 1980s and turned it into an empire after selling the "safety crowdsourcing" app he'd co-founded, OverCR, to a Saudi investment firm for somewhere in the nine-figure range. There was public outcry against OverCR from the moment it was launched, and a number of lawsuits claimed it violated every possible civil liberty in one way or another, but the outrage was dwarfed by the number of Americans who used the app to alert anybody in a five-mile radius whenever there was a suspicious-looking teenager or person who looked like they didn't speak English nearby. After that, Raphael Razumov-Augier was in the business of investing, with a side hustle as a motivational speaker who amassed an army of teenage and twentysomething male followers who wanted to know how to "Grind yourself into gold," as his catchphrase put it. His latest project, he told one reporter, was so massive in scale, there wouldn't be a traditional rollout "with all kinds of fancy press releases and stuff." When the reporter asked if he could be a little less vague, Raphael answered, "We're going to redefine the American city. And by 'we,' I mean Americans, not the government." He said his vision would put the people in control of making cites better, cleaner, more efficient places. All they needed to do was contribute—financially, of course. The article ended up being the magazine's cover story, with an illustration of a grinning Raphael standing over the city of Chicago with his quote "We're taking back our cities" next to his face.

Raphael didn't say hello when Elijah walked into his office, only "This thing is coming together real nice." He had on a pair of big black sunglasses and had obviously gotten hair plugs since the last time Elijah had seen him. He scratched a piece of dirt off his Air Jordan 3s. Every pair of the sneakers he owned was famously one of one, designed specifically for him. He loved to mention that in any interview he did. Elijah wondered what made them different from any other pair of Jordans as he struggled to come up with a nice way to ask Raphael what he was talking about, but he didn't need to. "I know you said you had to figure a few things out, but I got a few guys who don't have to think so hard about this," Raphael said.

A KAWS sculpture in the corner sat beneath a framed guitar on the wall above it that was signed by somebody, but Elijah couldn't make out who. The office looked like it was inhabited by a fourteen-year-old with expensive tastes. Elijah was wondering if the Uzi machine gun plated in solid gold sitting on top of the stack of art books actually worked when Raphael's voice picked up a decibel.

"That's the way it is. You either get on your knees for me or you don't. That's it," he shouted before taking the $10,000 big-tech-meets-high-fashion sunglasses off his face and whipped them onto his desk.

"They call those things smart glasses, but they're stupid as hell," Raphael said before starting to laugh at his own joke. Elijah figured it best to also laugh. Not too much, but just enough. A little smile with a chuckle would suffice. Raphael seemed pleased.

"So you're coming to me begging for a job," Raphael said as he picked up a baseball that was also plated in gold. He rolled it around the palms of his hands and glared at Elijah with the contempt of a spoiled child who'd been given another toy that wasn't much different from all the others he'd grown tired of.

The truth was that Raphael's CMO had reached out to Elijah about taking a role on an upcoming project, but Elijah wasn't in a position to turn anything down or tell the boss that he was wrong.

"I'm weighing some options while I'm in town," Elijah said with a hint of confidence that he had to pull from deep down to find. "My family is from here and . . ."

"Options? Buddy, last I heard, you couldn't even get an appointment at the unemployment office in San Francisco."

Thank God for the extra tab of Klonopin Elijah had taken before he walked into the building. He used to need a handful to get through the day but had gotten himself down to a single daily dose; taking a second pill for a big meeting felt like a healthy middle ground. He'd timed things perfectly. Raphael trying to be funny didn't faze him; Elijah could take being the joke if he had to.

Raphael smudged his finger on a tablet touchscreen. A woman's voice came through it asking what he needed.

"Send Tal in," he commanded.

Raphael sat back in his chair and studied Elijah's face.

"I thought it was a good idea, the whole CMUNTY thing. You got in right before Airbnb was everywhere. I heard VCs were chucking money at you."

Elijah opened his mouth to answer, but Raphael kept talking.

"Should have quit while you were ahead. Sold earlier, moved on to other things. That's what I do. You stay too long and you start to think you deserve more and more. I've seen it a hundred times, but never saw anybody fuck it up like you guys."

A bald man walked in the door. He was straight and tall; his torso reminded Elijah of a Renaissance sculpture, all marble and perfectly chiseled. It was hugged by a tight-fitting black T-shirt. Elijah looked closely and saw the little red monogrammed dragon on the right sleeve; it was the same brand of 100 percent Supima cotton shirts he used to buy ten of at a time at eighty bucks a pop. That used to feel so good to do.

"Tal takes care of all my security stuff. I had him check you out because what I'm gonna do is big, and I can't take any risks. Even with meetings like this I'm careful."

"I signed the NDA," Elijah said.

Raphael's attention was focused on something that flashed across his laptop screen. As soon it was no longer of interest, he had Elijah repeat what he'd said, then shook his head.

"Those things are a joke; you can wiggle out of 'em. But Tal checks out everything. Him and his guys keep an eye on you for a bit and then they get back to me with the thumbs-up."

If he'd started to think too much about it, Elijah would have melted into a puddle of neurosis. The fear would have neutralized the benzos in his blood, so he just convinced himself that Raphael's dictator-like paranoia was impressive and nodded at the private security man who looked like he'd done some truly terrible things to a lot of people in third-world countries without a hint of remorse. Elijah just nestled in his synthetic calm. It felt as though he were floating above everything that was being said to him, but then the one thing he should have seen coming sent him headfirst back through the windshield of reality.

"You still have a pill problem? Sounds like you were gobbling all kinds of shit," Raphael said as he glanced at his phone. "Not a big deal if you do; most of my top guys are junkies for something. Most of them do blow, and one has a heroin habit in the city, then goes back to his McMansion in Wilmette and is Joe Normal with his wife and three kids. I won't even get started on the sex stuff some of these guys are into. The point is I know all because I hear all and see all. I even know about your friend killing that family. You guys must have done some real work to get your name omitted from the report."

The extra Klonopin was no use against Raphael talking about Oliver, and the fact that he'd brought it up was purely out of cruelty.

Oliver was Elijah's best friend growing up. People called him "Ollie Party" since he was the first of the group to go to parties with older kids where beer, weed, psychedelics, and all other manner of intoxicants were available and consumed, starting when he was thirteen. By seventeen, he was in AA, had his first stint in rehab at nineteen; then he moved to Arizona to clean up before moving back to Chicago at twenty-two. After a few years of sober living and working for his older brother's online sports gambling business, Ollie started messing up again. During a business trip out in San Francisco he called Elijah. Things seemed normal and Ollie wasn't throwing them back the way he had, so Elijah had a cocktail, then another. He was going to settle up and get on his way to a party for another app that had received a five-million-dollar infusion that day. He invited Ollie as his plus-one, but his old friend said he had other plans, then told Elijah to stay for another drink—for old times' sake. They had one more before parting ways. Elijah went to the party while Ollie Party sat at the restaurant bar alone for another hour, downing three more drinks before getting in his car. He drove two blocks, veered into the other lane, and slammed straight into another car, killing himself, the woman driving the other car, and one of her two twin daughters in the backseat.

Elijah went numb when he found out the next morning. His only instinct was to tell his partners that the drunk driver in the news was his old friend and they'd had drinks together earlier that night. Within an hour, Elijah was in a room with two company lawyers and four "crisis management" PR people who told him they'd take care of everything. Their only advice was for Elijah to make sure he didn't say a word to anybody about seeing Oliver. He did as he was told and flew into O'Hare for the funeral. He got there the day before and stopped at a bar he'd been invited to by mutual friends who were gathering before Oliver's urn was placed inside a marble wall of some cemetery. When he walked in, Elijah noticed Oliver's ex-girlfriend glaring at him. When he walked over to the bar to order a drink, she approached him and said she'd gotten a text from Oliver the night he died that he was drinking with Elijah, yet somehow, nobody knew or mentioned that. Elijah's entire body burned. His pulse pounded and he couldn't think of what to say. He picked up his drink and chugged half of it to calm his nerves. Once he did, Elijah rushed out of the bar, texting his assistant to book him the next ticket back to San Francisco she could find, no matter how much it cost. He skipped the funeral, took a red-eye, and went straight to his office, where his partners called a meeting to tell him there was nothing to worry about. The police had contacted the company's lawyers, but they were only interested in the bar that overserved the drunk driver and understood Elijah was simply having a drink with an old friend. The gleeful way his partners delivered the news with smiles on their faces—like three people weren't dead—made Elijah queasy. That was the moment Elijah felt like he'd lost a part of himself. It was the break in his timeline that separated his old life from his new one. Before that meeting, he had money, a wife, friends, respect, and a nice home in Marin County. The after, Elijah believed, started as he walked out of the meeting with his partners slapping him on the back like he'd thrown the touchdown that won the big game. That was exactly when his journey toward divorce, loneliness, and living with his dying mother in Midwestern purgatory began.

"I just wanted to be up front with you before we started talking. I'm a big fan of trust," Raphael said. "But since Tal said you aren't a risk, then we're good."

Elijah could barely muster an "OK."

"I know California people like to talk about *impact* and *changing the world* and all of that crap, but this is Chicago. I don't pussyfoot around and I'll say up front this is going to make a ton of money for anybody involved, especially on the ground floor. You come on board, and I can promise you that you'll forget all your troubles from the past."

Outside the window, Elijah saw smoke rising up from the ground somewhere in the distance. It didn't feel like a good sign, but he still forced a smile and looked impressed as he listened to Raphael's pitch.

Hyde Park had never been the most exciting part of the city. It was "the place where fun goes to die," according to people in other neighborhoods, and Elijah couldn't disagree with the sentiment. Even though the area had added a few bars and restaurants that he normally wouldn't have minded trying out, they were so close to important landmarks—the house where Elijah had his first awkward kiss, the apartment where Elijah had his first awkward dry hump, and the playground where Elijah had his first breakup—that he didn't.

He was sitting with a three-week-old *New Yorker* when Eve walked in and sat in her favorite spot on the couch right next to the window. She cracked it open a bit, and Elijah saw how much doing a simple task took out of her, but there was no way she'd ask for help. She pulled from a purple vape, let the smoke drift slowly from her mouth, and then started reading a novel. It was the familiar routine, and Elijah felt like he was truly back home since reading in silence was how they'd spent much of their time together when he was growing up. When he was a child, Elijah never once interrupted the stillness unless it was an emergency; being an adult meant he had earned the right to speak up when something was on his mind—he just wasn't sure how to approach it. Something about his mother's steely concentration on what she was reading made him lose his nerve, so he decided to go another route. He picked up his glass of water and spilled some on himself.

Eve eyeballed him suspiciously.

"Are you doing all right?"

"Yeah, sorry. Didn't have lunch so I've got the shakes," Elijah said.

The information troubled Eve; if there was one thing she couldn't take, it was somebody missing a meal. She started standing up slowly. Elijah was caught off guard seeing the labor that went into her getting off the couch, but couldn't tell if it was her body breaking down or the weed.

"I'll make you a sandwich," Eve said, nearly to her feet.

"No, Ma. It's fine. I'm good."

"I don't want to be the stereotypical Jewish mother, but you need to eat."

"I know, but can we talk first? I'll eat after," Elijah said.

The suspicious look returned to Eve's face as she sat back down.

"I talked with Rabbi Ginsburg," Elijah started. He waited for a response beyond the annoyed look on his mother's face.

"Who?"

"The rabbi who keeps sending you letters."

"Why did you talk to him?"

"Because he's been trying to get in touch with you. The letters in the cabinet, remember?"

Eve took a long pull from her vape and exhaled. The smoke floated up toward the ceiling; she motioned with her hand for Elijah to keep talking.

"He had some things, papers and stuff like that. I've got the box in my car and was thinking we could look later," Elijah said. He hadn't gone into the conversation feeling the need to tread lightly, but his mother's tone was a sign to shift.

"Why would I want to do that?"

For such an unsentimental person, it was always funny to Elijah how much his mother saved. She was a pack rat who just did a good job keeping most of it out of sight. There were boxes in the cellar, the basement, and the bedroom her late sister had once lived in. Stacked in the corner by the washing machine were three boxes filled with copies of the book of poetry by members of the French Resistance that Eve had translated back in 1999. Another, which had been placed on the shelf in Elijah's bedroom after he moved out, contained an assortment of ephemera from his youth—newspapers from the Bulls' second and fourth championships in the 1990s, a Brooks Brothers catalog from 1996, ticket stubs from shows at the Metro in the late

2000s—that Eve must have found while cleaning up after he went away to college. She wanted things from the past close to her, yet she seemed totally uninterested in a mystery box with her late father's belongings.

"Maybe for research. It could be for your book," Elijah said. As far as he knew, the book was way past due and he always heard Eve complaining about lacking the inspiration to write.

"Why would I need anything in that box for my book?"

"Because it's a memoir. You know—*your history*. Seems like it could be helpful for a book about your life," Elijah said.

Eve sneered and told her son to be serious. "Nobody wants to read the story of some poet unless she stuck her head in an oven or jumped off a bridge. I'm just dying of cancer when I'm way past my prime," Eve said as she pushed herself with all her strength to get up and start walking. Elijah tried to stop her, but she ignored him.

"Come on, Ma. I want to help. . . ."

Eve didn't stop walking as she spoke. "Stop with your bullshit, Elijah. I don't have enough time left for it," she said before getting to the stairs. It took her a moment to make it up two steps and Elijah thought she stopped because she was winded, but she turned around again to look at him. "You don't know what you want. You never have."

He listened as she began climbing one step at a time, each cleared in nearly the same amount of time it once took her to ascend the entire staircase. When she finally made it to the top and he could hear her footsteps in her bedroom, Elijah didn't need to dig too deep into his memories to recall the last time she'd talked to him like that. If there was one thing he could say about his relationship with Eve, it was that they didn't fight the way he saw other kids and parents argue and yell. He could clearly recall being nineteen, the taste of charcoal and salt from the Japanese restaurant they'd been having dinner at that evening in his mouth as he replayed the scene.

He was going to bring up that he was taking time off school when the first parts of the bird were placed on the table, but something about breaking news over chicken gizzards didn't sit right, so he waited. The cooked small intestines with the crush of pepper on them weren't good, nor was the plate that was simply presented as "cartilage" by the server. As they watched the chef delicately season the next round of skewered chicken with light flurries of salt and twist the meat over a flame, Elijah decided it was time. He turned toward his parents, and ever-so-casually mentioned that he wasn't going back to school in the fall.

A small flame from the grill flickered up as Eve turned to her son and asked him to repeat himself.

"I'll go back, eventually," Elijah said.

Eve looked at her husband. They knew there was a possibility they'd hear those words come out of their son's mouth. He was a young person like a thousand others she'd seen in her classes, the ones who needed a little more exposure to the real world. Eve and Peter couldn't fault him; both had traveled when they were around his age. They gave their blessing.

The chef placed a single skewer on each of their plates and told them it was chicken thigh, before giving a slight bow. Peter and Eve ate while Elijah just looked at his. He had one more thing to ask.

"The bank account," he said. "I'd like to have access to it. I know I'm allowed to since I turned eighteen, but I wanted to let you know. I'm going to be doing some traveling and don't want to have to always call you guys for help."

Eve took a deep breath. The money had been set aside for Elijah by Sonny and had grown considerably from the initial $10,000 thanks to some smart investing over the years. All Eve could do was ask Elijah to be careful with it.

He promised he would be. "I'm starting a company with Nathanael and this other guy. It's seed money."

Peter started choking on his piece of chicken thigh.

"A company? I thought you wanted to travel," Eve said as her husband spit out the half-chewed piece of meat.

Elijah slid the chicken off the skewer into his mouth and nodded. He chewed slowly, and swallowed. "I will—for work," he said, before he explained that Alec, the third partner in the business, and a childhood friend of Nathanael, Elijah's dormmate, had started what he called a "dorm away from the dorm" for students who didn't like the campus living conditions and wanted something a little nicer. All they needed to do was pay $2,000 a month, and they could have access to a house on the water, with modern amenities, a fully furnished bedroom, and a space to do their schoolwork in peace.

Eve and Peter were confused. How did the students have all that money to blow on rent on top of their tuition and actual dorm fees? And who was this Alec? How did he have a house on the water in the Bay Area? It all sounded like a scam, but Elijah assured his parents it wasn't.

"Alec is Alec Kingsley," Elijah said.

"Yes. And? I don't know what that means," Eve said.

"He built DeweyD.com," Elijah said.

"The site that steals books?"

"They don't steal; they *provide*," Elijah scoffed. "Not everybody can afford books, so DeweyD made it easier for people to have access to them as e-books. I feel like you'd appreciate something like that. It's art versus capitalism, and art wins when it's free for all."

"I thought he sold the company for ten million or something," Peter said.

"He did," Elijah said.

"It sounds to me like capitalism came out on top," Eve said.

"Come on, Ma. You always said I should get a job. Now I have one."

Eve rolled her eyes and shook her head. "Wow" was all she could say. She said it again. *"Wow."*

"You're being so shortsighted and out of touch," Elijah said. "Within a decade, hardly anybody will work in an office and people will be free to roam the world, doing their jobs from anywhere they want. We're getting in early. The hope is that we can get enough investors on board to get properties in three cities and furnish them by the start of the new year."

Eve scoffed. "You're getting into the motel business?"

Peter asked what the company was called.

"Who cares what it's called? It's a terrible idea," Eve snapped. "Will it be pay-by-the-hour? Maybe you can get those machines that make the beds vibrate for a quarter. I don't know how you got like this, I swear to God."

Elijah looked around and saw people paying attention to the rising tension from near the counter. He tried to calm his mother down while still reeling from the shock of her response.

"Don't you think you're being a little intense about this? Maybe you should try being supportive," he said. "You always told me to make things. You wanted me to create, so that's what I'm doing."

Without even turning to look at her son, Eve let out a slight snort, a rejection of the absurdity. "You aren't *building anything*," she said. "You'll use the money you *didn't earn*, and you'll continue being unhappy. You've been cursed with the gift of good fortune, and it's not enough. That's called greed."

Eve told her husband to pay the check and walked out. Elijah and his father sat in silence until the server placed chicken meatballs in front of them and scurried off.

"I don't understand why she's like that," Elijah said. "She's maybe the only mother I know who would rather her son be a writer or somebody else that makes no money. If I had told her I decided to go to a liberal arts college to study puppeteering instead of what I just said then she'd throw me a celebration."

Peter Mendes was a lawyer. He was a great lawyer. Over his career he'd helped a number of poorer people successfully sue big corporations, but he always told his son that was just his job. He said that he liked the feeling of helping the little guy take down the bigger guy, but he still respected the bigger guy if he did things right. Eve hated the bigger guy, but Peter would routinely tell his son that the reason a country like America could exist was that little guys could become big ones if they worked hard. That lesson stuck with his son. Peter made success seem honorable, so Elijah grew up focused on the *idea* of success. He didn't know what he wanted to be successful at, nor did it matter much to him how others may have defined the word; to Elijah, making money meant success. Why didn't his mother understand that? How could she say that he wasn't earning anything when she was the one who'd inherited the house they lived in and was able to spend her life teaching and publishing the occasional poem in magazines that a hundred other poets read? It didn't make sense, Elijah said. It seemed hypocritical.

For a great lawyer, Peter Mendes was a man who used as few words as possible. He was a quiet, contemplative person who went out of his way to avoid conflict in his personal life. Elijah always found it funny that his father's job was to win arguments. Peter would say he only did what came naturally, that it was in his DNA because his own father's side were descendants of some famous seventeenth- or eighteenth-century Talmudic scholar from Morocco. He wasn't some rich, hotshot white-shoe attorney who fit his son's narrow ideas of what *success* looked like, but Elijah still valued Peter's opinion over all others. Surely he'd have some insight that could help.

"Your mother . . ." He paused as he picked a skewer up off his plate and put it in his mouth. "She has her reasons. They might be complicated, but they're her reasons. Someday you'll understand."

Peter liked to make things as clear and direct as possible. He didn't beat around bushes and was never vague, so his answer made Elijah boil. First his mother treated him like a child, then his father— the parent he always felt like he could depend on—had betrayed him by offering bullshit.

"No, I won't. And you know why? Because she never tells me anything and you just act like that's normal. Meanwhile, my normal is my mom waiting to tell me she has cancer or never opening up about herself to me, but she feels fine shitting on my ideas. I don't think that's normal, Dad. Nothing about our relationship is normal."

Peter took the skewer out of his mouth and placed it gently down on the plate. He straightened it so the tip pointed directly ahead.

"One day you'll understand," he said as he got up to leave.

"I doubt it," Elijah muttered.

Perplexed over how telling his mother a rabbi had given him a box of her father's things started a huge blowup, he took an Ambien and chewed up a melatonin gummy to fall asleep. The other option was to stay up all night replaying the whole thing over in his head, trying to figure out what set his mother off or how he could have approached things differently.

Eve woke at her normal time, just as the sun began to crack over the Illinois sky. After getting dressed and taking care of a few things in the house, she walked a few blocks to the coffee shop where she was the first customer every morning; the barista always had Eve's chamomile tea already steeping. The only decision she normally had to make was whether she wanted a scone or croissant, but she went with both and also a blueberry muffin. Food was always her way of making a peace offering.

Elijah was waiting for her in the kitchen when she arrived home.

"I assume this is for me," he said.

The box that the rabbi had given him was on the table in front of him. Next to it was another. It was also cardboard, but somebody had used so much tape to make sure it was shut that Elijah thought to joke about calling a locksmith to open it up. Eve put the coffee and bag of pastries down in front of her son and pulled up her normal chair. There was a little jar with pens and pencils on the table that Eve kept for doing crosswords and jotting things down. She pulled out a little flathead screwdriver that was in it, handed it to Elijah, and pointed at the box with too much tape on it. He stabbed the tool into the crease, ripped through the polypropylene, and opened it. On top was a manila folder that had sustained a little water damage on the right side. Elijah picked it up and saw a mess of papers, leather-bound books, and more folders spilling all over the place. It was as if all the things had been hurriedly crammed into the box, which was then packed up like it was going to Fort Knox. It looked as if nobody had any intention of ever unsealing it. Elijah opened the folder and found a photo looking up at him. It was in the sort of ghostly black and white that snapshots from the turn of the twentieth century always had and the only color to be found was the yellowing around the edges. It was of a young man wearing a suit. He couldn't have been older than a teenager, but he had that world-weary look on his face that people who lived back when you likely died by fifty always carried. A fedora was on his head and a blank stare on his face. Around his neck was a Jewish prayer shawl with its tasseled fringes. Elijah couldn't recall what they called those even though he'd also worn one at his own bar mitzvah. He knew as much about the religion his family once practiced as he knew about the man in the picture, whom he could identify only as his grandfather because he had the same cheekbones and eye shape as Eve.

"I know we've never talked much about him," Eve said.

He rummaged through the box a bit more, pulling out everything carefully and setting them in piles according to size. Wedged at the bottom of the box in a corner was a small antique leather bag. Elijah pulled it out and looked to see if his mother's expression had changed, but it hadn't. She just watched as he struggled to pull the rusted zipper back; little brown particles fell with each metal tooth that came undone. When it was finally opened, there was a small treasure trove of mostly worthless things from the past: pencils with hotel names on them, a notepad for TWA, and then Elijah pulled a ring of keys from the bag and looked at it. He pulled out an old matchbook for a place called Herzog's Fresh Seafood. The logo was a grinning fish, a cigar in its mouth, and an address for somewhere in the Loop made out of the stogie smoke. There was another matchbook for a place called Cantabile's Little Italy, and a business card for a place called Cafe Wilhelm. At the bottom was a plastic grocery bag wrapped around something. Elijah took it out, opened it up, and found some police paperwork in it. The paper was old and brittle; the handwriting on it was tough to make out, but it said something about a body being found, and it seemed to say that it was a possible drowning. He looked at another piece of paper from the bundle; it looked to be a facsimile of a death certificate from the Cook County coroner's office. He read the deceased's name: Rose Kaplan, his grandmother. He saw the date was sometime in 1963, but before he could read anything else, Elijah was startled by his mother grabbing the paper from his hands. She had moved with a burst of speed he didn't know she'd had even when she was healthy. He watched as his mother looked at the death certificate. A look came over her face that was somewhere between sadness and anger. She inhaled through her nostrils and exhaled the air the same way. Elijah counted as she did the same again, then again, and a fourth time until she had decided what she wanted to say.

"I wondered where this went" was all Eve said.

While she never talked of Yitzhak Kaplan or had pictures of her father up anywhere in the home, Eve's mother was, at the very least, acknowledged. There was a photo of her on the shelf in the living room, and Eve lit a candle every year on the anniversary of her mother's death, but did it without drawing any attention to the action, placing it in her bathtub overnight so it wouldn't catch fire. Rose Kaplan was at least allowed to exist in the Mendes household, but Elijah had to fill in her biography on his own over time. He knew that there was possibly some celebrity connection through his grandma he'd never met, information he learned while watching *Jeopardy!* with Eve when he was fourteen. "Who is Lauren Bacall" was the answer to Alex Trebek's clue. Eve looked at Elijah excitedly and told him that the actress, who was still alive at the time, was a distant relative of theirs, one of her mother's cousins. Then she dryly added, "Probably the only family member we have left."

By then, Elijah had also figured out some of Rose's story from before she made it to America. Eve and Peter had always used the vague term *survivor* when talking about her, and while Elijah knew what that meant, few other details were provided. He knew she'd been born in Romania, that her father was a teacher, and that Eve and her sister were raised by Rose's friend Sarah. Elijah met Sarah a few times when he was very young but had no real memories of her or how she became such an important part of her family's story since

Eve's relationship with Sarah deteriorated over the years. Part of it had to do with Sarah believing she was owed part of the inheritance that had been left to the girls after Rose died, but also because she didn't like Peter. Sarah tried to forbid Eve from seeing the young man who had his eye on law school because she didn't believe Peter—with his dark skin and fluency in Spanish—was a Jew. Eve hadn't talked to Sarah in nearly a decade when she passed, and although she'd been the closest thing to a tangible past that he knew of, Elijah didn't want to go to a funeral. He had better things to do like sit on the computer and start fights with strangers on message boards. Why should he have to go if he hardly knew the person and she wasn't even family? Eve seemed taken aback by her son's brattiness, but relented by telling him he was right and that he didn't need to go. She walked out of the room and Elijah saw the look of disappointment on his father's face, but couldn't understand why.

Peter walked over to his son and whispered "Sarah was in Ravensbrück with your grandmother" with a snap of anger in his tone before walking away. Elijah was confused. He waited until his parents left the house, went up to his computer, and typed the word his father had said into the computer, spelling it "Ravenbrook." A second later, the internet delivered the results for Ravensbrück concentration camp in Germany for women only. Elijah spent the rest of that morning reading about what went on in that horrible place and could only draw conclusions about his grandmother's experiences that were too awful to dwell on.

Eve took one more look at the police papers before handing them over to Elijah. "I probably should have talked about her more," she said. "I tried, but it felt better not saying anything. She was troubled—all those survivors were. I was too young to see or notice it, but Sarah said of all the people she knew who made it out of the camps, Mom was the toughest. I don't know what happened. No note or anything. They found her by the lake. She loved the water."

The only reason Elijah knew about his grandmother's suicide was that he'd once overheard Peter talking to one of the many shrinks the Mendeses took their son to when he was a boy, the one who had a mole on the tip of his nose and always smelled like cigarettes. He asked Peter if depression ran in Elijah's family. Peter answered yes, then added that Elijah's mother had taken her life years before her grandson was born. Besides that, Elijah and Eve never once talked about it, and as they sat at the table, he found it difficult to know what to say. To his surprise, Eve kept talking.

"The worst part was that back then they would often forbid people who . . ." She paused and grimaced. "They wouldn't let her be buried in a Jewish cemetery. The rabbi told Sarah he believed my mother was thinking rationally when she did it, which meant she couldn't be laid next to my father—*her husband*—according to some other rabbis who probably lived five hundred years ago. Can you believe that? The compromise was burying her in the nondenominational cemetery across the street."

Elijah picked up the photo of his grandfather as a young man.

"What about him? I don't know anything about this guy," he said.

"I didn't either," Eve said in a way that came off as dismissive. Elijah didn't think she'd meant it to, it was a reflex.

"He died when you were a kid. You got to at least spend some time with him," Elijah said.

"He wasn't around that much."

"But you had to know things about him," Elijah said.

Eve chewed the inside of her mouth for a moment; it was a habit that Elijah also had when he was nervous and thinking. She looked at the piles of things from the box arranged neatly on the table and pointed her finger at one of the folders protruding from its stack. Elijah pulled it out and opened it. Inside he found newspaper clippings. Some were old, a few were photocopies. He handed it to his mother, who looked through the papers until she found the one she wanted and handed it over to Elijah, who read it out loud.

"'Boy, fourteen, arrested in slaying of known criminal.' I wasn't expecting you'd say we should start a true crime podcast," he joked.

"Can you stop being a smart aleck and keep reading? You asked, so read," Eve said.

"'An immigrant boy was brought into police custody for the violent murder of known hoodlum Willy Porter. The police are withholding the name of the boy, only saying he is fourteen and of Jewish origin.'"

Elijah flipped to the second story and read it out loud.

"'The immigrant boy who was brought in for the violent killing of the criminal Willy Porter has been released to his family and cleared of the charges. Although the police didn't give the boy's name, one source identified him as Yitzhak Kaplan. The source said Kaplan is a good boy who sells newspapers to help his family and he deserves an apology from the police.'"

"Wrongfully accused. Happens all the time," Elijah said.

Eve said nothing.

"Is there something I'm missing here? It says they let him go," Elijah said.

"You asked me what I know," Eve said. She took the papers from her son and investigated them. "I also know he came from Ukraine, his friends called him Yitz, and my mother and Sarah's generic answer to my questions about what he did for a living, about how he was a *businessman*."

The rare bout of openness his mother was showing helped Elijah hold back from reminding her that a couple of times when he had asked what her father had done for a living, she also said he was simply a businessman.

"Well . . ." Elijah searched for something to say. He was having a hard time. "I guess it's good he didn't kill anybody."

Eve raised her eyebrows. "I suppose," she said.

Elijah was intrigued. He asked what she'd meant by that.

"I grew up aware that my father had a reputation and that some of the people I met or knew he'd been friendly with were bad people. But Chicago is a city where people blur lines all the time, and reputations can easily grow into tall tales, so anything I heard about him or his associates I took with a grain of salt," Eve said.

"That means you heard *something* . . ."

"Not much. He was in the movie business at one point. I think he owned a butcher shop with his brother or something like that," Eve said. She fished around her bag for a vape but couldn't find one. "But I know he wasn't on the up-and-up."

"So you know about his brother?"

Eve paused her search. She seemed taken aback; Elijah could tell she was trying not to show it.

"Solomon? No. Not really," Eve said as she shook a black vape pen that needed a charge. "Dammit." She got up and walked to the living room to retrieve another black vape. "My morning coffee," she joked.

Elijah noticed something off in the rhythm of the conversation. Almost as if he'd turned into an interrogator and his mother was a suspect trying to make sure she didn't say anything that would incriminate her. But why would she do that if she wasn't hiding anything?

"Did you know he's buried in a plot behind the Hebrew Benevolent Society on property we own?"

The smoke was slowly drifting from Eve's mouth. Elijah watched her face for the slightest movement, any tell that would give away her hand, but there wasn't even a tiny twitch or eyeball roll. She seemed to understand what her son had just said, but didn't answer. It was the classic Eve response, and it drove Elijah crazy when he was younger. He often felt that his mother was ignoring him on purpose, but he learned over the years that she liked to take her time to think about certain things. Every now and then she'd have an answer in minutes or hours, but there were certain questions she'd mull over for days. Elijah resigned himself to the fact that she wasn't going to answer and moved on. He studied the picture of his grandfather again.

"He looks a little like me," he said.

"I think you two are a lot alike," Eve said.

"How would you know that if you didn't know him?"

Eve sucked in a lungful of indica. As she blew it out, Elijah could see her eyes had started to water. He wasn't sure if it was emotions or the weed, but the topic she changed over to instead of answering his question had him thinking it was the former.

"Did you know that I blamed him for my mother's death? For years. I hated him. I really hated his guts. I didn't want you to know he existed. I felt like I was protecting you, but I know now it wasn't right."

Elijah was so used to his mother either leaving things vague and open to interpretation or saying nothing at all that he didn't know how to react. He'd once read a magazine review of one of her poetry collections that summed it up best by saying her work was "beautiful and mysterious to the point of being unknowable." After that, when people asked what his mother was like, he'd use the reviewer's quote as his own. She was beautiful and mysterious to the point of being unknowable, yet there she was, closing in on death and being truthful and open. All he could do was return the honesty.

"I always wanted to know more about him," Elijah said. "I've been curious my whole life. I don't know why."

Eve gave a solemn nod.

"You have every right to be. I don't know what I can do, and I don't know who else is around that could talk to you. Almost everybody he knew is dead."

"You mean like . . ." Elijah made a gun with his fingers. "*Dead dead?*"

"I didn't keep track. I read about a few people in the newspapers, but it's a little foggy who and how they knew him," she said as she got up and went over to the counter and opened the drawer that was stuffed with old menus, warranty cards that had expired a decade or two earlier, and other paper junk. She pulled out a business card and handed it to Elijah. It was white with blue ink and had a logo of a fox with a crown on its head.

"Fox Autos? Jerry the Fox? He's the guy in all the commercials that used to play on Channel 32 all the time," Elijah said before he launched into an imitation of a man ignoring the punctuation on the cue card he was reading from in a cartoonishly Chicago "*Dis, dat, da*" lifer accent: "Hello do you like deals because da Fox has da best deals on used 4Runners and Corollas and Supras in all of Lake County so come on down today because I'll let anybody outfox da Fox so dey can walk away with da lowest prices and best car off dis lot."

Eve began cracking up. Even though he knew it was mostly because of the weed, Elijah couldn't recall the last time something he'd said made her laugh that hard.

"He might be dead, but it's worth a shot," Eve said. "He worked for my dad once."

"Didn't he go to jail or something? I swear he killed somebody or maybe tried to," Elijah said.

"No. That was for extortion. It was twenty years or so ago," Eve said with a slight laugh. "I remember reading it was thrown out because the detective who arrested him owed an associate of the Fox's fifty thousand dollars in gambling debts or something like that. I think the cop was the one who ended up going to jail for entrapment and other corruption charges. It's such a Chicago thing."

4

1910S

The place was boarded up with slats of wood that had obviously been nailed across the windows in a hurry. Yitz told Sol to check the side door, but it was locked. After making certain nobody was looking, they got into the shuttered saloon by squeezing through a little window on the side that somebody had left unlatched.

It was disgusting in there; not even the cold could defeat the stench of mold and rotted meat. Nearly the entire floor was covered in broken glass that cracked under Yitz and Sol's feet as they looked for the little room with the desk. They ducked past all sorts of debris, walking from one door to another, opening one after another only to find little private rooms for hidden debauchery.

"Watch this," Sol said before spitting a glob of saliva at a window. It froze in seconds.

Yitz snapped at his little brother to cut it out.

After opening five doors, the sixth hid an empty room with another door inside it. The boys stared at the second entryway; both felt that something ominous waited for them if they turned the knob. Sol did it anyway. Yitz braced himself, but the only things in the next room were a desk and a chair. They opened each drawer, finding only papers, old cigar butts, and a deck of playing cards with illustrations of naked women on them. Sol flipped through, his eyes open as wide as a couple of open bear traps. He told his brother to look at the buxom lady as the Queen of Hearts, but Yitz was concentrating.

"I found the key! Let's get out of here," Yitz said as he rushed to his brother and grabbed him by the arm. They walked out the first door, then the second, but when they got to the main room, there was a sound of a key turning in a lock. Yitz pulled Sol underneath a table that still had a tablecloth draped over it. The thing was covered in spots of various colors, sizes, and textures. The brothers looked at each other, hoping the other would take charge and say what to do as the person walked across the floor and opened a door. It went quiet, and then there was the sound of a long fart slowly peeling out. Seeing their only chance of not getting caught or burned alive, the brothers crawled out from under the table and crept quietly but quickly toward the front door. They were halfway to safety when the sound of the toilet chain followed by a man yelling "Dammit" stopped them in their tracks. The man in the bathroom tried pulling the chain again but it wouldn't flush.

Seeing his only glimmer of opportunity, Yitz grabbed Sol and took off running. They made it to the door just as the man burst out of the bathroom. Yitz looked over his shoulder and caught a glimpse of a redheaded man pulling up his pants. His long legs helped him make up ground fast, and Yitz screamed to his little brother to run faster.

A few feet felt like two miles in the cold. Lungs shouldn't feel like a house on fire, especially when everything around him was iced over, Yitz thought as he signaled to Sol to cut through the patch of trees to the right. The newspapers said it was the coldest day of the year so far, and the perspiration around Yitz's head had frozen into an ice crown as the brothers looked for a place to hide.

There were fat swaths of land that had been cleared to extend Potter Palmer's waterfront road, where the city's rich would meander up and down without a care in the world. On a warmer day, the boys could have just run through the crowd and blended in, but the walkway was desolate because of the weather. The wooded area was their only option. They ducked behind a boulder.

"I thought Avi said the guy would be in jail," Sol whispered as Yitz snuck a look out from behind the giant rock. "Because he's not in jail, and he has a gun."

"Will you shut it? Avi didn't want me to tell you because you'd get frightened," Yitz said.

It was a lie. Avi assured Yitz that the man they were "taking something back from" was on his way to the penitentiary in Joliet as they spoke.

"What will he do if he catches us? Nobody can stop him from shooting us out here," Sol said.

The sound of feet crunching against the snow and debris on the ground could be heard somewhere in the woods. It stopped for a second. A man spoke. He sounded far enough that the boys could still make a run for it.

"Where you little shits at? I just want what's mine and I won't hurt you. What do you need a key for? How important can it be to you? Give it back and I'll give you five dollars. What's your boss giving you? Some candy? Come on out. Five bucks!"

Sol looked at his older brother with trusting eyes. Yitz had seconds to decide what to do, pushing aside the knowledge that their lives depended on him making the right call. He put one finger up, then a second, and signaled to run toward the lake that he knew was somewhere beyond the trees behind them on three. A third finger popped up, and he whispered, "Now!"

They took off running. It took the man a split second to register it, and the little fraction of time was what saved the boys from doom; he had been standing closer than where Yitz had calculated it sounded like his voice was coming from. Their legs moved faster than they ever had despite neither of them being able to feel their feet. Yitz wanted to just fall over, but his body wouldn't let him. Sol somehow found an extra burst of speed and got a little farther up. Yitz turned around and saw the man was mere feet behind him. Certain he was moments from death, Yitz closed his eyes and just kept charging forward. He ran until he couldn't run anymore, opened his eyes, and fell to his knees. To his horror, they were farther from the lake than he'd thought. Yitz resigned himself to his fate. He was about to know what death was. He turned to look him in the face, but the man was gone. The naked trees swayed as if they were celebrating an act of God. Yitz heard only the wind blowing past him for a moment. It was a terrifying howl of frozen air that screamed toward the lake, and when it stopped, he heard a human cry. It was the sound of a man crying for help. Yitz squinted his eyes and saw a body rolling on the ground not too far behind him. It was the man who'd been giving chase. As Yitz stood up, Sol walked back to his brother.

"Stay there," Yitz commanded. "If I yell to run, you go all the way back to Avi and don't stop."

Sol stood back as his older brother crept slowly and deliberately toward the man on the ground, who was in agony; he had thrown up all over himself and it had already frozen to his jacket with some chunks of vomit stuck to his face. Yitz got closer and could see that the bone was cracked and sticking straight up out of the man's left thigh; his right ankle had twisted itself in a way that didn't look normal. He'd knocked a tooth out and part of his face was swelling. The man must have tripped when he was running; maybe it was a miracle, Yitz considered.

"Please," the man begged. "Go get somebody. I'm not bad. I wasn't going to hurt you."

Yitz saw the pistol on the ground a few feet from the man. It must have flown out of his hand when he fell. He picked it up.

"Kid, I got a son and a daughter. Your age. They need their daddy."

The man had picked the wrong topic to try to save himself. Yitz didn't have any pity for other kids who'd grow up without a rat of a father since Yitz's own, a good man who always worked hard, wasn't around. He aimed the gun at the man's head.

"Yitz. What are you doing?"

"Schmuck! You said my name," he snapped at his little brother.

"Yitz? You're a Jew. Did Lippy or Avi send you? It's just a key for a trunk. They sent you into danger to save a few bucks? There's maybe two hundred bucks in there and some guns, that's it. He can have it. I'm sunk. The cops closed my place during the vice raids, so I'm headed west. He's never going to see me or hear from me again. I promise."

"The money," Yitz shouted. The echo of his own voice startled him. "You said you'd give us five dollars if we stopped. We're here. I want the money."

The man swallowed. "I don't got it, but I'll get it to you. I swear on my kids."

"You lied," Yitz said. He pushed down on the hammer of the gun with his thumb the way he'd seen some of Avi's guys do it when they'd go out in the alleys and shoot bottles. It took more power than he'd expected, and his clumsiness exposed his inexperience in handling a firearm. The man on the ground was still pleading, but seeing the kid didn't know how to shoot put him at ease.

"Kid. You shoot me and then you've gotta run like hell because the shots will be loud. The rich folks are a few feet down that way. They'll hear it and they'll call the cops. Do you even know how to fire that thing? Come on, kid . . ."

Yitz let the thought sink in. He lowered the gun and started to walk away.

"Thanks, kid. You're a good one. Good little Jew. Your parents must be proud of you. Now, go get me some help. Just say you found me here while you were playing and go back home and we'll never talk about this again," the man said.

Yitz walked back in the direction he'd entered the woods from.

"Do the right thing, kid. You're not a bad guy," the injured man said as Yitz walked past him. Between the broken bones and frostbite that was setting in, the man had seconds to decipher what the sound of rustling on the ground a few feet away from him was, and mere milliseconds to figure out that the galloping coming toward him was Yitz running at full speed with a piece of jagged rock in his hand. The rock connected with the man's skull and made a single, violent crack. Sol yelled to his brother to stop, but Yitz lifted his arm toward the sky and served another blow to the man's temple. He tried to direct more hits to the same spot, but the man moved his head slightly with the rock an inch away from his head and it caught his cheek instead.

There was still vapor trickling out of the man's mouth; he was still alive. Yitz was enraged. He picked up an even larger rock that took both of his hands to hold. He backed up a few feet, ran toward the man again, and with all his weight, anger, and hope, Yitz threw the chunk of ancient limestone straight down at the man's face, certain that it would finish him off.

And it seemed to, but it was impossible to tell how much damage the rock did with all the dark blood all over the man's face. His body twitched, but Yitz had heard that happened sometimes even minutes after a person had died. He leaned in to listen whether he could hear a heartbeat. He was inches away when Sol screamed something. Yitz turned to look at his brother and didn't see the man, who, with whatever was left in his body, lunged for Yitz's ankle with one hand. He got a grip on the boy and pulled a knife out from around his ankle with the other hand. It was a surge of adrenaline, pure animal instinct. Yitz didn't even see the weapon until the man was trying to pull his body toward the blade with what little strength he had. He kicked and flailed to break free, but the man had every intention of bringing Yitz to hell with him. Yitz stretched his arm as far as it could go and was about to pick up the man's gun on the ground when the hand that had been holding him slipped away. Yitz fell forward, face-first into the ground. He got up and saw his little brother, white as pure cotton, a few tears rolling down his cheeks. A large piece of wood was sticking up and out of the man's neck.

"I didn't . . ." Sol started. He sobbed and shook. "I didn't want to do that."

Yitz looked at the dead man's body. The face was hardly visible, and the way his blood drained out into the snow made it look like there was a red halo around his head.

"There was no choice," Yitz said. He looked up and saw the sun was starting to sink. "You had nothing to do with this, OK? We'll tell Avi it was me. This could end up being big trouble and it's not your fault. We're going to walk back to see Avi. And the whole way there you act like nothing happened. We walk, never run. Got that?"

Sol sucked up the snot that was turning to ice in his nose and he wiped away the frozen tears hanging around his eyes.

It was still for a moment. The branches didn't move. There was something unsettling about the Chicago winds ceasing on a freezing day that caused Yitz to think of the crazy old man who, back in Odesa, would walk around yelling about how when the Messiah comes the earth will be totally still for a few seconds before everything changes.

Yitz had the gun, he walked toward the water. The wind was fierce; it flayed the skin on his face. He walked down the empty beach to a part where the lake had frozen over, stopped right up at the edge where the waves died along the shore, took the gun out of his pocket, and hurled it into the lake as far as he could with all the power he had left.

The boys kept their heads down as they walked back onto the street from the woods. They ducked past a man pulling a cart with lumps of coal for sale and tried blending in with the crowd of cold and miserable pedestrians when a disheveled woman ran toward the brothers, pointing her bony finger and screaming, "That's them! That's them!"

The boys were so cold that everything they did was purely on impulse. Sol's lips hurt so bad he couldn't even open his mouth, and Yitz's throat felt like he'd swallowed sandpaper. He could barely croak out a command to his brother.

"Listen and don't say anything. Walk back to Avi. Don't tell him nothing that happened back there, except there was a problem with the guy and the cops nabbed me. Don't say you know anything else."

Sol hesitated; he didn't want to abandon his brother. Yitz whispered, "Go," then walked swiftly toward a group of cops that was behind the screaming woman. They grabbed Yitz by the shoulders, and the screaming woman, whose face was covered in blisters, lunged at him.

"That's him! The little thief! I need my money," she screamed. Two cops grabbed her and pushed her away. The two other policemen picked Yitz up, tossed him into a wagon, and started driving.

The entire way there, Yitz imagined what it felt like to be fried by an electric chair.

The next morning, Yitz awoke to somebody clanging on the jail bars.

"You're out, boy," a cop said as he unlocked the door. He led Yitz out to a waiting room where Avi was waiting in a gray checkered suit made by Paolo, the ancient Italian tailor. All the other Jews with money for nice garments went to Julius Spiegel, the man whose boxier suit jackets with three buttons on the front were popular among East Coast college students and heftier American businessmen, but Avi said the form-fitting jackets and tapered trousers Paolo cut were the best in the city. He used the finest materials and they didn't make you look like you were walking around in a potato sack. Avi's fingers were manicured, his slicked-back hair looked as if it was a day removed from its weekly cut, and the shave was fresh. The man the newspapers called "Gentleman Avi" had a spark and swagger that none of the other men around Jewtown possessed.

While Yitz stared up at the ceiling from his jail cot, he fixated on how Avi would deal with him. He'd hoped that Sol had done as he was told and kept his mouth shut, and that maybe he'd be spared as an unwitting accomplice. When he walked out of the police station with Avi and saw his little brother flanked by two of Avi's guys, Yitz had no idea what to think. It was warmer than it had been the day before—a balmy 35 degrees with light wind. Avi suggested he and Yitz take a walk. Yitz turned around and saw his brother getting in a car with the other two guys.

Avi said they should speak in Yiddish, something he had told the boys to speak only if they needed to talk about sensitive topics and they were sure other Jews weren't around. It was better to "speak like Americans," he had told them.

"Sol gave me the key," Avi said as he used an alley wall to hide him from a gust of wind so he could light a cigar. He blew some smoke out and picked a piece of tobacco off his tongue. "Good job. And my guys in there told me the cops who brought you in had to slap you around a little because you wouldn't even tell them your name." Avi licked his thumb and rubbed a speck of crusted blood from Yitz's forehead. The other side of his face was the tender one. "Next time something like this happens, telling them your name is fine, but nothing else. Probably save you a beating, but you never know with those bastards."

Yitz looked down at his feet. He quietly asked if he'd have to go back to jail. His attempt at masking the fear in his voice failed and made Avi laugh in the middle of a slow pull from his cigar.

"Nope," he said as he exhaled. "That whore who pointed the finger at you isn't exactly the most believable character. But we picked her up. And dropped her in Dunning."

The woman had either been committed or buried. Yitz knew those were the only two reasons anybody was brought to Dunning. He also understood not to ask which one, and it didn't matter because either way she'd never be heard from again.

"But you do need to tell me what happened. Sol said something about how you guys got into the saloon and the guy caught you snooping around. Then he chased you out. Am I right?"

Something in Yitz's head said to lie. The job was to find a key, that was all. But now somebody was dead, and as Avi always said, killing somebody always came with some sort of cost that had to be paid sooner or later. But if he got caught lying to Avi, the punishment was probably even worse, Yitz decided. He nodded yes.

"And that's where you did it," Avi said, thrusting his cigar at Yitz like a dagger. "You got Willy Porter into the woods, and you slaughtered him."

Yitz wasn't sure what to say.

"You know Willy Porter's a maniac?" Avi shook his head and smiled. "Sorry. He *was* a maniac. Son of a bitch knocked off somebody for every year you've been around, maybe more. Used to be really respected until he couldn't stop with the booze. Now they're dropping him in the ground with what's left of his head."

He let the last part hang in the air as a cable car passed by. The waiting made Yitz crack.

"Sol shouldn't have been there with me," he said once the car was gone, a trace of desperation in his voice. "I made him go."

Avi howled. He tossed his cigar into the street.

"That drunk putz owed money all over town. That's why they shut down his place. He couldn't pay back his creditors and word was that he'd already skipped town. You probably did more than a few guys a favor, including me and half the cops back there. We figured that we'd lost out, and then somebody gave me a tip about the trunk Willy left behind. We just figured that whatever was in it would cover some of what he owed us and that was the only thing that mattered." He pulled a cigar from his breast pocket and presented it to the boy.

"Yitzy, you just became a legend. Even the Big Man is impressed," he said.

When Yitz was adjusting to life in America, he'd heard Foxy Foxman say something interesting about how Lippy Shulman owned Maxwell Street. Yitz didn't understand it was a figure of speech and told other guys how impressive it was that a Jew could own land, but that he wasn't quite sure why anybody would want such a cramped and rotten avenue. Foxy, always looking for ways to make other people look stupid and feel small, spent several weeks feeding Yitz's belief that Lippy was lord of the land until Sol finally put it together that there was no document stating that Lippy owned the stretch of street where nearly all of the city's Jewish population moved about the days like trapped rats. Yitz was embarrassed, but never dared show it. Instead, he paid attention to the way people acted toward the man even Avi called "Boss," the way they looked at the ground when Lippy walked by as if they were bowing to royalty. Yitz decided one day he wanted people to treat *him* like that, reasoning that a man at the top had safety those below him weren't afforded. The people feared Lippy, yet they also needed him for protection. They hoped he'd notice and take pity on them, sparing an extra dollar or two just for the sake of being charitable; they also paid him half of whatever they made for the privilege of continuing to work and live in the dirty little part of town he lorded over at the same time.

Once the Big Man knew his name, everything changed for Yitz. He stopped being just another expendable little insect who made the neighborhood feel just a bit more crowded. Even though he'd been born and raised in a city like Odesa, Yitz and all the other greenhorns were considered shtetl pests by Lippy and anybody else that had lived in Chicago more than a few years. And he would have stayed that way if not for the thing with Willy Porter on that frozen day in the woods.

Within days, Yitz's legend grew. Locals told stories of how the kid from Odesa had fought off a few of Willy's guys and how he'd spit in a cop's face after they asked him to turn on Avi. All the while, Sol couldn't stop having nightmares of Willy Porter's headless corpse chasing him into the water, and of a demon boasting of killing Mother and Papa as retribution for Sol's sins. He suffered in silence while Yitz became the hero.

Yitz was just the guy Lippy needed, Avi said. The boss wanted somebody who had real brains and unshakable nerves for a plum assignment. Avi told him the other guys would be jealous, but it didn't matter because taking the gig meant Yitz was on track to become *their* boss someday. Without asking any questions, Yitz said he'd be there the next morning. He woke up at six like Avi told him.

Lippy lived in a nondescript brick bungalow west of Maxwell Street. It wasn't a large home by any means, but Yitz was sure it was one of the mansions he'd heard stories of.

Yitz showed up fifteen minutes early and waited in the living room for the ancient maid to bring him to meet the boss of the boss.

He'd heard the old lady was originally from Moscow and had served some aristocratic family years earlier, but didn't believe a Jew could have a Russian maid until he saw it with his own eyes. After thirty minutes of his sitting and wondering why Lippy didn't have a single book on the shelves, the maid came down and snapped her fingers for Yitz to follow her into the kitchen. She handed him a tray and told him to carry it up to Lippy's room, second door on the right. Yitz did as he was told, adding a "Yes, ma'am" that took the old maid by surprise. He made it to his destination and knocked on the door, but there was no answer. He knocked again.

"Mr. Shulman? Sir?"

He cracked the door open slightly, and what he saw squashed any excitement he'd once harbored about his new job. There, right in front of him, was Lippy, totally naked, his deformed penis hanging there, the saddest thing Yitz had ever seen. He'd heard rumors that there'd been an accident when Lippy was circumcised as a baby, but people told botched-schmeckie-snipping tales all the time, so Yitz didn't pay any attention to it. With the thing right there a few feet from his eyes, Yitz saw that it was much worse than anybody had described. It was like a damp carrot with a reddish hue that a horse had stepped on. The poor thing looked mangled, like a dog had gotten ahold of it.

"Who the fuck are you?" Lippy screamed.

"I'm—"

"The kid Avi sent? Well? Are you an idiot? What's your name?"

"It's—"

"That's not a name! Bring me my food."

Yitz hurried the tray over and put it on the small table next to the bed, then just stood there, not knowing what to do next. Lippy, still naked, glanced at him as he walked over to inspect his breakfast. He looked at the eggs, jabbed the whites with the tip of his finger. There was a moment of tense silence as Yitz tried to read the look on Lippy's face. Was it anger? Displeasure? Were the eggs not to his liking?

"Fine," Lippy said. "This is fine. Go wait outside while I eat. I'll call you when you're needed."

From that moment on, Yitz was "Lippy's boy," fetching the boss breakfast every morning and helping him get ready. It was hardly the grand career move Avi made it out to be. The King of Jewtown was a slob. Every morning his maid fixed him four eggs sunny-side up with a side of sardines, some toast, and a glass of prune juice. The lady was too feeble to make it up the high steps of the staircase that led to Lippy's bedroom, so it was Yitz's job to be there every single morning promptly at 6:30 to bring the heavy gilded tray up to him. The smells from breakfast would stick in Yitz's nose for at least two hours after. Lippy never thanked him and possibly didn't even know Yitz's name. He just called him "Boy." Yitz would sit and wait for the boss to finish eating. When he was all done, the boss would let out a huge burp that Yitz could smell from twelve feet away. Then Lippy would get out of bed and call out to Yitz for his clothes. The boss didn't have a wife and always slept in the nude. He'd get out from under the covers when Yitz walked in, then stand next to his bed to do a series of stretches until a little squeal like a dying trumpet came from his ass.

Then there was the matter of Lippy's famous temper. Yitz had heard the stories, like how the boss had once choked a man to death right in the middle of Maxwell Street because the guy accidentally brushed up against Lippy when they walked past each other and didn't apologize. Avi gave Yitz the advice to just do what he was told to, stay out of the way the rest of the time and he'd be fine, but it didn't take long for him to find out that part of his job included being a whipping post. If Yitz was in the general vicinity when Lippy got some bit of bad news, a call that the collection numbers were low or a cop was causing trouble looking for a handout, Yitz would brace himself. Sometimes it was a single hard smack across the face, but if Lippy was in a really bad mood, the beating would leave bruises and welts. All Yitz could do was take it and not say a word.

After helping the boss in the morning, Yitz bolted over to the Schvitz. He'd usually find Avi reading the newspaper, and on his second glass of tea using the same bag, which he'd use at least twice more before noon. Yitz would do anything—wash windows, light cigars, clean toilets—and never complain. The other boys mostly sat around waiting for Avi or somebody else to give them tasks, but Yitz didn't sit still. Guys like Jabby Wiessman and Foxy Foxman were working to help their families; Yitz worked with nothing in mind besides advancing. He wanted *something*. What that was, he could never define, but he did the most menial tasks as if his life would end if the shoes he shined didn't have mirror reflections or the toilets weren't milk white after he finished scrubbing. The only thing Yitz knew for sure was he wanted to be like Avi. He paid such close attention to everything his mentor did that Yitz could anticipate what was needed throughout the day. Two sharpened pencils were always at the ready for racing forms, a comb was available if a single hair was out of place on Avi's head, and Yitz could tell when his boss was going to need his coat and hat just by watching his body language. It was impossible not to notice the kid's drive, so Avi started taking Yitz out with him to collect from gamblers, business owners, and whoever else owed Lippy. On a few occasions when an old Yid couldn't give the proper amount, Avi would tell them not to worry, that he wouldn't charge them interest—but just that one time, he'd add. He also never raised a hand to anybody he was collecting from. "If you really need to get tough, you have somebody else dumb and strong do it for you," he told Yitz. "Fear is good, but it's more important to have people respect you. You'll last longer. The trick is to keep them guessing whether you're feeling charitable or not. Never let them know anything about you, but always let them know you're around."

That was the first big lesson. The second came quickly. A few days later, Yitz wondered out loud why Avi kept his money in a bundle in his pocket instead of a wallet like some of the men he'd seen around the market. Surely, he could afford one.

A smack landed on Yitz's face that was so hard, he thought his jaw had come unhinged.

"Stop asking questions," he snapped. "Questions are for dummies. Just watch and learn."

Yitz wanted to cry from the pain, but the knowledge his teacher had bestowed upon him made it smart less. After that, Yitz spent the next few years observing and never asking a single question. He mostly kept to himself, but also had a sarcastic streak that he found was a good weapon when he wanted to make others feel shame. He took everything he learned to heart and kept working, waiting for his chance.

Then, one rainy day as the calendar inched closer to the start of the 1920s, he had to work harder than ever to keep his mouth shut after Lippy and Avi finished up a conversation and the Big Man left the room. Avi noticed the look on Yitz's face.

"What's your problem? How come you're sour?"

Yitz shrugged. Avi demanded an answer.

"I don't think you should do it," Yitz said quietly.

"Do what?"

"The bank thing on Damen and Adams."

"You were listening?"

"I've got ears. Lippy talks loud," Yitz said.

Avi said an easy score is the best kind of score. Why wouldn't they take it?

"Because he said Johnny West set it up," Yitz reminded him.

Avi slammed his fist on a table.

"You're doing that disgusting thing again. Stop it," he snapped. "I'll smack the shit outta you next time."

The message was received loud and clear. Avi had doled out a few beatings over time—"lessons," he called them, usually with the back of his hand or his belt. He told Yitz it was for his own good, that if somebody had smacked him around when he was younger he wouldn't be such a wiseass all the time. But nothing drove Avi to madness like catching Yitz chewing on the inside of his cheek. It was a nervous habit, but what Avi didn't understand was that it meant the kid was thinking deeply about something.

Yitz explained that something wasn't right. Johnny West didn't do bank jobs; he was a small-time pimp who ran a few nothing poker games. Yitz was cautious as he spoke, making every word come out correctly.

"But the game he runs for some Greeks got busted up last week because he hasn't been on time with his payments to Sergeant Moody. He's been skimming from the game to pay off a guy on the North Side he owes."

Avi's eyes narrowed to the size of coin slots. He asked the kid how he knew that sort of information.

"Because . . ." Yitz started. He paused to make sure he said his next words with full confidence. He couldn't show a hint of uncertainty. "I listen. And Johnny West loves to run his mouth. He was bragging about it when I was sitting a few tables away from him getting lunch. The guy's a fink. I'd work with a rag picker before I did anything with him."

The kid wasn't kidding: he really did hear *everything*. Avi had been given intel just a few days earlier that Sergeant Moody had been helping Johnny West and a few other guys run some secret card games close enough to Maxwell Street that it could be considered infringement. It was small-time stuff, and Moody had just enough power to cause trouble, but Avi already had other issues with the cop.

Yitz knew that; his theory was that the sergeant and Johnny West were working together. He searched Avi's face and paid close attention to his every movement to gauge what his boss was thinking as he spoke, but Avi didn't give anything away.

"Go on," was all Avi said.

After swallowing a lump in his throat the size of a Buffalo nickel, Yitz explained how he believed that the cop went to Johnny West and said that if Johnny didn't do him a favor, and help him set up a robbery that he could trace back to Lippy, then Sergeant Moody would get word all over Greektown about all the money West was pocketing from their card game, and those guys from Athens had a real nasty streak over even the smallest infractions. Yitz had heard that the city was putting pressure on the cops to make more arrests since the newspapers loved nothing more than to print stories about how corrupt the force was, and Moody busting somebody big like Lippy would take a lot of pressure off him, and maybe even get him a promotion.

"He doesn't lose much if you and Lippy are out of the way," Yitz added.

"How do you figure that?"

"Moody told you he wanted a bump in his percentage. You said no, that it would impact Moody's captain's cut, and Moody had to take it up with his boss if he wanted a raise. Then you told him he only patrols a little section of Jewtown, and one call from you to his captain and Moody would be up to his ass in pig guts working the Back of the Yards beat. If you or Lippy get pinched, he doesn't lose much. He only gains."

On the inside, Yitz wanted to throw up, piss, and cry, but he fought the urge to let go of his bodily functions by telling himself over and over not to let Avi see how frightened he was, even as the man who had taken him and Sol in sat shaking his head in disbelief. When Avi said, "You're crazy," Yitz's eye began to itch, but he didn't dare scratch it.

"And what? We should just say no? Even if you're right, Lippy won't listen to you," Avi said.

Before answering, Yitz noticed Avi was wearing a new ring on his left pinkie. It was a gold band with a round diamond right in the middle. He thought of something his mother had said about men who wore diamonds but couldn't recall if it was that they were powerful or stupid.

"I know Lippy won't back out," Yitz said. He could feel some confidence welling up inside him. "What I think you should do is use some outside guys—don't use any of ours. I can get word to somebody without them knowing it's us setting it up. Then if it works, we give them a cut. If I'm right, then . . ."

"You'd set *somebody else* up because you think *we're* getting set up?" Avi asked with a different look in his eye. Yitz couldn't tell if it was anger or intrigue, but it didn't matter; he'd gone past the point of no return. All he could do was blurt out his solution to the problem.

"Finnish James," Yitz said in such an unaffected and detached way that Avi's eyebrows moved up, a familiar sign that he was interested in what he was hearing. Yitz knew he'd said the right thing, and for the first time in his life, the boy felt nothing as he talked. There was no sadness or remorse; his words weren't rooted in hate or a need for vengeance. He laid out how Finnish James owed Avi and Lippy a good deal of money that everybody knew he wouldn't pay back, and it looked bad to have some nobody getting away with not paying his debts. He told Avi to play friendly and get word to Finnish James that there was a way to take care of whatever outstanding money he owed and have a little for himself after, that the guy was small-time and a little bank heist was exactly the sort of job he loved.

Avi seemed impressed, but he still asked Yitz what if he was wrong. The only possible response was the honest one.

"Then Finnish James probably rips you off," Yitz said. "He gets away with whatever was at the bank and still owes you. He'll skip town."

As Avi's head slowly bobbed up and down, Yitz comprehended his own fate if he was wrong. He had a moment left to back up and say that it was a bad idea and apologize, but that would be as bad as his hunch being off. He'd have to leave town to get as far away from the shame as possible. He'd probably never see his brother again, and would end up a bum in some town in the middle of nowhere, but he'd still keep his skin. If he didn't take back what he'd said, then there'd be a sacrifice one way or another; either Finnish James or Yitz would go down.

In the end, Yitz decided there was only one way he wanted to live. Even if he'd sign his own death warrant, it sure beat ending up worse off than he'd been, he reasoned.

"But I'm not wrong. Trust me."

By the look on his face, Yitz knew at least he'd gained Avi's respect for not backing down. That wouldn't save his ass if Finnish James took more of Lippy's money, but it felt nice in the moment.

Avi tilted his head back and started to laugh.

"Odesa boys," he said as he pointed a finger at Yitz. "You're colder than I thought. A little ice block."

Avi walked out of the room. He was on his way to put plans into motion as Yitz stood in the same spot, tensing every muscle in his torso, pushing down the violence that wanted to force its way out his throat.

For three days, Yitz tried to fixate on the pain in his chest and stomach. He told himself nothing, not even death, could hurt so badly. Then, on the fourth day, word came that Finnish James and his two partners had all been shot dead by police as they walked out of the Calumet Savings and Trust bank on the corner of Damen and Adams. None of the five people inside the bank had alerted them; Sergeant Moody and five other officers were waiting outside from the moment the men walked in. Yitz had been correct about everything, and later that same day, Johnny West got a knife in the back while he was walking down Union Avenue on his way to the train station to get out of town. A few nights later, Avi had it arranged so Sergeant Moody, a deviant known for frequenting the cheapest brothels in the neighborhood, would have a most unpleasant encounter with his devout Catholic wife while he was in the middle of whatever depraved act he fancied that evening. Avi paid the guy who ran the place to clear everybody out of the main room for a couple of moments so Mrs. Moody didn't realize she'd entered a house of ill repute. A few minutes later, the cop's wife ran down the stairs shrieking and crying with a totally naked Sergeant Moody trailing behind her into the room that was filled back up with girls, their clients, and even a handful of Moody's fellow officers. Everybody in the room got a good laugh watching the bare-assed cop hustle out the door, except for Moody's wife; she packed her bag and left him that same evening. After missing three days of work, Sergeant Moody was last seen staggering out of a saloon on Harrison, and right into an oncoming streetcar.

Yitz didn't have a gambler's inclination, but he had hit the jackpot on the one very big bet he'd made. Just like the rumors around Maxwell Street about how he'd slaughtered bad old Willy Porter in the woods, people started talking about Yitz the Genius, about how they heard he'd been a Talmudic prodigy in Odesa, and every great yeshiva in Europe courted him. Avi began calling him the Maxwell

Maimonides and told him that his time working for Lippy was over; some other schnook can do that, he said. There wasn't any procedure or formal announcement stating that Yitz had been promoted to Avi's eyes and ears. He didn't have a job title or description besides telling Avi anything he heard about any person who had any bit of power in the city. It didn't matter if it was a Polack business owner, an alderman who was about to get outed for cheating on his wife, a pack of small-timers running schemes, or a meatpacking plant that was about to have a strike that could shut it down for weeks; every little piece of news, information, and salacious neighborhood gossip he heard was reported to Avi at the end of the day.

If the Yids of Maxwell Street were to have any influence in Chicago, they'd have to do what Jews had been doing for centuries in every single place they'd been the minority, and simply outthink everybody else. Avi deputized Yitz to get a few more of the boys to also get any bit of info they could, and then he gave the kid a little budget to grease palms and loosen lips. The other guys reported to Yitz, then he went to Avi with everything. Sometimes Avi would ask Yitz what he thought of something, never agreeing with or debating the answer. He wouldn't say it out loud, but the advice often influenced the outcome of whatever it was Avi had been considering.

The kid grew up fast. Yitz had learned to speak English like a native by mimicking the way other Chicagoans talked and had a natural understanding of the mechanics of the city, how it worked, who mattered and who didn't. He saw that in a metropolis filled with tribes, the Jews needed to do something different if they wanted to stand out. The Irish had gangs scattered from the North to the South Side; they also had political clout and so many city cops connected back to Cork, Donegal, Dublin, or any of the other Emerald Isle counties, that the police badge may have well been turned from a star into a four-leaf clover. Jewtown's neighbors in Little Italy had their rules and clans that stretched back centuries, while the immigrants that lived in Greektown, Chinatown, and the Bohunk neighborhood that were all a few minutes' walk from the Schvitz each had their own ways of doing things. Avi liked the Italians for their flair and style, but Yitz admired their organization. He stressed working with the other groups and not against them as much as possible, especially the masses of brown-skinned people migrating up from the South. Avi was dismissive of that idea at first, but was quickly reminded that everybody used the same color money.

The people of Maxwell Street all called Yitz "Avi's Guy"; Sol became "Avi's Guy's Little Brother." When people recognized him behind the butcher's counter, they'd stare with curious eyes, obviously confused about what the younger Kaplan was doing slicing their meat. Sol found it funny. He'd tease Yitz about being a celebrity; Yitz would grumble about how he just wanted to be left alone. His close proximity to the men who ran the neighborhood meant people were always coming to him asking for favors; some were small, others impossible, while more than half of the things people asked for hurt Yitz's heart. He became convinced the Jews were more miserable in Chicago than they were wherever they'd come from, and in his dreams he'd hear people kvetch about how there was no heat in their home or how some poor widow had been robbed of her life savings. The only thing he could do was try to avoid making eye contact and walk fast in the streets.

Middleberg's Dairy was his oasis. The little eatery wasn't a private club, but it had rules like one. Number one on the list was to not bother anybody who worked for Avi when they were in there. Yitz was at ease knowing he wouldn't have somebody talking his ear off about how they needed money to get their cousin out of Riga and into America. He was relaxed there, so the palm slapping him on the back, followed by the voice loudly proclaiming, "There's my boy," one afternoon as he was eating his bowl of noodles with cheese and butter shocked him to his soul. He spun his body around, ready to knock whoever it was in the jaw, but stopped when he saw it was Artie Berman, Avi's cousin from Detroit. People called the oldest Berman brother the Point because his nose was a perfect little slope that ended with a sharp tip that looked like it could puncture a tire. They just made sure to never say it around him. The last guy who did washed up on the shore of Lake Erie.

Artie's reputation crossed state lines. He was connected to a lot of violence and dead bodies. People died up in Detroit all the time, and more likely than not it could be traced back to the Berman brothers even though nobody could get anything to stick to them. Artie was cruel and quick to violence, but when it came to business, he could be shown the light. He knew how to make money, and most of it came from taxing liquor that came over the border from Windsor. After Michigan enacted the first statewide prohibition of the sale of alcohol in 1917, profits tripled then quadrupled.

"Mind if I take a seat?" Artie asked without waiting for an answer.

He had massive arms and walked with a swagger that was propelled by the belief that he couldn't be bested in any fight, but he didn't share his cousin's appreciation for good tailoring. His pants were wrinkled, fabric dangled from his jacket cuff, and his shoes needed a shine from walking the filthy city streets. He wasn't the tallest of the brothers, but he was the most intimidating. His wide eyes never seemed to blink, he had a slight tick that made his shoulder bop up suddenly, and he had gained a reputation as a feared bare-knuckle boxer in his younger days. Everybody got a little nervous when Artie was around.

Yitz was the exception; there was something about the guy that he understood and even related to. It was his talent he never told anybody about, how he knew so much even after the slightest interactions with people; he could pick up on their feelings, read little tells like what a hand gesture or head tilt meant. He knew that every person was afraid of something, and once he could pinpoint what that was, Yitz thought about what the person wanted to do to outrun the fear. Artie was easy. He was born poor and didn't want to be poor again. Yitz felt similarly about his own place.

"I was just talking to my cousin about you and all your good work," Artie said. "He really likes you. Know that?"

Yitz looked at the goon standing behind Artie. Artie noticed Yitz's glance and told the guy to go wait outside.

"New kid. Just got here. Born in Minsk. Speaks perfect Greek because he got stuck there for a few years trying to get to America, so it's good for dealing with stuff in Greektown, but he won't shut up about how cold it is here. All day with how he's freezing and kvetching about how he should have gone somewhere warm."

"It's the lake winds," Yitz said. "Nobody is prepared for those gusts."

Artie howled. His laugh sounded horrible, like it had started in the depths of his bowels and was meant to go down out his ass and not up through his mouth. It was like a dying foghorn.

"See, that's what I like about you. You like to be prepared, but you also think fast. I mean, the way you handled that Porter guy in the heat of the moment, you're tough, but that tells me you're the smartest guy around here. Avi knows it. He knows that about you, and you know everything about my cousin."

"Well," Yitz said with a smile, "it's not like I sleep in the same bed as the guy."

"And you're funny! A guy like you, young, good-looking, smart, *and* a sense of humor," Artie said. He bit off one of his cuticles and spit out the dead skin. "Listen, I know you're Avi's guy and I respect that, but he's my cousin and I'm asking you because I'm his family but you're *like* his family. His own brother, Hershey? I love him, but he's a putz. He needs a real job. Avi sees *you* as his little brother."

Yitz was moved. He could hear in Artie's voice some concern for his cousin, but knew it was also business; Artie's motivations were still selfish. He cared for his family, but he also had to protect and grow *his* interests. Yitz had learned that there was nothing wrong with being selfish. It was maybe the only way to get ahead in America.

"Avi's thing with Lippy," Artie continued. He thought for a second. He was making sure to choose his words correctly. "It's loyalty, right? I mean, Lippy is Lippy. I respect the old-timer."

Yitz could tell that the last part was bullshit. He sipped his juice to mask any look that would tell the man sitting across from him that he knew that. He put the glass down slowly and shrugged a shoulder.

"It is. But I think loyalty is a good thing, no? I'd rather know a guy is loyal and not scheming his way into your place," Yitz said.

"See, that's why everybody likes you: you're a wise kid. And since you're so smart, I think you know what's coming."

"Prohibition."

Artie threw his hands up.

"Exactly. They're gonna ban booze all over, and it's an opportunity. A big, *huge* one. Guys that get in on it early, especially in a place like Chicago? With the Bohunks alone, you could buy an island with all the beer somebody is going to sell to them. The way I see it, the Italians and Irish got their little parts of the city, and that's fine. Let them. But we—sorry, Lippy—" Artie grimaced; he couldn't hide his disdain. "He has a lot of space of his own. Between that, what we've got up in Detroit, and my brother-in-law with the Blumenfeld boys in

Minnesota bringing ethanol down Lake Superior from Bronfman in Montreal. It's legal and we're the only ones he's dealing with, but I've got some guys in Minneapolis have this perfume factory, they'll dilute the alcohol, make it smell all nice, and we'll make a mint. We've got something big in the works. But Lippy . . ."

Yitz didn't need to think about the next words that came out of his mouth. He'd been waiting for his moment since Lippy smacked him upside the head for the first time, but logic eventually got into the mix and he'd started viewing things differently. Yitz spent more nights staying awake worrying about what would happen if the old fat bastard screwed things up for everybody else. He could tell just by looking at the guy's face that Artie wanted the same thing he did.

"He's ready to retire," Yitz said. The period at the end of the sentence was audible.

A smile crept slowly across Artie's face.

"Go on," he said.

"He's been building that house of his in Lake Geneva the last year or so. That's why he's never around. He knows what's coming. He's ready to hightail it out of town. He won't admit it, but Avi runs everything now. Lippy is just the guy with the pen who signs off on things, and he doesn't like liquor. He says it's a bad business, but it's personal with him. His father drank too much, so Lippy thinks it's sinful."

"That's funny." Artie snorted. "He thinks booze is sinful, but some of the stuff I know about the guy . . ." Artie sat back. His eyes narrowed so the thinnest ribbon of white could be seen. "What should we do here? I can't force my cousin to do something he doesn't want to do. You said it yourself, he's loyal. And I appreciate loyalty, but I also know time is wasting. Some other guys are going to move in and then . . ."

The "and then" was always on Yitz's mind. He didn't want to find out what came after it, but had felt helpless to change it. Suddenly, the one damn thing he couldn't figure out a solution for was sitting next to him at Middleberg's. Yitz looked down at his noodles, which had grown cold and stiff. He wasn't hungry anymore, anyhow.

"Avi wants everybody to like him, but deep down he also knows what needs to be done. He just doesn't want to do it. But he knows. I believe he'd be happy with a different situation."

The grin on Artie's face went from one side of Illinois to the other. "That's why you'll go far. You know it's not important for everybody to think you're a good guy," he said.

"I'm not a good guy?"

Yitz was serious, but Artie let out one of his disgusting laughs as he stood up. He put a dollar on the counter. "Breakfast is on me," he said as he started walking toward the door. He put his hand on Yitz's shoulder as he passed by but said nothing.

Five days later, on Purim, as Jews drank until they didn't know the difference between blessed Mordechai and cursed Haman, somebody shot and killed Lippy Shulman as he was unlocking the front door of his home. His old Russian maid found the Big Man's body the next morning.

It took a week for everything to get taken care of: Lippy's funeral, the shiva, the eating, the crying, the laughing, more eating, more crying, the chatter to calm down about who did it, and more eating. When that was all over, it was time to make sure that what was Lippy's belonged to Avi. It was a fact that had to get beaten into a few guys, but that was easy.

Eight days after mourners said the Kaddish over Lippy's grave, there was a bang on Yitz's door. He shot out of bed and ran to open it up. It was Avi with two guys behind him.

"Get dressed and put this on over your eyes," Avi commanded as he handed Yitz a blindfold.

When they walked out of the building and into the street, Yitz tried to imagine he was looking right into the void. If the blackness was the last thing he'd see, then he was trying to make peace with it. Blocking out the chatter and laughter was difficult. He wanted to swipe at the hands that were under his armpits, helping direct him to which way he was supposed to walk. At least they'd let him put on a coat, he thought. Even if they were going to kill him, at least he wasn't being made to suffer by walking outside without much to cover his body against that horrid wind.

"We're here," Avi said.

Yitz could tell he was walking inside somewhere through a door. His face went from freezing to warm in an instant.

"I take off now?" one of the guys holding Yitz asked.

"This," Avi said.

"What's this?"

"It's 'I take *this* off now.' Learn English, you dummy," Avi said.

Yitz's body was all electricity. His breath sped up, he tried to focus on every particle of air, attempting to savor everything. All those seconds he'd lived were supposed to flash before his eyes, he thought as he tried to hold on to what he figured would be the last ones he'd ever experience. Where would all the memories go, he wondered as the blindfold was lifted from his eyes and in front of him stood Avi with a huge grin on his face. Behind him was a swimming pool with white tile all around it. Everywhere else there was white tile. Pristine. Not a spot of color that wasn't meant to be there could be found. In the middle of the eastern wall was a spot that read "Est. 1907" in black tile.

"What the hell is this? It's . . ." The pulse in Yitz's throat was pounding, making it difficult to finish the sentence.

"He asks what the hell this is. It's the Schvitz, ya schmuck."

"I can tell that, but why are we here?"

"It's yours," Avi said. "The Schvitz is your place. You're in charge of it. This is your domain; you're the king of the manor."

"Why did you make me wear that thing over my eyes to take me here?" Yitz asked.

"Because it was a surprise. Jeez. What did you think, I was gonna pop you?"

Yitz didn't say anything.

Avi stared at him for a second. "It was a surprise, Yitzy. Come on," Avi said. "It's yours."

"Mine? I don't know how to run a schvitz."

"What's to do? You keep it warm, make nice steam, you'll be fine. Everybody needs to start running legitimate businesses because we took in much more than we anticipated. We can work with the judges, the local cops, and even the state ones, but those country club bastards in Washington come after you and you're going away for a long stretch. Everybody gets to a certain level, and they need something on paper. So now you're Yitz the Schvitz Man," Avi said. "Maybe Yitzy Schvitzy?"

"Just Yitz, please. That's all I want to be, for God's sake. These names drive me nuts," Yitz said as he looked around.

For reasons he could never explain, ever since he was a boy, Yitz felt perpetually on the verge of tears. Whenever he felt like he was going to start, he'd hear his mother tell him that the Russians would find him and kill his whole family if he started up. But looking at the paperwork Avi had handed him, there was a slight bit of pressure behind his eyes. America had been a series of strange experiences, one after another in such rapid succession that he had just become accustomed to that being the way things were. He didn't understand much of anything besides how to get from one day to the next. There was violence, but there had always been that no matter where he was. He hadn't left it behind when he left Odesa, but it was in Chicago that he came to understand that if there wasn't violence, then that meant to beware of what was coming. Yitz didn't think there could ever be calm, but he also never had a moment to consider that maybe in the land of opportunity he could one day own a business.

"OK, then," Avi said. "You're Just Yitz now. That's what we'll call you."

Yitz didn't hear the joke. He was looking around, taking everything in. He'd had his doubts, but maybe anything really *was* possible in America, he thought as he looked around the business that *he* owned. A new decade had just started, and he entered it as an American. Yitz tried to allow himself a second to dream of a future, but he still wasn't sure what a future looked like. He shook Avi's hand, sat down behind his new desk, and took it all in. The pressure behind his eyes was gone, and for a moment, Yitz was content. It would come and go in an instant, never to return. The second he heard Avi whisper something to one of the guys, he knew it was over. The whole thing was all a setup.

"Oh, by the way," Avi said as he reached his hand out the door to grab something. "You know my sister, Leah. I got you two a table tonight at William Morton's new place in the Loop to celebrate your new job. It's all on me."

Avi's little sister smiled at Yitz. He'd known her for years, and not for a second did he feel even the slightest bit of anything. She was a good-looking girl, with fair skin and curly red hair. But she hardly talked, something Yitz would have normally welcomed since he enjoyed any silence he could get. But it would have been one thing if she didn't say much because she was shy; Leah didn't talk because she didn't have anything to say. She was dim. Boring. Dull. There was no way Yitz could ever say any of those things out loud to anybody since he knew Avi was trying to play matchmaker between them, but he had hoped to stall long enough that he'd find somebody else and then Avi might, hopefully, give up.

But when she said "Hiya, Yitz" in that office, he knew that time had run out. Yitz smiled and accepted his fate. It was obvious he'd been condemned a long time earlier but hadn't accepted it until that moment.

5

It felt like old times.

Elijah had nothing better to do besides sitting on the computer in his bedroom. Only he wasn't wasting time downloading music, and his libido had dwindled over the years due to age, crushing depression, and the cornucopia of pharmaceuticals he took to try to combat the sadness, so he didn't utilize the internet's vast library of porn.

Instead, he decided to keep himself busy by trying to find anything he could on his grandparents but spent the first hour or so looking at his ex-wife's social media and thinking about how much happier she looked. He chased the first round of torture by jumping headfirst down the wormhole of articles about him and his old company. The search engine told him that people also typed in his name with "alive or dead," "net worth," and "in prison." His name hadn't been mentioned in an article in eighteen months; he couldn't tell if his irrelevancy was mercy or a fate worse than death. There was no reason to type in his name with "CMUNTY," but he'd never quite figured out how to get comfortable with the feeling of relief. He'd read all the articles before, but sometimes it felt nice to pick at a scab. He found the one that first broke the news about his two partners being investigated by the SEC and FBI that incorrectly used a picture of Elijah and identified him as Nathanael, because he was curious to see if the letters from his lawyer threatening to sue if they didn't fix it got anything done—they hadn't, and the picture of twenty-five-year-old Elijah at some fundraiser holding a champagne glass was still up with the caption "Nathanael Hastings allegedly used company funds to pay for prostitutes, buccal fat removal, and a rare comic book priced at $25,000." Elijah had once counted 128 articles that correctly pointed out that he wasn't being investigated along with Nathanael and Alec, but that didn't stop thousands of people from plastering the picture of him with captions like "Greedy tech bro scum" or "Bring the guillotines back for guys like this" all across social media. Elijah knew it was coming; he'd cooperated with investigators and was actually a bit hurt that his partners hadn't at least tried to involve him in their little schemes. He knew he'd been a third wheel who was just in the right place at the right time with the right amount of money to invest to help get things going. It was a shock to everybody that CMUNTY got as big as it did, and keeping Elijah involved instead of buying him out was just the easier decision. His hope had been to make his mark, go above and beyond whatever they asked of him, eventually cash out, and move on to the next thing. All of that went to hell when a judge ruled that Elijah, as an acting partner, was also responsible in a civil fraud case. Two more cases went exactly the same way, and the day he received word of the third verdict was the day after Eve called to say the cancer had come back.

After growing bored of masochism, Eijah decided to finally look up his grandmother's name and got hundreds of results on Rose Kaplan, with none of them the one he was looking for. He tried to remember her maiden name, but couldn't. He thought about asking Eve but guessed they'd hit the limit on how much they'd talk about her long-dead mother.

He modified the search a dozen times, eventually finding a 1960 *Jewish Chicago News* bulletin with her picture in grainy black and white above it, on how Rose Kaplan had donated $100 to a local synagogue fundraiser, and then got her 1963 obituary. She was "survived by her daughters, Rebecca and Eve, and preceded in death by her husband, Yitzhak."

After that, he turned to his grandfather, only to find dozens of people with the name Yitzhak Kaplan, most of them on lists of Holocaust victims or survivors. He tried a few tricks to narrow the search down, trying a dozen combinations with Yitzhak Kaplan's name, Chicago, and a handful of dates. Elijah wasn't sure exactly when his grandfather had come over from Eastern Europe, so he just tried every decade of the twentieth century, and 1920 landed first. The result was for a book called *Early Speak: Hollywood's First Five Talkie Years*. He bought the e-book and went right to the index. "Kaplan, Yitzhak (Yitz), 33, 45." He clicked to the page and immediately saw the name.

Yitzhak "Yitz" Kaplan was a Jewish immigrant with Mob connections.

Elijah read it over to make sure he'd seen it right. That didn't sound correct, but then he remembered his mother's old newspaper clipping on her father's arrest as a kid.

Kaplan had no experience in the film business. There were a few like him, men who saw it as an investment. They were hustlers. His specialty was in other matters. Specifically, the illegal sort. Kaplan's ties to the underworld went back to Prohibition when he worked for the gangster Avi Kaminsky, leader of Chicago's notorious Maxwell Street Jewish gang that was known for unrestrained violence in the notoriously dangerous city throughout the Roaring Twenties. Whether or not he purchased the company legally or by brandishing his Tommy gun isn't known . . .

"Oh *God*," Elijah groaned. He'd inherited Eve's annoyance with writers who added unnecessary drama to their work.

. . . but what is for certain is that Kaplan was an innovator, a pioneer in the make them cheap, fast, and get them into theaters school of producers. It wasn't art, but it ended up being influential on later filmmakers like Ed Wood and Roger Corman.

Elijah flipped to the other page on which the index said his grandfather was mentioned.

. . . Kaplan was out of the film business by 1950.

He clicked back to the other page. Even after his mother showed him the news clipping about his grandfather's run-in with the law, and no matter how little else he may have known about the man, "Mob connections" and "underworld" weren't words he associated with his family. His late father helped people sue big companies, and Eve was a poet and professor who was leaving money to PBS in her will—not exactly the type of people who'd leave a horse head in your bed if you crossed them.

But there was that one name in the little bit about his grandfather that popped. Elijah took out a notebook, wrote down the name "Avi

Kaminsky," and circled it. He typed it into Google, and besides a tax accountant with the same name in New York and a lawyer in Ann Arbor, the results were dominated by a single person.

"The King of Maxwell Street" was the headline on a blog called "Midwestern Godfathers."

> Arnold Rothstein and Meyer Lansky might have taken up all the press for their exploits, but Avi Kaminsky and his cousin Artie Berman, a member of the feared Purple Gang out of Detroit, were the two most notorious and violent Jewish mobsters during Prohibition.

That was when Elijah decided to take the first Adderall and keep reading. He swallowed it without water and turned his attention back to the biography.

> Kaminsky came here as a kid from Ukraine. Not much of his early days in America is known, but by thirteen, he ended up in Chicago and started working for Lippy "The King of Jewtown" Shulman not long after. Shulman had moved to Chicago before the turn of the century after some time spent in New York and saw that the extortion racket was a lucrative one. Shulman understood there were these immigrants who didn't know anything and needed protection, so he enlisted a few other friends and started something called the Yiddish Black Hand. By all accounts, Shulman just showed up on Maxwell Street one day and suddenly he was mayor of the Jews. The term "Black Hand" is instantly recognizable to anybody who has seen Francis Ford Coppola's *The Godfather Part II*, an extortion racket developed by the Sicilian mafia; every culture in America

had their own version of the Mano Nera. Shulman was the first to do it among Chicago's booming Jewish population. Avi Kaminsky started as one of his younger enforcers. But by the time he was sixteen, he was considered Shulman's right-hand man.

Ironically, the connections to the second *Godfather* movie don't stop there. While Mario Puzo had based Don Fanucci—the Black Hand that Vito Corleone assassinates at the start of his rise to power—on a real-life Black Hand named Ignazio Lupo, or Lupo the Wolf, Lupo died of natural causes, a forgotten man with no power. Lippy Shulman, on the other hand, was gunned down during the Jewish holiday of Purim in 1919. He was last seen drunk as a skunk leaving a celebration at a synagogue off Halsted. Somebody shot him in the back of the head right outside the door of his apartment, just like Don Fanucci. His killer was never caught, but within a week, the word on Maxwell Street was Avi had taken over and was the new boss. Between Kaminsky's quick rise to the top and the partnership with Detroit and the Purple Gang, it wasn't hard to wager a guess who had ordered the hit on Lippy Shulman, if he hadn't done it himself.

"Gangs of Chicago: Ethnicity, Capitalism, and Survival," a college thesis, mentioned that Kaminsky was part of a group called the 12th Street Gang or the Jewtown Boys.

Long before the national media was obsessed with Chicago's Black and Latino gangs like the Vice Lords and the GD's, Chicago's Jewish gangs lived on and around Maxwell Street, a part of town that was almost always referred to as "The Ghetto" at the start of the twentieth century.

He even found a website dedicated to "uncovering the JFK assassination conspiracy" that connected back to Kaminsky.

All roads led back to the Chicago Outfit for Jack Ruby, the man who killed Lee Harvey Oswald. Born Jacob Leon Rubenstein, he grew up in a small apartment on Morgan just off "the most dangerous street in the world" according to one newspaper, Maxwell Street. Jack was just the sort of young man Avi Kaminsky liked. Smart and tough. His temper earned the son of Orthodox immigrants from Poland a reputation in the alleyways of Chicago, and by the time he was twelve, he was earning more money than his father by doing little jobs for known criminals like Kaminsky.

Kaminsky couldn't have had anything to do with the murder of the thirty-fifth president. The website also noted:

Kaminsky had been dead for about thirty years when Ruby shot Oswald. Kaminsky was gunned down after having dinner with his mistress, his killers were never caught. But you could say his DNA was involved since he'd been one of the first people to notice Ruby's unique skillset of violence and deceitfulness.

After a few hours of his brain buzzing from one thought to another, Ollie popped into Elijah's mind. One of his late friend's biggest quirks was his obsession with President Kennedy's assassination; he'd read dozens of books about the killing, his favorite movie was Oliver Stone's *JFK*, and he always wore a pair of tortoiseshell sunglasses like Kennedy had. The shock and sadness of Ollie's death were always present in Elijah's mind, but he rarely found himself thinking how he wished his friend were still around so he could tell him a specific thing, some strange bit of info that had him imagining what Ollie's reaction would be upon hearing the Mendes family may have had some sort of connection to the president's killing. Elijah's grandfather knowing a guy who knew Jack Ruby probably wasn't something that would show up in any secret files the government may have had on the assassination, but Ollie would have gotten a kick out of it.

While his grandfather seemed just unimportant enough to not have his biography available online, Avi Kaminsky was another story. His name linked back to more famous Mob figures including Al Capone, Johnny Torrio, and Dean O'Banion, as well as two Chicago mayors, the construction of three locally landmarked buildings, multiple heavyweight boxers, and the actor Al Jolson. The single page of paper that started with his grandfather's and Avi Kaminsky's names was filled in under an hour. Kaminsky connected to more than twenty-five well-known mobsters and politicians, and was such a topic of F. Scott Fitzgerald's fascination that there were several theories that Kaminsky influenced the author's Meyer Wolfsheim character in *The Great Gatsby* just as much as Arnold Rothstein purportedly had. The man was separated by less than six degrees to a who's who of famous Americans, which meant they also had some closeness to Elijah's grandfather. At some point during the long night of internet searching, Elijah decided he needed to figure out just who his grandfather really was.

After reading as much as he could online for ten amphetamine-fueled hours, Elijah finally gave up and slept thanks to a few hits of something called Chewbacca Fur that he bought in case of emergency when Eve sent him to pick up her order at the dispensary. He'd mostly given up on weed in his twenties, deciding meditation helped him better with focus. After he grew out of sitting and humming a mantra, he got into microdosing. First, it was psilocybin, then ketamine. After a few months, microdosing turned into full-on dosing and experimenting with psychedelics in hopes of never having to take a pill again. There was an ayahuasca ceremony held in the Santa Cruz Mountains, and the night he took Molly with his then-wife, Hannah. He did mushrooms on the first day of the month for over a year straight because a local psychedelic guru named Ram Adon told him it was the best way to clear out his "mental *mishegos.*" Elijah kept up the monthly regime for two months after Ram Adon, aka Elliott Schwartzman, was arrested on multiple counts of fraud. Then, one morning, Elijah woke up and swore he'd heard something that sounded like tearing inside his head as if some force had ripped apart his brain from inside his skull. Maybe it had been building up over time or was just a violent crash, but there it was: Elijah had snapped. Cold sweats followed, then a lack of appetite, and the feeling that all the joy in his body had drained from his pores as he slept. He didn't leave bed for five days and asked Hannah to tell his partners he had a bad case of the flu. When he finally got up and started to walk around, Elijah focused on his breath the way his instructor had always said. He may have stood in front of his open window for two minutes or two hours, he wasn't sure. But when he finally decided to walk away from the view of the outside world he hadn't seen in nearly a week, he typed out a quick e-mail to his partners that he was taking a sabbatical. He half-expected them to send a letter from their lawyers that he was in breach of some contract, but he quickly got a response of "Rest well, my dude" from Alec, and nothing else. He closed his laptop, put his work phone in a drawer, and called Hannah on his personal one. He said he'd booked a ticket to L.A. and that he was going to the place in Malibu his doctor had suggested. She said she could drive him; he said she shouldn't be silly, that it was a seven- to ten-hour drive depending on traffic. Elijah packed a bag, took a car to the airport, and got himself to the clinic. He checked himself in, took a nap, and then spent the next two months walking around the grounds, hardly saying a word to anybody, except to complain about how much he hated the ocean. Its vastness made him uncomfortable. He was more comfortable by a lake, like the one he'd grown up near. Lake Michigan deceptively looked as big as the Pacific, but to Elijah there was something friendly and calm about it. When one of the doctors at the clinic asked him to expound on that, he mentioned his grandmother Rose, and how she loved the lake so much that she decided to die in it. When the doctor asked him to talk a bit more about her, Elijah changed the subject to something else.

Rose was on his mind when he woke from his weed-induced coma. He'd had some dream involving her but he couldn't recall the details. The person at the dispensary with more than half a dozen piercings in their ears and face mentioned Chewbacca Fur was known to cause "crazy-ass thoughts when you sleep," but Elijah wasn't bothered. It was 4:00 in the morning. He felt rested and glad to be up before the rest of the world. He had an early-morning appointment in the suburbs and wanted to get ahead of the rush-hour traffic.

Driving up the Edens was a breeze. The expressway was empty save for some big rigs hauling ass, early risers getting a jump on the day, and the night owls retiring to their nests. Elijah arrived at Cafe All Day in the sad little shopping plaza earlier than anticipated and just sat in his car with the engine going to keep warm. The diner looked like it had taken over a space formerly occupied by a Pizza Hut, Taco Bell, or some other behemoth of suburban fast food from the end of the previous century. Its website said it opened at 6:00 every morning and it was 6:09. His meeting with Jerry the Fox was at 7:00. Elijah was on edge.

"You should strive to effortlessly own every space whether or not others know you are the owner," he said out loud. It was a mantra he liked to repeat to himself before any meeting. He'd learned it at a conference a few years earlier from some speaker whose name he forgot, but who was billed as an "Empathy Coach and Mountain Climber." He talked for an hour about his experience being the only one of his crew to survive an attempt at scaling Everest, and how the "principles of the journey could help in the business world." The speaker said that after the last of his group died on that mountain, he told himself to take ownership, that he'd own every inch of rock until he was back safe on the ground. Even though doctors had to amputate a leg and four frostbitten fingers, his mindset, he said, was why he survived.

The last time Elijah had tried to use the space-ownership wisdom was in his lawyer's office to sign his divorce papers. After that, he was so broke that it was hard to imagine he could afford real estate even if it was just in his head. But his meeting at the diner was different: Jerry the Fox was a local celebrity whose commercials were on during Bulls games in the glory years of the 1990s, and who was once so popular that he came in sixth in a radio station's unofficial call-in poll asking who should be the mayor of the city.

Elijah looked at himself in the rearview mirror. "The guy is a million years old and isn't even on TV anymore. Stop being an idiot," he said in an attempt to calm himself. He'd met famous people before, but that was when Elijah felt like *he* was somebody who was worth meeting. He also wasn't asking those famous people if they had any memories of his grandfather who had died decades before Elijah had been born.

Feeling just enough confidence, Elijah walked into the diner. He made eye contact with one of the servers, who was chewing on a pen, then looked to the left and saw Jerry the Fox had already taken ownership of the space.

He was dressed in a black Adidas tracksuit opened just enough to show two gold chains around his neck, one with a Chicago Bears helmet pendant and the other a Star of David. The brown toupee didn't match his white, impressively bushy eyebrows, and he had a bandage on his forehead.

"Got something scraped off," the Fox explained to Elijah.

He was in his late eighties, said his liver, kidneys, and heart weren't doing so well. "But I remember everything. Sometimes that's a beautiful thing, and other times, eh, not so much."

They made small talk for a few minutes before ordering. The Fox told Elijah he received lots of strange phone calls, but hearing from Yitz Kaplan's grandson beat them all.

"People call me up all the time looking for things. Sometimes it's just an autograph for their kid or something, but usually it's an ex-wife's lawyer or some surprise B.S."

The server placed their food on the table. Elijah looked up at the flickering fluorescent lights and old popcorn ceiling that was likely dusting diners' food with a little heaping of asbestos for added flavor. The old guy across from him radiated the sort of toughness Elijah believed he'd earned in his younger years but had tempered over time. He had a puffy scar on his neck that looked as if it had been put there intentionally, and his thick fingers were calloused and beaten up, yet he took perfect care of his nails. They were buffed, perfectly square, and his cuticles trimmed neatly. Elijah wondered if he went to a manicurist to get them done.

"How's your ma? Did she tell you I was one of the first people at the hospital to congratulate her dad after she was born? Showed up with this giant stuffed rabbit. Your grandpa busted my chops because he said it was an Easter bunny. How the frick was I supposed to know the difference? I'm a Jew."

The old man cracked Elijah up with his stories. He seemed harmless and sweet, but it was still strange seeing him sitting on the other side of the booth. The Jerry the Fox who claimed he would beat any price on used Mitsubishis in the Chicagoland area during his commercial spots was more of a character, an inflated version of the real Jerry Foxman. But he didn't seem like a car salesman to Elijah, either. In his mind, the men who sold automobiles for a living were all like Willy Loman or Jack Lemmon from *Glengarry Glen Ross*, an equal balance of cocky and dead inside. Jerry the Fox was confident and still had some spark left in him. He said "l'chaim" before taking a sip of his coffee, then showed off one of his rings that had been given to him by the late actor James Caan. He pointed out "real diamonds, not the fake stuff." It was a thank-you gift for helping with some research into a movie role.

"*The Godfather*?" Elijah asked.

Suddenly, the old guy's mood changed. He went from smiling and bragging about smoking cigars with a former Notre Dame coach to sullen and frightening.

"Why'd you think he'd come to me for that fucking movie?"

The harmless senior was gone. Elijah felt a type of energy he was unfamiliar with. It made him feel unsafe. As the old man stared a hole through him, Elijah started counting down. If he got to five, he was going to run out of the diner and head straight home, but Jerry the Fox broke out a smile at three.

"You kidding me? Who do you think I am? Marlon Brando? I'm much better looking than that guy!" He gave a laugh that turned into a cough. "No, it was this movie he did here in Chicago. I never saw it. All I know is Jimmy's gone. My dad's long gone. Your grandpa is gone. I'm here and you're here," he said before doing a total 180. "You adopted?"

Elijah gritted his teeth. He'd been asked the question more than a few times in his life, but it never came from so far out of left field. He shook his head no, then tried to explain his father's background, but

120

Jerry the Fox let out an "Eh," and added "Good for you. That's nice," that Elijah didn't know how to decipher.

"Oy, disgusting," the old man snapped as he gave a dissatisfied look to his piece of toast and mumbled something about how there was too much butter. He shook his head at the bread for a second, then he looked at Elijah.

"Did your ma ever get over what happened to your grandma? She was a beautiful lady. Shame what they did to her," Jerry the Fox said as he bit into a greasy piece of sausage that glimmered when a beam from the fluorescent lighting caught it.

It was a tough question to answer for a million reasons, and Elijah figured that by "they" Jerry the Fox had meant the Nazis. He gave the most honest answer he could, that Eve hardly ever talked about her mother. "She does still talk about how they wouldn't bury her in a Jewish cemetery with my grandpa. I think she wants to take care of that before . . ."

Elijah trailed off. He hated telling people his mother was dying because it reminded him of the inevitable.

"These rabbis," Jerry the Fox said as a fleck of spit shot from his mouth and clung to his lip. "My two girls, their mother is Italian. She's Catholic, so the rabbis say they're Catholic. But if the Nazis come and put me on the train, you know who else they put on the train?"

Elijah wasn't sure if he was supposed to answer "your daughters" or not, but it didn't matter because Jerry the Fox just kept talking.

"Your grandpa, boy, he was in love with her. Everybody knew it. Really adored her and his kids. Yitz was an old-timer when I was younger, we looked up to him. I wish I'd paid attention to how he kept things shalom in the home, because I've got five ex-wives now, and each one is worse than the last."

Elijah saw his in and started asking the questions. He started with the simple one of how they'd known each other.

"He came up with my pop. Guys like Yitz and my father started getting successful in the 1920s, and suddenly they were living it up. Nice cars, jewelry, fancy this and that. My dad bought my mom a few minks. But Yitz did things differently. You know what people don't remember when they talk about a lot of those old-school guys like your grandfather and my dad is they came from shitholes in Europe. They had nothing; they get to America and suddenly they have even *less* than nothing. It must have been a shock. You know what I'm saying?"

Jerry the Fox stirred the spoon in his mug slowly, then looked out the window. Elijah didn't want the old guy getting off track.

"Did you work with him a lot? My grandfather . . ."

The old man dug his finger into the little bush of hair in his ear. He thought for a second.

"Yitz taught me a lot after my dad died. He took care of me, felt bad about . . . things." Jerry the Fox laughed to himself about something, then shook his head like he was offended by the thought. The last part threw Elijah for a loop, but he figured that thinking about his father's passing was what got the man choked up. The old man squished his mouth tight and nodded his head before he started saying anything else. "My dad was doing another stretch in Joliet for racketeering. He was loyal and took the fall for some important people—then he really took a fall when somebody tossed him over a balcony. That was their world. Yitz, though, he was above everything. He knew just the right time to make a move. He knew everybody, had information on everyone."

Jerry the Fox stopped talking and grabbed the server by her arm as she passed by. He asked if she could take the eggs back to the kitchen because they hadn't been cooked to his liking. The woman snatched his plate off the table and conversation picked up where it had left off.

"Yitz took me in when I was eleven. He got me running errands for him. You know who he had showing me things? You ever hear of Jack Ruby? Yitz had me follow Jack for a few months. This was before he went to Texas."

"What sort of errands did you run? Like . . ."

In his head, Elijah pictured a young Jerry the Fox with a garrote, strangling an enemy, then saying something snippy out of Hollywood: "Leave the piano wire, take the blintzes." But he was disappointed with the answer.

"Eh. Nothing fun. Picking up dry cleaning. Dropping off packages. I was a messenger boy. Today you'd say I was an intern."

"Unpaid, I'd imagine," Elijah joked. He thought it was a clever quip, but all he got was a cold glare.

"Why wouldn't you pay an intern? That doesn't seem right," the old man said.

Elijah looked down at his food. He hadn't taken a bite and it was likely cold. Jerry the Fox asked if something was wrong. Elijah said no and asked how he'd gotten into the car business.

"I could thank your grandpa for that. I knew about the lifestyle. I saw the tough guys in their nice suits, and I thought, boy, those guys look great. They had money and girls, and I wanted those things. So I started boosting cars. Had a nice little hustle. Got them to a place over the border in Indiana and they paid per car. They'd scrap 'em and go and sell the parts for three or four times more."

Elijah asked if his grandfather knew. He was still trying to piece together what sort of person Yitzhak Kaplan was, and had a vision of his grandfather as a hard but wise older man teaching the younger Jerry Foxman some important life lesson about right and wrong.

Jerry the Fox croaked out a little laugh, the sort a man gives when looking back on a tender moment from his youth, like a summer with a first love or a memory with a buddy from the war.

"Yitz knew *everything*. For instance, one day, I went a little too far. This was '56. I was leaving this girl's apartment on Oak and I see this Cadillac just sitting there in an unlit area. I needed a ride, so I grabbed it. Couple of days later, Yitz calls me in. The guy knew every damn thing that happened in the city. He sits me down and says the car belonged to Mayor Daley's priest—the first Mayor Daley, not his schmuck kid. The first Mayor Daley was one of us—just Irish. He was a Hamburg before he got into politics. All the Irish guys were."

"Is that a fraternal order or something?"

Jerry the Fox lit up at the chance to teach a history lesson. He started talking faster, and his Chicago accent that he tried to tamp down on when having a normal conversation came spewing out. All *D*s in words where *T*s normally were.

"Back in the old days, what the Mick aldermen and business guys would do was they'd start these youth clubs, that's what they called them. But they were foot soldiers, the muscle who the politicians hoped to wise up and turn into the next generation. Daley was the best of them, and the priest I'd taken the car from was one of his oldest friends, so it made things a little hot. Stealing a car from a priest is one thing if you worry about going to hell, but ripping off the mayor's priest in Chicago is about as dumb a move as you can make. So Yitz tells me I got two options. The first was he could make all the mayor's priest's Cadillac trouble disappear. I coulda kept working for him and still do my little side thing, but I had to cut him in. He said he'd help me sell the cars instead of going to Indiana. The other option was I was on my own, and when a guy like Yitz said you were on your own, that wasn't a good thing. I would have ended up in a Joliet cell by the end of the week. I agreed and eventually the boosting business turned into my first dealership. A small place on Western Ave. We had a great big neon sign that said, 'Fox Cars and Trucks.' Your grandfather was my backer. A year after we opened, I paid him back with his interest and that was that. We did some good business together."

The server came by with the reheated plate of eggs and asked if they needed anything else. Jerry the Fox asked her if she was sure his coffee was decaf. "I'm an old man. My heart can't take caffeine," he added.

She held up the coffee pot with the orange handle that had "Decaf" written on the glass.

"It doesn't taste decaf," Jerry the Fox snapped.

"What's decaf supposed to taste like?" the server asked. She didn't wait for an answer and went right to the next table.

The old man shrugged his shoulders and looked at Elijah.

"You OK, kid? Your food looks lonely. A funny thing about your gramps is when they'd take his plate back to get washed after dinner, I bet the dishwasher would take one look and say that Yitz's didn't need cleaning. He ate every damn morsel."

Elijah was playing back what Jerry the Fox had said seconds earlier. The word *business* was in there, but the business was . . . stealing cars. Elijah asked Jerry the Fox if he had that right.

"It's just not a story I've ever heard. I mean, I don't know anything about my grandfather, but this is . . ."

Before he could finish, the sweet old guy he'd been talking to for over an hour slowly morphed in front of his eyes. Something came over Jerry the Fox. He was suddenly filled with the vigor of a man forty years younger than him. The drooping skin of his forehead raised as high and back as possible. He pointed an arthritic finger at Elijah. It was like a movie scene where a human transformed into a werewolf, except Jerry the Fox was the same old man he'd been a few seconds earlier, just filled with rage.

"Look, kid. All the stuff in the newspapers. Mobster stuff. The gangsters, the bad guys, *The Godfather*, the Soprano guy . . . I'm just somebody who tried to make a dollar. Did I cut corners? Sure. Did my dad and your grandpa?" He answered his own question with a nod. "But all that guys like them had in front of them were corners. Get around the corner and you got walls and signs that said they couldn't enter. What else were they supposed to do? This city is a cold place that turns people into animals."

Elijah apologized. He didn't mean to touch a nerve. The old man sat back in his booth. In an instant he went from violent back to being the sweet old man.

"Your grandfather turned a lot of bad into good. He had a lot of hardship. Over in Ukraine, God only knows what he went through. Back then, it was still Russia, and you know how the Russians are. Always bastards. Never trust a Russian with any bit of power, that's one lesson I've learned. One of my ex-wives was from Leningrad and she was a terror."

Elijah looked at the little trail of saliva on the left side of the old man's mouth; he thought about asking for the check, but the old man had one more thing to say.

"I know your grandfather wanted a quiet life, but sometimes we aren't dealt those cards, and he played with the hand he got without ever complaining. A man has to work. He has to do things he doesn't always want to do. That's life. That's why I understood what he did."

6

FIRST HALF OF THE 1920S

Not much that happened around Jewtown over the first few months of Prohibition was that out of the ordinary. In April, the very old man who sold brooms on Halsted Street stabbed his even older cousin who sold thread and string, but that was tied to a bad deal involving a hen that laid only yolkless eggs thirty years earlier in some forgotten shtetl. There was also the runaway horse that trampled two orphans to death as they crossed the street in the middle of May, and that same month, a man who drank some spoiled wine ran through the streets naked, shouting how he was the reincarnation of the seventeenth-century false messiah Sabbatai Zevi.

In June, it was said that a bolt of lightning hitting a small congregation on Shabbos was what started the fire that burned it down and took four other buildings on the block along with it. The firefighters took two hours to show up. Everything was smoldering rubble by the time they got there, yet not a single person perished in the blaze. The police said there was nothing suspicious they needed to look into, the people of Jewtown decided it had been a miracle that there wasn't a single death, and nobody put together that the policy claims on the buildings that kept burning down around the area were all owned by people with similar names: Isaak Caplan of Hobart, Ike Chaplin of South Bend, Newton Kapowski Holdings of Detroit, and the old man who ran the post office in the small Upper Peninsula town where a man named Ira Chaplain received his mail never met the guy, but he received more letters than the other 139 residents. Nobody batted an eye that none of the men actually existed, and not a single question was raised when it was Yitz, always flanked by two bigger men, who showed up to collect the money for all of them.

The money was good in the spring and early summer, and things were mostly calm until a muggy mid-August morning, the sort where all the scents of city life mix together in the air and create a sticky, sick perfume that coats the skin and nostrils. There was an act that seemed so brazen at the time, yet it was nothing like what was to come. The late edition of that day's *Chicago Daily Bulletin* reported:

Three hoodlums got out of a Studebaker Big Six on W. 13th St. in broad daylight this morning and opened fire for reasons unknown. One bystander was hit before another gunman or possibly multiple gunmen began firing back at the hoodlums. Two of the thugs were hit and later pronounced dead on the scene, while the third escaped and his whereabouts are currently unknown. Witnesses claimed to not have seen or know who the shooter or shooters that returned fire were, and the bodies of the two deceased men had no identification on them.

A couple of Polish jerks from Bucktown had tried to rob one of Avi's runners who was carrying the money made the previous evening at two nearby establishments. The only problem with their plan was the runner had been carrying a bag filled with scraps of paper. It was a setup. Yitz had gotten word that the Poles who'd been trying to make their mark were going to try to rob the places, so he had a few of his guys watching their every move. The plan was, since all the stickups had been taking place at night, they'd try to do it just as the sun was coming up.

At 6:30 in the morning, one of the Poles jumped out of the car and started blasting at the runner; he didn't even try to stop and stick him up. All three shots missed; the other two guys followed his lead, but were met by eight men from Jewtown who cut them down almost immediately. The last surviving Polack started shooting wildly and hit a Hasid who was rushing to morning minyan, putting a bullet in his leg. The Pole got away on foot. Avi told Yitz he'd negotiate with the Poles up in Bucktown to give the kid up, that it wouldn't be too hard since he was a nobody who wasn't connected to anybody of importance. Yitz disagreed. He said the old way of being friendly wasn't going to work anymore, especially when it came to some no-name Polack. If Avi asked for a single thing, Yitz said the Jews would look weak, and more nobodies would show up to see what they could get away with. An example had to be made, and there was one man to do it.

"If we don't do this now, then in no time America will be just like Russia or Poland. It's already happening. They're blaming us for Bolshevism. They blame us for wars. There are pamphlets being circulated all over town about how the Jews control the banks," Yitz said.

Avi laughed. "I've been to banks. No Jews in there."

"We *need* to take action," Yitz said.

Avi sighed, buried his face in his hands, and mumbled something about how he hated bloodshed, but conceded with a "Fine."

Without saying another word, Yitz put on his hat and walked a few blocks to the butcher shop. Sol was finishing up with a customer, an old lady who put her hand on his and said what a nice boy he was. Yitz rushed up to the counter as she walked away; he told his brother he needed some help.

"We've got some nice brisket today, and I know you like marrow bones," Sol joked.

"Shut up. I need you to come with me real quick. Just close up for a few minutes and go with me when I talk to the Mohel."

Sol stared at his brother as he rubbed his blood-soaked hands with his apron.

"You mean you need *me* to talk to Jozef," Sol said.

"He likes you. He'll listen if you're there."

"You could come study with us sometime if you want to make friends. It might do you some good to pick it back up."

Sol had started drifting back into shul. It surprised his brother, who had mostly abandoned exploring the Talmud or even keeping kosher. Sol wasn't enthusiastic about school back in Odesa, but something had changed in him after a few years in America, and he could be found at every morning prayer and Shabbos service. Yitz brushed off his brother's advice and asked again if he'd go with him. Sol agreed, and a few minutes later, they walked into Congregation B'nai Shalom, past the empty pews and the ark where the Torah slept. They walked into a back room where a group of men were sitting around a holy book, discussing something in Yiddish. Yitz shouted over them that he was looking for Jozef the Mohel. The men all looked at one another with surprise on their faces. One of them nervously pointed to another door and said he was in the kitchen making some tea.

It had been a long time since the Mohel had performed a circumcision. His name was once known all over the Romanov empire. He was the man you wanted to perform the ritual that started thousands of years back when God told Abraham to go in his tent in the arid desert, circumcise himself, then tell all the other men that wanted to be Jews to do the same. New parents far and wide begged and pleaded with him to take care of their newborn baby boys. They'd send letters, rich men sent gold coins with the promise of many more if he'd make the journey, and even a few gentiles of higher standing who'd heard rumors that the source of a Jew's brilliance was because God looked favorably on those who took part in the ritual wanted him to snip their boys. He did it with such precision and swiftness unlike anybody in all the tsar's lands that it was said some babies didn't even notice what had taken place. And if a parent showed the slightest bit of fear at what they were about to witness, Jozef the Mohel would turn to them, look them in the eye, smile, and say, "The blessed Torah teaches us that Abraham was ninety-nine when he did this." He'd wink, the parents would laugh, and without taking his eyes off them, Jozef the Mohel would snip.

He'd made the journey to America in 1905, smuggled out as a hero after he killed at least a dozen Russian soldiers. The story went that before the revolution, Jozef had never killed a man, but after a Cossack put a sword through his brother's stomach, the Mohel snapped. Killing became easy for him. When he came over to America and couldn't find much work in the foreskin-snipping business, he'd take small jobs taking care of low-level crooks who needed to be taught a lesson. He could slice off the top of an ear or the tip of a nose with a quick slash, but from time to time, he'd get a look in his eye, and just keep flicking the blade until the guy he'd been sent to teach a lesson had a face that looked like strands of bloody confetti. He made Yitz uncomfortable, but that was exactly what was needed for the job. Sol gave the terrifying man a warm hello, then let Yitz do the rest of the talking. All he had to say was some Polish guys had showed up, and that was the only thing that needed to be said.

The kid was tracked down an hour later. He'd been hiding in an alley a few blocks away, cowering behind some barrels, a bullet stuck in the fleshy part of his leg, hoping he could last until it was dark and try to sneak away. Later that night, he was tossed out of a car near Milwaukee Avenue. He was missing all his fingertips, and Jozef the Mohel added a deep slice under each eye going down the cheek that would eventually scar up and remind everyone of the mistake the fourteen-year-old Polish hoodlum from Bucktown had made.

That was when the rest of Chicago was put on alert that if you showed up in Jewtown, you'd better be on your best behavior. Everybody learned to respect the Jews. Everybody, that is, except for the Irish. They didn't care about anybody. Chicago was *their* town, and they called the Jews "Christ Killers," said the Blacks and Chinese weren't even human, but especially hated the Italians. They wanted nothing to do with them for reasons that didn't quite make sense to Yitz since they were mostly all Catholics.

Yitz kept a map of Chicago in his office. He wrote in pencil the predominant group in each neighborhood and added any gangs he knew of in each part. The Jews had made inroads with their Italian and Greek neighbors, and Avi and Yitz agreed they weren't too concerned with making nice with the Bohunks and Poles. Where they differed in opinion was on the matter of the parts of Yitz's map he labeled as the "Negro" sections. The populations of those neighborhoods were expanding each day as southern plantations emptied and the Black workers made their way to the Midwest to escape life under Jim Crow. Like every other group, they had their own ways of doing things and had plenty of money coming in through the numbers racket, but neither the Irish nor even the Italians would work with them because of the color of their skin. Not that the Black folks were quick to want to partner with whites, especially after what many of them experienced before they came up north from places like Texas and Arkansas. Chicago treated them just a hair better, but in the summer of 1919, when a Negro boy supposedly swam too close to a part of the lake that had been designated for whites only, a white man threw a rock that hit him on the head. It knocked the kid unconscious and he drowned. Even though there were plenty of witnesses, the cops arrested a Black man for the crime. There were protests in the Negro neighborhoods that were mostly peaceful until the Irish mobs started showing up. Fights broke out all over the city. The police tried to get a handle on things, but then came reports that brown-skinned mobs were going through Italian and Polish neighborhoods all over town and setting fire to homes and businesses. When the cops showed up, it turned out to be Irish kids from multiple gangs in blackface who'd been hoping to rile up the white immigrants. The riots lasted a few days. More than a thousand homes and businesses burned to the ground. Word quickly spread around Jewtown. There were plenty of people with memories of marauding Russian soldiers on horseback in their old country, and similar tricks pulled where the rich and powerful would find a way to blame people without any money or power for something. To Yitz and many others, if it looked like a pogrom, then that's what it was.

That's when Yitz started to find ways for the groups to work together and pool resources. Forget the South Side, he reasoned; all the power could easily shift to around Maxwell Street. Different languages and skin color be damned; everybody wanted to make money because that was how you built safety and security. It was the thing all the groups had in common.

Avi was skeptical. With the rush of money that had come in through bootlegging, the boss was optimistic they'd hit on something that would last forever. He even believed that he could charm the almighty Irish into working with Maxwell Street.

Hearing that was the first time the word *schmuck* popped into

Yitz's head while talking to the boss. Avi had obviously forgotten how bad things could get for Jews.

"Schmuck. Schmuck, schmuck, *schmuck*," he thought.

A week after the shooting on Thirteenth, word got around to Avi of the encroachment of Irish guys from the South Side on Fourteenth, in a block that had been Lippy's territory since back when it was just a sheet of mud and horse shit. It was a couple of guys not long removed from Ellis Island, the brogue of their homeland impossible to miss. Yitz had figured something like it would happen after the old boss was out but was surprised by how long it took. He had tried to push for preparedness, but Avi was confident that the old deals would hold up, that the other groups saw he was in charge and treated him the way they did Lippy. But he was wrong, and he admitted it, as he lit a cigar and blew a line of smoke out. "When you're right, you're right," Avi said.

The Irish guys had gone from a nuisance to a problem. They'd started out shaking down Meir's little delicatessen, but the thing was that nobody liked Meir because he always trimmed too much fat off his meat even when he was asked not to, and there was a rumor his beef came out tough because the cheap bastard had a deal on older steers. It also didn't help his standing that he allowed both of his children to marry goyim. There was much debate on Maxwell as to which of those things was Meir greatest transgression. Most agreed it was trimming too much of the precious marble off the meat.

Meir was one thing, but then it was the old couple that had scrimped and saved to open their own tailor shop next door to him, and then it was Chaim the pickle man next to them. Suddenly, everybody on the block was nervous.

Under normal circumstances, taking care of somebody else coming into Avi's area and setting up business would have been dealt with promptly. Yet the couple of Irishmen who were strong-arming the Jews along Fourteenth weren't just some everyday thugs whom Yitz could order some of his big boys from Romania or the two men everybody called the Irkutsk Bros—even though they weren't brothers, just two very large men who spent time in the same Siberian penal colony and only seemed comfortable in the world when they had some sort of weapon in their hands—to deal with. They were related to a couple of the higher-ups who operated out of the Bridgeport Arrowheads clubhouse on Thirty-third and Emerald. Distant cousins, but still under the protection of the Arrowhead brotherhood, a once-feared group for which Yitz had nothing but contempt. Before the war, they'd counted somewhere around five hundred members among their ranks, and their territory extended north beyond the river. But after things had calmed down in Europe, their numbers had dwindled to around seventy-five, and the Italians and Poles they'd held down before America joined the fight in Europe had moved in and taken over the areas all around the ballpark when the Arrowhead boys were off fighting. They desperately needed to show force, and letting their new members who had just come over from Ireland run roughshod—especially on the Jews, supposedly the easiest target—was their plan.

While the Arrowheads' membership numbers had dipped, they still had power through their founder, Alderman Frankie Walsh. He started the clubhouse the same way other Irish aldermen had founded their own little "athletic clubs" throughout the South Side. Walsh's boys had conceded some power to people they called "foreign invaders," but also had lost ground to rival Irish gangs.

Avi puffed on his cigar and said he'd work it out. The confidence in his voice annoyed Yitz. He knew talking wouldn't do anything, but the boss had made up his mind, and set up a meeting with the alderman. A day later, Yitz couldn't help but feel some small bit of pleasure after two of Walsh's underlings showed up in Frankie Walsh's place without apologizing or giving any reason for the boss not being there. The disrespect was followed up with the Arrowheads' pink-faced representatives cycling between calling Avi "Schwartz" and "Rothschild" instead of his actual name. Avi stayed diplomatic through the whole meeting, just smiling and ignoring the insults. The boss was trying to show his mental toughness, but Yitz could only think of how weak he came off. Avi thought of himself as a great politician, but he relied too much on appeasement; he considered himself a businessman, but it was really his cousin Artie who understood how to get things done. Yitz believed that without the Bermans, Avi wouldn't even have a street corner in the city to call his own, but at the end of the meeting, Walsh's guys agreed to call their boys off, and they'd pay back whatever they'd taken. Avi looked at Yitz and grinned.

"Now maybe you could do a favor for us, *Mr. Schwartz*," one of the Arrowheads said. Early in the meeting, Yitz had counted more than two dozen craters on the man's face and bald head, many of them splashed with orange freckles. He started counting the pox marks again to stop himself from laughing at the guy's suggestion that Avi owed him a damn thing. "We need a garage on Maxwell. Not for booze or nothing like that. It's for storing some things to send back over to Ireland. Trinkets, things of that nature. We won't need it for more than a month, and the alderman would consider this an act of friendship on your part if you'd be able to accommodate us."

The pleased look on Avi's face made Yitz sick. Walking from the meeting, all the boss could do was talk about how well he'd handled things. "President Harding should hire me to go talk to other countries. I've got a real knack. Lippy could have never done what I just did getting those dogs to heel. Now just make sure you're there tomorrow to open that garage up for them, and keep an eye on things. Take care of whoever they put in charge of that job, show him a good time. We keep playing nice with them and we've got a strong ally."

Yitz thought about reminding Avi that the Arrowheads had fallen pretty far down the local ladder, that they weren't the South Side powerhouse they'd been once upon a time. But he didn't. Yitz wanted to believe Avi knew what he was doing.

The very next afternoon a man named Murphy showed up. It wasn't certain whether his last or first name was Murphy, but Yitz didn't bother asking because the guy was just too difficult to understand. The accent was one thing, but he had only three teeth, all crooked and in the front. Whenever he talked there was a whistling sound. He was also always so soused that doing something as simple as unlocking the door to get into the garage was a nearly impossible task. Yitz decided to get one of his guys to help Murphy. There was a kid he'd liked who'd come up from Tulsa a month earlier after the Klan burned down his father's grocery store. He was looking to work as much as possible, had a good head on his shoulders, and could talk anybody into just about anything. His name was James Booker White, but everybody called him White Jimmy. Yitz got a kick out of seeing the looks people made when the kid introduced himself to white folks by his nickname, and he respected the way the young guy moved through the world. White Jimmy had been working cleanup at Sol's butcher shop, but he'd been hustling for Yitz's attention the way Yitz had once tried to get Avi to take notice of what an asset he could be. He gave him a little extra money and told him to act as Murphy's guide, helping him unload boxes, getting him food and drink, but most important, keeping an eye on the guy. There was something going on, but Avi was so busy acting like he'd negotiated the Treaty of Versailles that he didn't even care. The day after the month allotted to the Arrowheads passed, Yitz went to Avi and asked him when the Irish would be done using the garage. He mentioned how they were always moving boxes in and out, that something suspicious was happening, and he worried that Jewtown would end up suffering because of whatever it was. Plus, Murphy was drinking up all the liquor at the brothel, and he'd given at least two girls the clap. They were losing money by keeping him around, Yitz said.

"No luck," Avi told him, then changed the subject to something Yitz didn't want to talk about. "How's my sister? I heard Ma's coming to stay with you guys. Poor girl is slipping away. You're a mensch for taking her in."

Yitz was fond of his mother-in-law from his early days in America. She'd taken him and Sol in and remained the one Kaminsky that didn't drive him nuts, but it was one more headache he didn't need.

"Are you kidding? Of course," he said as he put on his hat and coat. A smile was hard to force, but he pushed all the muscles in his face to cooperate. "Anything for her . . . or you."

When Sol delivered the news of his new venture, Yitz smiled and said how proud he was of his brother. Three days later, Yitz showed up to the little butcher shop and told Sol he had a surprise. They got in a car to travel less than a block to another storefront. It had a large empty warehouse behind it that had initially been built to house one of the earliest fleets of taxicabs in the city; inside sat four shiny GMC trucks, each of them painted blue with "Kapovitch Sons Kosher Meats and Sausage" written on the side.

"I thought adding you do sausage was a nice touch," Yitz said. "It's a smart business move."

He called the trucks and warehouse a gift, and said Sol would be able to beat out all his competition by offering delivery, but failed to mention that the trucks would also be used to transport money up to Michigan, then booze back to Chicago, throughout the week. All he said was, "I'll use these sometimes."

A month later, Sol wrote a note to Yitz and handed it off to White

Jimmy, who was in the shop to pick up some steaks. It asked Yitz to meet him at an address at noon the next Tuesday. "And don't be a second late," he added.

It was obviously important, so Yitz made sure nothing held him up. He walked from the Schvitz to the address along a tree-lined street he'd somehow never seen before even though it was only fifteen minutes to the west. It was almost as if the stretch was purposely hidden from view so the people that lived in the row of stately townhouses wouldn't be bothered. He got to the address he'd been given. It was a three-story, creamy-colored home made with Joliet limestone.

"Yitzeleh," Sol shouted from down the block.

His little brother looked like a bear charging down the sidewalk with bull speed. If they'd only trained him to be a boxer they would have been able to print money from all the guys he'd have knocked out, Yitz thought to himself. Six-one, arms thick like logs, tight and solid middle, strong legs, and a pair of boulders for fists.

Standing outside the stately home, Yitz noticed something different about his brother.

"Look at this place. The tsar hiding out here?" he joked as he tried in vain to hug Sol's entire torso in his arms.

"I gotta ask you something," Sol said. He had cleaned himself up after work. Shaven, nice smelling, no bits of dried blood and cartilage under his nails.

Yitz rolled his eyes.

"Again with the trucks? I told you that soon—"

Sol waved his hands and told his brother to shush.

"We can talk about that later. But I need something from you. You're going to meet somebody when we go inside."

"Is it another rabbi? I told you, Sol, I can only give so much to these shuls."

139

"No. It's Julius Spiegel."

"The suit maker? Spiegel Suits and Shirts? *Bubbeleh*, I've got suits. You know I go to the Sicilian tailor."

"It's not for suits," Sol said. "It's for his daughter. I want to marry her, and he wants to meet my family first."

Yitz started to smile. The smile turned to a chuckle. Then a tear that he quickly flicked from his eye. "My brother. My baby brother," he said, pinching Sol's cheeks.

"Cut it out. I'm a year younger than you," Sol said.

"Two years younger," Yitz said.

"Year and a half at best. Either way, when you got married, I knew my time was up. Where's Leah, by the way? I thought she was coming."

"Eh, I didn't want to bother her. You know, with the baby and her ma and all."

As they stood waiting for somebody to answer the door, Sol put his hand on Yitz's shoulder and caressed it.

"Thank you for doing this," he said. "I've got a good brother."

A maid greeted them and brought them into a small study. The shelves were filled with religious books, and an oil painting of a rabbi sat over the chairs she told them to sit in before offering schnapps or cigars, which they declined. The old woman walked out, and a younger woman walked in. She was followed by an older man with a slight hunchback. Sol stood up and slightly bowed his head.

"Mr. Spiegel," he said. "This is my brother, Yitzhak."

"I see we both have small families," the old man said. The sadness wrapped around his words was impossible to ignore.

The girl's name was Devorah. Yitz tried to study her face without her noticing. She had crystal-blue eyes. Such a rarity to find a pair like them in Jewtown. Sol was talking, but Yitz hadn't heard a word his brother had said.

"Huh? Oh, yes. I approve," Yitz said.

Everybody stared at him. Sol leaned in and whispered "I haven't asked yet" in his brother's ear.

"You have to ask? He doesn't know that's what you're here for?" Yitz asked.

Sol shook his head.

"That's a very nice suit, Mr. Kaplan," Devorah said. "It doesn't look like one of my father's."

Yitz looked at the dark gray herringbone sleeve of his jacket. "You know, I forget. My wife's brother's tailor. I felt obligated."

"Is your wife Italian?" Devorah asked. "Because that's an Italian-made suit. You can tell just by the cut. The only Jews I've seen wearing that sort of suit are criminals," she said with a polite smile.

"No," Yitz said. "She's not."

It went dead quiet for a moment, until Sol took the sound of a glass cup clinking against its saucer as his cue.

"Mr. Spiegel, I've got a question . . ."

Later that night, as the two brothers were walking down Maxwell Street, Sol stopped, reached into his pocket, and pulled a half-pint bottle from his jacket pocket.

"What are you, a bum?" Yitz joked.

"This is special," Sol said. "It's from Odesa. The same vodka Papa used to make l'chaim with."

Yitz took the bottle and smelled it. He cringed and wretched, then examined the bottle.

"What are those? Pickle particles still floating around? You know we can get champagne. Whiskey. Gin? We don't have to drink that."

"Jews don't drink gin, it makes us too thirsty. Besides, I think Mama and Papa would like this," Sol said as he downed a little of the vodka. He swallowed it and let out a loud "OY" before passing it to his brother.

"L'chaim. To many years and many babies here in America for you and the rich tailor's beautiful daughter," Yitz said as he held his nose and took a sip. He tried to swallow the booze, but it shot right out of his mouth. Sol patted his brother on the back as Yitz laughed and coughed. "Putrid shit," Yitz said. "I can't believe our father drank that regularly. That vodka probably killed more Jews than the Cossacks did."

As they began walking toward their destination, a man approached them. He had a thin mustache, wore a suit that looked like it could use a date with the cleaners, and was smoking a cheap cigar. Yitz smiled at him and they shook hands.

"David Siegelman. No surprise I'd find you this close to the whorehouses. Let me introduce you to my brother, the best butcher in the whole city. Sol, Siegelman writes for the *Daily Chicagoan*, but he really is an artist. Working on his first novel for a publisher in New York."

"Pleased to finally meet the best butcher in town," Siegelman said as he shook Sol's hand. "Now I know the best bartender, and I've got the best editor, but I hate his guts."

Sol blushed. He hated being complimented.

"He just got engaged. A *terrific* girl," Yitz said. "We're going to make l'chaim at the River Club. Come with us."

"Well, I'm looking for a story . . ."

"Come on," Yitz said. "I'll help you find a better thing to write about."

"I suppose I can't say no to a man who just got engaged. Mazel tov."

Sol handed him the bottle of vodka and said he had to prove himself first.

"In order to join the Kaplan boys, you have to try this Russian petrol with floating pickle bits that some greenhorn smuggled across the ocean," Yitz said.

Siegelman took a big gulp and didn't even flinch.

"I've drunk much worse," the newspaperman said.

The brothers howled with laughter as they started making their way toward the River Club, when a woman's voice rang out from less than a block away.

"Mr. Kaplan! Mr. Kaplan!"

Yitz saw one of the girls that worked the private rooms behind the Schvitz. Streaks of eye makeup ran down her cheeks, and her black hair was a mess. She was out of breath and wearing a man's overcoat; from the looks of it, there wasn't much underneath. Her bare legs shivered and she was frantic. Yitz asked what was wrong. The girl caught her breath. "Harry Roth—" she said through a hiccup. There was a slight trace of a southern accent. Yitz couldn't remember if her name was Virginia or that was where she'd originally come from.

"He killed him. The Irishman killed him," she said through sobs.

Harry Roth was the barman in the brothel behind the Schvitz. He'd been a ballplayer as a younger man, a promising catcher whose career was cut short when he broke his leg. He got into tending bar before Prohibition to take care of his wife and three kids, always hustling despite his limp. He'd worked for a time at Fitzgerald and Moy's, a popular hangout for celebrities, politicians, and ballplayers on Clark Street near the river, but was fired after it came to light that he'd had a hand in introducing members of the 1919 White Sox to the bookmakers who wanted the team to throw the World Series. Yitz felt partially responsible since he'd been the one to relay the message to Harry that a few guys out east had hoped to talk business with some of Harry's old ballplayer pals, so he got him work at a few of Avi's spots.

The girl collected herself and explained that Harry wouldn't serve Murphy after he showed up smelling like he'd fallen in a still. The former ballplayer was calm as he told the Irishman that he was following house rules, that they didn't serve anybody who showed up as drunk as Murphy was. Murphy started yelling something; she said his drunken Irish gibberish made it sound as if he'd been speaking in tongues.

Trying to defuse the situation, White Jimmy put his hand on the Irishman's shoulder and kindly asked him to walk outside. Murphy pulled a knife from his boot, then screamed something that sounded like he never let a colored man touch him. He had murder in his eyes; ending White Jimmy was the only possibility the enraged man would accept. Harry Roth calmly crept up behind Murphy; the bartender had a few inches and pounds on the guy, but Murphy saw the old ballplayer coming and stuck the knife right into Harry's guts.

Yitz sprinted to the scene of the attack. He pushed past the crying girls and saw White Jimmy holding a slice of raw steak to the side of his face where the Irishman had clocked him. Harry Roth's body lay motionless, his mouth was open as wide as his eyes were; it was as if he had fully realized the final shock of death. There was a crimson pool that had settled from a small stream starting from his side. One of the guys who worked security in the back, whose job was to make sure customers didn't get too rough with the girls, walked up toward Yitz. He was like a bowling ball with arms and legs—bald, stocky, could knock you down. People called him Brody after the part of Poland he'd come from. He took his hat off and held it against his heart.

"Harry was smiling and laughing. Then he went back to the bar and a minute later there was shouting. It was Harry and the Irishman. I couldn't understand what they were saying. I get up and start walking and that's when I hear the thump. I start walking faster, and as I'm walking, I hear this banging. I get out here and the Irish guy's going through Harry's pockets, holding Harry's little gun he kept on his ankle. I knew it was his pistol right away because he was showing it to me the other day. Then the sonofabitch points it at me. I tell him to think about what he's doing, and he runs out the door still pointing the gun."

Yitz surveyed the situation. He was so possessed by rage that it took a few moments to remember that it didn't matter if they found the killer or not; nothing could be done until Avi gave the OK, and the boss had given strict orders not to be bothered while he was having a romantic evening with one of his girlfriends.

Then Yitz saw an even bigger problem in the corner of his eye. The damn newspaper reporter had followed and was recording everything in his head. Yitz had fed Siegelman some good information in the past for stories that got him pats on the back from his bosses, but he was still a newspaperman, and guys like him couldn't turn down a juicy story like a bartender getting murdered in a cathouse. The newspaperman held all the power, but Siegelman looked at Yitz with his kind eyes and nodded slightly. He spoke in a low voice.

"The reporters will be here sooner or later. That's just the way it works. But I'll be long gone by then, handing in my version of the story. OK?"

Siegelman stuck out his hand. Yitz shook it and thanked him. "You'll never pay for another drink in this town again . . . for a few weeks," he added, putting his free hand on Siegelman's shoulder and squeezing it.

After Siegelman left, Yitz kicked everybody else out of the room, then stood over the dead man's body. Harry Roth's eyes were wide open, a look of pure shock on his face, as if he couldn't believe it was happening right up until his last second. Yitz wondered if that was how it really was: torture and fear until everything went black.

As he looked at the dead man, Yitz started to hear the sounds of Odesa. He was suddenly a boy again, looking at the soldier whom his mother had just killed in their home. The urge to crawl and hide overtook him; he was terrified. His heart was a drum, and it felt like somebody had turned on a faucet in his armpits. He wanted to scream, and then, as fast as it had started, the urge was gone. He snapped back to reality, leaned down, and closed Harry Roth's eyes.

Harry Roth died on a Thursday evening; his body needed to be in the ground the next day before Shabbos. Yitz took care of all the arrangements.

The news had made the front page of the *Daily Journal* and the *Tribune*. The Friday morning edition of the *Chicago Daily News* had the headline "Violent Criminal Kills Former Ballplayer." But it was David Siegelman who had the best account of the whole incident. He'd made a name for himself as one of the best young reporters in the city, somehow always knowing where to be at just the right time. In his words, it was a tragedy, a senseless slaying, another failure not of the men, but of the system that produced them. On the next page was a blind item with the headline "Ward Boss Walsh's Clubhouse Tied to Beer, Crime." It described Murphy as just one of a number of thugs that were part of the Arrowheads network. The article didn't have a writer's name attributed to it, but it was clearly Siegelman's vivid and muscular prose. Yitz had supplied the reporter with the information he needed, deciding that while he couldn't make a decision on the fate of Harry Roth's killer, he could at least cause some heartache for the alderman and his goons.

They put the wooden coffin with the bartender in the ground at noon. More than a hundred people showed up for the funeral even though the Roth family had lived in Chicago for only a few years and didn't have many ties to the city. They gathered to pay their respects because the bartender was one of their own who'd been murdered. They helped lay Harry Roth in the earth because the words they read every year at Pesach—"in every generation they rise up to destroy us"—cut deep. They mourned because the destruction they thought they'd escaped had followed them to America.

His wife was hysterical. She threw her crying child to the ground, jumped in the grave, and had to be pulled out by three men. A fourth man, rushing to help pull up the others, bumped into the rabbi and knocked him to the ground. It was a commotion. As the scene unfolded, Avi leaned over to Yitz.

"The Arrowheads aren't budging," he said. "Their guy said there's no way they'd give up one of their own if he killed one Jew or a hundred. And since it was a Jew that was protecting a Negro, they're treating the bum like a hero. They've got him hidden somewhere. They won't even bother negotiating with us. Can you believe that?"

Yes, Yitz thought. He could believe it.

"We need to get them back," Yitz said. "We're losing any ground we've made."

"The Irish *are* the ground in this town," Avi hissed. "They've been here the longest. This is their town and they made the rules. That will change sooner or later, but for now—"

"Bullshit," Yitz spit.

They stared at each other for a second; neither one blinked until Yitz relented so he could argue his point. His tone was relaxed but confident as he spoke.

"Everybody hates Frankie Walsh. The Italians hate him because he's Irish. The Negroes despise him because of the riots in 1919. The other Irish don't like him because he's reckless. The cops don't even like him because his boys start so much trouble and the city has to pay for it. He's got his own breweries, and he doesn't have distribution out of them. He's turned his ward into a little island and he's not sharing the wealth with anybody. All he needs do is cut City Hall in and they turn a blind eye, but he won't. He's greedy. He thinks he's the tsar of the South Side."

Avi wouldn't look Yitz in the eye. It was obvious he was shocked by how he'd been talked to.

"I'm standing over the grave of a bartender killed by an Irish nobody whose people are willing to protect him just because they can. We start a war over Harry—may his memory be a blessing—we're going to be standing over a lot of other graves just to get this Irish nobody that means nothing besides the fact that he killed one of ours," he said.

Yitz had staked everything on his intuitions, but did so because he was certain. He never let emotion cloud his decisions, but Harry Roth was one of them, and Avi was treating his death like a minor statistic. He yielded to some of the rage he felt while speaking.

"There won't be a war," Yitz said. "I promise."

Avi spit on the ground.

"Don't get the Mohel for this" was his first command. "And don't fuck this up" was the other. He turned to the pair of stone towers who followed him everywhere and walked away.

An hour later, Yitz walked into Lev's Deli. There were three customers at the counter. Two older men sitting in silence, and Aaron Feigenbaum, the Golem of Maxwell Street.

Born a few blocks away on Thirteenth, Aaron Feigenbaum thought it was his duty as an American to join the army for the Great War. He fought in the Battle of Saint-Mihiel, watching a quarter of his division get gunned down all around him as they tried to make it down a stretch of muddy road. Feigenbaum, it was said, chopped down two dozen of the kaiser's men after he posted up behind a stuck American tank that was sinking into the ground and stacked a few of his fellow soldiers' dead bodies up around him like a little shelter as he shot. He came back to Chicago with medals, but he was hollowed out; there was nothing behind his eyes. When Yitz passed him on the street, he would wonder what, exactly, it was that took his soul in France. Whatever had happened on the battlefields of Europe had turned him into a monster who made a name for himself back home after he tracked down a pair of Bohunk brothers who had robbed old Moishe the cobbler. It was said he stalked them for almost two days, seeing where they'd be the most vulnerable, then he snuck up from behind and sliced them so badly that their mother couldn't recognize either of them.

Trying to contain the nervousness he felt around the Golem, Yitz sat down on the stool right next to him. He ordered a coffee and a liverwurst sandwich and couldn't take his eyes off the man's large hands, which were covered in burns and scars. It was as if he manicured his hands by dipping them in lava and glass. They were thick and discolored, like the entire top layer had been forever burned away. The man took bites of his sandwich and just swallowed. No chewing, just ripping big hunks of pastrami and bread and choking them down with a gulp. He stared forward, hardly blinking. Yitz wondered how much death you had to see and cause until you became the walking dead.

The Golem had been doing collections for Avi's numbers business; people found the money they owed quite quickly when they saw the monster that was once a man approaching.

But that was all arranged through somebody else. Yitz never had any reason to talk to him directly. He pushed a newspaper with a cash-filled envelope inside toward the Golem. As he did it, Yitz realized that the man, who seemed like a giant, was the same height he was. It didn't make him fear him any less; it made him seem even more terrifying.

There was an address written in pen on the newspaper. The Golem turned his eyes down at it.

"That's a big-money area," he said. "I assume it's a big-money person. Seems a little much for a dead bartender?"

Yitz nodded. He pulled out a little paperback and tossed it on the counter. "You know what that is?" he asked.

The title of the book read *Protocols of the Learned Elders of Zion*. The Golem said he was familiar.

The publisher's stamp on the inside was for the Knights of Arrowhead Press out of Chicago. Four boxes full of the booklets were in the garage they'd been borrowing from Avi; it seemed like a sick joke. There was also a small cache of guns and explosives meant for Ireland's anti-British fighters in the garage, and Yitz considered using some of the dynamite to blow up the Arrowheads' clubhouse as revenge, but decided not to let emotion dictate his actions.

"The man you're visiting is responsible for about five thousand copies of that being distributed all over Illinois and Wisconsin. You can consider your deed a mitzvah," Yitz said.

The old man behind the counter placed a liverwurst sandwich in front of Yitz. He gave him extra pickles, just like always. Yitz thanked him and the old man scurried away.

"It's better I don't know his name," the Golem added as he took a bite of his pastrami sandwich. He didn't even chew, just swallowed it. "Is it just one? A wife? Kids?"

Yitz started to feel queasy. The monster he was talking with was willing to murder anybody, even children.

"Just him," he replied. "He goes for a stroll at eleven every night on the dot to smoke a cigar."

"OK," the Golem said without a trace of humanity in his voice as he stood up to leave. "Good Shabbos."

It was another slow Sunday. Yitz sat in his office reading a short story in a magazine, something about a sad rich man and his sad rich man problems, chasing after an even wealthier girl who'd never love him back. He had a few lines to go when Avi burst through the door.

"What the fuck did you do?" he shouted as he slapped a newspaper on the desk.

Yitz didn't even glance at the front page; he knew what it said.

"You told me to do what needed to be done, so that's what I did. No Mohel involved, as you requested."

A vein bulged from Avi's neck. He seethed and screamed while Yitz calmly sat and said nothing. The silence enraged the boss further.

"You see what this says, smart-ass? At the top." Avi stamped his finger on the headline: "Butchery on South Cregier." He picked the paper up, flung it at Yitz, then started yelling again.

"The paper says he was stabbed to death, but from what I hear, whoever did it plunged the blade with such force into the left side of the alderman's throat that it went right through his larynx and tore through the other side. He was probably still alive as the knife was being pulled out. Poor bastard choked to death on his own blood."

Yitz feigned a look of disappointment.

"You're right," he said with a shrug. "It could have been cleaner."

Avi leaped across the desk and started slapping Yitz.

"You're making jokes? This is an alderman we're talking about," he shouted. "Frankie Walsh was dirty, but you can't kill a ward boss!"

Avi stopped his assault and straightened his tie. He motioned for Yitz to explain himself.

"There might be a few Irish that aren't happy that they're out of jobs, but they'll be fine. I made sure everything has been handled. *Our* reporters and *our* cops got there first. And by tomorrow, every paper in the city will be talking about all the things Walsh had his fingers in maybe more than they'll be talking about this. When everything calms down and people are finished being shocked, all they're going to remember is how he closed an orphanage so he could manufacture beer in the building, how he had kids with women all over the city, and all the money he stole to keep their mothers quiet. He was a bad man, and the public doesn't like bad men."

The answer didn't satisfy Avi. He was visibly shaken; Yitz felt powerful seeing it.

"*I* didn't do this," Avi said.

Yitz could feel the vein in his forehead furiously pumping blood. He needed to continue speaking and acting the same way, he told himself. He couldn't budge even a centimeter of room.

"That's right," he said. "The Golem did. And I told him to because you told me to handle it. That's what I do. I handle things."

Avi sucked on his teeth for a second. The sound of a band starting to play a tune came wafting in from somewhere outside. The two men looked at each other. Avi's eyes were filled with fire; Yitz projected a facade of serenity, even if his heart and adrenal glands were working four times faster than normal. Avi broke the staring contest as he looked away and gave a little laugh.

"You know why I picked you? It's not because you're from Odesa or how you hustled." Avi straightened his jacket and walked over to Yitz so they were face-to-face. "I looked at you and right away I knew that you were driven by something you can't put a number on. It wasn't going to be about money or women or any of that stuff. The truth is I couldn't quite put my finger on it then because I was also younger, but now I understand what sort of animal you are. You're a wounded one that will always be stuck in a corner. If anything gets too close, you'll do anything to defend yourself. But if you're left alone in your corner to tend to your wound that's never going to heal, then I know you're pacified. That's how I'll be able to go to sleep tonight and not worry that sooner or later you'll come for me."

"Never," Yitz said with a nod of his head. "It would never happen."

The two stared at each other again; Avi tried to read deep into Yitz's eyes and seemed satisfied with what he saw.

"OK. I believe you. Always a good kid, my little boychick," Avi said as he gave Yitz's cheek a light slap, then a harder one, and walked out.

The door shut behind him and Yitz stood motionless for a second. He could feel tears start pushing their way out of his eyes. There was no stopping it.

"No!" Yitz screamed as he smacked himself in the face. "No! No! No!"

The sting from his palm left his entire face red and thumping. It was the sobering up he needed.

7

Somewhere over Colorado or maybe Nebraska on his flight back
to be with his mother, Elijah started thinking about how if a poll
was held in Chicago, about 90 percent of the city's population would
probably say Elijah Mendes never had what they considered a "real
job." He'd never flipped a burger, couldn't change a tire, and had ham-
mered no more than a dozen nails in his life, almost all of them to
hang up posters when he was a bachelor. After that, he hired somebody from an app to do it for him. He just figured it was always good
to have professionals do jobs that involved tools.

Even though he'd been born in Chicago, rooted for its sports
teams, claimed its elevated trains beat any other American city's un-
derground subways, and loved to start arguments at parties in the Bay
Area by telling people he preferred the Mexican food in his hometown, Elijah never thought he'd move back after he left.

"You once said that you felt miserable as soon as you stepped off
the plane at O'Hare," Eve told him on his first night back in town as

they ate at a pizza place in the South Loop that prided itself on its tavern-style pies and house-made pierogies.

Elijah couldn't recall ever saying out loud that being in Chicago made him feel terrible, but he also didn't deny it. Instead, he tried to explain that a chance to work with Raphael Razumov-Augier was a great opportunity for him without bringing up the fact it had been the *only* opportunity he'd been offered in a long time. He told her it was the sort of idea people in San Francisco had long since abandoned, and added the lie about that's why it excited him. He mentioned the NDA he'd signed, but figured his mom wasn't going to blab to Tech-Crunch. He explained it was like Kickstarter, except instead of charity or backing some silly invention, people could invest in parts of a city that needed help getting cleaned up and safer. When his mother had to be reminded what Kickstarter was, he switched to company boilerplate text and mentioned "emerging neighborhoods," how areas of Chicago like the one they were sitting in were once considered dangerous, but because developers and small business owners took a chance, they were the parts of town where people wanted to raise families.

"He wants to give regular people an opportunity to do that. They invest in the neighborhood's future, helping with everything from paint supplies to cleaning up graffiti to paying for extra security features to make it safer. He buys the property in these neighborhoods, then with the help of investors—"

"Gentrification," Eve interrupted.

"No. Gentrification is . . ."

Eve stared sharply at her son.

"It's not the same," Elijah protested. He was about to explain how gentrification is when a bunch of artists move into a neighborhood, then the neighborhood gets cool, people with money start moving in, and eventually the things people with money want start showing up, and the people who don't have money can't afford to live there anymore, but Eve cut him off.

"Sounds like a pyramid scheme to me," she said as she typed the phrase into her phone and showed the dictionary website's definition of it to Elijah.

After thirty minutes of trying to convince his mother she was wrong, Elijah decided not to bring up the prospective job with Raphael Razumov-Augier again. Part of the problem was that he knew she was actually right. He'd become convinced that just about every startup was a scam one way or another, just new ways to get people to hand over money. But whatever Raphael was working on sounded especially like bullshit. Not only that, but the pay sounded too good to be true for a consulting job. It didn't add up, but Elijah didn't really have any other options. Everybody in the only world he'd ever worked in had turned their backs on him; people he considered good friends in San Francisco wouldn't call back or return e-mails about getting coffee, and nobody was even looking at his LinkedIn.

Waiting in line at the pharmacy, Elijah decided that it was time to call Raphael. He'd force himself to sound excited and say he was looking forward to working together and spending a year in Chicago. He took one deep breath and then let out a forceful exhalation. He waited a second and then sucked in more air, held it in his lungs, and let it out through his nostrils. Just before the third and final inhalation, his phone started to buzz. It was Eve.

"I saw your car is gone. Are you out right now? I need something," she said.

"I'm picking up my Lexapro."

"You're on Lexapro now? I thought you were taking buspirone," Eve said.

"Didn't you say you needed something?"

"The chocolate-covered popcorn and the honey-mustard pretzel bites," Eve said. In the few days since she'd stopped the chemo, his mother had gone from throwing up all the time to never having enough to eat because of the weed.

Elijah hung up as he made it to the cashier. As he waited for his prescription, the thought that he'd been granted a reprieve crossed his mind. Maybe he'd wait another day to call Raphael. Elijah was desperate, but *they* wanted *him*. That meant he had a little more time to give an answer, and it also filled him with a feeling of unease he couldn't quite put his finger on. It all made him wish that his shrink back in California would return his damn calls. He paid for his plastic bottle filled with pills, then went looking for Eve's snacks. He made it two aisles when a familiar face by the toothpaste stopped Elijah dead in his tracks. His first instinct was to turn right back around and find another way out, whether it was going down three extra aisles past the deodorant and the makeup to get to the exit, or just bolting through the doors that said "Employees only" and going out the back door. But he was too late. The other pair of eyes locked with his and the woman walked toward him.

"Welcome home," she said. Her face was expressionless. Blank. Nothing to read. Elijah sometimes fell asleep watching poker competitions on television and recognized the look of somebody who doesn't want to give away their hand.

"Hey, Shel," he said. He needed to pick up the snacks his mother requested and either he was going to have to grab them on the way out or he could just run out the door and go to another store.

"You look like shit," Shel said with an exaggerated grimace on her face. She always found a way to add a little levity to her insults. "I'm not trying to be mean, but you could use a shave."

He knew that, but Elijah had simply forgotten to go to a barber or drag a razor across his face since he'd been back in Chicago. He also knew that coming from Michelle Burton—who everybody called Shel on account of the two other Michelles in their high school friend group—it was just her inability to sugarcoat, one of the many things he'd found so attractive about her since they were both twelve. After living out west for so long, her bluntness felt refreshing to Elijah. God, he missed her sort of Midwestern mean whenever he had to deal with California passive aggression.

"I heard about you and Hannah," she said. The mention of his ex-wife made Elijah reflexively look down at Shel's hand and see there wasn't a ring. She was in great shape and she'd cut her hair. Besides that, she hadn't changed or aged a second. She had the most perfect skin of anybody he'd met.

They were both Jewish, but most people didn't guess that, with their darker skin and curly hair. Shel's Black father and white mother, whose maiden name was Ambromovitz, even eventually became friendly with Elijah's parents, making him think back to when he was young and romantic and thought that it was meant to be between him and Shel.

"I guess it wasn't a surprise to you . . . or anybody else," Elijah said.

The last time he'd seen her, Shel was visiting San Francisco and sent an e-mail saying it would be nice to catch up. Elijah said that would be nice, that he could use a familiar face, and he meant that. He swore he'd left his crush on her behind when he picked up his high school diploma; he was an adult and could have an adult friendship with somebody he'd known for so long.

He was wrong. The second he saw her standing up against the bar, nursing a martini, Elijah realized that the schoolboy crush had carried over into adulthood. Shel had also grown up. She was even more beautiful, confident, and still had the sardonic sense of humor he couldn't get enough of when they were younger. They decided to have their dinner at the bar. Elijah ordered a bottle of blanc from a winery in Napa he knew, casually mentioning that they'd been trying to get him to invest, that the winemakers were doing some really fascinating stuff with their grapes, and their philosophies behind what they produced were based more on midcentury designers and architects and not the French or Italian growers that everybody else copied. Shel feigned interest, but Elijah got the sense she couldn't care less that he had money now and talked about things like wine. Their food started coming out—house-made focaccia and also some little anchovies and peppers stabbed through with a small silver pick that Shel forced Elijah to try—as they finished their first bottle of wine and decided to move on to another. The sommelier walked over and presented a Syrah-Grenache blend, adding something flowery about his recent visit to the winery in the Ardèche, then opened the bottle to give Elijah a pour. He took a small sip and nodded approvingly even though he didn't really like how it tasted. While the sommelier poured the wine into their glasses, Shel asked how Hannah was. Elijah waited a second for the sommelier to walk away, then said his wife had packed a suitcase for three nights, but had been gone two weeks. Their only communication had been a few one-word text message responses. Elijah told Shel he'd resigned himself a few months earlier that their marriage was doomed, that Hannah had told him multiple times she was unhappy and didn't know if anything could change that. They drank more wine and talked about relationships not working out. Eventually, at some point before the server could ask if they wanted dessert or anything else, a car was called and Elijah went with Shel back to her place. It was nice and fun. They promised things wouldn't get weird between them and said they'd try to meet up next time Elijah was back in Chicago before he left to go to work.

Two days later, Hannah came home and said she had decided the marriage wouldn't work. She cared about Elijah but she thought that he worked too hard, obsessed over the future he couldn't control, and was in a toxic situation at CMUNTY. Elijah knew all of those things were true, but couldn't see a way to change his situation. It wasn't a shock that the marriage was over, he'd seen it coming. Still, there was a voice in his head telling Elijah that he'd feel better if he made Hannah feel worse, it yelled at him to tell her he'd slept with Shel. He was familiar with the voice. He knew it was anger, and he told it no.

Not long after that was when everything started to slide in Elijah's life. It all fell apart so spectacularly that he had to consider whether it was some sort of divine retribution. A side effect of all the psychedelics he'd taken was that Elijah couldn't shake the feeling he'd grown a spiritual side whether he liked it or not. That started him getting reflective and wondering if he'd been doing things wrong for his entire life, but never once did he ever let himself even entertain the thought that Shel was somehow complicit in his downfall. It was all his own doing.

"I still have hope for you," Shel said as some pop song from their youth started playing over the pharmacy speakers. "That maybe you'll figure out what it is you want."

"That makes one of us," Elijah said, trying to be funny, but only sounding like a sad sack.

"Take care of yourself, El," Shel said. Elijah couldn't look her in the eyes and focused on the display of nasal rinse kits that were on sale. She placed her hand on his shoulder and squeezed it before walking away.

As he watched her leave the store, a woman walked over and asked Elijah if he worked there. He gave her a look and wanted to ask what made her think he did, but his phone rang. It was Eve.

"I'm about to get your snacks," he said.

"You'll never guess who's here right now," Eve said.

A few names went through Elijah's head, all of them totally random. He was about to say "Disgraced former governor Rod Blagojevich," when Eve whispered the answer.

"Jerry the Fox. He's sitting on the couch."

"I was in the neighborhood and thought I'd stop and say hello. I haven't seen your mother in, Jesus, I don't know," Jerry the Fox said as he stood up off the couch to shake Elijah's hand. The old man somehow looked bigger than he had in the diner, and he moved like somebody who'd rediscovered their lost vitality and wanted to show it off. There was confidence despite his arthritis and the litany of maladies he claimed to suffer from. He had on a flat cap, the sort Elijah never knew the name of. Some people called them cabbie caps, others said they were golf hats; all Elijah knew was men who wore them were either the type you absolutely didn't want to cross or they were guys you couldn't take seriously because of how silly they looked. He was wearing a T-shirt with Muhammad Ali's face on it, and Elijah tried to recall why he hadn't noticed the old guy's arms were so thick the last time they'd met. It was obvious that before gravity did its thing and his muscle lost its definition, Jerry the Fox must have had a body like an old-timey strongman at a carnival.

"Jerry used to stop by the house a lot when I was a kid," Eve said to her son.

"That's right. I still know this place inside and out. Your father even gave me a pair of keys once because he had me stopping by to pick things up or give your mother a hand. I probably still have the set somewhere," Jerry the Fox said.

They made some small talk, the type that is specifically used to serve as a bulwark against encroaching awkwardness.

161

"So I was tellin' your mother I had to schlep out to Hammond. My pals got this scrapyard there with a couple of dogs that patrol it at night. Dobermans or Rottweilers, or maybe they're Doberman-Rottweiler mixes. Sweetest damn things when they're not trying to kill ya. Some guys say German shepherds are the best guard dogs, but I'm not bringing any dog the Nazis used. I see one of those things and all I can think about is how its great-great-great-great-grandfather was probably used to tear apart one of my family members in the old country. You know what I mean?"

Elijah and Eve both smiled and waited for the other one to say something. Eve took the initiative, holding up a key chain and a T-shirt with the Jerry the Fox dealership logo on it.

"Look, Elijah. He also brought us hats and a plastic coffee mug. You were just saying you needed one of those," she said.

"Some old crap I had lying around. I heard they sell for a lot of money on eBay," Jerry the Fox said.

Elijah wasn't sure what to do. He started thanking the old man for stopping by, hoping he'd take the hint, but it didn't work.

"I like to break up all the driving, and I figured you bought me breakfast the other day, so I wanted to return the favor."

"Oh, Mr. Foxman, that's really—"

"Call me Jerry, bud."

By the apologetic look on Eve's face, Elijah understood he didn't have any options to get out of the invitation, and a few minutes later, he was stepping into Jerry the Fox's jacked-up black Toyota Tundra. In his mind, he wondered why anybody, especially a senior who lived in the suburbs, needed such a big truck. He'd expected a guy like Jerry the Fox to drive a Cadillac or something classic.

"Now that we're driving, I'm craving corned beef. It'll probably take us fifteen minutes to get to Manny's. I haven't been there in a long time," the Fox said.

It had been years since Elijah had been to Manny's. It was his favorite childhood spot that Peter and Eve took him to every now and then, and the one thing Eve considered a family tradition. Sarah used to take her there when she was younger, and before that, Sarah and Eve's mother had a weekly lunch at Manny's, where they'd go and speak Yiddish with the old-timers and other survivors who sat there all day. Peter always got a bowl of soup, even in the dead of summer; Eve was a fan of either a turkey or salami sandwich, and always asked for extra pickles. Elijah liked the egg salad when he was younger, but eventually gravitated toward the pastrami with lots of mustard. Every now and then, Peter's father, Sonny, would come along, but he'd just complain about how everybody in America thought the food served at Manny's was all the Jewish food there was. He'd list off a menu's worth of dishes from Morocco, Egypt, and even some of the Spanish food his late wife cooked. Every single time he'd go on the same tangent while finishing off one gigantic sandwich, then leave with a grease-stained brown bag containing a second one.

All those memories rushed through his mind and put Elijah at ease as he accepted the offer. When they got there and walked in the door, it was as if a celebrity had entered. Somebody from near the counter yelled, "It's da Fox!" A hefty police officer walked over to shake the old car dealer's hand. A few more handshakes and conversations with three different guys working behind the counter later, they found a table and sat down.

"Rule is that ya gotta eat the whole thing or you're not allowed to leave," Jerry the Fox joked as he chomped his teeth into the rye bread and meat. He ordered a cup of black decaf along with his sandwich. Elijah couldn't decide if that was an odd pairing or a cool one. He asked if the Fox had been going to Manny's a long time, since he seemed to know everybody that worked there.

"Heh, I've got some friends. But with this place, not gonna lie,

I didn't start going to it until the last places around Maxwell Street closed. There used to be a ton of Jewish places." Jerry the Fox waved his hand dismissively. "Now you can't even get a decent bagel in this town."

It was hard to disagree with him about the observation. Elijah was so dissatisfied with the state of the Chicago bagel since he'd been back, that to cheer himself up, he had entertained the idea of a nice little life as a bagel shop owner, the guy who finally brought good bagels to the city. Maybe they'd call him the "Bagel King of Chicago," like a character out of a John Hughes film.

"There used to be this one place, Middleberg's." Jerry the Fox paused so he could swallow his food. Somebody shouted "Da Fox" from the other side of the room. He waved, then continued. "It was a dairy restaurant. Way back when, Jews had respect for our laws and keeping kosher was normal. So they had meat places and they had dairy places. Your grandpa was at Middleberg's at least once, usually twice a day. It was like his other office."

"Where was his regular one?"

"His regular one what?"

"Office," Elijah said.

"He worked out of an old . . . what do you call it? A bathhouse or sauna? It was called the Schvitz. It was by an old synagogue. Everybody went there."

It took a second for Elijah to remember why that sounded familiar. By the time his mind recalled the old building he passed as he walked to the Hebrew Benevolent Society, and the conversation he'd had with Rabbi Ginsburg about it, Jerry the Fox had changed the subject.

"You know, bud. The reason I swung by was because I owe you an apology. I can be a hard-ass when I first meet people. I'm not a big trust guy. You can trust me, but I don't trust people until I really know them. So when I get the message from you about how you're

Yitz's grandson and then you show up and I think you're Mexican or Muslim or something, it seemed strange to me. I go way back with your ma and family, so I wanted make sure everything was kosher, and she explained how your dad—may his memory be a blessing— was a Hispanic Jew or Moroccan or something."

"Both," Elijah said, surprised he'd gotten it right.

"Hopefully you can understand. I got ex-wives, the IRS, all kinds of people up my ass for things they say I owe them. I gotta be careful. So no hard feelings?"

A pinch of guilt started to form inside Elijah. He wanted to apologize but he wasn't exactly sure for what.

"I don't need any trouble. I just want to be done with everything. Go down to Fort Lauderdale for good. No more snowbird shit," Jerry the Fox added.

The openness caught Elijah totally off guard. He struggled to find the right thing to say or what question to ask. The guilty feeling only intensified when he started thinking of himself, envisioning an older version of the person he'd become, a man way past his expiration date, the mistakes of the past forever weighing him down. He took pity on the old guy, but he also didn't want to be like him someday. Elijah asked if there was anything he could do to help, as an act of charity as well as investigating what other corners not to back himself into.

"Nah. Just you coming out with me is enough. Makes me feel a bit better, ya know? Old people don't have a lot of friends. My daughters don't talk to me much, and my son . . ." Tears began welling up in the corners of Jerry the Fox's small, puffy eyes. He composed himself and continued. "When my son Brian was killed, it tore everything up. He's got two kids of his own. Boys. One is a good kid with a county job downstate. The other is about your age. I keep an eye on him because he reminds me too much of his dad: always trying to get rich, but not thinking too much about consequences."

The last words echoed in Elijah's ears for a second; Eve had said the same thing about him many times before. It was a charge he denied, but understood why she'd think that and not believe his claim that he never knew what he cared about. It sounded childish, but that was the truth Elijah had come to understand too late in life. Nothing brought him joy, and wishing that he could spark some happiness out of life was a fairly recent hope he was quickly losing faith in.

"Your grandpa was a guy who understood it wasn't all about money," Jerry the Fox said. "He didn't care about getting rich. He worked hard because it was all he knew how to do. He got to America and hit the ground running. Probably could have been anything he wanted to be. A genius, that guy."

"What *was* it about for him? I've been trying to figure that out," Elijah said.

There was a stray piece of meat on Jerry the Fox's plate that he had been eyeballing. He picked it up and held it in his fingers for a second before throwing it back to where it came from.

"I don't think he was ever really given the chance to figure that out. I think guys like your grandpa lived on instinct. Just surviving one day to the next."

Jerry the Fox said he needed something sweet because of his blood sugar. Elijah started feeling terrible he'd let the guy pay for his meal and offered him money, noting he didn't carry cash but could Venmo it.

"What the heck is a Venmo? This was my treat," Jerry the Fox said. "Besides, I can just put it on your family tab."

"What's that?" Elijah said with a slight laugh. He thought it was supposed to be a joke, but the look on Jerry the Fox's face said otherwise.

"It's old business. Nothing," he said with a wave of his hand. "I shouldn't have even brought it up." The Fox leaned back in his chair.

He picked a poppy seed from between his front teeth and wiped it on a napkin. Before he could answer, a man in a suit that drooped around his arms and needed desperately to be taken in came over to say hello. Jerry the Fox told him he looked great, that he'd lost weight. The man said he had cancer.

"That's terrible. Awful," Jerry the Fox said. "Get well soon, we'll get together." They shook hands and once the man was out of earshot, Jerry the Fox mumbled, "Friggin' jagoff. Used to have a few dealerships like I did. Now he's got five and I've got *bupkis*."

He got up without saying anything. Elijah watched as Jerry the Fox walked to the counter and bought a cookie. He made some small talk with the cashier, then walked back to the table. As he picked at his oatmeal raisin cookie, Jerry the Fox told a story that took too long to get to the point, but Elijah didn't want to be rude and try to speed the old man along. After several twists and turns, anecdotes involving former baseball players and a prostitute with a missing finger, the tale got to the part about how he wished he'd listened to Elijah's grandfather's advice to hold on to every penny he could.

"Guys from his generation, the great ones, they were smart about that. Guys from my time weren't. The ones now? Forget it—schmucks. The great ones saved their money."

"The rumor was your grandpa had everything hidden away, turned all his money into gold."

Elijah scoffed. Everybody had heard the mobster treasure tropes. Jerry the Fox picked up on his disbelief and shrugged.

"Maybe it was just a rumor, but I'll tell you what: that man always paid his debts on time. And the last time I saw him, right before he passed, I went to him to collect some money he owed me. And let me tell you, it wasn't just a little cash—I could have retired with that money years ago if I had it. He said he'd get it to me the next day and—I'll never forget this—then says, 'I gotta see my brother for it.' I didn't know he'd had a brother that was alive and never figured out what he'd meant."

As Elijah tried to process what he'd just heard—that Yitz said he was going to visit his brother to get Jerry the Fox his money—he just stared at the look on the Fox's face that Elijah had noticed the last time they'd sat across from each other at a table. It was the bright light of happy memories shining from his eyes. He loved talking about the old days he considered good and the people he thought of as heroes.

"That's why you hear about Lansky or Luciano leaving hardly anything behind when they died," Jerry the Fox continued. "You think those guys were gonna give the government any bit of satisfaction even after they were dead? The best ones know two things: how to survive and how to hide money so well that they can't find it when you're dead. Now that stuff is a little more difficult because everything is on credit cards and there's so much documentation, but back then, these guys were taking in God knows how much and they weren't telling the IRS about it. They told the government they had shnook jobs and didn't make anything. Your grandfather, being a *macher*—an important man in the community—had to show a little more, so he had the Schvitz in his name, some real estate or investments, stuff like that. You know he owned a movie studio once? Nothing big like Warner Brothers or any of the other ones. He hated California. Said the place made him sick."

"Sounds familiar," Elijah cracked.

"What's that?"

"Nothing. It's just funny. I lived in California and hated it. Maybe I inherited that from him."

Something about the way the old guy smiled warmly made Elijah think of his other grandfather, Sonny. He missed him every day.

"You remind me a lot of Yitz," Jerry the Fox said. "You know what you want, bright as hell. You're just like him. He'd be proud."

Kaplan's Plot

It was a high compliment coming from the guy, and a sense of pride overtook Elijah as he watched the old car dealer get cookie crumbs all over his shirt.

During his last night in California, Elijah filled the hours searching online to get a sense of where old friends and anybody who knew him before he left Chicago might live, taking four pages of detailed notes. The South Loop was a crapshoot, with one guy who wasn't part of his larger friend group, and another one Elijah just never liked to begin with. There didn't seem to be anybody in Wrigleyville he felt like avoiding, but he wrote the neighborhood's name down just because he hated going there. Logan Square and Ukrainian Village were totally out of the picture since at least eight people he knew—all of whom had some connection to Oliver—lived in those neighborhoods. They all seemed to own places not far from one another. He wondered if all those people from high school moved to the same part of town by design. How strange that seemed to him, bumping into some guy you had sleepovers with when you were nine as you stopped to get a beer after dropping your own nine-year-old off at whatever progressive-minded private elementary school they went to.

His research had paid off. Save for the run-in with Shel that he chalked up to a fluke, Elijah had successfully avoided anybody and everybody who'd known him once upon a time. But Stephen Morgan was an outlier. They'd known each other since the first day of kindergarten and had been friends since. They both left the city for college; Stephen moved back after graduation to write for a local magazine that folded two months after he started. He kept working, eventually becoming the Chicago reporter for one of the last national newspapers.

"They'll always pay a reporter to focus on Chicago because readers love stories of murder and corruption in big cities. It helps solidify their idea that places like here or New York are just cess-pools and they made the right decision moving somewhere with a lawn," Stephen started to explain as they sat in a cocktail bar that was drenched in neon lighting. The place was new, and all the local websites were hyping it, each noting how the owner's inspiration for the look was what people in the 1980s believed a future dystopia would be like, complete with an old analog TV/VCR playing *Blade Runner* on the bar. Classic Chicago house music blasted from the speakers, so they had to talk a notch below yelling. "I think I got a little more attention because I'm actually from here and they never hired a Black guy until me."

While he was chasing the murder and corruption stories, Stephen found time to write fiction. His brand of "hard-boiled Chicago" earned him the title of the "Millennial Nelson Algren," and a moderately successful premium cable show based off one of his short stories brought him Hollywood money.

"How's your mom's memoir coming? She had sent me some chapters to look over. Great stuff," Stephen said as he took the tortoiseshell frames from his face and cleaned the glasses with a napkin. Elijah had always appreciated Stephen's choice in eyewear, even when they were younger, but he was more focused on the topic of Eve's memoir, which he'd just assumed she'd given up on. "And why would she not let her own son look at it, but she'd ask for feedback from one of his oldest friends?" he wondered out loud.

"Are you kidding? Your mom has been a mentor to me since we were in high school. That essay collection she wrote is up there with old Studs Terkel interviews or Stephen King's *On Writing* for me. She edited the first short story I ever published when I was twenty."

Although she'd had several books filled with her work and multiple poems published in the *New Yorker* and *Harper's*, *How the Poet Writes*, her one nonfiction collection, was the book for which Eve was most famous. It had come out quietly in the mid-1990s but gained traction over the years with MFA students and writers who struggled to actually write. It was republished in 2000 with a foreword by John Ashbery that placed Eve and her work alongside Carl Sandburg, Gwendolyn Brooks, and Sandra Cisneros as the great poets of Chicago, and snuck onto the bestseller list. When people who were tuned-in to the literary world found out who Elijah's mother was, he could never quite wrap his head around the reverence with which they spoke of her; but he'd never figured Stephen as one of her fans, let alone a mentee.

The bar had filled up with people coming from the basketball game at the United Center down the street. Elijah could tell it was almost entirely made up of North Siders and people who'd drive back to suburbs with names like Lake Zurich, Crystal Lake, or Mount Prospect, even though it probably wasn't smart for any of them to get behind the wheel. They were mostly all white, and Elijah guessed they had all grown up in other states, then went to Big 10 colleges like Michigan or Iowa, got to Chicago, and had their sights set on a comfortable spot at the top of the middle of whatever it was they did for a living. It was a sea of guys who looked like they were named Chad or Brad with the occasional Jared from Northbrook mixed in, and Elijah was certain none of them would have been caught hanging out in the part of town they were in twenty or thirty years earlier. Back then, the Chads, Brads, and Jareds would have gone to see the Bulls or Blackhawks, then hurried back to their BMWs and SUVs sitting in one of the overpriced parking lots nearby so they could rush home as fast as possible. But things had changed.

Elijah had started going to Bulls games as a child when the team still played a few feet away in the old Chicago Stadium that they leveled and turned into a parking lot. The first time Elijah ever heard gunshots was a night after Scottie Pippen scored 30 points on one of

Michael Jordan's rare off nights. It wasn't the worst neighborhood in Chicago, but it wasn't great, was how Peter summed it up after the shots rang out.

Elijah was telling that story to Stephen when the server came by with another round of drinks and two shot glasses filled with some truly horrific-smelling yellowish liquid. Stephen picked his up and told Elijah to do the same.

"Everybody drinks Malört now," Stephen explained before tossing his shot back. He downed it and shook his head violently and made a sound like he was going to force the wretched stuff back up. "It's a thing people do to try and prove how Chicago they are, but usually it's people that grew up in Barrington or they moved here from somewhere else and think Chicagoans have been drinking it since this was swampland. They don't realize it was the stuff you found in a dead grandma's cabinet while cleaning it out and dared friends to try a sip of."

Hesitation nearly killed Elijah. He started to shoot the liqueur, then tried stopping the split second his mind registered the flavor on his tongue. He gagged on the little bit of Malört that had already started making its way down his throat.

"That's how I felt when you told me how you might work for Raphael Razumov-Augier," Stephen said as he sipped his Negroni made with mezcal instead of gin. "You can't be serious about that, man."

After taking a swig of his Hibiki Japanese whiskey highball, then another to make sure he erased any trace of the Malört, Elijah could talk without coughing.

"What choice do I have? Nobody takes my calls or answers e-mails. I'm pretty sure anybody who looks at my LinkedIn is doing it for laughs. I'm a tech world persona non grata."

"Maybe with Silicon Valley chumps," Stephen, unable to hide the look of disdain, said. "But San Francisco isn't the world. I know this is a *crazy idea*, but you could go anywhere or you can find something else here in a city you know where you have connections. Anything but working for Raphael Razumov-Augier. Not gonna lie to ya, El: the guy is a straight-up criminal who just knows how to not get caught. What's he trying to get you on board for?"

Elijah mentioned the NDA he signed, then struggled to change the topic.

"Is it that UtopiaStarter thing? I've heard all about it. His idea to remake entire parts of American cities—it's like Robert Moses in hyperdrive. He's saying he wants to privatize taking control of cities. Chicago is a big city, but it's like a small town, and word travels. From what I hear, your boy Raphael has gone from partying a little too much to letting Bolivia influence almost all of his decisions," Stephen said as he tapped his nose. "It's no secret the guy does blow, but I've heard he's getting to insane Alfred Molina in *Boogie Nights* levels. And if I'm being honest—"

"You are," Elijah interrupted. "Maybe too much." The booze was starting to get to him. He hadn't been out drinking in months and didn't anticipate how quickly it would get into his bloodstream. He was having a tough time holding his smart-ass comments back.

"He's going to bilk investors again, then when there's any sign of trouble, he'll throw you under the bus. Remember that guy Jeremy Abrahams? He was at that one movie streaming site that went bankrupt, then Raphael hired him to run that mental health startup. Two months later they had that massive data leak and all those users started reporting they were being blackmailed by hackers in some former Soviet republic who were threatening to make personal records public if they weren't paid off. It all fell on poor Jeremy Abrahams, but there was no way it was all his fault."

"I forgot about that guy," Elijah said. "Didn't he end up jumping from the roof of his building because of all that?"

Stephen nodded slowly. Two more drinks arrived. Elijah asked who ordered them.

"I'm going to get you drunk and you're going to call that Russian shit and tell him you're not taking the job. Now let's talk about the other piece of personal info I have on you," Stephen said with a grin, before bringing up how he'd heard Elijah and Shel had bumped into each other. Stephen saw her at a fundraiser and said she couldn't stop talking about the encounter. Stephen said Elijah should call her. Elijah laughed and told him to shut up.

"Everybody had a bet on how long it would take for you guys to hook up. I knew you liked her, but also that your virgin ass would never make a move," Stephen said.

Elijah was officially drunk. He opened up when that happened, which was why he hated drinking too much. He started by saying something about how he figured he'd messed things up by never calling Shel after that night in San Francisco, then stopped midway through. His head tilted down as he tried to pull a clear thought out of the booze pool his brain was facedown in.

"I started realizing how damaged I am after Ollie died. It was Ollie and then the divorce. I've always been this way. I knew it, but I was doing whatever I could to hide because I couldn't understand why. Then I came back to Chicago and I'm with my mom all the time, seeing this side of her I've never seen, and I realized I get it almost all from her. She's as damaged as I am. We shouldn't be, but we are."

Stephen asked why Elijah thought that. Elijah had lost track of what he'd been saying. Stephen reminded him. "You and your mom being messed up . . ."

"I am, yeah. My mom is also." Saying it again helped Elijah regain his initial train of thought. "I read all this stuff about intergenerational trauma a few years ago, like shit that's passed down from your ancestors. I didn't know why I found it so interesting back then;

I didn't know anything about my family besides they're Jews and from all these different places and blah, blah, blah. Now I'm starting to understand how deep the damage is. I always blamed myself, but I don't know if I do anymore."

He had to stop and collect himself. Another reason Elijah didn't like getting drunk was because he got emotional, and the impromptu unburdening of feelings in the dystopian future bar had his eyes feeling damp. He looked at Stephen, expecting his friend to make fun of him, but there was a sadness on his face that matched Elijah's feelings.

"It's like sins of the father, except it's the baggage of the great-grandparents," Stephen said. "I know all about it."

Elijah watched as Stephen got the server's attention and ordered another round. Something in him said it was a bad idea, but he didn't object.

"I've been doing all this research into my grandfather," Elijah said with a hiccup in the middle of the sentence. He could hear himself slurring when he spoke. "He was a bad guy. But you know who he was friends with? Jerry the Fox. Remember him? From the commercials during the Bulls game. *I'm da Fox. I've got da cars.* I had lunch with him today. He's a good guy."

The last thing Elijah remembered from the bar was Stephen just staring at him and saying something about how he was going to have to put a tracker on Elijah. Then he said something about how Jerry the Fox was a dangerous person. That he personally knew somebody at the state attorney's office who'd been trying to put the old man away for years. The prosecutor called Jerry Foxman his White Whale, saying his grandfather had tried to lock him up back when he was on the force, but the Fox was blessed with a cunningness that fit his nickname.

"Stay away from him. You don't need to be around people like that" was the last thing Elijah recalled Stephen saying before everything turned to liquid.

————————

At 11:45 the next morning, Elijah woke up on the couch in the living room. He'd successfully gotten his jacket and one shoe off before passing out and couldn't remember how he got home. He smelled awful, like he'd done at least two more shots of Malört and spilled another on his shirt. He looked at his phone to see what time it was, but the battery was dead. Vomit was coming soon, there was no stopping it. He tried to focus his eyes, and noticed a piece of paper next to a brown paper bag on the coffee table.

> I'm glad you had a good time. Please clean up the mess you made on the porch while you were noisily trying to get your keys in the lock at three in the morning. I got you a breakfast sandwich.
>
> —E.M.

Still a little drunk, Elijah crept into the kitchen and plugged his phone into a charger. It turned on as he took his first bite out of his turkey bacon and egg on a croissant, and it started to ding over and over. He had several missed calls, three of them from Stephen, one from the driver who picked him up saying he was nearby, and he noticed Raphael had called him at 9:00 that morning. He also had a dozen texts—most of them were also from Stephen. He clicked his friend's name and a video popped up. It was of Elijah. He was on the phone with a tamale in the other hand. It seemed they'd ended up in the part of town near the old meatpacking warehouses by the West Loop that had been turned into condos and offices. Elijah looked closely at the video and noticed that he was standing in front of the big glass tower that was in the exact same spot as an old meatpacking plant where he once watched a man hose a day's worth of pig blood into a drain when he was on a field trip in elementary school for Clean Up Your City Day. Raphael's voice came out of Elijah's phone. Elijah said something, but he was slurring so badly that it sounded like one very long word. He replayed it a few times and finally realized what he'd said after the fifth listen.

"Yo, man. I've decided not to come for your gentrifying ass . . . to work for your gentrifying ass. You're a bad person, Raphael. I'm trying to be a good one. I'm gonna be just fine, my friend."

The video cut out there. Elijah scrolled to the next one. In it, he'd eaten half the tamale and asked Stephen how he got Rahm Emanuel's number, then called the former mayor and Elijah said something in a voice like an Eastern European man that came out as mostly gibberish. The final video was of Stephen asking Elijah how he felt as he finished off his tamale. He said he wanted another.

"But how do you feel? You just told Raphael Razumov-Augier to piss off. That must feel good."

Elijah watched his former, much drunker self smiling and nodding. "I do. Now I gotta go home. I've got a long day of applying for jobs at Walgreens and Mariano's. I've got a blight . . . a bright future as a checkout girl."

The final text from Stephen was a link to a local grocery store's job site.

As he put the phone down to concentrate on finishing his breakfast without throwing up, Elijah thought about how just a few weeks earlier, seeing those videos would have made him spiral. He didn't just burn a bridge; he'd blown up the whole town. He had screwed up and done some stupid things in his life, but he'd never been a bomb thrower. Elijah had always operated as carefully as he could. He believed that every action could come back to haunt him down the road. He'd always gone out of his way to try to understand how he was perceived by others, believing he could use that knowledge to his advantage in both his personal life and business. He knew he couldn't control everything, but he desperately wished he could, and it ate away at him if he couldn't tell himself he'd done everything in his power to manipulate circumstances. Even though he'd known death and dying, he was never one to give much thought to how his own life would someday cease. He didn't dwell on what was or wasn't after he took his last breath, but the great contradiction was that, while the question of his own mortality didn't bother him, Elijah also felt that everything he did, every action, any conversation he had with another person, all the hours of work, it all had a life-and-death urgency. Everything felt so damn important and big, but there was never time to stop to think why that was, or enjoy any of the success. He could only feel any sense of comfort if he was constantly in motion, always busy, never not occupied with some project. It had never dawned on him to examine where that urge grew from, and then he found himself back in Chicago with nothing to do and no choice but to sit and stare the urge in its ugly face.

Elijah rewatched the video of him calling Raphael Razumov-Augier. It was ten seconds of him tossing dynamite at a possible future and just letting it all explode. It was something Elijah would never have done before, and he couldn't remember the last time he'd felt so damn happy.

8

1925

The leaves on the trees along Addison were the perfect shade of October orange as Sol plucked a brick-red frankfurter from a vat of boiling water that was heated by a small flame underneath. Supporters of the Chicago Bears, the young football club led by the local-boy player and owner George Halas, streamed into the ballpark that was home to the miserable Cubs baseball team in the warmer months. As he spread some yellow mustard across the sausage, Sol explained what made his product stand out in the crowded field of encased meats.

"More than a few folks have told me the best hot dog they've had besides mine is one you can find in Coney Island all the way in Brooklyn. A gentleman named Nathan serves them and charges a nickel. He puts some sort of secret sauce on top and tops it off with sour cabbage. I haven't tried one, so I can't make a fair comparison, but there's no secrets with my wieners. However . . ."

Sol paused as he spooned some chopped raw onions on top, then added some relish, and a pickle on top. A small crowd had gathered around to watch the demonstration, and Sol picked a young boy to receive the finished product. The child took a bite, then another. He smiled and thanked Sol while still chewing; another satisfied customer.

"For a few cents, parents can get their children to eat a healthy meal full of vegetables and protein. And my all-beef franks are kosher, so you don't have to worry about stray pig parts or chopped horse bits getting into the mix. My rabbi will confirm that for you if you need."

A lanky reporter who'd been sent by his editor to interview Sol about his popular hot dogs took a bite of a fresh one.

"That is incredible. Putting vegetables on top seems pretty crazy, but this is the best I've ever had," the reporter said.

"The combination possibilities are endless," Sol added. "I add tomatoes when I have them. I've even put a few spicy peppers my Italian friend gave me on top and it was delicious. The one thing I'd shy away from is that tomato ketchup sauce that I see everywhere these days. A gentleman from the Heinz company of Pennsylvania came in and tried to sell me on it, but the taste worked against the hot dog; the sausage is the main attraction."

The reporter stuffed the rest of his meal into his mouth and looked at the group of large, silent men all standing behind the butcher.

"Do these fellas go everywhere with ya?"

Sol seemed embarrassed by the question. He explained they were hired help, but it was obvious the reporter could tell they'd been sent to keep an eye on Yitz Kaplan's brother because he was so far up north, far from the safety of Maxwell Street. To get to the ballpark, they traveled through hostile Polish territory to get to a spot of land that was controlled by Dean O'Banion, the brutal bootlegger with a heavenly tenor voice and penchant for making flower arrangements.

The newspaperman tried to pretend that he accepted Sol's answer, but he still couldn't stop himself from saying how funny it was that Yitz Kaplan's brother was such an expert on all things beef.

"Given your brother's profession, that is," the reporter added.

There was a time when the comment would have bothered Sol, but he'd learned to take them in stride. He'd decided to just let people say what they wanted.

"My brother is a businessman. He doesn't like getting his hands dirty," Sol said with a smile as he started packing up his things. "I'm a butcher; I can't keep my hands clean."

Farther up north, past the Chicago city limits, up where remnants of the prairie were still visible, Yitz sucked in a deep breath of cold, clean lake air. The pastoral stillness and quiet unnerved him, but he put everything out of his mind as he waved at the blue Pontiac rumbling down the stretch of dirt that served as a road.

"That's Anderson and Anderson," he told White Jimmy. "No relation."

They'd driven up with Yitz's lawyer, Leonard Schwartz, a stout, anxious man who was always sweating. It was amazing to Yitz how he'd seen the man dripping perspiration on days when it was so cold that the pipes froze. He'd wanted to ask why, but Leonard's law partner, Morris Salamon, told him it was better left alone, that Leonard was touchy about it. Normally, that would only pique Yitz's interest; he loved seeing what poking a person in the most sensitive part of their soul yielded, but he had learned that of all the people you wanted working at their best, it was lawyers and accountants, and Leonard was no ordinary attorney—he was a genius, a savant, a mind bred from a long line of some of the most brilliant Talmudic scholars in Lublin. Leonard would have followed in the footsteps of his ancestors, but his father wanted his sons to learn about earthly justice, so he made them read and memorize all they could about the American legal system the way he'd once been made to recall ancient arguments like *Rabbi Shimon had this to say about goats as a sin-offering, but then remember something Rav Yosef said about the subject that may have contradicted Rabbi Shimon . . . but there was also Rabbi Asher ben Yechiel's thoughts . . .* For Leonard, with his limitless mind and argumentative tongue, it was the perfect calling. He was one of the few boys Yitz knew growing up who went to an American school instead of learning a trade or taking some peddling job to help make money for their poor family. And while the others shunned Leonard for being quiet, Yitz took a liking to him early on and always made sure to speak up when the other boys started in on him. He earned Leonard's loyalty at an early age, and when Leonard couldn't find a job after law school, Yitz introduced him to Morris and his brother, Solomon Salamon, of the Salamon and Salamon Law Firm, which their father, the first Jewish member of the bar association in the state, had founded. They saw right away what a talent they had in front of them with Leonard, regardless of how bad his perspiration may have smelled in the office on especially hot days. Yitz loved doing favors for people, especially if it helped him.

Yitz went to Solomon Salamon and said that he had an especially tricky situation with some land he had hoped to acquire up north. The Salamons put Leonard on it, saying none of them dealt in that area, but Leonard could pick it up after drinking a few cups of coffee and sitting with the right books. Yitz worried maybe they were overestimating his friend, but Leonard was confident there wouldn't be any issue with the sale.

Anderson and Anderson got out of the car. If they weren't related, it was hard to tell. They both had pink faces, weak chins, and thin lips. One was tall and gangly; the other was taller and round. They looked at the men standing there, and it was as if the Grim

Reaper was directly in front of them and they had no way of escaping their fate.

"Anderson," Yitz said as he vigorously shook the lanky one's hand, before turning to the other. "Anderson," he said as he slapped his palm hard against the fat Anderson's. "This is my associate and one of my partners in the acquisition, Mr. White. And I think you know my attorney, Mr. Schwartz."

"Good to meet you, gentlemen," White Jimmy said as he offered a hand that was ignored.

"Will Mr. Samuelson be joining us? That is who we've been dealing with," the tall Anderson said.

"Samuelson? No. He's a junior attorney at the firm. Just got him from Indiana," Schwartz said.

"Mr. . . ." the round one started.

"Sorry. Kaplan. Yitzhak Kaplan."

"Yitzhak. What sort of name is that?"

"Well, it's Isaac, like the son of Abraham and Sarah. But my friends call me Yitz. You can call me Mr. Kaplan."

"Yes. Well, Mr. Kaplan. I'm not sure if your attorney or . . . Mr. Schwartz explained to you or not, but there are certain rules in this area. . . ."

"Rules or laws?" Yitz asked.

"Pardon?"

"See, laws are laws. The city, state, or federal government can enforce those. Rules are something kids make up when they play games. Which one are you talking about?"

"Mr. Kaplan . . ." the fat Anderson blustered.

"Yes?"

"*Mr. Kaplan,*" the tall one said in a tone that was just slightly below a shout as he pointed a sharp finger at White Jimmy. "*He's* not allowed here."

183

Yitz let out a hearty laugh. He looked at White Jimmy, who also started cracking up.

"Of course he is, don't be silly. He's one of the owners of this land. A minority owner, but this land is *his* land. In fact, I believe if my associate wanted to shoot you right here for trespassing then he'd be within his legal right to do that."

Both Andersons went pale.

"Of course, that won't happen because we're businessmen like the both of you. And like any good businessmen, we had our lawyer go through everything with a fine-tooth comb, and he assured me that there's no actual law that says a Jew or Negro can't own property here. It's just that you have your little handshakes and agreements with each other. And that's fine. But . . ." Yitz held up a finger. "Buuuuut. The prior owner of this land felt differently, and he was within his legal right—by law—to sell this land to anybody he saw fit. And here we are."

Both Andersons went from white to pink to beet red in seconds.

"You'll hear from our lawyers," the fat one said as he stormed off to his car. The other Anderson followed behind, slammed the door, and the car peeled out, kicking up a cloud of dust in its wake.

"You think we'll hear from them again? They seemed pretty hot," White Jimmy said as he popped a cigarette between his lips.

"Who cares? They're just mad we fooled them into thinking we were some nice Christian businessmen. There's nothing they can do now, but I'll give you some advice," Yitz said. "When you're up here, if you see some guys on horses with white hoods on their heads, I'd run."

"Didn't think I'd feel like I was in even more danger when I *left* Chicago," White Jimmy said with a laugh.

"There's nothing to be afraid of," Yitz said. "Everything is working out beautifully." He tugged at the waist of his pants and made sure his shirt was tucked in, then walked to the edge of the small cliff that overlooked the beach and took in another deep breath of clean lake air.

White Jimmy walked up next to him and asked why Yitz had brought him on as a partner.

"I appreciate you giving me a no-interest loan and all, but it feels like some other people might be better suited to partner with you on an investment like this," he said.

Yitz patted White Jimmy's shoulder and chuckled.

"What can I say? I like helping good people get a leg up, and I loved seeing the looks on Anderson and Anderson's faces when they saw you. Getting a rise out of jerks like that is worth whatever I'd get from you in interest."

While Yitz felt comfortable aggravating the Andersons on land he owned, it was safer to sit in the backseat of the car while White Jimmy drove back to the city to make it look like the white man was being chauffeured back home. A few miles into the ride, White Jimmy brought up a topic Yitz was hoping to avoid.

"This Foxy thing," White Jimmy said casually. "How can we handle it?"

It made Yitz's head hurt just hearing the name Foxy Foxman. He'd disliked the guy since they were younger for minor reasons that he'd mostly forgotten, silly transgressions that fell out of the realm of business. Foxy was a schmuck and a sucker who had always talked behind Yitz's back, but was never wise enough to figure out that Yitz knew everything he said. He was bitter that Yitz was indispensable to Avi, and remained desperate to get in the boss's good graces, always hoping to move up from his place in the middle of the pack but never doing anything that made him stand out. He lacked talent, had no charisma, and while Yitz walked through life believing anybody save for Sol had it in them to betray him, he was especially guarded when it came to Foxy. He'd felt that way from the moment they'd met, and it only hardened the dislike into an impenetrable rock in Yitz's mind over time, but feelings didn't matter when it came to business, and Foxy still was a decent earner.

Then Foxy had started muscling in on some of the policy games White Jimmy ran out of the Golden Shovel pool hall on Forty-first and Wabash. Yitz's hands were tied because for all his faults, Foxy had put in a lot of time working for Avi; while the boss was always calling the guy a putz, he also considered Foxman steady. When Avi said that about somebody, it meant he trusted them, and that trust earned Foxy the opportunity to explain how they should consolidate some of the stuff they had a hand in and have guys from Maxwell take charge. Despite being a Yid whose own family had left their home in search of safety abroad, Avi had been poisoned by the same prejudices so many other whites across America felt. Yitz saw that duality as yet another sign of Avi's weakness, but Foxy used it to his advantage. Even though White Jimmy had tripled profits with the policy games and a few other rackets he'd inherited, Foxy told Avi he'd read somewhere that the lighter a person's skin, the better at business they were. It was complete foolishness that Yitz would have pushed back on had he been in the room, but Avi was convinced and gave his blessing.

If it was anybody else, a few words from Yitz and everything would have gone back to normal. But Foxy had an insurance policy thanks to a rare screwup by Yitz that ensured his safety, and he knew it. It had happened just a few months earlier, when Yitz walked past the sauna door and overheard a conversation between some of the guys led by Foxy, who spent a solid five minutes making fun of Sol. He called Yitz's brother all sorts of names, talking about how he was dim, and how he'd ended up a butcher because he was too stupid to do anything else. Yitz boiled as he eavesdropped on Foxy's slander.

In any other situation, he would have just put it in the wastebin of his mind, but he couldn't let it go. He waited for Foxy to walk out of the room, and attacked him. He jumped on the guy, slapping him in the face, yelling at him to repeat what he'd said about Sol, daring him, begging him to say it again. It was a side of Yitz nobody had ever seen. Foxy knew better and didn't fight back, but even after he finally calmed down, Yitz still promised himself that he wasn't done with the son of a bitch. The guy was a stain that needed to be wiped away, but so many guys saw him go after Foxy that it would be hard to make any other action not look personal—even though it was.

He tamped down on the hatred just enough to be cordial. Yitz was businesslike and kept his conversations with Foxy to mostly one-word answers, but there was nothing he could do for White Jimmy at that moment.

"I know it takes away from your pocket," it pained Yitz to say. "Just hold off a little bit. I'll get you something else, but we need to wait."

White Jimmy said OK, then changed the topic. Yitz caught a glimpse of his disappointed eyes in the rearview mirror. He balled his fist so tight that the skin on his knuckles cracked and began bleeding.

Sol walked into his home. He always brought flowers for Shabbos that he got from a woman on Maxwell Street, and walked through the front door exactly an hour before sundown every Friday. Devorah would normally be getting ready in the middle of a spare half hour between cooking the meal and serving it so she could dress appropriately for the occasion. But since he'd gotten home a little later than usual due to a last-minute rush of customers who needed more meat than they'd thought for the holy dinner, she was already in her black dress with her hair up. She caught him looking at her and shrieked.

"You! Are you trying to terrify me? I thought a burglar was in the house for a second," she cried.

He scooped his wife up, then planted a deep kiss on her before handing her the flowers.

She put the flowers in a vase and asked how things had gone with the reporter, saying how proud she was that her husband was being interviewed by one of the big newspapers.

"I could tell the reporter only talked to me because he wants to know more about my brother. Either that, or Yitz arranged to have the guy write about me as a favor."

Devorah told her husband he was being silly, but Sol could see in her face that she didn't actually think that. She knew Yitz was a person of interest since he was connected to Avi Kaminsky, but unlike his boss, Devorah's brother-in-law went out of his way not to get mentioned in the newspapers. It was a small blessing, Devorah always thought. How shameful it would be if everybody read about Sol's brother as some seedy criminal, while Solomon was such a good and honest man who went to work every day and took care of his family.

Sol started to walk toward the stairs to get changed, but stopped to look out the window at his little front yard that he loved to stare at and think of how when he was a boy, everywhere he looked there was dirt; just dirt and death. Yet even in the middle of autumn, when all the foliage was brown and dying, that little bit of Chicago ground represented life and growth; it reminded him that there is always possibility; he couldn't have dared to even dream of such a thing back in Odesa.

9

After fixating on the idea of digging up the earth in an old tomb for a few days as he got things in order, Elijah felt almost unaffected as they walked to the Kaplan plot at the Greater Chicagoland Hebrew Benevolent Society. He had a Percocet wrapped in a piece of paper towel in his pocket just in case he needed to go blissfully numb, but settled on a pair of over-the-counter, all-natural Peace Out Stress gummies instead of chasing his benzo with an opioid.

There was no pomp and circumstance, no ritual, and the gathered audience was made up of Rabbi Ginsburg, two guys who didn't speak any English who he'd hired out of a nearby hardware store parking lot, and the dead in their graves.

Elijah and Eve stood to the side as the pair of day laborers walked to the door of the Kaplan tomb. The rabbi undid the lock, one of the men crossed himself before walking in, and then they began digging. The whole thing took no more than thirty minutes before one of the men came out and said in broken English that there was no coffin, but

189

their shovels had touched something hard in the ground and they were afraid to keep digging. The other man kept using the word *pecado*; Elijah knew enough Spanish to translate for the rabbi that the pair worried what they were doing was a sin. Rabbi Ginsburg tried as best he could to calm their nerves and explain it was totally fine, but the men asked to be paid and left. Elijah said he'd finish the job.

"I wish I could help, but my back isn't so good," Rabbi Ginsburg said.

Elijah got to digging with the rabbi standing over him. Eve sat on an old log, reading a book and taking the occasional small hit from her vape pen.

The remaining earth came up without much effort, and after a few scoops, the tip of Elijah's shovel touched the solid thing the men had mentioned. He got in the little hole that had been dug out around it and started using his hands, pulling out dirt and flinging it into the nearby pile. He got his grip on the side of something that felt like a handle and began pulling at it, but the thing wouldn't budge. He took the shovel and dug out a little more room, got the tip as far down on the other side as he could, and then put all his weight into trying to get the thing in the ground to pop up. It was obviously a two-man job, but Elijah had gotten the top part out and could see the lid of a steamer trunk. He shoveled out a bit more until he saw the front of the trunk, an old rusted brass lock that served as its second round of deterrence after the dirt. Remembering something he'd seen in a movie, Elijah grabbed the crowbar and screwdriver that the two men had brought in with them. He shoved the tip of the flat head into the keyhole, gave it a couple of good smacks with the crowbar, and the lock broke. Elijah called out to Eve, figuring she'd want to know the verdict, but nobody responded. He called out again and got nothing. He looked at his phone and saw a text from Eve saying she'd gone to sit down inside. He thought to wait, but impatience got the best of him. Elijah lifted the lid of the trunk just as a ray of sunshine slid through the mausoleum's open door and a golden beam reflected onto his face. He looked for a second, awed by the absurdity of it all, of finding a gangster's buried treasure, proving it wasn't just some urban legend, but not being able to tell anybody about it. The gold continued to shine but the wonderment quickly wore off; Elijah was unmoved by the sight of the riches before him and was in no hurry to know its value. As soon as he shut the lid, Elijah was gripped by melancholy. He'd begun to find that he didn't like conclusions; the concept of finality filled him with dread.

Eve wanted to make a few extra stops after the digging was finished. The first was a few miles over the Chicago line into Skokie. They went from one cemetery to another, visiting a second resting place meant for multiple people filled only with a single corpse. Eve joked that the unfilled plot must have been a Kaplan family tradition as she placed a rock atop the gravestone.

"Kaplan" was at the top of the gray marble monument. It sat underneath a Star of David. There was room for two names, but only Yitzhak's was on there. It said he'd lived 1899 to 1962 and had some Hebrew lettering on there.

"I don't think the dates are right," Eve said as she plucked some weeds that had sprouted in front of the grave. "Maybe he was older, but Sarah once told me he was younger and 1899 was just the date somebody wrote down at Ellis Island."

"It's a nice spot here underneath this," Elijah said. He pointed up at the large sculpture of a candle that served as the center of the Jewish cemetery.

"Not sure what the point is since he can't see it," Eve said without taking her eyes off the grave. "But I guess he earned it."

A hundred questions went through Elijah's mind; the one he went with was: When was the last time Eve had visited her father's grave?

"I'd say when Clinton was president. Before the whole scandal thing," she said. "You know, I heard Monica Lewinsky's single. She always seemed like a really nice girl."

They looked at Yitzhak Kaplan's grave once more, said nothing, and walked back to Elijah's car. As they drove across the street to the nondenominational cemetery, Eve mentioned she needed to eat after.

"Maybe we do drive-through," Elijah said. "I'm just a little uncomfortable with what's in the trunk."

"We're in the suburbs," Eve said as she pointed Elijah where to park. "Nothing will happen."

They got out of the car and walked down a little path toward a big weeping willow. Underneath it was Rose Kaplan's grave.

"Beloved mother. July 9, 1922–December 9, 1963."

As Elijah laid some flowers on the ground, he noticed how clean the grave was and asked Eve the same question he'd asked about her father's resting place and the last time she'd stopped by.

"Three months ago," Eve said as she wiped a glob of mud off the grave marker. "She was a tough woman. I didn't like it when I was a kid, but I appreciate her much more now that I'm older."

Elijah put a rock on it, then stood next to his mother.

"When I was younger, I used to look at that one picture you have of her up in the living room, and I'd think about how much I wished I could have met her. Sometimes I'd walk by it and say hello like she was right there," Elijah said.

He turned and saw a smirk on Eve's face.

"If we were characters in a movie, right now I'd say something cheesy like, *She is! She's always there watching us*," she said. "And maybe that's true. Who knows?"

Elijah was still getting used to his mother making so many jokes, but he wondered if there was some truth in her words. He asked if she believed her mother's spirit had hung around to keep an eye on things; Eve nodded.

"I think so. And not because I'll be joining her soon, but I've always had a feeling even if I didn't want to admit it. She had such an energy, and I always felt it was hanging around and unsatisfied with something. If she had wanted to go on that she'd still be here. The only thing that could kill her was . . ." Eve cleared her throat. "Probably not great to talk like that here."

Eve wanted pancakes, the rules regarding what counted as "lunch-time" food be damned, she said. Elijah suggested the Golden Nugget he used to sit and study at when he was still in high school, but his mother had somewhere else in mind. There was a place not too far from the Loyola campus that she had started going to years earlier when she taught there. It was a little out of the way, but the radio said the traffic wasn't so bad. Elijah tried suggesting a place in Wicker Park that made its own syrup, got its buckwheat from a hippie com-mune in the southwest part of the state, and cured all its meats in a smokehouse out back, but his mother just laughed at that idea. Elijah started driving when he remembered there was one big issue with leaving his car unattended.

"You realize what's in the trunk, right?"

Eve was so stoned that her mood seemed to verge on euphoria. She'd been puffing on the indica pen like a nervous chain-smoker and it made her fidgety.

"How much do you think was there? I'm reading here that they measure gold bullion in troy ounces, and there's a difference between that and regular pounds," she said, glancing at her phone. "But there were also all those coins . . ."

"I didn't bring a scale, Ma. We can get this stuff home and then go get one."

"It's so funny," Eve said as she stared out the window and watched the suburbs pass by. "I figured if you put a bunch of gold in the back of a car it would weigh it down, but we seem to be moving fine. What do you think?"

His mother was blazed, that was what Elijah thought. And he was fine with it. She'd earned the right to be as high as she wanted without anybody giving her a hard time, but that didn't change the fact that they were driving around in the second-most-stolen midsized electric vehicle in the country.

"We can't exactly claim your dead dad's gold that was hidden away for years when we fill out insurance forms if somebody steals this thing," he said.

"It will be *fine*," Eve said as Elijah pulled into the parking lot of the Pancake Grotto.

The place was immaculately clean, but looked as if it hadn't been redecorated since the late 1980s. There were plaques going back thirty years for local Little League teams the restaurant had sponsored, and a glass refrigerator cabinet with slices of pie spinning around like they were being shown off as "the cars of tomorrow" at some Eisenhower-era world's fair. Everything was illuminated by fake Tiffany chandeliers hanging from the ceilings. The teenage server looked to be the only person who'd smoked more weed that morning than Eve. The poor kid just wanted to take the order, but Eve was feeling chatty. She asked if it was true the Guinness Book of World Records didn't accept the restaurant's claim of all-time leader in different combinations of pancakes served. She thought she'd read the number was somewhere past 250,000, but the server just nervously chewed on his pen and muttered, "Uh-huh." Elijah figured he'd throw the kid a line and said he was ready to order, going with two eggs over easy, hash browns well done, dry wheat toast, and then asked if they had any avocado.

"I think we have guacamole," the server said.

"Is it real?"

"What do you mean is it real? It's *guacamole*," Eve said.

"Like that premade stuff. You know what, never mind. No avocado."

Eve ordered the Banana Split Pile: five pancakes topped in whipped cream, fresh strawberry, and bananas.

"*Extra* whipped cream," she said. When the server walked away, Eve leaned in and started talking in a low voice to Elijah. "My goal is to go way over the calorie count every day. Give the worms something to feast on."

Eve had recently signed off to have a natural burial in an eco-friendly casket made from biodegradable materials, and no embalming fluids. His mother's choice of burial didn't surprise Elijah as much as when Eve gave him the number of a rabbi that she'd been talking to who was going to perform the services. Elijah had just figured his mother's friend who owned the women's bookstore and was an ordained minister in the Church of Life would oversee the process of putting Eve's remains into the earth and hadn't considered for even a second that she'd ask for anybody connected to an Abrahamic practice to preside over her gravesite.

As they waited for the food, Eve excused herself to go to the bathroom. Sitting alone with the sounds of clanging dishes, random chitchat, and Channel 5 news on an old television from the predigital 1990s blended together and composing a comforting anti-harmony, Elijah felt himself getting lost as he watched his mother fade from view.

He tried to tune out the voice in his head that was telling him soon she'd be gone forever and that he'd be an orphan with nobody left to call family, but it started screaming too loud to ignore. Fumbling with his phone, Elijah saw there was a missed call. It was from Raphael Razumov-Augier, but there was no voicemail. Elijah tried to run down every possible scenario that would explain the call—from an accidental butt-dial to Raphael calling to personally deliver the news of his comic book villainesque plan to get revenge on Elijah for turning him down—but the one that seemed most plausible was that Raphael didn't care about Elijah's drunken messages and still wanted to hire him. If that was it, Elijah wasn't sure what he'd say, especially without the influence of liquor or his friend goading him on. It could be a fresh start, a chance at starting a second life after the first one had burned down to embers. And maybe Raphael had some ideas about how to invest Elijah's share of the gold. . . .

He stopped himself. Elijah looked at the phone and blocked Raphael's number. The only way to move was forward and not look back.

The food was on the table a few minutes later when Eve sat back down. She took one bite of her pancakes, grinned, let out a little "Mmmm," and then asked Elijah what he planned to do with his newfound riches. It was as if she'd sensed his moment of temptation.

"Just please don't tell me you're going to invest it in some new app that lets you review other humans on how likable they are. I'm a dying woman, so lie to me if you must," Eve said with a stoned chuckle.

"They already tried that app idea, and I'm sure they will again," Elijah said. "I had an idea for one, though. But I think it would have to be some sort of nonprofit deal."

His mother's eyebrows crinkled upward. She mouthed *nonprofit* with a look of disbelief on her face.

"I've been thinking about a way people could record their family stories on their phones. An easy way to keep these stories alive. I thought you and I could spend the next few weeks trying out a few. Maybe it could be material for your book," Elijah added.

Eve ignored what her son said and called the server for another spray from the whipped cream can.

"I also think I'm going to go back to school. Probably DePaul," Elijah added.

Eve picked up a piece of banana and popped it into her mouth. She chewed for a long moment, then asked Elijah why he would go back to school.

"I think I'm too old to start a new career, so I figured I'd become a middling academic," he said.

"The family business," Eve said.

Elijah explained how he'd been inspired after he'd watched a video online of some conference panel, "Generational Trauma and Academic Curriculum." It was fascinating to him, the idea of transferring distressing experiences through the generations, the belief that trauma can live in the DNA of descendants of violence and oppression even a century or more after the passing of their ancestors that experienced it. Once he started reading up on it, he started to wonder if he'd been missing something about his own mind. Maybe the past offered more clues than he'd ever thought.

His mother looked impressed for a moment. Elijah smiled awkwardly. He asked if everything was OK.

"I'm just proud of you," she said, before adding that she'd watched the same panel video featuring a young professor of African American studies as moderator, who explained her interest in the subject came when she started relating her own battles with depression and anxiety back to her ancestors' experience as slaves, her grandparents' time living in the South during Jim Crow, and her parents coming of age in the Civil Rights era. There was also a linguist and *New York Review of Books* contributor whose parents were Holocaust survivors, an author and psychoanalyst whose American-born Japanese parents were put in internment camps in California during the Second World War, and a fourth panelist, a historian from a Jesuit college in Ohio whose only function seemed to be talking about "cancel culture," and leading the discussion into a full-blown shouting match after about fifteen minutes.

"Pure comedy," Elijah said before explaining his motives, about how there had been plenty of study on the topic among Jewish descendants of Holocaust survivors, as well as some on children and grandchildren of victims of the Armenian genocide, but, strangely, not too much on African Americans or native peoples.

"America hates to admit its mistakes," Eve said.

After they finished eating and waited for the check, Eve asked if she'd ever talked about the dreams she'd had about her father. Elijah told her she hadn't, but he was getting worried about leaving the car unattended even though they could see it through the window where they were sitting. They put money on the table and walked out. As they did, Eve began to talk about her dream.

"My dad is standing on the ledge of a bridge. My mother is there. She's not smiling—I don't know if she ever did—but she doesn't seem upset, either. She's calm. That's something she certainly never was. My father is more of a presence. I don't have any concrete memories of what he looked like in the flesh, only the photos I've seen. But I know it's him in the dream, and he has this feeling, like he's OK. And I'm OK. I can't see his face, but I know he's better. Is that strange?"

"I don't think so," Elijah said. "But I wish Dad were around to hear this. He would have had a field day telling you what Freud might have thought about your dreams."

"God," Eve said with a laugh. "I miss him all the time, but I don't miss the Freudian obsession." She got quiet for a second. Elijah could tell she'd landed on a happy memory of her husband, and he wanted her to be able to savor it as long as she could. "So the dream. At the end, the presence of my father smiles. I can tell it's smiling at me. Then it jumps off the bridge."

Eve looked up something on her phone. Between that moment

and the new topic of conversation she'd start up a few seconds later, Elijah thought about how he'd had an eerily similar dream involving his own father. Except he could see Peter's face, and his father didn't jump off a bridge; he fell into a hole in the ground. Despite his mother's misgivings about psychotherapy, Elijah's experiences with it in the past had been mostly positive, so he went online after he woke up and read Freud's thoughts on absurd dreams. He read about the doctor having a patient who dreamed they saw their father—who was dead in real life—alive and riding a train for a moment, then watched as there was a horrific accident and the already-dead father was killed in the dream. Elijah agreed with Freud's theory that the patient was memorializing their father, then added his own addendum that it also had something to do with finding peace and closure.

As they started driving, Elijah had one other thing he had to ask. It was about something Eve had said to him when he was about seven or eight, a quote she used to explain that the family didn't do a Thanksgiving dinner like other families because it was a celebration of genocide. She knew the one.

"History is a nightmare from which I am trying to awake," she said. "It's James Joyce. Why?"

"I'd had a vague memory the other day of it and how I felt directly challenged when I heard it for some reason, but I couldn't remember the quote," Elijah said. "Now I get it."

As they got on the expressway, Elijah wondered if he was finally waking up.

10

1926

It was the same thing every morning at 7:00 on the dot. Yitz walked into Middleberg's Dairy, sat at the stool all the way at the far end of the lunch counter, and ordered his usual of coffee, dry toast, and whatever fruit they had. He'd speed-read the newspapers and eat his food quickly. Middleberg made the same joke once a week, wondering if Yitz had ever enjoyed a bite of food in his life; Yitz would always answer there wasn't any time to, and that he didn't like to fill up on breakfast. He'd leave the same amount on the counter (thirty-five cents for breakfast, plus a generous tip of two quarters) and walk over to the Schvitz. He went into the changing room to peel off his clothes, wrapped a towel around his waist, and got into the sauna. Yitz figured if there were 1,440 minutes in a day, that he was awake for about 1,260 of them. The ninety between 7:00 and 8:30 in the morning were the only ones he enjoyed. He'd eat in quiet, then go and sit in the sauna, letting all the toxins just drip out without anybody to bother him.

When he was all finished sweating, he showered, put on a new change of clothes, and got to work. By 9:00, the men in charge of all Avi's operations in the area would report to Yitz either in person or by phone call, though he preferred the former since it gave him the opportunity to look the guy talking to him in the face. He'd take the nightly total from each spot, add everything up, then he'd report the amount taken in to Avi with a quick phone call. They'd talk in Yiddish, no small talk, and never for more than a minute. Even though he'd never dare touch a cent, Yitz had learned that Avi would double-check the numbers Yitz told him every now and then. It would have been insulting if Yitz didn't do the same thing with the numbers he got from the guys who reported to him.

Avi ran more than a hundred speakeasies around Maxwell Street. Some were hidden in basements or behind fake walls in grocery stores or pharmacies, while others weren't that difficult to find if you knew what alley to walk down or who to ask. There were also seventeen brothels, not including the one behind the Schvitz, and two dozen clip joints that mostly hosted card and dice games. Even though it brought in barrels of money, Yitz hated dealing with the gambling. Those addicts were even sadder than some of the drunks he'd seen; they'd risk everything they had just to prove something to themselves that Yitz could never understand. Gambling just didn't make sense to him. He didn't bet on horses, baseball players, the roulette wheel, or even the stock market—*especially* the stock market. The way he saw it, all the schmucks on Wall Street were as bad as the idiots that went into any clip joint, except they were gambling with other people's money. And for what? The whole idea just seemed so absurd to Yitz, that whenever somebody brought up stocks, he'd ask them if they knew anything about the panic back in 1907 or the one in 1873, telling them that all it took was one domino to fall and that paper money was worthless. And anybody who asked, he'd tell them the same thing: buy gold. It was a lesson from his childhood. Everybody wanted gold, his father once said; money was just a bit of metal or paper, something a king or government could say was worthless with the snap of a finger, while gold would always be valued the world over. Yitz tried to remind his brother of that lesson, but Sol laughed and told Yitz that he always appreciated the business advice, but he was making more money from the market than the meat.

There were other parts of the business, ones that went beyond Jewtown. Avi was involved with the unions, the protection money locals gladly coughed up, the policy games, and he also had a small army of bookmakers on his payroll. All the things he considered "extracurricular," especially the real estate and any business investments, he'd let Yitz handle. Avi didn't want his name on anything, partially because he had never bothered to become an American citizen, but also because he told Yitz that not being tied to anything made it safer for him.

Something had changed in Avi. He'd gotten even more enamored of himself, and loved seeing his name in the papers—so long as it was positive. Yitz stayed quiet, doing what he was told even though it enraged him that his signature was on a number of legitimate contracts and accounts for tax purposes, and any paper trails would lead back to him. Avi would have sacrificed Yitz in a second; he was so delusional that he thought he'd survive a day on his own.

It was the day before the first seder. Sol walked the last customer to the door, then locked it behind him so nobody else tried to get in for one more order of brisket. As he turned around, there was a knock on the window. Sol didn't want to see who it was, but he couldn't help it. What was helping one more person before the holiday?

The customer was Foxy Foxman. Sol smiled warmly as he undid the lock and hugged Foxy after he came in; he apologized that they didn't have much left in the store, but he'd help him however he could. Foxy said he didn't need meat.

"It's the trucks. I've got a delivery to Rockford due before morning. Avi will be fine with it, trust me."

Sol never asked questions; he especially didn't want to know anything about the trucks and the deliveries. The keys were hanging on the wall. Foxy grabbed them as Sol washed up, said thanks, and began rushing out the door.

"Hey, wait a second," Sol called out.

Foxy had one foot out the door. He turned around and answered with a slight tone of annoyance in his voice that Sol didn't catch.

"You need anything for the seder? We've still got some nice tongue, also enough shoulder to feed your whole family," Sol said.

Foxy said he had everything he needed, then left before Sol could wish him a happy Passover. Sol walked over and locked the door. The phone began ringing. Sol usually didn't pick it up when the store was closed, but he felt certain obligations during the holidays. If somebody needed something, he wanted to help.

"It's me," Yitz said when Sol picked up. "What time should we be over tomorrow?"

"I think the candle lighting is at seven fifteen and . . ."

"Is this going to be another of those seders that takes four hours before we eat? You know I get cranky if I don't have food," Yitz said.

His brother had always kvetched about Passover, even when he was a boy. It was as much a holiday tradition as leaving a cup of wine for the prophet Elijah was named after. Sol was tired and knew there was no use answering a question his brother already knew the answer to. He changed the topic instead.

"I just saw Foxy. Haven't seen him in a few years and he just showed up for the truck," Sol said.

"What he want with the trucks?"

"He needed them. Said Avi was OK with it. Something about Rockford," Sol said.

"Did he say Avi was OK with it or Avi told him it was OK?"

"I don't remember exactly, but I think he said Avi was OK. What's the difference?"

"There's a *big* difference," Yitz snapped. "I gotta go."

The line went dead. Sol didn't think anything of it, hung up the phone, and finished closing up.

A few blocks away, Yitz was stewing at his desk. There was no way Foxy went to Avi and asked for the trucks, and if he had, Avi would have just told him to go to Yitz. There was an order to things that son of a bitch had purposely ignored, and Yitz quickly put together why. It was all so clear: there had been a robbery in Aurora a night earlier, two trucks owned by some Swedish bootlegger named Janson. It was the sort of heist somebody needed to clear with the boss first since DuPage County was tricky territory into which Avi and Artie had been trying to make inroads. Yitz deduced that Foxy had pulled off the job and was going to unload the booze as quickly as possible so he could go to Avi with a bigger-than-usual cut that would placate him for doing something without cluing him in first. The worst part of it all was Yitz couldn't help but feel a little bit of respect for Foxman. It was a smart move, one the boss would look favorably on because he made a profit.

Yitz chewed on the inside of his mouth and concentrated on the pain he felt in his stomach. He reminded himself that, like everything else, taking care of Foxy was a work in progress. All he had to do was continue trying to make Foxy obsolete, just keep pushing him out to the edge of the earth in small nudges and then watch him drown. He'd been bleeding him slowly with paper cuts since the thing with White Jimmy's policy games; whispering poison into the ears of Foxy's allies, making sure to always get him edged out of any potential new business, and always looking for ways to set him up for failure without it connecting back to Yitz. Foxy must have figured out what Yitz had been doing and now it was simply a game of human chess. Yitz still had the upper hand, and had to use it any chance he had. Maybe it was getting the cops to bust one of Foxy's card games, or giving some small-time crew the jump on a scheme the guy was working on. Yitz would eventually hold the guy's head underwater until he couldn't talk anymore.

11

When Elijah was eight, he cried in the elevator all the way to the top of the Sears Tower. When the doors opened, he was so terrified to walk toward the observation deck that he took baby steps, then stopped and refused to budge no matter how many adults said he was perfectly safe inside the skyscraper.

"I'm also afraid," Ollie whispered in Elijah's ear and put his arm around him. "But it will be OK."

Before the two boys walked over to the window together to look down at Chicago from more than a hundred stories up, Ollie's dad snapped a picture of his son comforting his friend from behind. The photo was eventually framed and placed directly in the middle of a dozen other memories above the fireplace in the home Ollie had grown up in.

"I still won't call it Willis Tower," Ollie's mom, Sandra, said when she noticed Elijah looking at the photo. "It will always be the Sears Tower. Anybody who says otherwise isn't from Chicago."

He tried to remember the last time they'd seen each other. Maybe it was ten years, possibly eleven; either way, time hadn't been kind to her. Sandra had her own demons that only intensified after Ollie died, and had signed the papers for her third divorce a month earlier. Eve had stayed friendly with her, and when Elijah said he wanted to visit her, she mentioned that Sandra had been clean for two years, but the way she said it lacked any trace of confidence that the sobriety would last. Every family had their curse.

"I saw Shel Burton when I was running an errand in Lincoln Park," Sandra said as she poured some coffee from a French press. "Ollie always used to tell me he was sure you two would get married one day. She's such a great girl that it's hard to understand why she doesn't have a husband."

"She seems to be everywhere these days," Elijah said.

He thought about giving her some context, about the one night they'd spent together, running into Shel in the pharmacy, and Stephen pressuring him into giving her a call. He felt comfortable around Sandra; she was the "cool mom" among all the parents, the one who'd let Ollie have parties at the house, drove the kids to punk concerts, and was always easy to talk to. But he hadn't shown up at her front door to look for love-life advice.

"Why haven't I seen you for so long? I never told your mom this because you know how she is, but I always felt like you were part of our family. Gosh, you were here at least four nights a week from third grade until . . ." Sandra didn't finish the thought, but Elijah knew when he'd stopped coming over so much. It was around sophomore year of high school, not long after the night Ollie dropped a tab of ecstasy in Elijah's drink at a house party without telling him. Ollie thought it was hilarious; he told Elijah it would lighten him up. It didn't, and when he'd look back, Elijah knew that was the night their friendship really ended. They continued sitting at the same table at

207

lunch, and Ollie would sometimes show up at the Mendes house to crash on the couch when things were rough at home, but Elijah was relieved to say goodbye one last time to his old friend a few days before he went off to California for school. Ollie had been up doing coke and smelled like a mix of vodka and fruit punch that made Elijah feel a sense of good riddance and thankfulness for the distance he'd finally get. He figured Ollie would grow out of his partying ways or get over his addictions by getting really into some new age wellness movement, but he never did.

What Elijah didn't expect was the feeling of guilt that would overtake him whenever he went online and would see some social media update or pictures of Ollie holding a beer, his eyes glazed, and the company he kept. He watched from afar as his oldest friend got worse, and Elijah didn't know what to do. He considered an intervention, but then things got so busy with the new company that he forgot. When he'd heard that Ollie had cleaned up his act, he felt relieved; but the news of him falling off the wagon hardly surprised Elijah. When Ollie showed up that night in San Francisco, there was a little of the original version sitting there waiting. It was Oliver, not Ollie Party. He'd had a couple of drinks, but he seemed unfazed and was pleasant to talk with. It was like old times, and it dawned on Elijah only later that the guy's tolerance must have been so high that the cocktails he'd had before they met up took longer to work into his bloodstream.

In the days and weeks after the accident, Elijah went through all the stages of grief, but when it came to acceptance, the guilt remained. No, he didn't exactly ply his friend with booze or give him any of the cocaine that was in his system when the coroner drew blood from Ollie's corpse, and Elijah had been under the impression his friend was meeting other people at the same place a little later. He swore that was what Ollie had told him, and just assumed somebody else would be responsible to get the drunk into a cab. There was some guilt over that, but not enough to make Elijah culpable for the crimes Ollie committed after getting behind the wheel. Instead, Elijah's guilt had been building years earlier when his friend was still alive. Every moment he didn't try to help his friend, all the times he just stood by and watched him do a keg stand or say "hell yeah" when somebody offered any pill or powder, Elijah held on to the belief that his silence and then abandonment of his friend was part of what led to the horrors of that evening on a San Francisco street.

He went to visit Sandra to explain all that, and then apologize. He wasn't looking for forgiveness, but he hoped maybe admitting his sins to Ollie's mother would help *her* find some peace. His delivery wasn't elegant, and he caught himself rambling from time to time as he often did when he was nervous. He said what he wanted to say, and then when he stopped, he wondered if anything he said mattered. What if he'd made things worse and made the poor woman sitting across from him confront her grief anew?

But Sandra smiled as a few tears rolled down her cheeks.

"I figured that's why you've been avoiding me," she said. "But you never did anything wrong. Oliver was his own person, you know that. As soon as he could talk I knew there was no arguing him out of anything. He was a stubborn little guy, and I was a little too easy on him. His father gave up trying even before the drinking and drugs started. My son made up his mind early on that things were on his terms, and I tried to be respectful of that. But you were there for him . . ."

"No, I wasn't. That's the thing," Elijah said as he barely held it together.

Sandra shook her head.

"You would let him stay over when the marriage was in its last days. You stayed by him as long as you could, and you tried to tell me what he was up to. It was after the party with your drink. You told me he was messed up. I didn't take it as seriously as I should have," she said.

"I didn't tell you because I was concerned; I told you because I was pissed."

"You still told me. You tried. That was all you had to do. Nothing else. But if it helps you out, I absolve you of all your sins, my child," Sandra said as she made the sign of the cross. "Does that make you feel any better? You're a good guy, Elijah. You always have been. You were the best friend Oliver could have asked for and I'm glad he had you in his life, but you need to go on living yours. If anything, he'd be mad knowing you were walking around with this hanging over your head."

Much to his surprise, it had made Elijah feel better. He almost felt guilty about Sandra's words making him feel good, but he decided to embrace the feeling.

12

END OF THE 1920S, START OF THE 1930S

David Siegelman walked into Yitz's office ten minutes early. He'd gotten into town ahead of schedule and wanted to beat the freezing rain, but from the look of his soaked clothes, his timing was off. He'd taken a train back from Los Angeles after making the move out there for a few months after a studio purchased his second novel, *The Emerald Trail*, and wanted to make it into a film. Except that after a dozen rewrites and a lifeless, perfunctory shoot, *The Emerald Trail* movie was nothing like the novel except in name, and David was back in Chicago to work on his next book.

Despite the frustrating experience with the studio, California's positive impact on Siegelman was noticeable. Gone was the little bit of protruding belly and pale complexion; he was tan and taut in his gray pinstripe suit and blue tie with white dots on it, a red square folded with two sharp points sticking out from his breast pocket. It was a long way from his drab brown suits that hardly fit him and his dusty loafers that looked as if they'd been stolen off a corpse that

211

had been in the ground for a few weeks. He also wanted to get back out west. The first round didn't pan out the way he had wanted it, but Siegelman said Hollywood wouldn't get the best of him. He told Yitz he knew there was money out there, about how just a year or so earlier, Herman J. Mankiewicz had wired a telegram to Ben Hecht, an acquaintance of Siegelman's from his time as a reporter for the *Chicago Daily News*, and offered Hecht a job in Los Angeles, working for Paramount Pictures for $300 a week. He claimed that the princely sum was nothing compared to what could be made writing for the pictures. It was a game of attrition, Siegelman reasoned.

"How much did they pay you so they could massacre your book?" Yitz asked.

Siegelman mumbled that it was $150 a week.

Yitz shook his head and mentioned his offer to step in and negotiate for more.

Siegelman admitted he'd been stupid. He'd respectfully declined Yitz's first offer to help him out, but since he'd fired his manager for not protecting his work, Siegelman was uncertain what to do. He was desperate for something that would pay the bills while he worked on his books. He had told Yitz that his new novel, the one about love, power, and corruption in Chicago that he was calling *The Machine*, was going to be his masterpiece, a great American novel.

Yitz brushed off the artist talk and asked how much time he needed to finish and how much money he wanted to make. Siegelman said he was having trouble working because Hollywood had given him a bigger appetite. He wanted to see *The Machine* published as a book above all else, but he knew that it also had to be given to actors and turned into something audiences could watch—that was the nature of business and the way to make a living. He added that after

The Emerald Trail, he'd settle for having it on a small stage; it didn't necessarily have to be Broadway, but that would be nice. At least the theater respected art.

"Nonsense," Yitz said. "We'll get it made into a movie, and it'll be to your liking. Don't settle—only schmucks do that."

Siegelman scoffed at Yitz but regretted it immediately when he saw the cold stare that was being returned.

"You think I'm joking," Yitz said. "But you seem to forget that I'm not that funny. I can get you back to Los Angeles by the end of the week and have you on salary for double what you were making by next Monday."

Siegelman decided he had no choice but to play ball. He asked how Yitz intended to do that even though he'd never even been to California, let alone past the middle west toward the Rocky Mountains.

"I'm going there in two days and getting into the movie business," Yitz said. "Me and some partners purchased Butler Pictures, know of it?"

Siegelman was familiar, but only vaguely. It was one of the countless sad little studios that made up Hollywood's Poverty Row, the type that turned out little pictures that they made on the cheap, about cowboys shooting Indians and Bowery tramps getting into trouble. Though he couldn't name a single picture they made. Yitz said he loved the pictures, that he snuck off to the Tivoli, the grand movie palace built by Balaban and Katz, with its interior made up of gold leaf and expensive marble and its facade that made it look like a cathedral from seventeenth-century France—except in Chicago. Yitz had seen *The Jazz Singer* there, and in a flat tone claimed he'd been very moved by it. He loved the new talking pictures, they were far more enjoyable than the silent ones. There was one he'd seen a few months earlier, *The Mob Boss*. When the film started, he watched as the names came up on the screen; they sounded like the members of a prayer minyan. Blumberg the director, Schulberg the associate producer, Blumfeld and Cohen presenting the movie—what a feeling seeing your name up on that screen must have been, Yitz thought. And even better was the money the studios must have been raking in; it had to be a big number given the fact that men were willing to spend one or two million to build theaters just to show the films. Yitz decided he wanted to find out for himself.

"Never struck me as that easy to just buy a film studio," Siegelman said. "Even if it is a smaller one like Butler Pictures."

Yitz smiled and sat back in his chair. He loved it when smart guys like Siegelman underestimated him.

"Anything is easy to buy if you've got the money and you're smart," Yitz said.

The whole thing had been planned out a few days in advance. Yitz always got gossip about people with deep pockets who were visiting Chicago. Usually it didn't lead to much, but the stock market crash a few months earlier made it so a person could buy nearly anything they wanted at wildly steep discounts if they had the funds. The British Butler Pictures founder was already running out of money due to a costly divorce, three children out of wedlock, and a notoriously long-running streak of bad luck at the poker table. The studio was another costly investment that the Brit was looking to unload. Yitz had been smart about saving, and did everything in his power to make sure the boorish Brit made it into one of his joints, specifically one with women and card games. Initially, Yitz had hoped to get the Brit good and liquored up, cozy up to him, feel out what he could. But when he showed up to introduce himself and heard his guest was more than $10,000 in the hole after several hours of poker, Yitz changed plans. He didn't normally like to use his power to sway outcomes; he didn't want to get a reputation for running unreliable clip joints where the only way a player could walk away with money at the end of the night was if they held the place up. But he was the man in charge, and the Brit was both rude and obviously impetuous in a way brats who had been raised with all money and no care often were, so Yitz gave word to the staff to make sure the red-faced Englishman kept playing and to make sure he kept losing. By the time he was twenty thousand deep in the red, Yitz moved in and made his pitch for how the guy could clear his debts with a few pen strokes. The next morning, Leonard Schwartz of Salamon and Salamon was ready with the paperwork. The studio owner, still soused from all the cheap gin and losing, signed away without any remorse. He said he was happy to be rid of the burden.

Yitz didn't mention any of that, but Siegelman was still a journalist who needed answers. He asked if Avi was involved; the question annoyed Yitz. He waved his hand and grimaced.

"Who cares if he is or not? He doesn't know a thing about movies. And the best part is we're only going to make talkies, so a brilliant writer like you is necessary."

"Talkies? Even Irving Thalberg, the wunderkind head of production at MGM, had called movies with sound nothing but a gimmick," Siegelman said.

"Who the fuck is Irving Thalberg?" Yitz, slamming his fist on the table in a rare display of controlled anger, yelled. "He doesn't know what guys like me, Americans that pay to buy tickets, like. He thinks he does, but he doesn't. He's a pretentious prick who just wants to appeal to the few with big bucks, but what he doesn't get is those rich folks are spending the same cash to see movies as everybody else, and there's a lot more of everybody else than the wealthy people in America. We're going to give them *stories*, something they can all relate to, but also look up to. That's what people want, and let me tell you, this schmuck Hoover is making things worse with the economy. It's gonna get bad, and people will want to take their minds off whatever is coming."

The idea was simple. Things would be done inexpensively, but Yitz emphasized "never *cheap*." His movies would be about heroes and villains, about cowboys, Indians, criminals, cops, whatever the public wanted. He said they'd be shorter and wouldn't cost as much to make, and every smaller theater in the country needed them because they couldn't justify showing only movies from big studios like Paramount and MGM. Plus, people wanted more for their buck, so places were starting to show two movies for the price of one. The problem was with the new technology of talking pictures, there was a rush to get movies made. Yitz said there were only one or two smaller studios getting their stuff out there, but they were making *dreck*, absolute garbage.

"I'll give them *good* dreck, and you'll get three hundred a week to be my main writer. In six months, once everything is up and running, you get five hundred weekly, and I'll give you room to work on your book, which I will personally help you sell to a bigger studio and make sure they don't take you to the woodshed. I'm leaving for California in two days. You have until tonight to let me know if I need to get you a ticket to go with me," Yitz said as he stuck out his hand for Siegelman to shake.

The writer didn't have time to think over the offer, not that he really needed to; it was a lot of money and freedom, but he'd also be working for Yitz. He knew so much about the man that he had to consider the massive downside.

But in the end a job was a job, Siegelman figured as they shook hands.

"Great," Yitz said as he sat back down. "We'll figure out all the details when we're out west. In the meantime, I've got another meeting in a few, but I was wondering, since I assume you're going to see your old editor at the paper for a liquid lunch, could you give this to him?"

He handed over a thick manila envelope. When Siegelman went to grab it, Yitz pulled it back gently, looked him right in the eyes, and sternly said, "But so help me God, if you open it, I'll fucking kill you."

Siegelman's face went pale.

Yitz smiled. "I'm joking with you! I can be funny occasionally," he said. "I'll send a car to pick you up for the station. Take me somewhere nice to eat when we get to Hollywood. I want to go where the important people go."

As Siegelman walked out of the office, Artie Berman, flanked by three guys, walked past. Berman nodded at the writer, and Siegelman watched as he walked into Yitz's office. All he heard was the elder Berman brother say "We're good to go" before the door closed.

Five days later, as Yitz sat outside at the Garden of Allah Hotel eating the freshest, juiciest grapefruit he'd ever had, Siegelman ran over to his table. He was out of breath. Yitz handed him a glass of water and asked what was wrong. Siegelman asked if Yitz had read the papers.

"I started," Yitz said.

"Did you see any Chicago ones?"

"Why do I want to read about Chicago when I'm out here in the sunshine?"

Siegelman went pale. He cleared his throat but couldn't get the words out. Yitz asked if he needed something stronger than water, but he'd composed himself enough to talk.

"It's Avi. Your brother-in-law. He was shot . . . killed. He was eating dinner at some place on Clark Street. When he walked out, some guys ran up and . . ." Siegelman was shaking and couldn't continue. Yitz sat motionless as Siegelman showed him the headline, "Chicago Hood Kaminsky Killed."

"Terrible," Yitz said without even a drop of grief in his voice. "May his memory be a blessing."

Siegelman was puzzled by the reaction. He figured it was the shock.

"I know how important he was to you. I'm sorry, Yitz."

Yitz took a slow, measured breath.

"A real tragedy," Yitz said calmly. He took a sip of water, then placed the glass back on the table gently. "Lot of tragedy in that family. First his mother passed, then his brother Hershey cracked up and we had to send him away. Did you know I met Hershey first? On the boat over from Odesa, in fact."

Siegelman read something from the paper out loud, a claim that Avi was working with police by feeding them information to keep himself out of trouble. He looked at Yitz, who remained unmoved.

"That envelope, the one you had me deliver in Chicago to my old boss," the writer said. "You had me do your work for you. This stuff in the paper about your own family is from you. *You* did this."

"You could have asked what I was having you deliver, and if you told me you didn't want to, I'd have respected that," Yitz said.

"You said I was dead if I looked!"

A rhythmic hum of laughter flowed from Yitz's nostrils and evolved into a full-throated howl. David Siegelman took a step back and looked on in awe at evil manifesting itself right before his eyes. The writer didn't believe in God, but in those moments he understood that he'd been keeping company with the devil the moment he met Yitz Kaplan.

"I said I was joking. Can't I make a joke? Next time know what you're getting into. Don't be a schmuck." Yitz's laughter halted. He looked back down at his paper.

"Chicago is such a violent place. It's never smart to talk to cops. They do more harm than good," he said before going back to finish his grapefruit. He took a bite, started looking at the funny papers, then asked if Siegelman needed anything else. If not, Yitz said he had work to do.

Siegelman slunk back to his bungalow. He muttered, "Dear God. I'm part of this," to himself as he turned the key to open his door.

He picked up a bottle of whiskey and started drinking until he fell asleep. For the three weeks that followed, David Siegelman spent his life in a drunken haze. The booze didn't hinder him from typing words and scenes and making little stories for his murderous master, but he felt nothing. The only moment of clarity he had was the second before he pulled the trigger of a small pistol that he'd bought at a pawnshop and got bits of his skull and brains all over his typewriter. In that last second, he realized he'd had nobody to blame but himself.

It was business as usual on Maxwell Street in the months after Avi Kaminsky's murder and the new decade began. The killers were never found, but the guys who'd worked for the dead boss kept showing up for collections. Beer and liquor continued flowing, the brothels and clip joints still ran night and day, and not much around Jewtown changed to the casual observer besides nobody on the street knowing who was running things. Word had gotten around that Yitz Kaplan had been living out in Hollywood, and Foxy Foxman was doing two years in Cook County Jail after getting caught with a small bag filled with stolen jewelry. As soon as Avi was in the ground, Jakey Jake Malamud started talking big, telling people that he'd always been Avi's second-in-command and was taking charge. He tried convincing a few of the Maxwell Street gang to side with him, but nobody considered Jakey Jake a serious guy, and it took a few months for anybody to even notice he'd gone missing not long after he started making claims that he was the new boss.

It was a new era of things being done quietly. The days of bosses smiling for the cameras and trying to get the newspapers to like them were over. The public had turned; it was something Yitz believed would happen when the cops discovered seven dead bodies in a garage on the North Side a year earlier on Valentine's Day. People had enough to be frightened of with all the talk of the economy sliding even further into the abyss; they didn't want an extra side of violence in the streets and started getting vocal for the city officials to take charge. Yitz knew that Avi getting knocked off in public didn't help matters much, but there was no other choice in that matter.

Things had changed and would continue evolving with the plans Meyer Lansky and Lucky Luciano had laid out in a meeting of all the big-city guys in Atlantic City the previous May. It had been sold as a chance for men from all over the country with like-minded interests to come together and form something large, like a corporation or syndicate. Luciano started things off by giving a speech where he told the men who'd come from all over the map that before 1929, anybody could get rich ruling over a neighborhood in some city; thinking provincially wasn't the way to do things in the new decade. All the fighting that was going on in New York and Chicago wasn't worth the trouble when people could work together and triple their profits within a year. He gave a toast; a *salute* and also *l'chaim*.

Two days later, as they took a morning walk on the boardwalk, Yitz and Artie Berman discussed how things had to be. They liked what they'd heard from Lansky and Luciano, but Avi wasn't going to be convinced. He wanted to stick to the old way of doing things just like Lippy had, so Yitz and Artie had a conversation in Middleberg's Dairy similar to the one they'd had about the old boss years earlier. That was the day Avi's fate was sealed.

After months out west, Yitz was inspecting his office at the Schvitz to make sure it had been kept clean, but that nobody touched anything they weren't supposed to. The phone rang. It was Artie telling him everything was in order and that Yitz could go ahead with his "spring cleaning."

"There's a few things we need to deal with right away," Yitz said to White Jimmy after he hung up the phone. "Westy Mendleson needs to be done by no later than tomorrow."

White Jimmy grimaced. He looked at Yitz, who sat stone-faced, unmoved by the fact that he'd just ordered the end of somebody he'd known since first coming to America.

"He's an Avi loyalist," Yitz said. "It can't be helped."

White Jimmy nodded. He tapped his fingers nervously.

"You got a question? Go ahead," Yitz said.

"Foxy," White Jimmy said. "He'll likely get out on good behavior a year early."

"So? You got your policy games back. That was the whole point of planting that bag on him."

"You aren't worried he'll get out and raise a stink about Avi?"

Yitz shook his head.

"He has no loyalty to anybody but himself. Even if that wasn't the case, we couldn't do anything until we're totally out of the booze. He's too deep in the business and we need a few reliable guys for that. But once things start to change with the laws and all that, he'll have less use and fewer friends. Then we'll take care of it," he said.

White Jimmy didn't look so sure; Yitz told him to read the newspapers every single day like he did.

"Repeal is coming. If the Democrats make it part of their plans for next year's election they'll win in a landslide because it's jobs for people to make and serve it, and also it numbs the pain of everyday life. If it's legal, then what good is it to us?"

White Jimmy was impressed as he walked from Yitz's office to make the call that would mark Westy Mendleson for death.

———————

Devorah could see the sidewalk from her kitchen window. She kept busy near it while keeping lookout. When she saw Yitz walking toward her house, she excused herself and rushed out to greet him even before he made it to the steps of her porch.

"I was hoping I could have a word with you before you go inside," she said.

Yitz squinted his eyes, then nodded his head. He told her to go on. She asked if he'd known a man named Vincenzo Ciccarelli.

Yitz cocked his head back and laughed.

"Stink Lip Ciccarelli? Sure. Haven't heard from him in a few years," he said.

The guy was an old con artist. A cockroach among the rats. He'd worked for the local Black Hand once, but that had been about twenty years earlier, and he didn't carry much weight even then. The only reason Yitz knew him at all was because Ciccarelli's nephew was a guy everybody called Nicky Chops. He ran the Four Jacks on Wabash but wasn't anybody of great importance.

Devorah explained how Ciccarelli had walked into her father's store with two men. Julius Spiegel said they looked Russian; one of them was possibly Jewish, the other had a tattoo of a cross on his hand and letters branded there. Yitz knew the sort of Russian she was talking about. Criminals, likely stowaways who didn't go through a port like Ellis Island or Baltimore and were roaming America without documents. There had been more than a few of them showing up in Chicago; the cross on the hand meant they'd deserted the army, and the brand usually meant they'd done forced labor in a penal colony. They weren't usually very talented, but they were very good at being dangerous.

Devorah explained what they told her father, about how they

said they'd make sure nothing bad happened to his store if he paid them. But if he didn't give them money, then something surely *would* happen.

"My father is a gentle man," Devorah said. "He doesn't understand how people in your world work."

"*My* world?" Yitz stared at his sister-in-law. They'd never had a conversation that lasted more than a few minutes, and it was never just the two of them. "You think I'm the same as some old dago and a couple of pieces of liverwurst?"

"I didn't mean . . ."

Sol walked outside. He greeted his brother. Devorah looked down at the ground, excused herself, and walked back inside. Sol asked what was going on. Yitz stared at the beard his brother had grown since the last time they'd seen each other. He'd started wearing a yarmulke all the time, and Yitz noticed the little bits of strings from *tzitzit* he was wearing hanging around his waist the last time they'd seen each other.

"When did you become a regular old *tzaddik*? Business must be bad if you're dressing like a Hasid," Yitz joked. "Is that a stunt or are you hoping God will look favorably on you?"

Sol wasn't amused. He asked what had happened between Yitz and Devorah.

"Your father-in-law has *your wife* coming to me asking for favors? Julius Spiegel looks down on me, always has." Yitz spit. "What balls that man has."

Sol stared blankly at his brother. He had no clue what Yitz was talking about.

"I told you," Yitz said, his voice a notch higher. "Didn't I say that part of town he was opening his new store in is strange? It's all old money or newspapermen. They're not part of our world. But you didn't listen to me."

Sol was taken aback. He tried to say something, but his brother kept talking.

"Because *she* despises me. You know that. And don't try to deny it. You can't even come in my place of business because you're worried that she'd find out. Her father, that little worm, he can't even ask me for a favor. He hides behind my brother's wife."

"Yitzhak . . ."

"I'll take care of it. I'll tell Ciccarelli to scram and he'll never bother Julius Spiegel again. But I won't do it for that schmuck. I'll do it because I can't have some vermin bothering my brother's poor old father-in-law."

Sol pleaded with his brother, saying Julius Spiegel was a good man, and Devorah was only trying to help him by going to Yitz, that she didn't know what else to do. Surely he'd understand that she was only trying to help their family.

Yitz stood on his toes and got in his younger brother's face. "Your family? *I'm* your family. Me. Your wife is *your wife*, and her father isn't your blood. You need to—"

Before he could finish his tirade, Sol's palm slammed into Yitz's chest. It wasn't all of his power; Yitz likely would have been implanted into the facade of Sol's home if he had. Instead, he tumbled back and fell on his ass, dropping the babka he'd brought from a bakery that was near the Schvitz.

His little brother had never put his hands on him. Yitz was shocked as he got up and brushed himself off.

"You're becoming cruel," Sol said. "I've seen it happening over time, but I haven't said anything because I know you're under lots of pressure. You didn't used to be this way and it's not who you are."

"Who am I? I'm the guy who makes everything in our lives possible," Yitz said before spitting on the ground. "Believe me, every day of my life I wish that wasn't the case, but this is how things are, and you're fine and silent because you're safe and secure. You would have been wiped out last year if not for me. Your family would be out on the streets, but you're *my* brother, and I've always made sure you're taken care of. I just want some damn respect from you and your wife."

It had rained a few hours before and the sidewalk was still slick. Sol looked down and moved the front of his right foot around. He was wearing waterproof boots, and the rubber against the wet pavement made a slight squeal. Something about the sound made Yitz laugh. It was involuntary, he couldn't help it.

"Your wife and child are inside waiting for us," Sol said before turning his back to his brother and walking away.

13

Elijah pulled up to the Lincoln Park Rehabilitation Center. Eve got in on the passenger side of the car in her workout clothes. Her sunglasses were on, and an old Bulls hat that once belonged to Peter was pulled down almost to her eyebrows. She had never been much of an exercise buff, claiming that the only reason she liked the palliative rehabilitation program was because there was a sixty-minute massage included at the end of every session and it was covered by insurance.

"I need a little bit of quiet," she said as she turned the volume on the radio all the way down. "My head is killing me."

"Does that mean you don't want me to talk?"

"Of course you can talk. Just in a low voice," Eve said. "And if you can take the local streets and not the expressway, that would be good. Take Halsted down."

Starting discussions with Eve was always tricky. World events, a painting Elijah saw in a museum, even sports so long as it was the

White Sox or tennis, those were all good ways to kick things off, but he was struggling to come up with anything banal enough to lead into talking about Jerry the Fox. They drove toward home to the familiar score of silence all the way until passing the Mr. Greek Gyros that Elijah ate at by himself the day after Peter's funeral.

"Keep driving toward Jim's Original," Eve said. She often gave directions according to food landmarks.

"You want a Polish sausage or something? I haven't had a char dog in forever," Elijah said.

"Turn left here," Eve said as she pointed at a small alley that was almost totally obscured by the college administration building that looked like a small glass city. Elijah recognized the direction they were going in as the one he'd taken just a few days earlier to get to talk with Rabbi Ginsburg. Another turn later, and they were in front of the little building for the Greater Chicagoland Hebrew Benevolent Society.

"If I recall correctly," Eve started before craning her head to get a better look. "Little Italy started two blocks to the south, but they bull-dozed most of it to build the campus in 1961 or so. I think Manny's original location was right over there. The one that's there now isn't the original location. I may have gone to the old place with my mom or dad, but I only remember the one that's still on Jefferson. Sarah took me for soup. I think it was maybe two years after my mom died. I always remember that because it was the first time I remember not feeling miserable."

"What about that one?" Elijah pointed to the building that housed the Greater Chicagoland Hebrew Benevolent Society.

"My father took me there once when I was three or four. It's the clearest memory I have of him. He brought me to the tomb and didn't say a word. He just placed a rock down in front of the door. I remember it was freezing that day and I wanted to go home, but there was something about the way he looked, it was the saddest I'd ever seen a man before or since. He just had so much pain on his face, I . . ."

Eve pulled a vape out of her bag and examined it before putting it back and fishing around some more until she found the rose-gold-colored one that she'd wanted.

"You don't have to keep talking if you don't feel like it," Elijah said, instantly regretting it. He wanted her to talk, but he guessed it was probably better she not use up too much energy.

"Maybe now you understand why I don't talk about this," Eve said.

"I do. I still don't get why you withheld that we own a piece of property near the college that's probably worth a million dollars. That feels like a big oversight."

"It's one point seven million, I think. We also have some property up in the suburbs that my father bought years ago. It's just sitting there, overgrown and waiting for a developer to build a couple of ugly mansions on it. If I had told you that earlier, you would have told me to sell it because all you think about is money."

"That's not true," Elijah protested.

"Maybe not now, but only because you know there's a personal connection. But soon I'll be gone and it will be up to you to decide," Eve said.

"I mean, I think we could probably charge the Benevolent Society *some* rent. And if the property in the suburbs is just sitting. . . ."

"Exactly my point," Eve said.

When they got home, Eve fell into the couch and let out a loud sigh. She took a long drag from the rose-gold-colored vape pen that she had taken to clutching like it was a set of rosary beads.

"It's so funny that I used to do this stuff in the 1970s and then totally stopped in the '80s except for a concert we went to at Ravinia a few years before you were born," she said. She exhaled a cloud of smoke toward the ceiling. "I suppose even I bought into Reagan's whole War on Drugs thing."

"As long as it helps," Elijah said.

Eve tilted her head to the left and made a disappointed face. "It does the trick."

"I had a chance to invest in some cannabis-ordering startup a few years back, but I thought the idea was dumb. Now it's valued at just under two billion and I'm living with my mom in the house I grew up in."

Elijah wasn't sure if Eve had even heard him. Her eyes were barely open. He was hoping she'd doze off, but she started talking, very slowly.

"The thing about my father . . ." She smacked her tongue against the top of her mouth. It sounded dry. She took a sip of water before continuing. "I was curious for years. I mean, I assumed things. It was obvious he wasn't exactly on the up-and-up. He was an immigrant who didn't speak the language when he came here. He had it hard, and we . . ."

There was still part of Elijah that wanted her to keep talking, but his sympathy was stronger than his curiosity by that point. She needed to sleep. He told her it was fine, and they could talk some other time, but Eve kept going.

"He was a businessman; he had business. I took my mother and Sarah at their word until I couldn't any longer. I had ideas of the sort of people he associated with, old family friends whose names you'd read about in the paper or hear about on the news when there was a killing or Mob raid, that sort of thing."

With her eyes almost totally closed, Eve explained that not long after Elijah was born, she got a call out of the blue. It was from a man who said his name was Nathan and that he was her half brother. He was a few decades older than Eve and explained that their father had been married to Nathan's mother, and then left her for Rose in the early

1950s. Eve had no idea, but it turned out that Nathan had known about his half sister for years and had a private investigator find her. He never contacted her until after he found himself in the doctor's office hearing he had maybe a year left, and it would be good to put his affairs in order. They met for lunch once, a month and a day before Nathan died. He was sickly, with tubes hooked up to an oxygen machine by his side. The meal was cordial at first. They talked about their lives, and how it was so odd that they had lived fifty miles away from each other all those years. Nathan explained how their father wasn't around much when he was a boy, and that one day he just didn't live in the house anymore. His mother's name was Leah; there had been another brother who was killed in the Second World War. Eve said she'd never heard of a first wife or other family. Nathan wasn't surprised, but said their father sent them a check every month and put the boys through college. Besides that, he hardly had any part in their lives. As he told the story, Eve could tell her long-lost brother was getting more upset with every word.

"He started talking about what a horrible man our father was, how he ruined lives. Nathan was happy when he heard that the man who made both of us had died. It wasn't a very comfortable meal." Eve started to laugh but began to cough again. It wasn't good to get her worked up. She tried to talk some more, but her eyelids were too heavy. "I think I ordered salmon. It was overcooked."

"Go to sleep, Ma," Elijah said.

"I always felt terrible for her," Eve said. "Poor Leah." She started to drift off. Just as Elijah was about to get up and walk away, she remembered one more thing. She said it with her eyes closed.

"I hate that they didn't bury my mom in the same cemetery," she said. "Those rabbis with their ancient laws . . ."

She was nearly out. Elijah sat for a few minutes and couldn't recall the last time he'd seen his mother sleeping. She'd always been the last to bed and first to rise.

His mind flashed to some generic scene from any number of movies he'd seen, a part where somebody falls asleep and the other person who is still awake puts a blanket over them. He crept over to the closet where the linens were kept and found an old afghan that his aunt had knitted when she was alive.

14

CHICAGO, EARLY 1930S

There was a movie house a few blocks past one of the countless shantytowns that had sprung up seemingly overnight across the city. Yitz told his driver to stop when he saw *The Navajo Ghost* advertised on the glowing marquee. It was the latest Butler Pictures release, and Yitz had never seen one of the films he made play in public. He felt funny enough buying a ticket for himself for one of *his* films; there was no way he was paying for the two goons that followed everywhere he went. He made them wait in the car, and walked into the Congress Theater on his own.

When he opened the door to the room where the movie was playing, Yitz couldn't believe what he saw. Even though the box office numbers were reported to him daily, seeing the packed movie house on a cold, gray day was something that he couldn't have understood without witnessing it live. It was the sound of hundreds of people totally enthralled with what they saw on the screen. They laughed and shrieked as if all the troubles that awaited them outside the Congress didn't exist. They didn't have to think about how America was broke, or the troubling news coming out of Germany.

Yitz was so enthralled with watching the audience that he didn't pay attention to *The Navajo Ghost* on the screen. Even though he'd made himself late for his plans, he stayed right until the end, long enough to see his name in the credits.

Devorah had everything in order: a meal fit for a king . . . or at least for her brother-in-law, who lorded over everybody like he was royalty. First, he wasn't eating beef, then he wasn't eating chicken and only wanted fish—but nothing that swam in the lake. Sol told her that his brother said the local water was disgusting and he only ate ocean fish. The only reputable place she knew of to get it was on Western and Division, so she had to schlep all the way there to find stuff that had been caught in the salt water of the Atlantic and shipped halfway across the country overnight. When she saw the price, Devorah joked to the man behind the counter it was too bad her brother-in-law didn't eat beef anymore, because she could find a calf made of gold for less than the Atlantic cod she purchased.

It was nearly noon by the time she'd gotten home and began preparing dinner, much later in the day than she usually liked to start. She hoped to work fast enough that she could get a couple of moments of peace, and maybe a few bites of food, but it wasn't about her; the dinner was for her husband. He'd been talking for weeks about seeing his brother and how it had been ages since Yitz last got to sit with his own wife and children to eat a meal.

That poor woman, Devorah thought of her sister-in-law. Yitz left the entire family in Chicago while he was out in California. When she'd brought it up to her husband, Sol said there was nothing to worry about. He said that his brother didn't have many vices, that he wasn't drinking all night with the Hollywood stars or carrying on affairs with other women. All he cared about was work, Sol said.

That was the problem, Devorah thought: only *work* mattered to her brother-in-law. She didn't say that, of course. The one time she had mentioned that she worried Yitz didn't pay enough attention to his family, Sol kissed her condescendingly on the forehead and joked that he had also grown up almost entirely fatherless, and she liked how Sol turned out. He said it was some greenhorn logic that she didn't quite understand, having been born in America with her father's business finding success not long after she came into the world. What she could appreciate was that Sol and his brother had experienced things in Odesa that she couldn't fully grasp and wouldn't have wished on her worst enemy. All she could do was try to be understanding and patient. Patient for what, she wasn't quite sure, but the whole point of being a Jew is patience. You're always waiting for something; it's either the messiah coming or for the next disaster to strike. The best Devorah could imagine happening was somewhere in the middle of those two things.

Cooking the dinner felt like a minor mitzvah. It wasn't a holiday or Shabbos, but she treated the weeknight meal as if it were. She used the nice china; the meal was *parve* since it was fish, so she decided to bake a chocolate cake. It was her first time trying out such a big dessert, but the smell coming from the kitchen told her it would be a hit with everybody. When she took it out of the oven, before adding the frosting to it, Devorah looked at the cake and smiled at the beautiful thing she'd made. She was still admiring it when a voice called out to her.

"Mrs. Kaplan," the maid interrupted as Devorah gazed longingly at the cake. "That was a call from the other Mrs. Kaplan. She said that her Mr. Kaplan wouldn't be able to make it this evening, but she'd still be coming around with the children at the same time."

All Devorah could do was shake her head.

"Of course he can't," she said out loud. "Why should I have expected anything else from Yitzhak Kaplan?"

Even God's houses were depressed. The churches and synagogues had joined the other beggars in line for handouts. Yitz had heard plenty about how the Jews supposedly controlled all the money and the banks, but all he saw around Maxwell Street was poverty. Even though Henry Ford had shut down his *Dearborn Independent*—the newspaper he bought so he could spread the idea of some Jewish conspiracy to control everything that had dated back centuries—after threats of boycotts, it was rumored that he was the money behind a million copies of *The Protocols of the Elders of Zion* that had been printed and spread across the United States. They'd had some impact: people Yitz dined with would casually ask him if it was true, if *the Jews* really had *all that power*, like it was some normal topic of conversation. All those educated, well-bred business types he dealt with were actually very stupid. Between that and the things he'd been hearing about what was happening in Germany, Yitz was worried. He wished other people would take things seriously. He'd seen what happened when Jews just waited for the next terrible thing.

"All I'm saying is that you can have my money, but I'd also sleep easier if the shul also accepted my other donation," Yitz said to the rabbi sitting across from him at the table.

The rabbi squirmed uncomfortably in his seat. "Mr. Kaplan," he said. "While we appreciate the thought and your much-needed generosity, the police . . ."

"Police?" Yitz laughed. "Rabbi. You're American-born, correct? Your parents are Bialystockers? I knew your father. A nice man. Very quiet. I heard he was like that with everybody, not just me. But I've spent a lot of time reading into the silence of others, and I know why men like your father didn't say much."

"My father's English was never very good," the rabbi said.

"That's not why. I spoke Yiddish with him, and he was still a man of few words. He didn't say much because he knew not to, that talking could get you in trouble. I knew some people that came over with your parents. They all arrived in '06, after the pogrom when a hundred Jews were killed. The Russian army blamed the start of things on Jewish anarchists. Members of Black Hundreds, who loved the tsar and hated the Jews, saw an opportunity. They *were* the policemen. They didn't help the Jews; they killed them. They raped them and burned their businesses. Now, you might think that can't happen here, but I know for a fact there are plenty of Chicago police officers who are in the Klan, and if they aren't, it's likely they read some of Ford's drivel or they've heard that Jew-hating preacher on the radio. You think *they'll* protect you if things get bad?"

Yitz turned to the stone-faced brute in a double-breasted suit behind him. The big man walked out of the room.

"Take both donations, rabbi. You take one, then you take both. Please don't say no to me about this," Yitz said as the thick man walked back in carrying a steamer chest. He put it on the floor in front of the rabbi.

"I don't even know how to use a gun, Mr. Kaplan," he said.

"Me neither, but I bet you can learn," Yitz said. "You memorized the entire Torah, right? How hard could squeezing a trigger be?"

The rabbi pleaded. He said a shul was nowhere for weapons to be kept.

"If you'd like, I have some friends who would be able to move your, um, donation, to people who truly need it. A cousin of mine is part of the Haganah . . ."

"That's a pipe dream, rabbi. This right here is as close to the Jewish holy land as we're gonna get," Yitz said as he circled his finger in the air. He looked around proudly at the great big synagogue. "And why would I want to schlep to the other side of the world to live in *the desert*? I live *here*. I make my living *here*, in America. I already left one place and have no intentions of leaving here with my tail between my legs."

Yitz got up and walked to the main sanctuary of the synagogue. He was rarely awed, but the polished wooden pews, grand bimah in the middle of the room where the prayers were led from, and the stained glass windows had him looking over the precipice of wonderment. On the opposite end of the long room, the mahogany ark that held the Torah scrolls sat proudly under a pair of gilded Lions of Judah bookending the Ten Commandments. Above the ark lived the centerpiece of the shul, a massive circular window made of kaleidoscopic stained glass with a Magen David in the center. The rabbi caught up and stood beside Yitz as he looked around.

"And to think, this was once a Christian church. That wouldn't have happened in Europe," the rabbi said.

Yitz ignored him and walked toward the wall in the back. There was a brass plaque in it. He read it out loud.

"'From Solomon Kaplan and Yitzhak Kaplan, in memory of their parents and sister. Moshe, Raisel, and Chava. May their memories be a blessing and may their ancestors know their names.'"

Yitz looked at it for a second, then took a handkerchief out of his pocket to wipe a smudge from the brass.

"When I was a boy in Odesa, there was a grand shul like this, but we were too poor to go to it. Now look how things change: I'm paying to help these places renovate, and you know what happened to the big, beautiful synagogue in Odesa my father believed we weren't worthy of? They kicked the Jews out. Put a portrait of Lenin over the

Ten Commandments and call it the Rosa Luxemburg Workers Club now. Isn't that funny?"

The rabbi fumbled his words while searching his brain for some ancient story to connect to the conversation.

"Come on, rabbi. It's *hilarious*," Yitz said with a grin. "Think about it. A Jew writes *The Communist Manifesto*, then he dies in exile; Trotsky, a Jew, helps the Communists get into power and the Bolsheviks kick him out. All these Jews aligned themselves with Communists; the Communists took power and kicked the Jews out of their synagogues. It isn't funny like Buster Keaton, but Buster Keaton's not a Jew. It's the sort of humor Jews have always understood and lived through. *Mann tracht, un Gott lacht*."

Yitz looked at the large man in the double-breasted suit who was standing guard over him.

"Rabbi, my friend here was also born in America. Doesn't speak the *mama loshen*. Can you translate what I said?"

The rabbi muttered, "*Mann tracht, un Gott lacht*, it means—"

Yitz interrupted him. "Man plans and God laughs. Tehillim. Chapter Fifty-nine. I remember some of that stuff."

Yitz looked at his watch and headed for the door. When he got to the bottom of the synagogue's staircase, he looked up at the gray sky.

"I'm back five minutes and it's all meetings," Yitz grumbled as he got in the car. He looked out at the frozen landscape, at the naked trees, snow covering everything, and the hanging icicles that made great weapons that wouldn't leave a trace after use. There was something so calming about it to Yitz. "It's nice to be back," he said.

The good feelings washed away twenty minutes later as Yitz walked into the Schvitz and was told that Lefty Gianino was waiting to see him. In a city of more than three million people, about ten could walk in and say they needed to talk to Yitz and they'd be granted the time of day, and the former welterweight who'd bulked up to a light heavyweight's size since his boxing career ended was one of them. He worked for Paul Ricca, the guy who'd become the big Italian since the feds looked to have finally figured out how to neuter Capone.

"Mr. Ricca needs this wine situation taken care of imm-de-itly," the big lug stuttered. Yitz could never tell if it was from so many hits to the cranium or because the guy was just an idiot.

The whole thing was funny to Yitz: Bunny Berkovitz, a guy who'd started out working for Avi when he was a kid, had exploited a loophole to legally make and sell wine. Bunny had been running his own fencing business for years, but since he was a Jew who lived near Maxwell Street, Ricca and his *paisans* decided he was Yitz's problem.

It was an old trick. The First Amendment's promise against religious discrimination made it so the Eighteenth Amendment couldn't ban Jews from the sacramental wine needed for weekly Shabbat dinner or the Passover seder, so rabbis were allowed to purchase wine and dole out ten gallons a year to every family in their congregation. Bunny couldn't read much English, let alone Hebrew or Aramaic, but he got the government believing he was a rabbi, and he'd rebottle the kosher wine and sell it as imported stuff from France or Italy at a higher price. He'd even enlisted a few guys to help him and had a Black rabbi, two Greeks, three Italians, and a Rabbi Callahan. It wouldn't have been a problem, but one of the bottles made its way into one of Ricca's favorite restaurants. He took one sip and told his men to find out who'd bottled it. Bad gin or whiskey was one thing, but you never tried to put one over on an Italian with his wine.

"Mr. Ricca believes this guy has made at least twelve grand on the wine, which infringes on Mr. Ricca's import business. We understand this Berkovitz fella has a small merchandise business off Halsted which should cover that," Lefty said as he stood up and walked out without saying goodbye.

Yitz chewed on a hangnail for a second. He needed a manicure. He picked up the receiver, asked the operator for Lawndale 2260, and waited a second for Bunny to answer.

"I got something that could be big. It can't wait," Yitz said. "Meet me at that Chinese place on Wentworth in thirty. It's one thirty now and I want to get there before the lunch rush. You ever have chop suey? I'm craving it."

The tongue was long and slimy, but there wasn't a single trace of salt left on it. The blood had been cleaned off completely, and Sol could only smile at what a job he'd done. Some butchers paid off crooked rabbis to let them get away with using cheaper salts to soak up the blood or to look away from slaughtering practices, but Sol was adamant that he used only the strictest *bodek* to inspect every muscle and tendon that he put in his case. The old rabbi he hired literally used a jeweler's eye to go over every rib and cut of brisket. Sol didn't want a single person saying he didn't sell the best kosher meat in Chicago.

He was about to finish wrapping the tongue for the old lady on the other side of the counter when Devorah opened the front door so hard that the bell above it almost flew off. Sol greeted his wife, but she didn't answer as she walked behind his side of the counter, mumbling angrily as she took out a few cuts of beef and put them on the table. Sol thanked the customer he was helping and went to his wife.

"Your brother," she snapped. "He makes me go all that way to get him fish from the ocean because lake trout isn't good enough for him, and now he can't even make it to dinner. He always does this. I don't know why I expected him to even show up in the first place. How can you two be from the same mother?"

Sol could only smile. He'd heard his wife get angry about Yitz so many times that it felt like a routine. He took the meat she pulled from the case and started to cut into it, giving her the fatty pieces that she loved, as she ranted. He listened while he cut, never taking his eyes off the beef he was holding with one hand and the knife he had in the other. By the time he was done slicing off the chuck steaks and finished wrapping them, Devorah had calmed down.

She asked him how he did it.

"Practice. Training. I watched my father do it when I was a boy," Sol said.

Devorah laughed. He was good at making her do that. Such a sweet man. How she got such a lovely husband, especially when he was related to a criminal, was so hard for her to understand.

"How do you always stay so calm? That's what I meant," Devorah said.

Sol handed her the beef wrapped in white paper. He took his knife and started to clean it as he thought about an answer, but he could only repeat himself. "Practice. Training. I watched my father do it when I was a boy," he said with a smile. "Besides, what do I have to be in such a hurry for?"

Yitz was back on Maxwell Street by 3:00. The stench and frantic pace felt like home to him. Every person he passed said hello to him as he walked to Izzy the Trout's fish shop. The two old friends embraced, but the fish man was obviously nervous.

"Mr. Hollywood," Izzy said.

Yitz grinned. "I need something from you, Iz. Tonight."

Izzy stood motionless. He tried to speak, but the only thing he could say was "OK" and "Yes." He had hoped the moment wouldn't come. He had prayed the moment wouldn't come.

Izzy had gone to Yitz a year earlier with grand plans to take his stand and turn it into a store. He'd heard about how in New York there were shops that sold just fish. He said they were selling chubs, kapchunka, salmon pickled herring—the Jews *and* the gentiles loved it. Izzy had been catching whitefish in the lake that his mother said was as good as the kind she'd had when she was a girl in Chornobyl, and he'd learned to cure trout that he could catch by the barrelful on a good day of fishing. He'd be the first person in Chicago to open one of those shops, and all he needed was another $5,000. Yitz told him that even though they'd been friends for years, $5,000 still carried interest. But also, since they were old pals, he knocked it down from ten points to six. Even with that, Izzy had a hard time keeping up payments. The fish shop wasn't catching on, but he swore it would. Yitz chastised him, but also showed pity. He told him they'd work something out. That put Izzy's mind at ease until the moment he saw Yitz walk into the store that afternoon.

"Right now, with the interest, you're almost back where you started," Yitz said as he poked a dead fish in the eyeball with his finger. "I put it on hold, but these are hard times for everybody. I need you to take care of this debt."

"Of course. And I promise, I'll do whatever . . ."

Yitz held up a hand. "I know. I got a real easy way for this to be all done. Real simple."

There was a truck at Yitz's brother's garage near his butcher shop. That night, all Izzy had to do was pick it up and drive it to a warehouse on Harrison. Twenty minutes of his time and the big debt would be cleared. He'd follow behind another truck. Jerry Knish would be driving it. Yitz asked if Izzy knew who that was.

Izzy the Trout said he didn't, but he was lying. Everybody around Maxwell Street knew Jerry Knish. Most recently, word was that he was responsible for the slaying of a small-time boxing promoter whose body had been found facedown in a pile of half-melted snow with two dozen stab wounds around his chest and stomach.

"I'll even have a car waiting to pick you up and drop you back to your home," Yitz said as he put on a pair of leather gloves. "Beautiful, right?"

Izzy the Trout nodded and croaked a yes.

"You sound like you need a drink," Yitz said. He walked over to the sink and filled a glass with brown, lukewarm water that he handed to his friend on the way out.

Sol had broken down the hindquarters of the steer in no time. The modern equipment made things move faster, but he hated the way convenience felt like one final disrespect to the animal beneath the blade. The nature of his profession had never bothered him before. The blood, bits of muscle, and chunks of bone were part of a process. His father had done it, and his father before him had as well. But Sol had been taught when he was an apprentice that one of the things that separated the Jews from the gentiles was meat. The *shochet* had to study before he could pick up the knife. And when he did finally get to do his job, when he picked up the *chalif* with its long rectangular blade, he'd have to run his fingernail along its edge to make sure there wasn't the slightest chip. Even the slightest imperfection meant the knife couldn't be used. There was a rule for everything, even how one sliced the trachea and esophagus of the beast in a swift motion following the same laws that had been followed for centuries. He had to be present for every moment of the ritual; the slightest slip or mistake, the smallest pause, could render the animal unkosher.

Back in Odesa, Sol's father did the entire thing, from the *shechita*—the slaughtering—to the inspection of the animal's dead body, the removing of the veins and tendons that was *halakha*, and the kashering of the meat by drawing out all the blood with kosher salt. Then his father would break down the carcass, all of it by hand, a special relationship between the man and the meat, nothing like the workers at the stock houses who killed endlessly without giving it a single thought. The men on the Chicago killing floors were employed to be part of a *process*; Sol took part in a *ritual*, and he used his hands for it. But the new equipment and the promise of even better technology not far off to make it easier for the "modern" kosher butcher to do more in less time made Sol wonder if he was committing some sort of sin. He could admit that he wasn't the most learned man, but he'd always found time to study and was certain the old rabbis in Jerusalem and Babylonia didn't have a bandsaw you only had to push the meat toward with a little effort in mind when they were debating the Torah.

When he looked up at the clock, Sol realized he had been thinking about the right and wrong of slaughtering cows for ten minutes. It was time for a walk when his mind began to wander. He took off his white coat, hung it on the hanger, then walked to the front. He told the two workers behind the counter he'd be back in fifteen. They knew the boss liked to take walks, but that was about it. He didn't talk to them much, never told them anything about himself save for the things he'd learned on the job. They knew who his brother was. They assumed things and talked about how lucky they were to be working for Sol Kaplan, because that meant they were connected to Yitz. Sol knew they talked about it, a couple of the guys even placed bets with Yitz's bookies, but he never interrupted their private conversations about his brother to correct them and say Kapovitch Sons Kosher Meats and Sausage was his business. He was quiet around his workers, but he treated them well and always paid them on time. That was all that mattered.

Sol stepped into a strand of sunlight. The wind blew the smoke from the factories his way. The little bit of light felt like a miracle on such a cold day. Chicago often felt dark, but especially in the wintertime. He'd always wondered if it was the same way everywhere in America, and dreamed of finding out someday. He was thinking of taking his family on a trip the following year. Perhaps Wisconsin or toward the Catskill Mountains out east. He'd heard the quality of kosher meat out there was outstanding and the air was fresh. His daydreaming of America's spacious skies, amber waves of grain, and majestic purple mountains was interrupted by a familiar voice.

"Look at the boychick with his eyes toward the sky."

Sol turned his head to the left and saw his brother. He was so overcome with emotion that he wrapped his arms around Yitz and lifted him off his feet with a hug.

"I didn't come here to have my ribs broken," Yitz said as Sol put him back down.

"You look like you've gotten into shape," Sol said as he looked his brother over. "But you're still pale as a dumpling."

Yitz rubbed his stomach. "I eat a lot of grapefruit. One every morning, usually with toast and cottage cheese. I have an egg or two for lunch, and that's it. The only decent place I've found out there to eat is this steak house called Musso and Frank. The rib eye there is like heaven."

"Is it kosher?"

"Kosher? Of course. Musso is short for Mussoberg. Frank's last name is Cohen. Mussoberg is a descendent of the Baal Shem Tov and Frank is the wise man from Chelm," Yitz said. His brother wasn't great at catching sarcasm.

"Really?"

"Solly. Come on. You know I don't care about that stuff," Yitz said just as he noticed the yarmulke on his brother's head and was reminded that his brother had rediscovered the practices and beliefs Yitz had left back in Odesa.

"Have you seen Leah since you've been back?"

Yitz winced. He told his brother he had hoped to but had to get back to California as soon as he wrapped up a few things.

"I don't even have a lot of time today as it is, but I've come to personally deliver some good news," he added.

"*Nu?* Go on. Tell me, Yitzhak. What's with the suspense? You wait too long, and the messiah will come and bring the cow I'm working on back to life," Sol said.

Yitz licked his thumb and bent over. He rubbed a piece of dirt off the sole of his oxford, then stood back up slowly. He'd always loved driving his little brother crazy.

"OK," he said. "I'll tell you."

"Yes?"

"Say please."

"Yitz . . ."

"Sol."

"Yitzhak ben Yeshayahu, *please* tell me your news."

"Very well . . ."

Sol huffed and turned to walk away.

"Fine. Fine. I'm selling the trucks," Yitz said.

"You mean . . ."

Yitz nodded.

"No more with the transport? That's it?"

"That's it. They'll be taken from your garage and dropped off to the new owner this evening. A guy I know in the wine business," Yitz said.

Sol couldn't believe it. He had often entertained the idea that all it was going to take was one time for a police officer who didn't know any better to pull over a truck with the name of Sol's business on the side, and that was it. He'd be ruined. Yitz told him that would never happen, but his brother hadn't been so sure. Sol could also never kick the feeling that the introduction of those trucks marked the beginning of a change in Yitz. Maybe getting rid of them would offer a correction to the way things had been.

"*Baruch Hashem*," Sol said.

"Thank God? *Baruch Yitz!* Thank me! I did this, you ass."

"Yes. You as well."

"I just had lunch with the buyer. My men will likely be by when you close. Have one of your guys take them around to the garage and open it up. Then it'll be done. All finished. And I'll stop by and see you soon. Save me a nice piece of flanken," Yitz said as he took a step to start walking away. His brother grabbed him by the shoulder.

"Our parents would be proud of the man you've become," Sol said. "A mensch in America."

Yitz was unmoved. He looked down at the ground.

"I spend a lot of time doing nothing by myself out in Los Angeles. Just a lot of time to think. And you know what's funny? My life, all this, it's because of you," he said.

Sol told him to stop being silly, that his brother had worked hard. But Yitz disagreed.

"Everything started with Willy Porter in the woods. You did what you had to do, but the way you did it, the way you didn't want anybody knowing it was you . . ."

"Willy Porter was basically finished," Sol said with a disgusted shake of his head.

"*Basically* finished isn't *finished. You* stuck that piece of wood through his neck. *You* did what I couldn't do. *You* had to take care of it for me and I'm the one that got the reputation."

Sol looked down. He cleared his throat. There was nothing he could say. He tried to not think about that day that felt like a million years in the past. He knew that he'd taken a different path from his brother, but remained haunted by the thought of that frozen afternoon in the middle of a patch of wild land that had long since been cleared to make way for more buildings. He didn't hold anything against Yitz—how could he? Everything his brother did, all the work, the decisions he made, the terror a yes or no from him could cause . . . Sol decided years earlier that wasn't his business. But he also knew that if it wasn't for all his brother had to do, then Sol wouldn't have anything. No business, no family, nothing. The only reason he could stay afloat after the market crash was because of Yitz's help. Sol knew it was dirty money, but he never said a word about it. Things that were unspoken were that way for a reason, and Sol made peace with the fact that their relationship would always be the way things were, even if the two brothers made it to old age together. Hearing Yitz talk of the man in the woods brought a rush of emotions Sol wasn't prepared for, so he stood there trying not to say anything, holding it all back.

Yitz looked up at the sky. The clouds had come and covered up the sun. He threw his cigarette at the ground. "Nobody here knows you've always been the brave one." He put his hand on his brother's cheek, smiled, and walked to the car that was waiting for him.

Izzy the Trout stopped into shul to get closer to God before he walked over to the butcher shop. He had no idea what he had gotten himself into, but the only conclusion he could draw was it was illegal. Booze, guns, or something worse. All that he could hope for was that it was over quick, and he could return to his store the next day with all his limbs, a man free of debt.

He arrived at the butcher shop at 6:30 exactly as the second hand on the clock passed the 12. He found Sol Kaplan, scrubbing soap over his walnut-sized knuckles, trying to get the last of the bovine blood off his hands. He turned and looked confused when he saw Izzy.

"Didn't expect him to send you for something like this," Sol said.

"Like what, exactly? I wasn't given too much information."

"Relax, Iz," Sol said as he poured a small shot of vodka and handed it over. He'd known the guy long enough to understand how nervous a request from his brother probably made Izzy even if it was harmless. A little l'chaim would stop his hands from shaking.

"The other guy coming? I need to close up," Sol said.

"He should be here by now," Izzy the Trout said.

Sol looked up at the clock. "Yitz told me Jerry Knish was driving the other truck. He's ten minutes late. He used to drive these trucks all the time and was always early. It's not like him."

Jerry Knish wasn't coming. He'd gotten too comfortable in an opium den on Twenty-fifth Street and fallen asleep, but nobody except the lady handing him the pipe knew that.

Sol and Izzy waited ten more minutes until Sol said he'd drive the other truck. Izzy asked if he could just call his brother. Hopefully he'd postpone the whole plan, but that was exactly what Sol didn't want.

"It'll take at least an hour or two to get somebody else, and I've got to lock up. I sent my boys home already. Besides, I've been waiting to get rid of these damn things for a long time. Knowing Yitz, if it doesn't happen tonight then he'll make me wait another year or two. I'll just drive it. If I'm twenty minutes late then Devorah won't be too mad. I'm sure the soup will still be warm when I get home."

Sol knew where they were going and said he'd take the lead. A calm came over Izzy knowing Yitz's brother was leading the way. Sol was a good man. He loved his wife and kids, and everybody in the community talked of what an upstanding man he was. A real mensch. The Meat Macher of Maxwell. Thick flakes of snow started to die against the windshield. As Izzy watched where the other truck turned into a warehouse on Harrison, he felt better. A good snow always made him happy.

He pulled the truck up behind the one Sol was in and killed the engine. He just sat there for a second before he noticed a sound to the right of the warehouse. He strained his eyes to see and could make out the front of a car facing the street; the little puddles of rain that had collected on its black hood caught just enough of a nearby light that he could tell what it was. The headlights were off, but the engine was on. Izzy hopped out of the truck and walked toward it to get a better look, but stopped when he heard Sol call out, "Is that Bunny Berkovitz? I haven't seen you in ages!"

He looked inside the warehouse and could see Sol talking with somebody. He was laughing. Suddenly, everything was peaceful and still for a moment. Izzy looked around at the virgin snow covering the naked trees and the sidewalks; he started to smile, then looked to his right and saw a man running from where the car was parked to the first truck. He threw something in it, looked at Izzy, and yelled, "Run!"

The word was so simple to understand. And yet Izzy would spend the rest of his life wondering why instinct didn't kick in and he didn't do what the man said, why it took him an extra second or two or five or ten—he didn't know how many. It felt like a lifetime when he looked back on it, the moments between the man yelling to run and the explosion that threw Izzy's body backward in the air and knocked him on the ground. He looked up and saw thick snowflakes had started falling again, then everything went to black.

Yitz couldn't even close his eyes for a second that night. He spent the night behind his desk at the Schvitz, getting up every so often to mutter to himself, trying to think up any possible outcome, no matter how plausible or far-fetched. He hadn't heard back about the thing with Bunny and the truck like he was supposed to. He called Jerry Knish but didn't hear back. He rang White Jimmy nine times between 11:15 and 3:00. Finally, at 5:00, he walked over to the sink in the room and splashed his face with some cold water. He needed protein. Some eggs. Toast would also help. Coffee for sure. "Thank God," he said as he found his pants neatly folded on a hanger. He had a few clean shirts hanging in the closet, and he plucked a gray tie off the rack. Then there was the watch, a new addition to his wardrobe. He almost forgot his wristwatch; he often left home without it, and breaking that habit had become a minor concern in a life filled with countless major ones.

It was black outside. He walked a few feet, then came upon a frozen man lying with his head against a wall. He'd likely fallen asleep drunk; it happened often in Chicago during the winter, and enterprising locals who acted fast enough could snatch up his body and sell it to a local medical school for a nice profit. He stepped around the body and walked up the block until he saw a newsboy carrying his stack of papers to the corner to start his day. The kid put the bundle down and, before he could undo the string around them, Yitz put three cents in his ink-stained little hand. He pulled a paper out for himself and looked at the front page. Right there next to the news of a blizzard killing some folks in Minnesota, "Building Explosion on South Side." He scanned it and saw the name of the street, Harrison. Six bodies pulled from the rubble, "one confirmed was bootlegger Chaim Berkovitz, better known as Bunny Berkovitz."

He let himself feel sorry about it for a second, then reminded himself that he had no choice. Bunny dug his own grave, and it was a matter of time before somebody kicked his carcass into it; but when you crossed the Sicilians, everybody had to see a big, gaping hole where Bunny's business had been as a sign not to try to do the same. That was how things were done. The Italians had their ways, and even if he didn't agree with them, Yitz had to abide with the laws.

Yitz sat down at Middleberg's counter and ordered a coffee from Zederbaum, the stumpy Litvak with the long beard and tiny glasses who worked the morning shift. He knew just enough English to ask orders and every word that started with a *w* was replaced with a *v*.

251

"You vant eggs? How you vant done?" he asked Yitz.

Yitz nodded. "Do you have any kasha left? Can I get a side of that? Cut some apple into it."

The old man rolled his eyes like Yitz was pulling his leg. "Yes, kasha. You vant juice? Kvass?"

"Orange."

"No kvass?"

"I don't need a cold glass of bread," Yitz said.

The old man walked away shaking his head and grumbling. Yitz opened the newspaper to "Little Orphan Annie." His food was in front of him a few moments later. He got one bite in his mouth, then a little girl ran into the restaurant.

"Uncle Yitzhak," she said frantically. It was Sol's oldest. Yitz forgot her name. He confused his brother's kids. He guessed Rachel, but she didn't confirm whether he was right or wrong. Instead, she kept speaking frantically. "My mother is looking for you. She said she's been trying to call you at work. They said to check here." She paused to catch her breath. Before Yitz could ask what was wrong, she kept going. "It's Papa. He didn't come home last night."

Yitz assured the girl that everything was fine and sent her home. He went to use the phone in the back at Middleberg's to call Stern Benny, whose real name was Benjamin Stern, but there was already a guy named Benny Stern as well as a Ben Sternberg, so when Benjamin Stern showed up one day, somebody just gave him the new name on the spot. He was the guy that decided on things like how to handle the Bunny situation, but Yitz never was the one to talk to him. He'd tell White Jimmy, who'd relay the message to somebody, then that person relayed it to whoever made the arrangements for how things were carried out. That's why Stern Benny sounded surprised when he heard the voice on the other end. Yitz never talked to him, and it was terrifying to hear his voice. Stern Benny stuttered through the conversation, said it had been taken care of, but there was a problem.

"The guy you sent, salmon or whitefish . . ."

"Izzy. Izzy the Trout."

"Yeah, right. He got hurt bad. He's in a coma."

"What happened?"

"The guy who threw the grenade in the truck said he didn't hear to run. Got blasted back about five feet. But Yitz, there's more . . ."

Yitz's throat started to close.

"Jerry Knish was in the other truck. He was inside the garage when everything went up," Stern Benny said, adding a series of apologies and a "May his memory be a blessing."

Yitz had known Jerry Knish for a long time. Never in a million years would he have ever thought he'd find himself smiling at the news of his death. He was relieved.

"That's . . . that's awful," he said. "We'll figure something out for his wife. What was he doing in there? He was supposed to drop the truck off and walk away, right?"

"I was very clear about that. I said load the one with the explosives in the back just far enough into the garage and walk away fast. It was supposed to be timed. They were supposed to turn off the engines then walk away within thirty seconds. We've done this before."

Yitz hung up. He walked back to his breakfast and dipped his finger into the kasha to measure the temperature. It was cold. No matter, his appetite was gone. Something strange was going on.

When he got back to the Schvitz, White Jimmy was waiting for him. Izzy the Trout had woken up. The doctors said he'd make a full recovery, but he was having a hard time putting words together and would probably stay that way for a few days.

The phone rang. Yitz looked at it and took a deep breath. It rang again.

"You're going to pick that up," he told White Jimmy. "It's going to be Sol's wife. Tell her I went to deal with something near Uptown and you don't know when I'll be back."

He was right. Yitz could hear Devorah's voice on the other end. She was hysterical. White Jimmy said he'd tell Yitz to call her as soon as he got back, hung up, then followed Yitz out the door.

In the twenty-five minutes it took to get from the Schvitz to the hospital, Yitz once again found himself running down possible scenarios. His biggest worry was that some small-timers nabbed Sol and were going to deliver a note to Yitz saying they wanted money for his brother's safe return. That had become a big business as of late, nobodies looking to make a few bucks and a name for themselves kidnapping. The problem with small-timers was they could get sloppy, and people ended up dead even once the ransom money was delivered. Word through the grapevine was the Kraut carpenter they'd fingered for the Lindbergh baby thing was just an unlucky mark, and that it was a crew of schmucks from Trenton who didn't know what they were doing, and one of them dropped the kid from the window as they were nabbing him. Yitz could believe it. People were getting desperate.

But Sol wasn't a baby. It would take three guys to nab him. He was thick and strong, not to mention he had countless sharp objects around him he knew how to use if they grabbed him in the butcher shop, and Yitz knew he carried a little pistol around his ankle because he was the one that did the nightly bank deposits.

They ended up at Cook County Hospital, walking up two flights of stairs to Izzy the Trout's room, where they gently nudged him awake. He was startled when he opened his eyes. Yitz tried to calm him down, telling him he did good and that everything was taken care of, but he wanted to know what happened. Izzy's eyes started to water. He tried to speak but had a hard time muttering even a single syllable.

"It's OK, Iz," Yitz said. "Everything is taken care of. I just gotta know what Jerry Knish was doing in there. Was it an accident? Was he taking a leak or something?"

Izzy the Trout looked confused. He shook his head slightly and whispered "No" as he tried to wave his finger. "No Knish," he said, but couldn't bring himself to say any more.

Yitz shot up and rushed right out the door. He asked a nurse which way to the deadhouse. He could only come up with the colloquial name, but the lady knew what he meant. Everybody knew the city morgue, where the dead bodies of the last decade piled up day after day. Yitz seemed to know how to get there almost instinctually, White Jimmy followed behind. After multiple turns, one flight of stairs up, three more turns, then two flights down, they arrived at the desk where a young blond nurse sat looking over paperwork.

"You have a John Doe," Yitz muttered.

The nurse raised her eyebrows.

"We've got about twenty guys by that name on any given day, sweetie. You need to be more specific," she said.

Yitz could hardly say the words. "Explosion. Harrison. Couple of guys . . ."

She looked down at a sheet of paper, then flipped to another before excusing herself. Another minute or two or maybe a week went by. When the nurse came back, a man in a white jacket followed. The man led Yitz down what felt like an endless hallway. The echoes of feet hitting marble played like a dirge. The man opened a door and turned on a light. Four corpses under four sheets were lying there. A smell hit Yitz's nose. It was a wicked perfume of burnt flesh along with some mixture of chemicals. Vomit shot right from his mouth.

"Sorry," the man in the white coat said flatly. "I should have warned you." He walked to the first corpse. "This one is the worst. Do you need a moment?"

Yitz shook his head. The man pulled the sheet back. It took a second, but Yitz recognized what was left of the face. It was Bunny Berkovitz. All his hair was gone, and it looked as if his lips had melted off. But he saw the scar on his neck from a broken bottle some guy had run across it once.

Yitz said he didn't recognize the corpse.

The man walked to the second body and peeled the sheet from his face. Yitz couldn't have recognized the man with what was left of him, but he was too short. The third body was so tall that the sheet only went to its ankles. The man in the white coat removed it, and there he was, the person Yitz had watched come into the world as a bloody baby on the floor of their old home in Odesa. He looked so peaceful. There were no burns or blood. It seemed impossible.

"How did it happen? It can't . . ." Yitz struggled to find the words. He held his hand to his mouth. "How did he die?"

The man looked at a chart. He was unmoved by the whole situation.

"Smoke inhalation. It's likely he was trapped when the explosion happened, but it says here his knuckles were bruised and bloody and he had wood splinters all under his fingernails like he was trying to get out. He put up a good fight, but the smoke was too much. His lungs couldn't take it."

Pulling his brother's huge hand from underneath the sheet, Yitz held it for a second before flipping it over to confirm what the man had said. He rubbed Sol's wounds gently for a moment.

"He was always the tough one," Yitz muttered. "Everybody thought it was me . . ." He placed the hand back under the sheet, wiped the tears from his eyes, then said he'd be taking the body within the hour.

"I can't let you do that. There's an investigation . . ."

"Fine," Yitz said as he took out a roll of cash. "Investigate. You investigate these men over here. But he will receive a proper burial today," he said as he handed the man in the white coat a hundred-dollar bill.

"Mister, I can't. I'll lose my—"

"You'll lose your *fucking legs*," Yitz snapped. He got control of himself and continued. "One hour. I will have men here to take him away and you will be on your break. This is just another John Doe to you. In your records, he's in the pit you throw all the others in. Got it?"

The man in the white coat said nothing. Yitz commanded White Jimmy to get Sol's body away from the others. "Nobody except us knows about this for now. Got that?"

White Jimmy snarled at the man in the white coat to help move Sol's body off the slab and onto an embalming table, then rolled him out. Yitz stayed behind with the corpses. The sick smell of chemicals and multiple ways of dying mixed in the air, but he didn't even notice. "You motherfucker," Yitz whispered as he tore a hole in his shirt. "You haven't taken enough from me?"

It was the first time Yitzhak Kaplan had talked to God since he was a boy in Odesa.

Everything was in place before the sun fell and Shabbos started. Sol's body was washed and placed in a plain wooden coffin. When Yitz arrived, White Jimmy and one of the Berman brothers were waiting for him. He was joined by a rabbi and a group of shuffling elderly men wearing yarmulkes who were there to help round out the quorum of ten men necessary for a Jewish funeral. They kvetched in Yiddish and shivered as they bunched together near an open grave. Somebody whispered, "Oh, God." Everybody looked behind them and saw an ashen-faced Jerry Knish, the cold-blooded killer, slowly and nervously walking toward them. White Jimmy rushed over and said something to him. Jerry Knish nodded solemnly and started walking. The rumor that went around town was he walked a mile in the cold, then another. He walked to the train station and asked for a ticket for the next northbound train. Nobody ever saw him on Maxwell Street again after that.

The men recited the Mourner's Kaddish before White Jimmy and the Berman brother each took turns shoveling some dirt onto the coffin. Nobody asked where Sol's wife and children were.

When it was Yitz's turn to toss earth onto the humble wooden box holding his brother's corpse, he crept toward the grave, picked up the shovel, threw one heaping of dirt on top, then another, and another, and another.

"You son of a bitch," he shouted. "What the hell were you doing there? Who told you to go? You were supposed to be at home. This wasn't meant for you."

Yitz stopped shoveling for a second. He tried to bury the blade of the shovel, but the ground was so frozen that it barely made a dent. Yitz gripped the long handle with both hands and swung it like a baseball bat against a tree. He shouted out in pain before slamming it against the trunk a second and third time. He dropped the shovel, turned around, and looked at the rabbi.

"I want a crypt built around my plots. Whatever has to be done, I'll take care of it. I want it done in two weeks. Money is no object," he calmly said as he fixed his hair with the hand that was obviously injured. He walked to his car. White Jimmy followed and started driving.

They drove toward the lake, to a place not far from the old Palace of Fine Arts, left over from Daniel Burnham's White City for the

Columbian Exposition of 1893. Julius Rosenwald, co-owner of Sears, Roebuck and Co., had spent nearly five million dollars of his own money on repurposing it into a museum of science and industry.

It was nighttime. Snow was falling again. Yitz told White Jimmy to keep the car running to stay warm, saying he'd only be a few minutes. He walked out toward the water and disappeared into the dark within seconds. White Jimmy waited five minutes, then ten, and fifteen. After twenty he got out of the car and called Yitz's name but didn't get a response. He walked out a little farther and yelled again but didn't hear anything back. The wind was whipping ferociously from what felt like all directions. The little bit of moisture on White Jimmy's eyeballs felt like it was turning to ice, so he got back in the car, turned on the headlights, and started driving toward the beach in hopes of finding his boss.

Chicago is a city of legends; of Mrs. O'Leary's cow supposedly kicking over a lantern and starting the Great Fire of 1871, the Devil Baby of Hull House, or Resurrection Mary, the ghost in all white, hitchhiking her way to nowhere on Archer Avenue. But on the frozen night after Yitz buried his brother, a handful of people around the Near South Side reported hearing the same deathly wail around the same time, not long after the day had turned to night. It ended up a small item on the *Tribune* two days later, one man claiming it was the ghosts of dead soldiers who were killed in the Battle of Fort Dearborn back in 1812, while another, more skeptical man who worked overnight security at Soldier Field said he heard it, but claimed it was "just Hawkins," making it the first known use of the nickname of the city's infamously cruel winds. It was just the Hawk and nothing else.

The next morning, Yitz sat in the living room of the house Sol had bought with the idea that he'd continue to grow his family and his life with Devorah. Yitz recalled how it had always been filled with warmth and love inside thanks to his brother's adoration of his wife and kids; now it was dark and unwelcoming. There was a feeling of everything being put in a certain place, as if somebody had prepared the home for the coming of tragic news. There were no signs somebody was sitting shiva; none of the low stools that mourners sat on or curtains at the ready to drape over the mirrors. Nobody wanted to tempt the evil eye, after all.

Devorah walked into the room carrying a tray with a teapot and two glasses on it. Yitz liked his tea with a little milk and honey the way his father drank it in Odesa, but he learned early that taking it that way was a sure way to let people think you were a greenhorn. He thanked his sister-in-law and took it black.

She poured herself a cup and sat down. The steam drifted up past her face. There was a clock ticking somewhere that was driving Yitz mad.

"Maybe he was overworked or something. It could be a temporary thing," Yitz said. "Men snap sometimes. Could be he just needed to get something out of his system."

Devorah narrowed her eyes. "I suppose that's a family trait."

Sol had never muttered even a single bad word about his wife. He loved his Devorah, doted over her, made sure she had everything and more. Yet with her brother-in-law, she was an absolute *balabusta*. Yitz found comfort for a second sitting there when he realized that his mother would have respected the woman Sol had married, but the comfort died quickly as Devorah put her cup of tea on the table in front of her, stood up, and tore at her dress. Tears were streaming down her face, but she wasn't sobbing; they just fell from her eyes. She had the same look she'd had throughout their talk, one of steely resolve and a deep hatred that Yitz only at that moment realized was all for him.

"If what you have told me is true and he has run off with some shiksa, then that's one thing. But I don't think you told me the truth. You're a liar, Yitzhak. My Sol is a good man. He's happy and I know you are lying to me. I know about this explosion and how they found his trucks there. You're a coward, Yitzhak. A coward! All I want is to know where my husband is!"

Control the breath. That was something Avi had taught Yitz. People could see if your breathing speeds up and it's a sign of nerves. Don't blink. Don't give her anything. Yitz had always been great at doing what he'd been taught, but at that second, when he needed it most, he lost control. There was a voice in his head that wasn't his; it was Avi's, then it was Sol's. Yitz couldn't make out what they were saying; it was a muffled scream, a static in his brain, but he could tell it was them. On the outside, all he could do was take a deep, quiet breath that pushed the muscles in his face that were holding back tears to their limit, but Yitz couldn't stop the slightest tremble that gave everything away. Devorah had all the proof she needed. She shook her head and muttered a curse that sounded dredged up from a gutter. Something about a ball of cancer the size of a balloon growing inside Yitz's stomach. Then she spit. "*You* are dead to me," she said with a calmness that Yitz had only heard from men who took money to kill other men. "Your family is dead to me and my family," she said as she tore another part of her dress. "Let your children know and let their children and all the children after them know you are a murderer! I hope all your descendants suffer for what you've done. You wicked man!"

She screamed for him to get out. Yitz stood up and put on his hat. He took another deep breath; it was measured and stable. The voices were gone. "When I find out where my brother is, I will let you know first," he said as he turned around and walked out without looking back. "I promise."

261

At the same moment Yitz was walking out of the home his brother once lived in, Izzy the Trout was walking out of the hospital with White Jimmy and into a sedan that had been sent for him. They told him to sit in the front seat. In the back was a horrible sight. Aharon the Golem sat silently.

Izzy couldn't muster the strength to yell and didn't have the energy to run, and even if he could, he was too in shock. There was no way what he thought was happening was taking place. He got into the car quietly, almost falling into his seat. White Jimmy started the car and they drove east toward the lake. When they got there, as the Golem marched him out toward a part of the water that wasn't frozen over, Izzy the Trout asked for one moment. He wanted to imagine himself and where he'd be in just a few seconds. Izzy's last thought before the Golem fired two bullets into the back of his skull was how funny it would be if somebody went fishing and ended up catching him. What a prize he'd make, was his final thought before he hurtled into the void.

Later that night, his store burned down. The insurance for the building was in Yitzhak Kaplan's name.

15

Elijah found Eve sitting at the table reading the latest issue of the *Atlantic*. He sat down and didn't waste any time launching into the whole crazy story. He told her about how her father owed Jerry the Fox, and how it was Foxman who'd told Elijah the story that some old family money was supposedly buried somewhere. Before she could say anything, he said he knew it sounded nuts, but he'd also been spending some time doing research of his own, and he'd located three more people directly related to both Yitzhak and Solomon, and even several more relatives of James White's. He said he wanted to cut them all in on the sale of the property up north, but also give them a portion of the gold in the mausoleum. One of White's descendants, a great-great-granddaughter, was an Afghanistan war vet, single mom, and vice principal who lived twenty minutes away. Elijah had found her on a genealogy site message board after hours of searching, and decided the story she wrote about the James White she was related to fit the profile. They all deserved something, he said. And so did

Jerry the Fox—no matter what, he deserved what he'd been owed all those years.

"I also want to give some to the Hebrew Benevolent Society, help clean it up. We should take care of it."

Elijah explained his idea, but convincing his mother to agree wasn't necessary. The smile on her face told him everything he needed to know.

"This all sounds absolutely crazy," she said. "Maybe stupid. Honestly? I haven't heard something this wild out of your mouth since you told me you wanted to stop going to college so you could start opening overpriced hostels with those criminal partners of yours."

Eve's hand hovered over the vape pen on the table for a second. She didn't pick it up, and decided to put both hands on the table, one resting on top of the other. She continued talking.

"The one thing I ask is you should make it quick. I've been talking with Grace, and she's willing to let us move Devorah's remains in there to be next to Sol's."

"Who's Grace?"

"One of our relatives I found online and . . ."

Elijah glared at his mother. How had she known? She shrugged.

"I was bored and started doing research a few years back on one of those DNA sites. I met this lady named Grace, a descendant of Sol's and a really sweet woman. We'd had our guesses what happened to him, but we were both wrong. When you told me, I messaged her and told her I'd found out what I should have known the whole time."

Elijah asked what that was. Eve looked down at her hands, shook her head, and started to chuckle to herself.

"Maybe if I'd answered that rabbi's letters then I would have figured it out faster, but there was something holding me back. I really figured you'd find out about it after I was gone and I wouldn't have to die worrying you were just going to sell it off to make a quick buck. So if I wanted to put my aunt's old bones back in there so they could be next to my uncle's skeleton the way they should have been, then I couldn't judge you for wanting to at least know what or who is in that unmarked grave in there."

Things had ceased making sense to Elijah since he'd been back in Chicago, and saying anything else just felt like wasted air. But he was curious, and they'd both laid things out on the table, so he asked his mother about Devorah Kaplan. He understood why she'd want to move her body to be with Solomon's. What he couldn't quite get was why it felt like a necessary endeavor in her own dying days.

Eve unfolded her hands and went right for the emerald-colored vape pen before answering. She took a hit and put it down. Elijah picked it up and sucked a pull of whatever vaporized strain of weed was in there, partially because he needed it, but also because it felt nice to share something with his mother in the moment.

"You shouldn't do drugs," Eve joked.

They both laughed for a second, and when it died down, she started explaining her reasons. It was all very simple, she said.

"Devorah came to visit me, this was a few years before you were born. She was so old, but she looked even older than I assumed she was, like she'd lived a full century of misery. She just showed up here one day, knocking at the door, this tiny Jewish woman. I had absolutely no idea who she was. Her head was covered with a shawl that was all tattered, and she was in all black. Now when I think about it, I can't help but think it was like she went to a funeral years earlier and never left the cemetery until she showed up at my door. She explained who she was and I invited her inside. I'd never seen anybody so broken down by life, and it really affected me—then and now. I wasn't sure what to say to this person, so I let her talk, and she told me this story. This horrible, awful long story about our family, my father, and her husband. Then she started to cry. She begged me to tell her where her husband was. I tried to tell her I'd never even heard of him until she told me her story, but she didn't believe me. She flew into this rage, this broken little woman was all of a sudden possessed. She was speaking in Yiddish or tongues or maybe both, and she said something about how she cursed my father and all his children, then left. It was . . ."

"Jesus. That's traumatic. *I'm* going have nightmares," Elijah said, shaking his head in disbelief.

"That's why I need to do this. Because it's righting a wrong, but also because I don't know what to expect when I finally go, maybe it's nothing. But I don't want her waiting for me, and I don't want her haunting you when I'm no longer around. So you can think wanting to give people their inheritance is strange, but I've got you beat with my little ghost story."

Eve was shaking. It was like she'd attempted an exorcism on herself by telling Elijah so much, but the ghoul still had a grip on her soul. Elijah knew there was no point to even try to say anything. Instead, he stood up, walked over behind his mother, and put his hand on her shoulder. It was instinct, not something he'd ever done before. His ex always brought it up when they tried couples therapy, how Elijah seemed almost totally incapable of physical intimacy, how she could almost have dealt with how emotionally unavailable he was if he'd just put his hand on her shoulder or rub her back sometimes. The thought of it made Elijah cringe when he was in the therapist's office, but it felt like the right thing to do for his mother in the moment. She needed comfort, but Elijah second-guessed himself as Eve looked down at his fingers. Had he made things weird? They'd never been much for hugging and touching. Peter was a hugger, a trait he'd picked up from Sonny; Elijah and Eve usually greeted each other with a kiss on the cheek if they hadn't seen each other in a bit. But usually it was just a "Hi," "Hello," or "How was your day" even when he was younger. He was about to just come out and ask if he'd made things weird, a funny attempt at salvaging the nice moment, but it didn't come to that.

She put her hand on his.

"Thank you," Eve said.

16

YITZ, 1950S

Nostalgia was cruel; it tortured Yitz wherever he looked. Walking slowly down streets he'd known his whole life in America reminded him of how he was once young and his knees and back didn't hurt so much. He watched Dick Daley ascend to Cook County clerk and remembered when the guy was just a rising star in one of the South Side Irish gangs that had figured out how to consolidate their power and take over the city's Democratic Party in the 1930s. White Jimmy was on the run from the law and living up in Canada, and the Italian friends he had left had moved to Cicero, Florida, or back to Italy. The Jews were following suit, going north to Rogers Park, Skokie, or even farther, to the gentile lands along the lake. Sometimes he wondered if he should follow and get out of the city, but never more than when a memory snuck up on him. He'd see men walking with the couple of fish they'd caught from the lake and it would remind him of Izzy the Trout's genius for getting the perch and bass to take his hook; he'd read the newspaper and long for the days of David Siegelman and

Ben Hecht truly *writing*. He enjoyed the new sounds on Maxwell, the music Black men played in the streets with harmonicas and old guitars that were usually missing a string or two; but he often missed the sound of the old klezmer musicians even though they drove him crazy when they used to play in the same spots. He couldn't drink whiskey because it reminded him of his youth, and every now and then he'd catch a whiff of a certain type of tobacco in the air, then turn around to see if Avi was behind him. Yitz never saw his old boss standing there, but that didn't assuage his feeling that a spirit was nearby.

He tried to never think about his brother, but that didn't stop Sol from showing up in his dreams all the time. He never said anything; only flashed that kind smile and stood there looking at Yitz. It went on for two decades. Sol never spoke a word, and Yitz would wake up in the morning and remind himself that ghosts weren't real.

His family didn't help any. Leah never dared say her deceased brother-in-law's name out loud, but she'd always tell her husband that he'd changed after "the loss"; the kids asked why they never saw Uncle Sol or Aunt Devorah so much that Yitz took to ignoring the lot of them as much as possible. He'd heard one of his nephews had died in the war and thought about reaching out to Devorah, but decided against it.

As for his sins, Yitz was fully cognizant of all of them, and accepted what he'd wrought. Lippy, Avi, Jerry Knish, Foxy Foxman, and countless others were waiting to have a word with Yitz if death really wasn't the end. He tried not to think what Sol would say to him in the next world. Yitz's hope was his brother was with his son, Mother, Papa, and their sister, dear Chava.

There were times he felt guilty about being the last of the old gang, but would combat the remorse by telling himself that there had to be some logical reason he'd survived while everybody else was in the ground. Yet the only conclusion he could draw was the curse that Devorah had placed on him; she'd damned him to a miserable existence. His whole life had been about survival, and there he was as the only one of the old Maxwell Street gang left, wishing it could all just be over.

On paper, he was doing well. The government saw him as lawful; he'd sold the movie studio for a hefty sum and owned a few dry-cleaning joints and some real estate up and down the lake, but men like him couldn't retire from their business that couldn't be defined. A thousand strings that could be severed only by death clung to Yitz's back. He was ancient in his middle age, a relic in a young man's game. All he could do was fossilize and hope nobody came looking for revenge. And since all his known enemies were dead, Yitz had decided to make sure to pacify the next generation into thinking he was a wise old sage who wanted to help them advance. Jakey Jake's boys, Jerry Knish's kid, and especially Foxy Foxman's son. That one had something inside him that Yitz saw immediately as hate. What the kid knew about Yitz and his father wasn't certain, so keeping him close and under heel was the best course of action.

All Yitz knew was that he was walking around people who'd someday bury him, and it was only decades of survival instincts that stopped him from handing them shovels. Devorah's curse had worked; he despised every moment of life. He wondered how long it would keep going as he splashed his face and then frowned at the face of the old man staring back at him in the mirror. He was in the bath-room of some diner that he'd ducked into when he was walking down the street and thought his heart was about to explode. Everything in his body was pulsing; he was sweating, dizzy, and felt like throwing up. It took seconds to realize it wasn't a heart attack; he'd felt the same way many times before and chalked it up to his blood sugar being low.

He steadied himself as he walked out. He wasn't hungry and had no plans on ordering anything, but then he saw somebody sitting alone at the counter and something forced him to walk over, take the seat next to her, and order a coffee. She looked at him for a second, smiled, and that was all it took for Yitz to believe the curse had been lifted.

17

The house was quiet when Elijah went downstairs after a particularly bad night of sleep. He was trying natural ways to doze off, but the melatonin chews just didn't work like Ambien. He was groggy when he noticed a piece of paper on the table with a note written on the bottom.

Take this. Look at it.

—E.M.

The way the little thumb drive sat in the middle of a white piece of printer paper made it look like it was lying on a clean sheet. He took it upstairs, put it in his laptop, and clicked the single file on it, called "Book." When the document opened, there was a note at the top for Elijah from his mother.

You used to love mystery stories as a boy, so I should have guessed you'd be able to find out as much as you did. Far more than I was able to find. But I think we were looking for different answers. I finished this a few months ago, but held back sending it to my publisher until last week. Partially because I wanted to figure out a way to prepare you for what I wrote about, but also because I was at a hip coffee shop the other day and saw some cool young girl with one of those tote bags from the literary blog with the picture of me from 1979. I decided you'd learned enough and maybe that girl and a few other people actually would want to read this, so it's with my editor. All I ask is you don't tell me what you think.

—E.M.

The book was titled *The Inheritance: A Poet's Memoir.* The initial idea, as Eve had explained to Elijah after she sold the book, was simple: it was to be a look at Eve's early life and work as a poet just before she had any acclaim. People she knew, influences on her work, and how a moderately famous poet and translator found her artistic voice.

The first words on the first page told an entirely different story:

People love the sad poet. They read the sad poet, but never ask where the sadness came from, choosing instead to believe that it was simply the muse who'd given the poet some otherworldly power with words that they'd have to suffer for if they wanted to write. I think that makes the experience of reading a poet more interesting for people, and the poet just accepts it and keeps writing until they can't continue.

But I needed to know where it came from, both for my sanity and for my work to evolve. What I came to learn was that my sadness was inherited, it was something my father, who died when I was young, passed down to me.

Over the next 250 pages, it became just as clear how much Eve had known about her father the whole time as it did why she didn't want to talk about him, and it wasn't because of what he did for a living.

I hardly knew him, but I always knew we had a connection. He died when I was a girl, but I can still see his face in mine when I look in the mirror. My mother had her own sadness, but I believe that was something else. She was a different person before the war, a happy person. My father never knew happiness a day in his life. He had the black bile inside him, and it drained into me.

To Elijah's surprise, his mother's book was as much a mystery as a memoir. It was Eve's tale of trying to learn about the person her father was, of trying to understand the origin of the sadness she believed they shared. She wrote of meeting old friends of his, and multiple sessions with different hypnotists, including one who focused on bringing up events of past lives. In true Eve fashion, she spent three pages explaining how embarrassed she was for even considering that such silliness could work, but felt obligated to include it in her story. She never once mentioned her father's work or called him a violent criminal. She wasn't concerned with any of that in the seventy-five or so pages she dedicated to trying to understand where her depression and mania came from and how they influenced her own work. Elijah understood that the rest of the book had to focus on other parts of her life and career, but it was obvious that she wanted to know more about her father and would have written the entire book about him if she could have. Eve was seeking closure, but her son wasn't sure she'd found it yet.

18

ROSE, 1950S

American food was so tasteless. No wonder so many of the men died of the heart attacks, she thought. All the cream they had to pour in their coffee, all the salt that had to be shaken into the soup. If there was anything she missed from home, it was the meals. Over a year in America and the closest thing she'd found to familiar was a chicken paprikash that was so dry and overcooked that she wondered if the chef was trying to make certain the bird was truly dead. One of the girls she worked with—also a Jew, but American—took her to a cafeteria and told her she'd find some familiar dishes, but all she recognized was borscht, and she never much liked that soup to begin with. She went with a bowl of fruit. The grapes were mushy, and the melon just tasted like semisweet water.

One of the things she liked about him was that he knew where to get good food. He certainly looked like it with that belly of his. When they first met, he had tried to tell her he wasn't married, but between the tan line on his ring finger and his stomach that had obviously been fattened up by a woman who knew her way around the kitchen, it was obvious he was lying.

She looked him dead in the eye and said she knew he wasn't telling the truth. He said she was sharp. She didn't quite understand what that meant, but the smile told her it was a compliment.

That was the night she'd seen *Peter Pan* by herself in the theater. It was her first time seeing Walt Disney's magic on a movie screen. She found the whole thing silly, but it was hard not to be moved by the dazzling colors and promise of retaining childhood innocence forever.

When she locked eyes with him at the diner afterward, it looked as if he'd never experienced boyhood. He was older, maybe twenty-five years older than her. There was the belly, but also his nose looked as if it had been smashed once or twice. And his eyes, those tragic eyes. She'd seen eyes like his before, but the odd thing was that in America, it made her comfortable, like they had something in common. When he sat down next to her and ordered a coffee, she listened to the way he talked. He was a Jew, that was obvious. She could also detect a slight trace of Europe, possibly Romanian, like her, but more likely Kyiv, Odesa, or some shtetl. He had the rough manner of one of those Yids who came from a time and place when the tsar was in charge, that was all she knew. But the tsar and his family had been dead more than thirty years—the man was basically an American.

The way he started talking to her, asking if she wanted some company, gave it away that he'd been away from wherever he'd originated for a long time. He was cocky. She liked it.

He was also rich. That was obvious. She could spot a rich man a mile away. Her mother had trained her eye for it. The one daughter who came after three brothers, all they really had to offer a potential suitor was her looks, her mother would say. Then she'd always add,

"Your problem is that you're so smart that you're stupid. No man wants a smart girl."

But that night in the diner, her mother and brothers were all dead, and hardly anybody knew she was smart because her English was so poor. She could speak German, Romanian, and Yiddish fluently, but those languages were worthless in America because the only people she found who spoke in those foreign tongues were bumpkins, mostly religious fanatics and people who believed they'd end up somewhere around lots of other Jews again. Some of them thought it would be in Palestine, others longed for the Europe they once knew. All of them were idiots, she thought. They were hoping to find a world that she knew was dead and gone.

That's why she gave the man an inch. She knew what he wanted, and it wasn't to go back to wherever he came from. He had something else on his mind, and she appreciated that. Men liked her, but it took seconds before they usually were frightened off.

But not him. He didn't run. He started asking her questions in Yiddish. It made her happy. Nobody asked her questions, and she hadn't had a normal conversation that wasn't with her cousin she was living with or the couple of girls at the dress shop she'd gotten a job at. They talked for two hours, and when she thought he'd make his move, he looked at his watch and said he had an appointment. It was 10 p.m., who has appointments that late?

He did, unfortunately. But if she didn't have plans the next night, he wanted to buy her dinner. He knew somewhere she'd enjoy.

She told him OK. But if she didn't like the food, then she'd never speak to him again.

He laughed and gave her the address. The next night, they went to an Italian restaurant. Everybody there knew his name. He told her she had to get the veal. She reminded him of her promise to never talk to him ever if the meal was bad, so he was taking a big gamble

278

suggesting it. He flashed a smile. His teeth needed some work, but she felt turned on by how self-assured he was. She assumed they'd sleep together later that night, but he just paid for her to get a cab home by herself. Before she got in, he gave her another address and said to meet him there the same time the next night.

She looked at the address, said nothing, and went home. The next night, they dined at a place where the waiters brought a large bowl filled with lettuce to the table, and prepared the salad by whipping the bowl around and around as they added ingredients and dressing. Then they ate prime rib. He told her it was the best in the city, and he knew meat because his father was a butcher. When the main course was over, he asked if she wanted dessert. She said no and stared into his tragically dark eyes. He got the picture, paid the check, and took her to a nearby hotel. When things were over, she assumed he'd gotten what he wanted, she knew how men were. But no. He gave her another address, and said he'd have a car pick her up at 6:30.

Every night after that for three months, it was the same routine. Restaurant, then hotel. She was enjoying herself enough that she didn't want to ask questions, and since they didn't talk a lot to begin with, that was easy. But then, one night, he casually said that he was leaving his wife. He never loved her and explained the marriage was an arrangement, sort of like the ones they used to make back in the places they'd come from. He was younger and had no choice. It was something he'd wanted to do for years, but he'd grown lazy. He didn't know how to exist in the world, he told her. He'd been an orphan since childhood and had no family. He had some nieces and nephews, his late brother's kids, but their mother was crazy and had forbidden them from ever talking to him. He told her he'd always felt alone and didn't want to anymore.

The honesty poured out of him. It was the first time he told her so much. She wanted to weep with joy that a man would be so forthcoming and open. What she didn't realize was that it was the first time he'd ever totally opened up to a person, but that it would also be the only time she'd see that side of him. They'd marry two months later, the day after his divorce was finalized. She hoped that with that albatross lifted from his neck he'd be able to start talking again like he did that night he laid out the future he wanted to share with her.

They went down to Miami for their honeymoon, and it was wonderful. They spent two nights dining, dancing, and making love before boarding a boat that took them to Havana. When they pulled up in front of the grand Hotel Nacional, he took a roll of money from his pocket.

"I've got a house account, but in case you need a little petty cash," he said.

"Aren't you going with me?" Rose said.

He kissed her on the cheek.

"I'll catch up with you tonight. I've got some business to deal with."

"What business? It's our honeymoon," Rose said.

"*My* business is none of *your* business," he said with a grin as he reached across his wife and opened her door.

Rose watched the car drive off, not knowing then that the last thing her husband had said to her would define their marriage and the rest of her life.

19

"You look great, kid," Jerry the Fox said. "Beautiful. What are ya? Thirty-five?"

Normally, any sort of flirtatious joke of that nature would cause Eve to insult the person who had made it, but there was something about the charming old guy that made her laugh with delight.

"I'm sorry it took so long to get this to you," Eve said.

They'd made a quick stop at a Target to buy a scale on the way to meet the old man at the dealership, and weighed out a portion to pay back Yitzhak's debt.

"I know you said you'd round it down to an even number and forget the interest, but you can keep whatever extra that is," Elijah said.

The gold on the desk shined under the fluorescent lights. Jerry the Fox shook his head in disbelief. "I really figured this guy would have been smart enough to screw me out of it, or he'd have me committed for being a crazy old fart, but here he is. This is a mitzvah. Your son is a mensch."

"Thanks, Jerry. I hope you enjoy Florida," Elijah said.

"I'm gonna try my best, bud. But, uh, before you go, I felt like I owed you something for being honest. You and your mom," Jerry the Fox said as he took an envelope from the desk drawer. "Reading material, for later. I got it printed at the library. It's about a guy named Tommy Rosetti. You ever hear of him?"

Eve was hazy, but Elijah had seen the name a few times when he was researching the Chicagoland underworld to which his grandfather was connected. Rosetti was the first guy executed in Indiana after they reinstated the death penalty in the '70s. He was a Mob hit man that got caught on the run after killing a police officer execution style not far from Eve's home.

"Yup. They fried him up good," Jerry the Fox said. "He went in back in '71, right before the death penalty had been ruled unconstitutional. He thought he could cut a deal, so he told the state all kinds of crazy stuff about guys over in Chicago, how they contracted him a few years earlier to knock off a bunch of people, he said it was around a dozen. But it wasn't underbosses or politicians or nothing like that. Some very important people decided that a few very unimportant people needed to go away."

"I remember seeing Rosetti's name connect back to my grandfather when I was doing some reading," Elijah said. "But what does this have to do with him?"

"It's about him," Jerry the Fox said with a slight head tilt. "And also isn't. See, back in the '50s, before Castro, guys like your grandpa and some of the other old-timers had a lot of coin invested in Cuba. Havana was gonna be Vegas and Miami, but bigger. Then everything went to hell, the Communists took over. A lot of guys in Chicago and New York lost tons of money and wanted to get it back, then Kennedy happened."

Visions of Hyman Roth and Michael Corleone in *The Godfather*

Part II flashed through Elijah's brain. Eve asked if Jerry the Fox meant "Kennedy happened" was about him being elected or assassinated.

"Yeah," Jerry the Fox said.

"Which one?"

"Both."

Elijah saw he and Eve had the exact same confused look on their faces. The old man kept talking.

"So Yitz and a few other guys had some ideas how to fix things. I don't know all the details, but things didn't go as planned. There was all sorts of stuff going around. Investigations, things like that. After the first Kennedy was shot, the FBI was all over Chicago. It was an excuse for them to finally go after some of the big fishes, and guys were worried. Things were so hot that the guys at the top of the Outfit decided they needed to cut off any possible ties to anything that could have incriminated them, so a lot of people started to die off. A couple of them were more old-fashioned, like Antony Schivone. He was a made guy, and they put his body in a shallow grave in Gary. Then there was Artie Berman. Him and Yitz went way back, and Artie was probably seventy-five then, basically harmless and out of the game. He used to run Detroit back in the '20s, then ended up in Chicago at some point. He showed up to Thillens ballpark on the North Side to watch his grandson play his first Little League game, and as he's walking to his seat, somebody shoots him right in the head and runs off."

Eve's face had gone white. "I remember that," she said. "I hadn't thought about it all these years, but I remember seeing the newspaper and my mom was crying. She said it was one of my father's friends."

There was a pained look on Jerry the Fox's face. "He was a good guy, Artie. Served his time and just wanted to spend his days playing with his kids. But guys like him didn't have retirement plans."

Elijah noticed a familiar look in Foxman's eyes. He worried the story was going to start going in a million different directions, so he interrupted. Elijah tried to sugarcoat it, joking that the suspense was killing him, but he could see right away his grandfather's old associate was getting visibly agitated. Jerry the Fox lunged across the desk, ripped the envelope from Elijah's hands, and waved it.

"The loose ends this Rosetti had to tie up, it was a lot of innocent people. The bosses didn't want to take any chances, so they told him to make each one look like an accident or suicide. When they reinstated the death penalty in '76, and brought him up on more old murder charges, Rosetti talked all about it. He named a few of the people he'd done: two housewives, even some poor secretary who gossiped a little too much about her boss who'd been a capo back in the '50s. You know how they did her?"

Elijah said no, but he had an idea what was coming. Eve was fighting back tears.

"Made it look like a suicide. Dumped a bunch of pills down her throat. Forced her to swallow, waited until she stopped breathing, and just left. It's right there in the paper. The lady lived in Valparaiso, so the Indiana cops had no idea that a few weeks later, when the Chicago cops found your ma dead from an overdose, that the deaths looked familiar. They were both ruled suicides."

"But you're saying they weren't," Elijah said.

Eve started to sob. She asked where the bathroom was and excused herself. The door slammed and the water started to run. Jerry the Fox had tears in his eyes. He looked at Elijah.

"I'm telling you this because you did the right thing with paying me back. But also because your grandma was a nice lady. She didn't deserve it. I remember you said your ma was upset because they didn't bury her with your grandpa, and that she didn't get the proper Jewish burial. I've always felt bad about that; maybe now you can fix it. I know some rabbis if I've gotta talk to anybody, but I want the right thing done by your family now."

20

CHICAGO, 1962

Nothing much of note happened the day Yitz Kaplan died. As he was walking out the door of his home, his daughter Eve stopped him to show him a drawing she'd made. He looked at it and was filled with the feeling of wonder he felt whenever his girls did just about anything. They were amazing to him, so smart and sweet. So innocent and safe. He wanted them to stay that way forever but knew the world would eventually disappoint them. All he could hope was that he'd never be the one doing the disappointing. Whenever he walked out the door, he would think about the idea of retirement. Before the girls were born, he'd never given much thought to the idea of not working, but as he watched his daughters grow up Yitz began wondering how a man like him could walk away from the work that had been his life since he came to America. He had a plan, a series of small actions that he believed was his way of paying any final dues and cashing out. There had to be an end to that life and the beginning of a new one, he thought as he kissed Eve's cheek for the final time.

There were thirteen hours left in summer before it officially switched to autumn, but it was still sweltering out. The conversation on Maxwell Street was either about the intense heat or the upcoming fight between Sonny Liston and Floyd Patterson just a few miles south at the ballpark. There were posters for it on every lamppost and in almost all the shop windows along the avenue. Outside the barbershop, a singer who called himself Calumet Johnnie Lee strummed a guitar plugged into a fuzzed-out amplifier and sang his songs. He'd heard the local legend Muddy Waters was inside getting a shave and had rushed down in hopes of catching the blues singer's attention and convincing him to introduce him to the men who put out his records.

It wasn't Waters; it was a guy who'd played drums for him a few times, and he'd left the barbershop five minutes before Calumet Johnnie Lee had strummed his first chord. The drummer was nearby watching a dice game and talking to some guy about how the champ was going to beat Patterson worse than the last fight when there was a commotion. An old white man staggered down the street. He was grabbing his chest and gasping for air before he collapsed into a table filled with secondhand leather boots and sneakers. The table flipped up, tossing the salesman's wares all over the place. The old, toothless boot man was about to start yelling at the guy who had ruined his makeshift shop, but then he stopped as soon as he got a good look at the face. A small crowd gathered.

"I know this guy," the boot man said. "Yeah, I know him. That's . . ."

Another man leaned in. "That's a fella that smells like he shit himself," he said.

Everybody was standing around, trying to figure out what to do, when a younger man stepped through the crowd. He was clean cut, dressed in a light blue Oxford and striped tie. He spoke in a way that immediately told everybody he'd been born down south but educated up north. It was a calm and friendly voice with a drawl from somewhere around the Delta, but spoken with big-city certainty, every vowel and consonant pushed out. Somebody asked if he was a minister or alderman, but the young man ignored the question. All he said was he needed room as he checked the old man's pulse. The young man was studying to become a doctor and had recently learned of a technique called cardiopulmonary resuscitation that combined mouth-to-mouth breathing with chest compression for cases just like the one he was faced with. He was about to start when the old man told to him come closer.

"Don't let me go," the old man said.

"We'll take care of you, Mr. Kaplan," the young man whispered. He gave a reassuring smile

"That guy is right—I think I did shit myself," the old man said. He squinted at the young man. "I know you. Cecil's kid. Your father was a good man; used to work for me in the '40s. He'd be proud of you."

"Thank you, Mr. Kaplan. He always said you were kind to him. You're why I could go to college."

Yitz didn't have time to revel in any good deeds.

"Some guys are coming for me. They're real bad. Make sure they . . ."

The old man coughed up a small bubble of blood and tried to say something but couldn't get it out. The young man shouted to the crowd to give them some room so he could lay the old man down all the way. The old man told the younger one to lean in so he could whisper.

"I need to take care of things with Sol. My brother. He's alone."

"What do you mean, Mr. Kaplan?"

Before the old man was able to answer, a pair of linebacker-sized white men broke through the wall of onlookers and pushed the younger man aside.

"Come on, Yitz," one of them said to the old man. His ugly face was filled with craters and his skin flaked off around his mouth; he was wearing a handsome, gray checkered suit with a slim tie. His partner was in a black suit with a white shirt and black tie; square faced with a wide nose, and baby blues that sat below a single bushy eyebrow that looked as if it needed hedge shears, not scissors, to trim. He was chewing on a toothpick. They weren't cops, that was obvious.

Crater Face leaned down and looked closely at the old man, then put his hand in front of his mouth to feel for air coming out.

"I don't think he's breathing," he said.

"Check his pulse," the man in the black suit snapped.

Crater Face did as he was told, holding his fingers up against the old man's neck. He waited a second, shook his head, then said, "Nope. Nothing. Dead."

"Shit," the man in the black suit said. He took the toothpick out of his mouth, then scratched at his cauliflower ear and thought for a second. He told Crater Face they had to go.

"What are you gonna do with that man on the ground? You can't just leave him there in front of my damn shop," the barber hollered.

The men ignored him and hurried away, leaving the locals to figure out what to do with the body. Normally they'd just call the deacon to handle it, but this wasn't normal. They had a dead white man, and a few of the older folks knew who he was, snapping at the younger boys not to touch the ring on his finger or take his wallet. Whatever they'd get from him wasn't worth half as much as they'd likely have to pay back later, they said.

"That's Yitz Kaplan," an old-timer said.

There was a hush. Everybody in the crowd looked at one another and then down at the dead man. *The* Yitz Kaplan? Right there on the ground? "Damn," one of the younger guys said. "I've never seen him before."

"Well," the barber said as he draped his apron over the body, "you got your look. Now, go get the man from the deli. He's a Jew; he'll know what to do. And bring me back a corned beef sandwich. I'm starving."

They all walked away. Yitz Kaplan's body lay alone in the street for more than an hour. The barber's apron flew off it and perched atop a nearby lamppost, waving in the wind like a flag of surrender. The rats were circling the corpse, crows were circling in the sky, and the crowd had all gone back to whatever they were doing before; another dead body in the streets wasn't of much interest.

According to the laws of his people, every Jew is to have a person watching over their lifeless body until it's in the ground, a centuries-old tradition known as the *shemira*. But for the two hours it took for authorities to arrive and collect his earthly remains, Yitz Kaplan's corpse continued the lonely existence that the man who once inhabited the body experienced every moment of his life.

You could replant the entire Garden of Eden with all the flowers people sent. And all the kugel, soup, cookies, and cold cuts people brought to Rose's home could have fed the entire inner city. One man showed up, offered his condolences, then handed her a 12-pound brisket. She smiled and brought it to the kitchen, where she tried to squeeze it in with the 10-pound and 13-pound briskets other people had brought.

Two hundred people attended the funeral, then the house was packed for the memorial after. Little Eve read a poem she wrote for her father without crying, while Rebecca had locked herself in her bedroom and didn't go out to say hello to anybody. When it was all over and the last guest had left, Rose sat down on her couch, still in her black mourning dress. She kicked off her shoes, put her head on the pillow, and fell asleep.

She went about her business after that. Making sure the girls had all their needs met, that they kept their grades up and stayed out of trouble. They were such good kids that it wasn't much work for her, and Rose often found herself trying to figure out what else she could be doing with her life when she decided she missed writing poetry. Every single morning for more than a year after Yitz died, she'd write for an hour right after Eve and Rebecca were out the door and down the block. She didn't like anything she wrote, but that wasn't the point. The age of poets having meaning burned alongside everything else in Europe. She did it purely for enjoyment, and kept her streak going until November 22, 1963, the day of Yitz's headstone unveiling. It had taken a little longer than she wanted because the first one they'd carved had a misspelling of his Hebrew name. When she got home, sat down and was about to touch her pen's tip to paper, she heard a muffled announcement coming from a neighbor's radio that the president had been shot in Dallas. She couldn't write anything that day or the next. What a horror. Her girls wouldn't stop crying. Rebecca locked herself in her room again; Eve—always with a melancholy familiar to Rose's own—sat looking out the window and said nothing.

The girls decided to go for a walk the following morning. Rose was relieved and was going to try to sit down and get some writing down when there was a bang on the front door, a single loud knock with a fist. Rose was slow to get up, so the person pounded against the wood several times.

"Wait, wait," Rose shouted as she unlatched the locks. "There's a knocker you could use instead . . ."

As soon as the door was open even a little, an old business acquaintance of her late husband barged through. His name was Morton Goldberger. She'd always been fascinated with Morton, with his droopy eyes and nervous nature; he was a simple bail bondsman, but Yitz treated him the same way she saw him treat lawyers, judges, politicians, and other men of power. All Yitz ever said was Morton "isn't just any bail bondsman," and nothing else. It always seemed a little out of the ordinary, even more than some of her husband's other dealings. But his policy that his business was none of Rose's kept the marriage running smoothly, she reasoned.

"Files," Morton shouted. Spit flew in every direction. "Where did Yitz keep his files?"

She didn't know what he was talking about and had a hard time getting an answer, so Morton grabbed Rose's shoulder and shook her violently. "The fucking files!"

He wasn't so strong. At least not as strong as Rose. People were always surprised to find out how much strength she had, but Morton wasn't impressed. He removed his hat, patted his brow with a handkerchief, removing only a quarter of the sweat that was all over his face and head, and shook his head.

"Lady, if you don't lead me to where your husband kept his files, some very bad men are going to come in here looking. And they won't ask like I am, believe me."

She knew where to look and led him up to the top floor. There was a filing cabinet. On top of it was a box. It had been sitting there for at least a month before Yitz had died. Morton Goldberger went over to it, looked inside, and started fumbling around. "Thank God," he said as he pulled out two folders before turning around and heading down the stairs and to the front door. Just before he walked out, Morton Goldberger turned to Rose and said, "You never saw me, this never happened. Got that?"

She nodded, closed the door, and locked up. Shaking, she walked to the kitchen to make herself some tea, hoping it would calm her down. She put the kettle on the stove, then turned on the radio while she waited. The DJ was frantic.

"The killer has been identified as a Jack Ruby, a nightclub owner in Dallas. And ladies and gentlemen, let me be the first to say that this Ruby fellow is a hero and should be treated as such," he said.

It took a second for her mind to fully understand what she'd just heard; the adrenaline was still coursing through her body from the encounter with Morton Goldberger, but then the DJ said the name again. Ruby. Jack Ruby. From Dallas.

She'd been introduced to a man named Jack Ruby. Yitz had called him a business partner of his down in Texas, but nothing else. He was an odd man, Rose thought. There was something not right about him that she couldn't put her finger on. He gave her such a bad feeling that later on that night when they were back home, she mentioned it to Yitz. Under any normal circumstance, she'd never say a word about somebody her husband said he did business with, but she couldn't stop thinking of how uncomfortable his presence made her. She remembered him laughing, then his words came flashing back to her like he was right there in the room telling her.

"I've known Jack since he was a kid. We always felt bad for him because his mom was sent to an institution for being bananas and his dad was a drunk who ran off. He was a hard worker, but just never got anywhere in Chicago. I sent him to Texas a few years ago and he's been doing better. He's never gonna do anything big, but guys like him aren't meant to."

Two weeks to the day of Morton's visit, Rose Kaplan looked down at the waters of Lake Michigan. As it all came to a close, she couldn't stop thinking about how the day had started off like any other. How had it come to this?

Up until then, it had been the same routine of waking up, walking outside, and waiting for the newspaper to hit her porch, then making some tea as she looked through the *Tribune*. She left the house at exactly 7:30 so she'd make it to the grocery store by 7:45, just as the fresh produce was being unboxed. After decades in America, she still couldn't believe how bland everything tasted. Her early shopping meant that, at the very least, she'd be able to say the fruits and vegetables she bought had a freshness to them. Whether or not that added to the taste, she never could tell. It all tasted bland to her.

When she got back home, she put away the groceries and then sat down. In front of her there were some brochures for homes in Miami. The man she had talked to asked if she was interested in what they called a "retirement village," which made Rose laugh. She was barely in her forties! Forty-one, maybe forty-two or forty-three, it was hard to tell since all the records of her birth had long been burned to ashes in some pyre of documents that proved her existence back in Czernowitz. But retirement age? Young men still flirted with her all the time. She never reciprocated because just about every man repulsed her even before Yitz—it only took having a single German getting on top of her without permission for Rose to feel that way forever—but he ruined her. A good lover, but he was older than she was by about twenty years, so everything on him started sagging not long after they were married. He looked like an old man by about fifty, while people still seemed truly surprised that she was even a day over twenty-five. Good genetics, she'd joke. In her head she'd think about how the women in her life all lived long and stayed well-preserved as long as cancer, pogroms, or Nazis didn't show up. On the way out of the man's office, she looked at herself in the mirror and could understand why he'd assumed she was older. Rose had aged years over the course of the last however many months since Yitz died.

But retirement? Absolutely not. She lived through hell in Europe and her family didn't die just so she could survive and go through life as the walking dead. Maybe she'd travel or perhaps it was the sunny beaches of South Florida where she'd start a new life. Her girls would love it down there. Life would be different, she thought.

Rose looked down at the newspaper. A name popped right out at her. Morton Goldberger.

"A bail bondsman and insurance agency owner with reputed ties to Mob bosses from Paul Ricca to Sam Giancana was shot to death while walking out of a Jewish temple in Skokie."

She had to read it again. Just as her eyes got to "reputed ties to Mob bosses . . ." she felt something hard and soulless touch the back of her head.

"Up," a man said.

Rose did as he said, rising slowly to her feet without turning around. The voice was familiar, but she couldn't place it.

"Where do you keep your pills? Show me," he said. There was a slight tremble in his voice.

"Upstairs," she said.

"Let's go."

They marched up the stairs slowly. She never turned to look at him, but she wanted to. The voice was so familiar.

They made it to her bedroom. He told her to walk into the bathroom and then get on her knees in front of the toilet. She stiffened herself and did as she was told. This feeling was familiar to her. She'd been in a situation like it more than a few times. She'd either die or she'd live. That was all she knew as she listened to him rummage around. He grabbed a pill bottle, filled a glass with some water, and told her to take all the pills.

She put the pills in her mouth, took a sip of the water, and then his hand grabbed her nose from behind and pinched her nostrils shut.

"You swallow? Tell me you swallowed," he screamed.

"Yes," she said. "You coward."

He put his huge hand over her nose and mouth and held it there. That was it until she woke up and found herself barely conscious. She was somewhere dark and loud and couldn't move. Things started to come to her, she could see them right before her eyes. A boy she kissed when she was nine, reading "The Raven" by Edgar Allan Poe for the first time, her mother smiling at her, and then Yitz was there. He was smiling and told her it would be OK, that it wasn't her fault, and nobody blamed her.

"Blame me for what? I don't understand," she said just as the darkness turned to light. She moved her head slowly and could see two figures standing over her.

"Are you fucking kidding me? I thought you took care of her. You moron," a man said.

"I've never done this, Rosetti! I thought she stopped breathing," the other man said. His voice was so familiar.

Rose could feel her body being lifted. She was floating. Were the Christians right about what happened when you died, she wondered. Was she going to heaven or hell? Had she done everything on earth wrong?

No. She was going in wet sand. The men let her down and she could feel the waves as they rolled up and soaked her body. She knew it was cold but couldn't feel it. Her vision started to go. Her breathing slowed, the feeling in her body started to disappear, and all she could do was hope that whatever was out there in the blackness would let her pass through without her memories.

"This wasn't what I was expecting today" was the last thing Rose said before she slumped over face-first into the water.

A voice behind her saying, "Tell your husband that Jerry Foxman says this is for his father," was the last thing she heard before everything went black.

Epilogue

Elijah was thinking of changing things up. He'd seen a guy out a few days earlier and liked the way he'd tied his tie, and later identified it as a Prince Albert knot. But after two dozen attempts guided by a mustached man with a Hitler Youth haircut in a YouTube video, he gave up and just went back to the way he'd always put on a tie, a thicker knot that he learned was called a Windsor. As he was flipping his shirt collar back down, his mother knocked on the door. Elijah said he was almost ready.

Eve walked in slowly. She'd started using a cane and walked slowly to her son so she could straighten his tie.

"I thought after owning your own company you'd know how to wear a suit by now," she said.

"Have you seen how guys in the Bay Area dress? Billionaires mostly go for hoodies and T-shirts," Elijah said.

"That's a shame."

Eve ran her hands down the arms of her son's jacket. She made it seem as if she was getting any creases out, but Elijah noticed the time she took in doing it. He wondered if she'd always been that much shorter than him and was surprised he'd never realized it before. He swore she'd been taller before. She said she had a question, adding that it was an awkward one.

Elijah's stomach tensed up at hearing "awkward." Things had been anything but between them for weeks, and with such an uncertain, but certainly limited amount of time left, he had hoped for things to be smooth and calm.

"Do you think you'll ever forgive me? I know it's a horrible thing to ask," Eve said. She tried to say more but couldn't get words out.

"Ma, come on," Elijah said.

She shook her head, then sat down on the bed. A look of shame had overtaken her face.

"I could have—should have been more open with you. I don't know what I was afraid of. When you were born, I guess I wasn't ready. But you've always been a good boy. I just saw so much of myself, and maybe what I thought I knew about my parents, in you. Then when you got older, I realized I'd been wrong, that you are your own person, and I just couldn't move past . . ."

"There's nothing to be sorry about," Elijah said.

Then, driven purely by instinct and nothing else, Elijah put his arm around his mother and leaned into her shoulder. He began to cry. She ran her fingers through his hair and rubbed his head. The first clear thought in his mind was to wonder what was going on, but then his memory kicked in. Suddenly, he was three or four again and it was the same situation. He was crying and his mother was comforting him. He cried out everything he could, and when he was finished, he understood that it wasn't a cry out of sorrow or mourning; with every tear, Elijah was letting go of the past. She handed him a Kleenex. He didn't see a box nearby, then remembered that she always had a few in her pocket. Elijah blew his nose and dried his eyes before asking a question of his own.

"What about you? Do you forgive him?"

Eve nodded.

"I've come to a place where I understand it's no longer about forgiveness; it's about blame. I can't blame him. My father was alive when I was born, but he was also already long gone. I only have a little idea what this world did to him, how it broke him and forced him to do what he had to survive, but he was too young and full of energy to realize it. A little Oliver Twist, I suppose."

"Who's the Fagin in this scenario?"

Eve thought for a second. She chewed on the inside of her mouth. Then the answer came to her.

"America."

It felt like a sign. There was an early-season Cubs game going on at Wrigley Field and traffic was terrible. It was as if Peter had played a little cosmic joke on them, Eve noted.

When they finally arrived at their destination and found a decent parking spot, Rabbi Ginsburg was in front of the Benevolent Society building waiting for them. Behind him stood about a dozen old men he'd brought with him from the nearby retirement home for the prayer minyan; all of them were wearing yarmulkes on their heads, two had fallen asleep on a bench nearby, and one asked when they'd have the lunch the rabbi promised. Next to them stood a group of people Elijah and Eve had never seen before, but instantly recognized as descendants of Solomon and Devorah. A woman was walking around taking pictures with her phone but screeched with joy when she saw Eve and Elijah; it was Grace, the long-lost relative Eve had found. After a few pleasantries, the group walked toward the Greater Chicagoland Hebrew Benevolent Society's cemetery, fresh with its new landscaping, fence, and sign thanks to a generous donation from an unnamed source. They walked to the Kaplan mausoleum. Another one hundred years of maintenance had been paid for by another unnamed donor just under the wire of its previous century being over. The weeds in front of it were gone, so was the ugly turf that was as dead as the people buried around it. In its place, big bluestem, switchgrass, and wildflowers had been planted and allowed to grow around it, reconnecting the little part of the cemetery in the sprawling city back to its prairie roots.

"The Talmud says that miracles don't happen every day. I feel very lucky to be able to see this one happen," Rabbi Ginsburg said before he stepped back, opened his prayer book, and started talking about one of the most famous stories in the Jewish canon, about Moses and the Israelites wandering the desert for forty years. He said everybody knows that story, about how after all that wandering, Moses sat down on the ground of Mount Nebo, looked out onto the Promised Land, but never got up to make it there. "What happens when we die has been debated for as long as man could speak. We Jews believe in the *olam ha-ba*, the world to come, but we can't even fathom for a split second what it's like when we close our eyes and take our last breath. Are we happy? Do we spend our days studying Torah with the great masters? Are we floating on a cloud with angels playing harps around us?"

The assembled crowd all let out a muffled laugh in unison, and only one man hacked something up from his throat—the desired effect. The rabbi, understanding the laws of comic timing, let the laughter die down and then continued. "Is there sadness? Do we carry the weight from this world into the next? I don't know. None of us do. All that is for certain is that we are here, right now. All of us together in this moment are gathered to see something happen that might not have any bearing on things in the world to come, but here on earth, as we reunite Solomon and Devorah, as well as Yitzhak and Rose, back together after all these years, it's hard not to feel like we've done something good in this world that we're living in. Something has been made right by letting them all rest in the place where they were supposed to be in the first place. It is the Jewish idea of *tikkun olam*, to repair the world. However tiny this might register on the list of things that need fixing, we are still repairing. We're healing. Elijah and Eve, you've done something good, and I hope you can take a moment or two to appreciate that. For the rest of us, let us take that with us from this place after we leave and try not to forget it."

An old man said "Amen," then coughed some phlegm up. The rest of the crowd repeated the utterance. The rabbi bowed his head and started leading the group in the Kaddish. Elijah didn't understand the words of the Hebrew hymn, so he just listened, letting the words flow through him. He looked into the door of the crypt and could see the graves next to each other. Devorah's was still open, awaiting the dirt that would seal her remains in the ground next to her Solomon for all of eternity. So were Yitzhak and Rose's. All three coffins were picked up from hearses and carried into the tomb, then put into the earth.

After it was all done, Elijah wondered if he'd set things right, if maybe he'd at least patched up a tear in his family's history. There was no changing what was, but maybe repairs could be made even if they couldn't be seen. Just a few months earlier, he would have scoffed at such an idea, but as he picked up the shovel and scooped up some dirt, Elijah Mendes was willing to give himself a little room to believe in something bigger, something he couldn't possibly contemplate.

Acknowledgments

At some point between my last book and this one, somebody told me it's tradition to thank your partner last. I don't know if that's true, but I've always thanked Emily Goldsher-Diamond first, and I certainly won't stop here. She not only helped keep my brain from cracking while I wrote this, but she also carried our first child while I tried to get this novel right. Em, you're my hero, and I love you.

Peter Steinberg: You elevated the agent game and helped as both an editor and a friend. I'd never even shown anybody my fiction before you looked at the first draft of this book, and I'm forever grateful how much you did to make this happen. Zack Wagman, editor extraordinaire and fellow Kaplan through birth: I can't tell you how happy you've made me not just because you bought this thing but because your constant encouragement and feedback have made me feel comfortable calling myself a novelist. Megan Lynch and everybody else at Flatiron: I appreciate what you do and I'm glad you brought

Acknowledgments

me into the fold. Maris Kreizman, my older little sister: You are my literary consigliere. Kelly Farber, Philly's finest: It meant the world to hear your opinions. Isaac Fitzgerald: You're a brother and I appreciate you letting me unpack my mental mishegoss. Jami Attenberg: You know you're like my older sister, but I've been paying close attention to everything you've said and done as a novelist, and I fully understand why people are so inspired by you. Jesse David Fox: Talking to you is always enlightening, and it helped me remember that when all else fails, I should try to be funny. In my case, I usually fail, but at least I've made the attempt. Nicholas Heller, Jeremy Cohen, and Jess Flores: You sat in various cars with me for over a year and heard me drone on about this book, and I appreciate it. Josh Gondelman: I learn a lot from you about being a better writer but also a better human. Alexander Chee: You're the other fiction writer whose work and words I've paid attention to over the years, and although I've never taken any of your classes, I hope you'll consider me a student. Noah Rinsky: I hope there's enough OJM content in this book to pass your test. Helen Rosner, Dodai Stewart, Kristen Arnett, Sarah Seltzer, Jaya Saxena, Matthew Specktor, Rachel Syme, Matt Starr, and Lincoln Michel are writers I'm glad to call my friends because conversations with them and reading their work always push me to do better. Sophie Garcia-Cubas Assemat: Thank you for dealing with all my begging for just one more day to look over the manuscript. Mika Kasuga, Dorothy Berry, Michael Weber, and Mattie Lubchansky each inspired something that ended up in this novel whether they know it or not. Maybe it was helping me find out something for research or possibly just something they said in conversation, but a little piece of them is in this book. Michael Sebastian at *Esquire*; Jeff Gordinier, Sam Schube, Adam Rathe at *Town & Country*; Alan Sytsma at Grub Street; Nitsuh Abebe at *New York Times Magazine*; and all the editors who push me to be a better writer. Harry Sherer for the helpful feedback on the

Acknowledgments

last draft, Chris Smith for letting me ask publicity questions waaaaay before the pub date. Katherine Turro for being a marketing genius. Aaron Lefkove, Tom Kretchmar, Dan Saltzstein, Bryan Reisberg, Dave Schilling, Noah Segan, Jayson Buford, Adam Chandler, and anybody else who responded to my annoyingly cryptic text messages like "I'm losing my mind" while I was in the middle of writing this book. To Tessa, Lacey, Harriet, and Barry Goldsher for being wonderful in-laws. Thank you to Chicago, the city that gave me life. I will go to my grave saying you're the Great American City and that your importance to American literature is underrated. In some small way I hope this book adds to your legacy that includes (but not limited to) Theodore Dreiser, Ben Shahn, Carl Sandburg, Ring Lardner, *Poetry* magazine, Richard Wright, Ernest Hemingway, Meyer Levin, Margaret Walker, Nelson Algren, Studs Terkel, Saul Bellow, Bette Howland, Gwendolyn Brooks, Frank London Brown, Mike Royko, Lorraine Hansberry, Shel Silverstein, Leon Forrest, Sara Paretsky, Roger Ebert, Ira Berkow, Gene Siskel, Michael Mann, Stuart Dybek, David Mamet, Margo Jefferson, John Hughes, Edward Hirsch, Harold Ramis, Sandra Cisneros, George Saunders, Adam Langer, Michael Hainey, Aleksandar Hemon, Bob Odenkirk, Rich Cohen, Dave Eggers, Joe Meno, Steve Krakow, Jami Attenberg, Mikki Kendall, Dan Sinker, Arionne Nettles, Rebecca Makkai, Adam Levin, Clare Zulkey, Nnedi Okorafor, Megan Stielstra, Samantha Irby, Jac Jemc, Christopher Storer, Angelica Jade Bastién, Lindsay Hunter, Eve L. Ewing, Leor Galil, Catherine Lacey, Jeremy Gordon, Halle Butler, Dana Schwartz, the *Chicago Review of Books*, and a bunch of novelists, poets, essayists, journalists, and screenwriters from and of Chicago that I have for sure forgotten to mention. A couple of you I know, a few I've never met, and the rest are dead, but you've all helped create the Chicago literary canon, and I'd humbly like to submit this novel for consideration in it.

Acknowledgments

And finally, to Lulu. This book was started before you were born, but maybe someday when you're old enough and I've collected my thoughts, I can explain how you coming into the world helped me finish it. I love you, and I love our family.

About the Author

Jason Diamond is the author of *Searching for John Hughes* and *The Sprawl* and is coauthor of *New York Nico's Guide to NYC* (with Nicolas Heller). His work has been published by the *New York Times*, *Esquire*, the *New Yorker*, *GQ*, the *Paris Review*, and many other outlets. He publishes the newsletter the *Melt*, was born in Skokie, Illinois, and lives in Brooklyn with his wife and daughter. *Kaplan's Plot* is his first novel.